The Mountains Wild

ALSO BY SARAH STEWART TAYLOR

Still as Death

Judgment of the Grave

Mansions of the Dead

O' Artful Death

The Mountains *Wild*

Sarah Stewart Taylor

MINOTAUR BOOKS
NEW YORK

First published in the United States by Minotaur Books, an imprint of St. Martin's Publishing Group

THE MOUNTAINS WILD. Copyright © 2020 by Sarah Stewart Taylor. All rights reserved. Printed in the United States of America. For information, address St. Martin's Publishing Group, 120 Broadway, New York, NY 10271.

www.minotaurbooks.com

The Library of Congress Cataloging-in-Publication Data is available upon request.

ISBN 978-1-250-25643-0 (hardcover)
ISBN 978-1-250-75413-4 (ebook)

Our books may be purchased in bulk for promotional, educational, or business use. Please contact your local bookseller or the Macmillan Corporate and Premium Sales Department at 1-800-221-7945, extension 5442, or by email at MacmillanSpecialMarkets@macmillan.com.

First Edition: 2020

10 9 8 7 6 5 4 3 2 1

For the women of Rosary Terrace

The Mountains Wild

PROLOGUE

....

My mother singing. That's one thing I remember.

"Molly Malone," "Red Is the Rose," "Danny Boy." She likes what she calls the "rebel songs," songs that tell stories: "The Rising of the Moon," "The Wind That Shakes the Barley," "The Foggy Dew," "Come Out Ye Black and Tans." I like these too. Her thumb rubs soft circles on the back of my hand when she sings to me at bedtime.

I remember my cousin Erin in patches of color, light, sound, and scent. My Erin. Erin, fast and laughing. Erin, running, disappearing around a corner. Erin shrieking. The warm yellow smell of Erin when we sit close together.

My father carrying me out of the car to bed, the laundry smell of his shirt collar.

The soft voice of my grandmother Nellie, my Nan, her warm, purple, lavender hand cream smell, the way she swirls hot water in her white china teapot and says Mo ghrá. *My love. She tells Erin and me about her girlhood in Ireland, a friend named Ellen and a cat with three legs and a spilled can of paint.*

Erin's elbows and knees sharp against me in bed when she has to sleep over because Uncle Danny's working late.

Chocolate pudding for dessert, a treat, the sharp starchy taste of it, the warm skin on top, the cold metal taste of my spoon. Eating it outside in the backyard, Erin and I saving the skin for last.

The first time Erin disappears, it's summer, a fan whirring on my desk by the screen window, hot, wet air drifting in from the beach, the sun baking the driveway outside. I wake up to find her gone, the top sheet on her side of my bed peeled back, the bottom sheet still warm and rumpled.

No Erin downstairs. When my mom realizes she's not in the house, she runs up to Uncle Danny's, her face pressed in worry. I follow behind in my nightgown, my feet hopping on the already hot asphalt. Uncle Danny stumbles out of bed, still smelling of the bar, cigarettes and the sharp dusty smell of the basement. He can't find her and suddenly, everyone is running down to the beach, checking the water, neighbor moms coming out of their houses in bathrobes, holding cups of coffee, their feet bare.

The grown-ups are yelling and running, spreading out on the beach, but it's me who finally finds the line of shells and rocks she's dropped on the far side of the pavilion. I follow them, counting, until I see the top of her head, hiding in the lifeguard dinghy. When she hears me, she sits up and grins. Her nightgown is polyester pink and yellow, Easter colors. Her hair is wavy in the humid air. The summer has already brought up the freckles on her nose and cheeks.

"You found me, Maggie," she says. "I knew you'd find me."

1

Uncle Danny is calling from the bar. I can hear the sound of glasses clinking as he stacks them from the dishwasher. My phone says 3:04 a.m.

"You there, Mags?" he asks. *Clink. Clink.* I can see him, unloading highballs from the racks, *one, two, three, four.* Next row. *One, two, three, four.* I can see the shiny wood of the bar, the damp towel over his shoulder.

"Yeah. Uncle Danny? Everything okay?"

"Maggie, baby, I was gonna call before but it was busy tonight and I didn't want to, you know, the guys was there. Clyde, you know, the divorce got whaddyacallit, finalized yesterday. He needed to drink."

I let him talk. He'll get around to it. It always takes Uncle Danny a few sentences to warm up to his story, the anecdotes a slow first mile, his Long Island accent getting even thicker as he settles into his tale.

"I got the message when I got in. On the bar phone. Byrne. That's the guy, right? The one who updates us."

I'm wide awake now, scrambling for the light on the bedside table.

"What'd he say, Uncle Danny? What?" My bedroom is suddenly filled with yellow light. I shut my eyes tight for a moment before opening them slowly, letting them adjust.

"I don't know. I didn't talk to him. He left a message. On the phone here at the bar. It was just, ya know, 'Mr. Flaherty, this is Detective Roland Byrne with the Irish police whateveryacallit, the Guards whatever.'"

"Garda Síochána." I remember the pronunciation. *Garda Shee-uh-cahna.* Guardians of the Peace.

"Yeah. He just said I should call him as soon as I got the message."

"Nothing else?"

"Nothing else. Whaddya think, Mags? Ya think they found her?" I can hear him starting to choke up. He has high blood pressure, a failing heart. I can't let him get too worked up.

"I don't know, Uncle Danny. I don't know. Don't get all . . . Let's wait till you talk to him."

He takes a great big raspy breath, trying to calm down. "You gotta call him, baby. You gotta call him. You know him and I can't take it. I can't take the stress. You gotta do it for me."

I check my clock again, do the math. "It's three," I say. "Over there it's eight a.m. He's probably not in yet. Is it the cell or office line?"

"Both. He left both."

"Okay. I'm heading over. Stay at the bar. I'll be right there."

Clink, clink, clink. "Thanks, Mags. Thanks, baby."

◆ ◆ ◆

I dress, let the cat out, leave Lilly a note on the kitchen table: *Went to help Uncle Danny with something. If I'm not back, have a good day at school. EAT BREAKFAST!!!! I'll see you later. Your dad is picking you up after track and bringing you back. See if he can stay for dinner. EAT BREAKFAST!!!!*

The night air coming off the beach is wet and salty and full of spring. I open my car windows to breathe it in and hug the Shore Road, keeping the water to my right all the way to 25A. I'm used to being out late at night for work, but it feels strange to be out going to see Uncle Danny. The border between night and morning is quiet, the streetlights lining up in a yellow row. Town's empty. On a Friday or Saturday, there'd still be a few stragglers making their drunken way down from the clubs on New York Avenue. But early Tuesday morning, even the drinkers are home in bed. The breeze blows litter across the sidewalks. There's no moon and the sky is blue dark, not a sliver of light above the horizon. It's 3:27, 8:27 in Dublin. I try to remember Roly Byrne's face and get a cubist amalgamation of features: Blond hair. Small, brilliantly blue eyes. Sharp face. Needed to be on the move. Needed to keep things interesting. Roly Byrne.

I almost smile. He'll be up.

Uncle Danny's Toyota is the only other car in the lot at Flaherty's and I pull in close and go in through the back door, past a pile of cigarette butts and what looks like an old pool of vomit.

He's still behind the bar, wiping it down. The radio's on, some '80s station, Billy Joel singing "You May Be Right," and the only lights in the whole place are up over his head, making the seating area look like a dark ocean and Uncle Danny a tall hunched figure in a boat of light. The old cordless phone is sitting in the exact center of the bar. He has a smartphone but he doesn't like it.

"Hey," I say, coming up behind him to stand with him in front of the phone. He picks it up and pushes a few buttons, passes the handset to me. I listen to the familiar voice say, "Mr. Flaherty. This is Detective Inspector Roland Byrne ringing from the Garda National Bureau of Criminal Investigation in Dublin. I would appreciate it if you would give me a shout as soon as possible." He gives the numbers. I gesture for a pen and Uncle Danny shows me he's already written them down. I hang up and think for a moment. Twenty-three years. My cousin Erin has been missing for twenty-three years and now Roly Byrne is calling us to say he wants to talk "as soon as possible." Either they've found something—*a body*, I force myself to think, *or remains*—or there's a suspect, some guy who was trying to get a reduced sentence by admitting to earlier crimes or a witness who hadn't wanted to talk to anyone way back when but wants to come clean now.

Roly's voice opens up the filing cabinet for the case in my brain and suddenly the names come flooding out like they've been waiting for me: *Gary Curran, Hacky O'Hanrahan, Emer Nolan, Daisy Nugent, Niall Deasey, Conor Kearney . . . Conor Kearney.* I take a deep breath, mentally shutting the file drawers. This isn't the time. Instead I look up at the framed photographs and posters on the walls of the bar: Bobby Sands, Gerry Adams, the tricolor, a framed copy of Yeats's "Easter, 1916," some newer stuff too: a *Michael Collins* movie poster, a signed and framed Dropkick Murphys album. The standard American Irish bar kit.

"Okay, give me the paper." I dial the cell number. I don't have to look up the country code for Ireland. I remember. For some reason I don't want to do it on my cell.

He answers on the third ring. "Byrne here."

"It's Maggie. Maggie D'arcy. Uh, my uncle, uh, Daniel Flaherty, asked me to return your call."

"D'arcy." His voice is tight, stressed. "Thanks for ringing. I wanted to let your uncle know that we've found something in Wicklow. The forestry lands, not far from Glenmalure." An image swims up before me, dark trees and sky and a narrow road, lined with rusty bracken.

"Something?" I see Uncle Danny wince, but we need to know if this is it.

"No remains. A scarf," he says quickly. "Printed with butterflies." With his Dublin accent he says it *booterflies.* "Crime scene woman says it's been here a while. Maybe twenty years. There's blood on the scarf. Quite a bit." There's a long pause. "It was deliberately buried."

I can't stop a memory coming to me. *Christmas. Erin unwrapping the scarf, ripping the paper to get to it, her crazy hair in her eyes. She looks up, delighted. "Thank you, Mags. I love it."*

Roly Byrne hesitates, then says, "One of the lads checked the old cases, found your description of the scarf in the original report." The line crackles a little.

I meet Uncle Danny's eyes. He turns his head. The lights swim together. My eyes fill up. I swallow hard. I focus on Gerry Adams.

I can hear Roly Byrne breathing across the line, across the air, across the sea. He's not finished.

"What?" I ask him.

"There's a woman after going missing," he says.

I look down at the floor. I know these boards better than the ones in my own kitchen. There are two shiny depressions where Uncle Danny likes to stand. "Another one?"

"Yeah. Her name is Niamh Horrigan. She's twenty-five, a teacher from Galway. She stayed at a youth hostel near Glendalough and told someone she was going to walk to Glenmalure. She was seen on the path and then she just . . ." *Disappeared.* He doesn't say it. "We don't have a body. Nothing like that. This was just Sunday the family rang us up."

"So you were searching for her and you found the scarf?"

"Well, one of the local lads." He's tired. I can hear it now. They would have launched the search immediately. He probably didn't sleep last night. "We're going to get right onto it. We'll look for additional evidence of course. We'll . . . uh, see if there's anything else. Nearby."

Anything else. Erin's body. Her remains.

I'm already thinking about how it's going to go down. They'll conduct a search in the surrounding area, see if they can find anything. They'll test the blood on the scarf, look for other biological material that might yield DNA, look for fibers, though after this much time there may not be much to find.

"This hasn't been widely reported yet—though with all the reporters down here about Niamh Horrigan, a few of 'em know we found something. We had to tell 'em the, uh, the evidence wasn't related to Horrigan's case. For the family, like. But I thought I'd let you know. We'll keep you informed. And I wondered if your uncle might need some assistance from us, if he's going to travel." *I tot I'd letcha know.* His Dublin accent has softened a bit but it's still there, his *th*s disappearing into the ether.

I glance at Uncle Danny. He's watching me, his right hand on automatic, still wiping the bar. It strikes me suddenly that I've been wrong all this time. I thought we knew. I thought we'd accepted it. But we haven't.

I have a thousand questions, but now's not the time. "I'll get back to you," I tell him. "Let me talk to him."

I meet Uncle Danny's eyes. He looks away and drops the cloth into the sink.

"Okay," Roly Byrne says. "I'm sorry, D'arcy." I click off. *D'arcy.* Only Roly Byrne calls me that.

I don't wait. "They found her scarf," I tell Uncle Danny. "They're looking for remains now."

I watch him take it in. He holds the knowledge for a long moment and then I see him grasping for something, some little drop of hope.

"They're sure it's hers?"

"I think so." I hesitate, then I say, "There's blood on it."

He winces. "Maybe it's not hers. Maybe it's someone else's. There must be a lot of those scarves around. It's been so long. How can they be sure?"

I can feel it too, the tiny seedling, growing toward the light despite my job, despite everything I know. I need to stop it.

"Uncle Danny, I'm so sorry. It's near where I found the necklace when I was over there in ninety-three. It's near where she was walking. With the, the . . . other women, I think we have to face that it does indicate that . . . something happened." He sobs then. This is it. I hug him hard, struggling to get my arms around the breadth of him. "I'm so sorry." He cries for a little bit and then he pulls away from me, picks up the towel again.

"There's something else, too," I say quietly. "Another young woman has just disappeared. Close to the last place Erin was seen."

"Oh, Christ. What do they . . . ? Do they think it's connected to Erin and the others?"

"They don't know anything yet. It's all new."

"You gotta go, Mags," he says. "You gotta go and make sure they do this right. Can Brian take Lilly for ya?"

"Uncle Danny. Let's wait and—"

"It would kill me, trip like that," he says. "My doc says I can't exert myself at all, my heart's so bad now. You gotta go and find out what's going on. You went before. You were there a long time. You know everyone. You know the deal over there."

Our eyes meet.

"Mags."

My mind slides back. *Cold air whipping my hair across my face. The smell of peat smoke. A gray street, the sidewalk dark, a door painted a shade of blue so alive it vibrates through the rain.*

"Okay, I'll go," I tell my uncle Danny for the second time in twenty-three years. "Okay." And then I hug him again hard, sinking into his huge middle, my arms wrapped around him, my hands rubbing circles on his back. He's wearing one of the slippery golf shirts he likes and he smells like Guinness and lemon oil.

"Of course I'll go, Uncle Danny. Of course I will."

2

I help him clean up and close the bar and we go for eggs and bagels. Lilly's gone to school by the time I get home and after I check in with the homicide squad and let them know I'll be away for a bit with a family emergency, I dress for my run and Google Niamh Horrigan.

I find a bunch of stories, in the *Irish Times*, the *Irish Independent*, the local Galway papers, all of them covering Niamh Horrigan's disappearance with barely contained excitement: "Galway Girl Niamh Loved the Out of Doors." "We Just Want Our Niamh Back—Hillwalker's Mam." And then, "Is Niamh Southeast Killer's Latest Victim?" along with small photographs of Erin and Teresa McKenny and June Talbot and a bigger one of Niamh, dark-haired and sporty-looking. If I squint, she looks a little like Erin.

Don't go there.

Niamh's an avid hillwalker, the papers say. She's climbed all of Ireland's highest peaks and goes mountaineering or walking every weekend.

Her hair looks naturally wavy. She has a spray of freckles across her nose. In the picture she's grinning and holding a walking stick, trees behind her.

Don't go there.

Alexandria is right in the middle of a little C-shaped bay on the North Shore of Long Island. Jogging on the wet sand, I can see the gray line of Connecticut across Long Island Sound. I love this run. I've been doing it almost my whole life and I know every house along the beach, every barking dog and every old man fishing for stripers from the shore. I run fast, putting in six miles on the streets around Fleet's Cove and then heading back along the beach. When I come around the turn of the coastline, I stop and look back at the peppermint-striped LILCO stacks in Northport. I can't help but think of the Poolbeg chimneys in Dublin, how you could see them from all over the city.

My memory has been doing funny things since Danny woke me and I have a sudden image of a long stretch of wet sand, the red-and-white-striped stacks in the distance.

Sandymount. It strikes me suddenly that they're bookends to Erin's life, these stacks. Long Island. Ireland. *Here. There.*

A gull drops a mussel shell on a rock by my feet, then hovers overhead, waiting for me to leave.

◆ ◆ ◆

I'm half packed by the time Lilly comes in at five.

"Where's your dad?" I ask her. Dinner's in the oven and the table's set. I have a bottle of red open, Brian's favorite.

"He had to go pick up some milk and bread. He'll be here in

fifteen. What?" She can see it on my face. I go over to her and tuck a stray piece of dark brown hair behind her ear, smelling strawberry shampoo and fried food. She's taller than I am now. I have to reach up to do it. Lilly looks more like Brian than she does like me, with his father's family's Southern Italian coloring and softer features cancelling out his mother's and my Irish genes, though she's an original, too, and I've always been glad of that, and a little jealous. That she has her own face and no one else's.

"We heard from Dublin. They think they may have found my cousin Erin's scarf. She was wearing it when she disappeared while she was living over there."

"No way. After all these years?"

"Twenty-three."

"What does it mean? Did they find her body?"

I hesitate. "No, not yet. But they think it may be close by. They're searching for another woman, who was hiking there and disappeared. They found Erin's scarf while trying to figure out what happened to her."

"Is it connected to the other two women? Is there any evidence?" Poor Lilly knows a lot more about forensics than any fifteen-year-old should have to.

"We just don't know," I tell her. "Uncle Danny wants me to go and see them and try to figure it out. You okay staying with Dad for a week or so?"

"Yeah, I guess. Can he stay here, though? I can't sleep with the trains going by his apartment." She looks down at the table, feeling disloyal.

There are a bunch of reasons I'd rather they stay at Brian's, but I know it's better for Lilly to be at home. "'Course. I'll ask him, anyway. How was school?" She's a sophomore this year, past the storms of puberty, though somehow even Lilly's worst seemed fairly mild. One of the benefits of being a cop, I guess. A thirteen-year-old yelling that she wishes you'd leave her alone forever because you're too nosy never seemed that serious compared to a thirteen-year-old who's addicted to heroin ending up as a witness to the murder of another thirteen-year-old who was sex-trafficked and killed.

"What do you think happened to her?" Lilly asks me seriously. She has a way of looking at you, her head tilted a little, her huge brown eyes watching you, that makes it impossible to lie.

"I think . . ." I start. "I guess until last night, most days, I was pretty sure something happened to her, Lil, that someone killed her and hid her, I guess I'm saying. But then there were days where I thought maybe she started a new life somewhere, that she didn't want to tell us. I pictured her sometimes, with a daughter . . ." I smile at her. "And bad, unfashionable jeans, just like me."

"But why wouldn't she tell you?" Lilly has a tight group of best friends who share all their secrets. She can't imagine why Erin would have kept something that big to herself.

"I don't know. Erin was complicated, sweetheart. She could be mysterious. She'd gone off before. It was hard to know what she was thinking."

I think she's done asking questions, but then she says, "What was she like? Uncle Danny told me she looked like you. But what was she like?"

Wavy brown hair, stiff with the salt, threads of gold where the sun bleached it. Freckles across her nose. Her hand tight in mine.

"We grew up together. We were like sisters." That doesn't answer her question, though. "Erin was . . . We did look alike, enough alike that people sometimes thought we were twins, but she was really beautiful, in a way that people noticed. She was wild, a risk-taker, troubled, creative. Fun." Lilly doesn't say anything. I still haven't really explained Erin. "When I say *Erin* to myself, I have this sort of picture that I see, of her running down a beach, her hair flying all around her, the sun behind her. She loved the beach. When we were little we spent all our time there." *Erin running, too fast for me to follow, turning to shout back at me.*

While Lilly finishes her homework, I head down to the basement to find the boxes of notes and files I've kept on Erin's case. Twenty-three years. I've gone back to it over the years, when Roly Byrne called me with an update, and a few times on Erin's birthday, when I was feeling melancholy and frustrated. But it's been a while.

They're over in a dry corner of the basement, up on wooden pallets, in front of a pile of other boxes of my mother's and father's things and a bunch of Brian's stuff from when we sold his parents' house that I keep forgetting to return to him. Lilly likes to come down here and look through it; she pulled some of my mother's clothes out and wore them for a bit, and decorated her room with things from Brian's boxes, old Red Hot Chili Peppers posters from his University of Delaware dorm room and posters and soccer jerseys he bought while backpacking in Europe or the time he and his brother, Frank, and our friends Derek and Devin O'Brien spent spring break in Mexico.

There are papers everywhere, old postcards and letters and receipts, and I have to stop myself yelling up the stairs at Lilly for making such a mess. I find the box that has all my notes from Erin's case, but Lilly's gone through it and it's mixed up with things from the other boxes. It takes me twenty minutes to sort through Brian's college papers and my mother's old purses and find my box of notebooks and files. I open up the box and put them in a separate pile.

In a plastic tub are the things from the house Erin lived in in Dublin, books and clothes and postcards and jewelry. The police in Ireland—the *Guards*, I remind myself, the *Gardaí, with a little* th *sound added to the d*—had gone through it. After she'd been missing for six months, her roommates had shipped her things home. At some point Uncle Danny had asked me to keep them since he couldn't stand having them in the house. There are a few items of clothing, a white satin jewelry box that had held Erin's claddagh necklace, a little fabric pouch of earrings, a four-leaf clover embedded in glass, some makeup, and some books and stationery.

In another box, there's a paper envelope of photographs and I open it and fan out a random assortment of pictures of me and Erin. It was my mom's; she had kept some pictures of us on her bedside table when she was really sick, once we'd moved a hospital bed into the den.

There's one of Erin and me at the beach. I'm five or six; she's a year older. We sit on little chairs on the sand, looking up at the photographer. We're pink from the sun, our red bathing suits caked with sand. Erin's grinning and waving. I'm clutching a little plastic sand shovel.

Another is us in our Irish dancing costumes, onstage at an all–Long Island feis. There are school pictures of me from fifth grade and seventh grade and eighth grade.

There's one of Erin at seventeen, sitting on the beach and looking out across the water. Her long hair is wildly curly, the wind whipping corkscrews across her face; she's in half profile. I seem to remember that her best friend Jessica took the pictures, that they were supposed to be a present for a boyfriend, though I don't think Erin ever gave them to anyone. They're too solitary, too dark, the expression on Erin's face sad, stormy.

And then there's one of me at twenty, just before my mom was diagnosed, standing in front of the student center at Notre Dame. I'm wearing jeans and Doc Martens and a tweed blazer I got at the thrift store in South Bend and I look basically the way I looked almost two years later, in 1993, when Erin disappeared and I went to Dublin to try to find her.

I look at the photograph for a few more minutes, trying to remember what it was like to be that person, before I put everything away and head back upstairs to finish dinner.

3

....

1993

I was twenty-two that fall, a too-thin girl with shoulder-length brown hair that I always wore scraped back in a ponytail, working at the bar to help out Uncle Danny, training for a marathon, and trying to stop my dad from drinking too much. I'd graduated from Notre Dame the spring before, after taking a semester off as my mom was dying and then finishing up the last of my coursework at the bar when things were quiet. I think I can say with complete honesty that I had no inkling, at that point, of my future career path, but I was curious about people and I knew, from bartending and from studying literature for four years, that people lie all the time, and that the interesting thing is not that they lie, but *why* they do. Now I know that this is a lot of it, of being a detective, and that perhaps I was setting off on some inevitable path that night we got the call from Dublin.

I was working a long shift with Uncle Danny, serving beers and vodka and rum and Cokes to the cops and the plumbers and the bankers off the train, when the phone rang at the bar.

"Is Mr. Flaherty there?" I recognized the accent as Irish, real Irish, and for just a moment I thought it was Erin, that somehow she'd picked up an accent since moving to Dublin almost a year before. I handed it to Uncle Danny and listened as he said, "Oh, no, I haven't heard from her. She didn't leave a note? No. Okay. Thanks. We'll . . . yes, we'll get back to ya."

"That was Erin's roommates over there in Dublin," he said, hesitating for a moment and then starting to wipe the bar down. "Eeemur or somesuch, one of those real Irishy names. She hasn't been back to her place for a while. They got worried and thought they oughta call. Whaddya think, Mags? Ya think she's okay?" His voice caught and I rubbed little circles on his shoulder. I could already feel the anger rising through my throat.

Do you know how fucking worried Uncle Danny is about you?
Why do you always do this, Erin?
"I'm sure she's fine," I told him. "I bet she'll be back."

But Erin wasn't back the next day.

My dad came by the bar after work to talk about what to do. *Two old men.* That's what I thought when I came up from the basement and saw them. Uncle Danny was wearing one of his shiny golf shirts and the fabric was lighter where it stretched over his belly. My dad was just off the train from the city, still in a gray suit that had gotten too big for him, his blue eyes the only alive thing in his face. My mom had been gone for a year and a bit and he wasn't over it. He was pale, shaky. He didn't sleep much. I watched him stir the gin in front of him on the bar.

They tossed it around for a bit, Uncle Danny going over, maybe my dad.

"I wish Father Anthony was here," Danny said. "He'd know what to do. God rest him. I guess I'd better go over."

I stepped in after Uncle Danny started coughing and couldn't stop.

"I'll go," I told them. "I can go look into it. Uncle Danny, your heart."

They barely tried to stop me.

Two old men. I felt guilty for thinking it, but it was true. Uncle Danny. I kept finding cigarettes hidden in his desk in the office at the bar. He reeked of them. His doctor said he was a heart attack waiting to happen if he didn't cut out the smokes and lose some weight.

"I'll go," I told them again. "And then once I figure out what's going on, you can come over. Hopefully she's just . . ." We let it sit there, all the possibilities contained in that *hopefully.*

"Okay, baby. Thanks. That's a good idea. I can come when you figure out what's going on."

◆ ◆ ◆

I arrived in Dublin on a wet, gray morning, the first of October. The airport was a '70s movie, psychedelic carpet, cigarette smoke thick in the arrivals hall. *Ireland.* Cold wet air swept through me when I walked outside to find a cab. The accents were familiar from the bar, where we always had a guy or two just off the plane, but they took on a different quality when they filled all the spaces around me, looser, more confident. Changing money, I was conscious of my own accent, the nasal of it, the loud upward pitch of my words. The cabdriver was a skinny, leggy old man who said, "God bless you now, love. Take care o' yourself," when I got out at Erin's house.

Gordon Street was a little side street near a canal, a twisting narrow lane of squat little stucco one- and two-story houses, almost in miniature, with brick or red-painted facades and a few doors painted bright blue, a few shabbier ones painted black or dull red. Looming over the rooftops was a huge round structure shaped like a crown, and there was a Virgin Mary statue tucked into an alcove on the sidewalk. Children played and shouted in the street, their cheeks pink from the cold. With a little thrill of recognition, I thought, *The cold air stung us and we played till our bodies glowed.*

Ireland. It wasn't the way I thought I'd get here. I'd been about to spend my junior year studying at Trinity when my mom got sick. Lately I'd been thinking about graduate school. The brochures from Trinity and UCD were still in the top drawer of my desk.

Ireland. I could smell the ocean and something like woodsmoke and I inhaled deeply, clearing the stale odor of the cab from my nose. As I stood there, the sun broke through the clouds for a moment and illuminated the wet sidewalks, throwing the little row houses and brightly painted doors into impossibly beautiful color. It stopped me for a minute, the sheer magic gorgeousness of it, all the saturated reds and browns and blues, the light, the proportions of the houses, the shine of a silver car parked against the curb.

Erin's roommates were named Emer Nolan and Daisy Nugent. Emer, blond, round-faced, cheerful, was the one who had called the bar, and she took the lead once they let me in, showing me Erin's tiny room, barely a closet, with a small twin bed and a folding table set up as a desk.

They showed me the work schedule pinned on the wall over the desk and wrote down the address of the café where Erin worked.

I got out my agenda book and had them show me the day she left. September 16. I circled it in green pen. "She didn't tell you that she was going on a trip or anything, did she?"

They shook their heads.

"We got home from class and she'd gone already. Her rucksack wasn't in the press, so we thought she'd just gone traveling. She'd done it before."

"Did she ever talk about friends from work?" I asked them.

They glanced at each other. "There were some girls she went out dancing with a few times, and your man came by to see if she was sick when she missed work. But other than that, I don't think so."

"My who?" I was tired, jet-lagged from the red eye, off center in this unfamiliar place, their accents taking all my concentration.

"Sorry, the fella at her job. Conor. He came by Monday and we said we hadn't seen her. That's when we thought we should ring up your uncle."

It didn't take long to check her room. I didn't know what she'd brought with her to Ireland when she'd moved over in January but there weren't a lot of clothes in the closet: a couple of short black dresses that I knew she wore to go out, two floral blouses, a couple of pairs of faded Levi's. There was a heavy Aran sweater folded on the shelf over the hanging clothes, and a couple of cotton sweaters. Wherever she was, she must be wearing her brown leather jacket. She got it for herself for her birthday the year after she graduated from high school, and when you hugged her, the jacket smelled of new leather, cigarette smoke, and faintly of her perfume; the leather always felt cold to the touch. The velvet scarf I gave her for Christmas, green and blue, with thicker velvet butterflies gathering at one corner, wasn't in the room, either, so she must be wearing that. Her claddagh necklace, a high school graduation present from Father Anthony, wasn't in the little white box printed with a claddagh on the front that I found tucked into her underwear drawer. I could close my eyes and picture her wearing it, the delicate silver chain, the silver hands and purple amethyst heart in the center. I hadn't seen her without the necklace in five years. She must be wearing it too. Wherever she was.

A blue paper packet of photographs sat on top of a stack of bank statements and papers on the makeshift desk. They'd been printed at a photo shop in Dublin, and when I took them out and leafed through them, I found a few of what I thought were Dublin landmarks—I recognized Trinity College—and the rest seemed to have been taken in the country, trees and mountains and what looked like an abandoned school: gray buildings, empty windows, grass growing up around the foundation.

I sat on Erin's bed for a moment, then brushed my teeth and washed my face in the tiny bathroom at the end of the hall. I told Emer and Daisy that I was going to the café and didn't know when I'd be back. "Conor, right? That's the guy she worked with?"

"Yeah," Emer said. They were staring at me, their faces in shadow in the dark little hallway.

"What?" I asked.

"It's, it's only," Daisy stammered, "you have the look of her. It's a bit weird."

I pushed down a flash of annoyance. "I know. Everyone says that. What are these pictures of?" I held out the stack and Daisy took it from me, looking through them slowly.

"Four Courts, Grafton Street, Trinity. Here in Dublin," she said. "The others I don't know about. Wicklow maybe. She has a little camera." I tucked the packet of prints into my backpack.

Outside, the clouds were racing across the sky, a time-lapse movie. When they made space for the sun, the slightly shabby street was saturated with color and life again, the white lace curtains in the windows pristine before the clouds covered the sun and they went back to a dingy gray.

◆ ◆ ◆

It took me twenty minutes to walk to Trinity College and the center of the city. I walked into a stiff wind the whole way, past a square of sober gray houses and a small park, and men in overcoats walking fast, their heads down, and old ladies in rain bonnets pushing shopping trolleys. I breathed the sour smell of beer pouring out of empty pubs and the steam rising from the backs of buildings. It was late morning now, but I had the sense of a city waking, a few students returning from nights out, long coats clutched around them. I didn't linger outside the gray walls of the college or wander the lanes around Grafton Street, brimming with bookshops and little businesses behind glass windows.

The café—"The Garden of Eating," Emer had told me, rolling her eyes—was in a section of the city labeled "Temple Bar" on my map, a close little collection of narrow streets between a broad avenue called Dame Street and the river Liffey. It was grittier and more bohemian than the streets around the college; the colorful shopfronts and tiny lanes made it seem like a separate section of the city. Wild drumming came from a second-story window; a band practiced behind half-open garage doors. Workmen sat on buckets and smoked in front of a construction site.

A bit of graffiti on one wall read, "Long Live U2!" Someone else had written, "Wankers!"

At eleven a.m., the pubs lining the little streets were mostly quiet. The Garden of Eating, down a narrow, cobblestoned street called Essex Street, was open, though, and a guy behind the counter was dumping coleslaw and bean salads from huge aluminum mixing bowls into rectangular containers. The place felt more like a cafeteria than a café. There was a hammer and sickle painted on one wall and a sign over the counter that read, "No Man (Or Woman) Shall Go Hungry! Ask And Ye Shall Eat!" A tattered poster of a neon-haired troll with the word *Norge* was thumbtacked on one wall.

"Can I . . . ?" the guy started, but as soon as he saw me, he stopped and stared openly at my face. He looked confused, terrified, happy—all of those things in one moment and it made me pay attention immediately. It felt like a jolt of caffeine, sharpening all my perceptions, speeding my heart. He thought I was Erin, and he was happy to see her and somewhat surprised. *Remember that*, I told myself.

He was tall, dark-haired, and dark-eyed, a face full of interesting angles and dimples, Irish-looking in a way I'd never be able to put into words. He was wearing an apron and black jeans and a wool sweater in heathery shades of blue and brown.

"I know what you're thinking," I said quickly. "I'm Erin Flaherty's cousin. I know I look like her."

He exhaled and put a hand down on the counter to steady himself. I watched his face. For whatever it was worth, he was really surprised.

"Sorry." I stuck out a hand. "I'm Maggie D'arcy. I'm here trying to figure out where Erin went."

"Conor Kearney." His hand, when he took mine, was cool. I could feel a callus on his right thumb.

"Her roommates called my uncle to say they hadn't seen her in a while. He couldn't come over so I came instead. I'm hoping I can figure out where she went."

"She's not back, then?" His eyes met mine, then darted away.

"No. Can I just ask you a couple questions?"

"Sure. It's quiet now, but I'll have to go if a customer comes in. We've just had someone leave and I'm on my own at the moment." His accent was somehow both softer and stronger than Emer's and Daisy's.

He pointed to a table and we sat down.

"How long had Erin been working here?"

"Since the winter. Uh, she must have arrived in January. I think."

I wasn't sure, but I thought maybe he was only pretending he didn't know exactly when she arrived.

"Did she fill out an application or something?"

"No, it was all a bit . . ."

"Under the table? Don't worry. I don't care."

He almost smiled. "Nobody really bothers with that stuff. The Revenue doesn't go after places like this. She came in one day, asked if we needed anyone, said she had lots of experience, and that was it. She's good. Really good. Fast. Knows her way around a kitchen, understands how to close out the cash, all that. I guess her da has a bar in the States. Of course you'd know that. We're delighted to have her."

"Is it your place?"

"Ah, no. No. I've been here since my second year of college so I'm sort of a manager, I suppose you'd say."

"Do you work the same shift as her a lot?"

"Twice a week, Fridays and Sundays. I'm doing my M.Phil at Trinity, so my schedule's around when I have classes, but she works a pretty regular schedule, Thursdays to Sundays, three to closing."

"Were you seeing her?" I said it quick, no preparation. He was already nervous. I met his eyes and he looked away in alarm.

"No." His cheeks flushed pink. "No. We worked together. I saw her home a few times." His eyes were very dark and thickly lashed. I was sitting close enough to him to see each individual pinprick of black stubble on his cheeks.

"You live in Ringsend, too?"

"Donnybrook. Not far. I've only got a bedsit, like. It's a tip but it's not far into college." I wondered why he felt like he needed to explain.

"Erin's roommates said you called to check on her. Why did you do that?"

He hesitated, but just for a moment. "She hadn't shown up for her shifts for a whole week. It didn't seem right, somehow. At first I thought maybe she quit and didn't want to say. But then . . . I don't know, really. I thought I should just ring up." His eyes darted away from mine.

"Was she seeing anyone? Anyone ever come here looking for her?"

He flinched. "I thought you said you were her cousin. You sound like you work for the Guards."

"I'm just trying to find her."

"Yeah, 'course. Sorry." He looked down at the tabletop, embarrassed. "I don't think she was seeing anyone in particular."

"Where do you think she went?"

Someone out on the sidewalk shouted and he looked up and watched as a group of teenage boys ran up the street. "I . . . I've no idea. I hope she's all right."

"But if you had to say?"

"I don't . . . Why would you think I would know?"

The words erupted out of me before I could stop them. "Because you know her and you're a human being and sometimes human beings get ideas about other human beings. Or maybe she told you and for some reason you don't want to tell me."

He looked back at me quickly, then down at the table. "I don't know where she is. And look, maybe she just needed to get away, find some peace and quiet, like."

I studied him, trying to figure out if he knew something. I couldn't tell. I didn't know him well enough to know if he always bit his lower lip, if the guarded way he watched me was normal for him.

"I'm sorry," I said. "I haven't slept in about three days now." I took a deep breath and got the packet of photographs out of my backpack. Leaving out the Dublin ones, I handed them over. "Do you know what these pictures are of?"

He looked carefully, then handed them back with the abandoned school on top. "Down in Wicklow. That's Drumgoff Barracks, I'd say, though I can't be sure."

"What's that?"

"Glenmalure. It's the next valley over from Glendalough. The monks and the round tower and all that?" I nodded. He looked away, thinking, then said, "How much do you know about what happened in Ireland in 1798?"

"A little. The United Irishmen, right?" It came back to me as

I talked, a class from my sophomore year. "The Irish planned to rebel against English rule all over the country. But the English found out and put the uprising down everywhere except for a few places where it went on for another couple of months, right?"

He looked surprised. "Yeah, that's about the shape of it. Glenmalure was a bit of a symbol, I suppose you'd say. Before that, it was the site of a famous ambush in 1580, during the Desmond Rebellions, one of the few victories we could claim out of the whole yoke. Lord Grey was the English commander who was supposed to put down the Wicklow uprising and—"

Suddenly I remembered the song. "'Grey said victory was sure and soon the firebrand he'd secure. Until he met at Glenmalure . . .'"

"'With Fiach McHugh O'Byrne,'" Conor Kearney finished, grinning. "Right. The O'Byrnes and all the mountain men picked off the English in the mountains in 1580. Then in 1798, it was where the United Irishmen leader Michael Dwyer escaped after the risings. He had a network of hiding spots and safe houses and relatives in the hills who protected him. Anyway, after 1798, the English built the Military Road down through the Wicklow Mountains, so they'd have a military presence in the hills. Barracks were built in a couple of different places and they made sure to have a presence in Glenmalure, to keep an eye on the mountain men. It was kind of symbolic. I'm pretty sure that's the Drumgoff Barracks, just down the road from the Glenmalure crossroads. It's a lovely spot. That's where you go if you want to walk up Lugnaquilla. The Wicklow Way goes through there and there's a state forestry plantation. Good pub, too. My da used to take us walking there."

"Did she ever tell you she was going there?"

He hesitated, then he shook his head and looked away. "Not

exactly. But she once asked me whether I'd ever heard about a rock marking the place where a priest had been killed, somewhere near Glenmalure, she said. I hadn't. I think I told her there were lots of stones commemorating various massacres and killings around there. She didn't ask any more questions." There was something else, but he didn't say it, whatever it was. He was wary now.

I asked, "What's your degree in? What are you studying?"

He looked relaxed again. "History."

"Like, world history, all of it? The entire progression of human existence?" I let myself smile at him, let the tension go a little, and a big grin cracked his face.

"Yeah. I've got a ways to go now. I'll be an oul' fella by the time I've finished."

"So, what is it? Mesopotamia? Modern Turkey?"

He grinned again, then held his hands out at his sides. "Not that interesting. Here. Ireland. Twentieth century."

"Ah."

There was an awkward pause and then he said, "It's funny now. You look so much like her, but your . . . I don't know, your energy is really different."

"How would you describe Erin's energy?" The café was very quiet. All I could hear was an appliance humming somewhere in the back, radio classical music on the other side of a wall.

He ran a hand through his hair, looked away. Then he said, "I was raised in Clare, in the country, like, where there are oul' ones who go to mass every day but still put out offerings for the fairies, and one of my aunties believes that people have colors. Auras, I guess you'd say, but she just says 'colors.'"

He studied me for a minute. "Erin is yellow and orange. I know it sounds mad . . ."

"No, I get it. She is." I breathed in slowly. "What am I?"

He met my eyes. His were brown, but flecked with amber and green. He looked amused. "You're blue, but a sorta greeny blue."

"Yeah? Is it like, emanating from the top of my head? Or kind of a blue light all around me?"

"Neither." He grinned. "It's more intangible than that. You wouldn't understand. Not being a mad witch like my auntie."

I waited a minute, gathering my courage. "What color are you?" I asked him.

He looked serious again.

"Blue," he said. "Greeny blue. Like you. So she says, anyway." I liked his face. His eyes were suddenly alive with something. I could see him thinking.

The bell on the door jingled and we both looked up. A big group of students came in, smelling of cigarette smoke and the cold. "Sorry. I should . . ." he said.

"No problem. Thanks for your help."

"Give us a shout," he said. "I hope you find out . . . I hope you find her."

4

Emer said she'd drive me down to Glenmalure.

Daisy's brother had a little Ford hatchback that he kept behind his flat in somewhere called Dolphin's Barn and he let them use it once in a while to drive home to see their families or to visit a school friend of theirs who was going to university in Limerick. Daisy had work the next day but Emer didn't so we drove down in the morning, the Dublin suburbs quickly giving way to countryside. The sky was a clear, chilled blue, and the air, when we stopped for gas in a little town called Roundwood, smelled different from the air in Dublin, like trees and mountains rather than sea. As we headed south and then west, the land opened and rolled, turning into the Ireland in my mind, green fields, little cottages tucked into the folds of the hills.

"This will be Laragh, now," Emer said as we came to a junction where there was a hotel and a little craft shop. I was holding the road map Daisy's brother kept in the glove compartment and

I told her to take a left toward Glenmalure. The road started to climb after a bit, cottages and farms nestled into the wooded hillside. In five minutes we'd come out on top of a series of rolling hills, the fields broken into patchwork, white sheep clotting together against fences, the roofs of cottages bright against the brownish-green grass. A stone wall traced the road on one side, wild hedges on the other, a few last yellow flowers hanging on here and there.

"It's lovely, isn't it?" Emer said. I was tired; I hadn't slept well the night before in Erin's bed, and even as a passenger, I was having trouble getting used to the traffic being on the other side. Cars seemed to come out of nowhere, from the wrong place, and it felt strange to have the hedges and trees up against my left side.

We came to the crest of the hill and started down the other side. It seemed suddenly darker, the road now surrounded by orderly rows of dark green conifers. There were sections where all the trees had been cut down, exposing brown, wet-looking ground, and others where the trees seemed to crowd in around the road.

"That's the state forestry service," Emer told me, pointing to the thick forest to our right. It opened up a bit as we drove down, with different kinds of trees along the road. "We must be nearly there. What does the map say?"

I checked the map. "We'll come to an intersection up here and you should go through it. Stay on the Military Road and the barracks should be just there."

We descended through the trees to the intersection, just a tiny crossroads, a long whitewashed hotel hard against the hillside to our left, and went straight through. I took out Erin's pictures and compared them to the scene in front of me. I was pretty sure one of the pictures showed the view right in front of me, but in springtime: the

narrow country road, bright green fields, the yellow bushes blooming along the road the same but brighter and washed with sunlight.

"There it is," Emer said. "Up there." She pulled the car over onto
the left shoulder and turned the key. The barracks rose up from
the ground, a slim, tall, gray barrier. There was something ghostly
about the building, the way it was so obviously of another era, the
walled-up windows and the fence around it. We stood at the fence
for a minute, looking at the building. If Emer hadn't been there, I
might have yelled, "Erin!" but it was so silent, so still, I didn't say a
word.

"What do you . . . ?" Emer asked, watching me. "Do you think
she's here?"

The wind came down the valley and whistled around the old
structures. The clouds had covered the sun and Emer and I both
pulled our jackets more tightly around us. When I looked over at
her, her eyes were worried, her forehead set in concentration. "No,"
I said finally. "There's no one here. Let's go ask at the hotel."

*   *   *

The lower level of the hotel was a pub, empty at eleven a.m., but
warm and welcoming just the same thanks to the blazing fire and
the wood paneling and stone hearth inside. A young woman—our
age or even younger—was drying plates behind the bar, and she
gave a big smile when she saw us, and called out, "Hiya. You're back
again, then!"

I stopped where I stood. Next to me I felt Emer stop, too. The
room seemed to close in on us, the heat from the fire washing over
me in a wave.

"Erin's my cousin," I said. I could already see confusion crossing her face. She was seeing the differences. "Was she here recently? I'm looking for her."

The woman looked shocked. She put the plates down on the bar with a clatter and stared at us. "She's not . . . Is she all right, then?"

"I don't know." I forced myself to cross the room to the bar. "She left Dublin a week or so ago and we don't think she came back. Was she here recently?"

The woman was still flustered but she turned to a large calendar hanging on the wall behind the bar. "Yes, she . . . It must have been a Thursday because we had a big walking group arriving the next day, for the weekend." She traced a finger over the boxes, then said, "The sixteenth. It must have been the sixteenth."

I glanced over at Emer. That was the day Erin had left Dublin. "Was that the first time you'd seen her? She took these pictures but these look more like spring." I put them on the bar and the woman looked down at them quickly, fanning them out like cards.

"May. She came in and had lunch back in May and she was asking me about the barracks and the Wicklow Way. She wanted to do some walking and she asked me how to get to the path. I pointed her in the right direction and she set off. I remember it was May because it was my mam's birthday and it was nice she had such a lovely day."

"Okay, and then on September sixteenth she came down again?" My mind was racing. Obviously Erin had made it back to Dublin from the May trip. What we needed to know about was the more recent one.

The woman glanced back toward the calendar, remembering.

"Yeah, she came in and was talking to Deirdre, who does the cleaning. I came in and saw her and I recognized her from before. She said she wanted to walk the other direction on the Wicklow Way, like she'd gone south before and now she wanted to go north. So Deirdre and I told her to walk back up the Military Road and she'd see the signposts."

"How did she get down here?" I asked. "Did she tell you?"

"She must have taken the bus and had the driver stop. If it's not busy, you can sometimes ask the Glendalough bus drivers to drop you here. We can call ahead and arrange it with Bus Éireann, but we hadn't that day so she must have just asked once she was on the bus from Dublin. Or maybe she hitched. People would hitch around here quite a lot."

"And you didn't see her after you told her which way to go?"

"No. Is she all right then?" she asked again. "The Guards were in a few months ago asking about a German girl. I think they found her, though. They didn't ask about your cousin."

"No, they . . . We just don't know," I said. "I want to walk up that way."

Emer cleared her throat. "Do you not think we should ring the Guards?"

"I want to look first." I pointed back the way we'd come, along the Military Road. "Back that way. That's where the trail is?" I asked the girl behind the bar.

"Yeah, you'll see the signs." She looked worried. "Take care. Come back and let us know, will you?"

Outside, the wind had picked up and the temperature had dropped. The air was heavy, suddenly teetering on the edge of rain.

"You don't have to come with me," I told Emer. "I just want to see where she went. If I don't find anything, we'll call the police."

"No, I'll come along," she said, without hesitating.

We started walking up the road, climbing gradually back the way we'd come. The road was narrow, lined with moss-covered stone walls, the ground obscured by fallen leaves and mud-brown bracken. After ten minutes of walking, we came to a little turnout on the left. "There's the marker," Emer said, pointing to a wooden sign with a little yellow hiker icon. The trail disappeared into the woods ahead of us. "Do you think she's here?"

"I don't know. Let's just walk up there a bit," I said. "Okay?"

Emer nodded and we set off.

The clouds crowded in around us; I had the sense of the looming shapes of mountains ahead of us and all around us, but I couldn't see them through the mist. The woods got thicker as we went. We were back in a fir tree plantation now and there was something menacing about the uniform shapes of the trees, the way they reached toward the sky. When I turned around, I could no longer see the road. We were all alone in the woods.

Where are you, Erin?

Emer trudged along. I could feel her annoyed energy behind me but I wanted to keep going. I felt something in those woods. I knew Erin had been there.

"Maggie, do you not think—" Emer started.

"Hang on." I'd been scanning the ground next to the trail, but it was only by chance that I caught the glint of silver, the sliver of purple an alarm against the brown and dark green.

I fell to my knees, scrabbling in the leaves on the side of the track.

A silver claddagh necklace, tangled and nearly buried. The chain was broken at the clasp, the small silver link on one side now in the shape of a C; whatever force had done it had bent the metal until it gave.

At the center—a pale purple amethyst.

Erin's necklace.

5

TUESDAY, MAY 24,
2016

While I try to get the boxes back together, I think about giving Brian his stuff tonight, just to get it out of the basement. But his apartment doesn't have much space and I'm about to ask him a big favor, so I leave them where they are and bring my notebooks and a few of the files up and tuck them into my leather messenger bag for the trip. I'll have the six hours across the Atlantic to go through them.

The lasagna's in the oven when Brian comes through the door. He knocks first, always trying to be respectful, which annoys me, unreasonably, and he has a bottle of white, which is my favorite. We've gotten relatively comfortable with each other since the divorce, but we're not huggers or kissers. I take the bottle and say, "Can I talk to you for a sec?"

Lilly melts away to her room and I pour him a glass of red and we head out to the backyard. It's up a bit from the beach; my dad always said that the more expensive houses with beachfront down on Ocean Street were likely to get flooded but that we had the benefit of the view without the risk. The patio table's in the corner and we sit down and he leans back in his chair. He looks middle-aged, his hair thinning on top and his chest and stomach newly soft. I suddenly remember the desperate crush I had on him when I was sixteen and he was seventeen. I loved how tall he was, how the veins ran down the inside of his arms. I can still see that seventeen-year-old in his face.

"What's up?" he asks.

"Uncle Danny got a call from Dublin last night. They found Erin's scarf. Not far from where she disappeared. He wants me to go over."

He doesn't say anything, but he reaches out and touches my shoulder, just for a second. "Oh, Mags," he says finally. "I'm so sorry." I can feel his emotion. He cares about me, about Danny. He's a good guy. He really is.

"And there's another girl missing. That's how they found the scarf."

"But . . . is it connected to the other two? Did they find anything else?"

"No." But now I'm wondering what Roly hasn't told me. "Can you take Lilly for a week or so? Maybe more. I don't know how long it will take."

He hesitates and I know it's his embarrassment about his apartment. "Yeah, of course."

"It's probably better for her if you just stay here, since it's for so long. Do you mind?"

"No, no, of course not. Probably better for her." I can hear the relief in his voice. I'm supposed to pay him spousal support, but he won't take it. He was okay for a few years, after the divorce, but lately he's had bad luck with jobs, layoffs and workforce reductions and so on. His family had money once, a lot of it. Brian and Frank were like royalty at our high school, their house one of the biggest and most expensive along the beach. But his dad went bankrupt in the early 2000s and he now lives in Florida with a twenty-six-year-old girlfriend. Lilly tells me that Brian gets into a bad place sometimes, thinking about that.

He was angry for a while, after we split up, but now he's forgiven me for my together life, my career success, the nice house, inherited from my parents, which was half his before the divorce, the fact that I stopped loving him before he stopped loving me, the fact that maybe I never loved him at all. I flash back to an afternoon in the counselor's office, Brian spitting out the words: *I never had a chance. You loved someone else the whole time. I don't even know who it is.*

He wasn't wrong. But that's a long time ago now.

"Thanks, Bri."

"'Course."

After we eat, Lilly asks if we can go down to the beach. She's hesitant, not sure what we'll say, but Brian nods and I say, "Great idea!" a little too enthusiastically. The three of us walk down and stand on the sand. The beach is busy tonight; everyone in the neighborhood can feel spring on the air, the new sweetness of the days.

We watch the sun coming down over Long Island Sound. The gulls are calling overhead. A clam boat's coming in. We watch a lone fisherman against the horizon.

We're about to head back to the house when Jessica and Chris Fallon and their twins come down the beach, their dog running circles around the boys. Jessica and Chris were in Brian and Erin's high school class; I was a year behind them all. They wave and Lilly runs to say hi to the twins.

"Hey, guys," Jessica says. When she leans in to hug me, I can smell her perfume, too strong, even in the fresh air. Jessica was always thin, but middle age has rounded her out and like me, she's suddenly got a lot of wrinkles around her eyes and across her forehead. I saw her once on Main Street and thought, *That's an old lady*, before I realized it was her. But now, looking at her small nose and greenish eyes and the high cheekbones she always put too much bronzer on, I can see the sixteen-year-old she was. Chris has thickened, too, his football player's body gone to fat. I feel a sudden surge of affection for them, for Brian, for all of us. We're the parents now. We're the middle-aged fogies.

We watch the three kids throwing rocks into the water for the dog.

Something on my face makes Jessica turn serious, searching my eyes. "Is everything okay, you guys?"

I glance at Brian. "Yeah, we just . . . Uncle Danny got a call from Ireland last night. They found something they think belonged to Erin. I'm flying over tomorrow." Brian rubs my shoulder again. I think about how we must look to someone coming down the beach. Two couples, talking, watching their kids.

"Oh." Jessica's eyes go wide. She was Erin's best friend in high school, but it's been so many years. I can see it's completely out of the blue, that she'd stopped thinking we'd find anything. "I'm so sorry, Maggie. Do they think that . . . Do they think it's her?"

"They just don't know. I'm heading over. Brian's going to stay with Lilly." I nod toward the house.

Her breath catches. Her eyes fill with tears. "I just keep thinking about the last time we saw her. When we were all Eurailing over there and stopped in Dublin. She seemed different, but good. Like she was happy there." She looks up, meets my eyes. "Settled, I guess. And you know, for Erin . . . that was . . . I guess even once they found those other women, I always wondered if she might not just walk in someday and have some crazy explanation. I'm sorry, Maggie. This must be awful."

"No. I think probably I always thought that, too," I tell her. "Hopefully we'll get some closure. For Uncle Danny." The dog barks and we all watch it run down the beach, back toward Jess and Chris's house. Chris calls to the boys to head back.

"Bri, let us know if we can help with Lilly this week," Jess says. She hugs me again, too tight. I can feel her tears on my cheek.

"Nice time of year," Brian says once they're gone, his voice heavy with sadness.

"Yeah. It'll be summer before we know it."

He nods.

A gull calls somewhere over the water. The sound tosses me back—*a low, gray skyline, the air damp and touched with peat smoke, gulls wheeling over the Liffey, Mespil Road, Raglan Road, Sandymount Strand, Leeson Street, Sutton, The Four Courts, Delgany, Roundwood, Glenmalure.* I walk the maps in my mind.

Brian coughs. We watch our daughter walk toward us.

"She looked so old to me tonight," he says. "I mean, I just saw her last week. But when she came out to the car after school, she looked up and she was just . . . older."

"I know. It's crazy. That's been happening to me all the time lately."

"She's a good kid. We're lucky. She's got her head on straight." I know what he means. *Not like Erin.*

The sun hovers for a moment and then it's gone. We stay there, watching the empty stretch of sky as it changes color, purple, then pink, then orange.

6

The Aer Lingus nonstop to Dublin runs overnight. I sleep a little and when I wake up they're serving tea and coffee. The coffee is strong and dark, and I'm awake and on edge, teeth brushed and face washed in the airplane restroom by the time we land. Ready. I get through immigration and customs quickly, with a wink and a "Don't work too hard now, love," from the officer when I say I'm here on business.

This time, I arrive on a perfect day. Blue skies. White clouds. Sun shining. One in a million. The airport seems completely new, shiny silver and glass, a chic restaurant with pale wood décor just outside the passenger arrivals area. There are huge black-and-white pictures of Irish men and women lining the hall, some pale-skinned, red-haired, freckled, but not everyone, not anymore. There are little stories below the photos. *I grew up in Lagos and came here for medical school. My family is from Enniscorthy.* Not a psychedelic carpet to be seen.

I've read the stories. In the twenty-three years since I was last here, Ireland's been up and then down and now, maybe, from the looks of things, up again.

Roly Byrne is waiting for me. I catch a glimpse of him through the crowd. He's craning his neck, looking around, and when he sees me, his face breaks into a huge grin.

He surprises me by wrapping me in a tight hug. He smells good, lemony, like expensive soap and aftershave.

"You're looking great, D'arcy," he tells me, taking my carry-on without asking and leading the way through the waiting crowds. "Getting on agrees with you. Myself, on the other hand . . ." He runs a hand through thinning blond hair, cropped short, and makes a funny face that emphasizes the lines fanning out from his eyes. He's fit, still wiry, a greyhound of a person.

"You're no worse than you always were," I tell him.

He puts a hand on my arm and says, "What do you want to do? I need to head down to Glenmalure. I can take you to your hotel, you can have a shower and then I can tell you what we've got once you've had a sleep."

I think for a moment. "Let's head to the scene and you can brief me on the way."

"I won't be able to take you up to the site," he says, giving me a sidelong glance. "You know that. At best you'll be able to see the staging area for the search."

"I know. But it's been so long. I just want to remind myself of the place, see how far it is from where I found her necklace, that kind of thing." I force myself to make it sound breezy.

He hesitates for a minute and then says, "Cool." *Kyooooool.* I completely forgot about the way Roly Byrne pronounces *cool* and I smile in spite of myself. He points toward the airport exit. "I'll take you through the city center so you can see the changes. Let's go."

His car is a late-model silver BMW, so clean I can practically see my reflection on the door. I run a hand over the hood. "Fancy car, detective."

"Feck off," he says good-naturedly and tosses my bag in the back seat. The interior of the car smells strongly of lavender. "Sorry," he says, noticing me sniffing the air. "The wife has some special oil she plugs in. She says the car smells of stinky runners after I've been in it." He grins, looks over at me. "It's a bit weird, isn't it? We've both kids, you're a cop now. It's twenty-three years."

"It is weird," I say. "Getting older is weird."

Once we're out of the airport, he hands over a paper cup of coffee. "That's for you there, D'arcy."

"Thanks. How thoughtful of you."

"Oh, I'm a very thoughtful lad these days. You should see me, always doing the washing up, doing the school drop-off. I gave Laura a week at a yoga retreat for her fortieth, so."

"Yoga? I never would have thought it."

"You wouldn't find me *doing* the yoga, now." He winks at me and I laugh.

"So," he says. "Do you even recognize the place?"

Coming down O'Connell Street, it's almost the same, the wide bridge ahead, shops and neon signs, Dubliners crossing in every direction, but as we cross over the Liffey, I lose track of where I am for a second. There are new buildings, a new bridge, shaped like a harp. But then I see Trinity and the Bank of Ireland and the bottom of Grafton Street and I get my bearings again before we turn. "You should see her old neighborhood," Roly says. "It's all Facebook and

Google offices down there. They're even making some kind of skyscrapers out of Bolands Mills."

We head south, through quieter Ballsbridge and Donnybrook. I'm off center from the changes to the landscape, the new buildings, the jet lag.

"I'm glad to see you happy," I say. "Tell me about the job." I'm not ready to talk about Erin yet.

He follows my lead. "Yeah, job's good. I'm detective inspector on our Serious Crime Review Team, which is our cold-case squad. It was formed in 2007 and they put me on because I was a detective on the task force looking at the Southeast disappearances. I must have told you that. I'm hoping for the homicide squad at some point, but it's good, so. Now, I've a bit of irony for you. My superintendent will be a familiar name to ya."

"Wilcox?"

"That's the one. He's all right, though. Mostly leaves me to it. He'd rather play golf most days. But when I mentioned you were coming over he warned me off letting you get too close to the case. Again." He looks over at me, serious now. "I've to watch myself, D'arcy. Just so you know."

"Of course," I say, feeling my spirits sink a bit.

"Anyway, I've a good team. You'll meet them. I have a sergeant and two detective Gardaí I've assigned to the discovery. They want to ask you some questions about your . . . about Erin. They're just getting up to speed now. The scarf's only just been found. We have a tech designated to the team and she's working away. Hopefully she'll have something for us. It's all a bit more reactive than the way we usually work. Normally we'd identify evidence for testing or witnesses to be interviewed again, but because of Niamh Horrigan we're working parallel to the missing persons investigation. It's a bit mad, to tell the truth, but if there's a possibility of uncovering anything from the other cases that might help find her we'll keep at it."

"Of course. I'd like to help however I can." The look on his face makes me add, "However Wilcox lets me."

"How about you, D'arcy? How's the job for you now?"

"Yeah. Job's good on this end, too. I'm still working homicides. I like my team, like the work. Nothing to complain about. I made lieutenant a few years ago. Sometimes I don't know how I got through the years after I got divorced, when Lilly was little, but she's fifteen now and it feels like I've got room to breathe again."

"Fair play to you," Roly says. "Laura was home full-time during all the years ours were little. There were weeks I hardly saw them. But she kept things going. She's a great woman now. You'll meet her." Roly and Laura have four kids, two girls a little older than Lilly and two little boys. He sent me a picture a few years back, the boys blond and impish, the girls tall and pretty, everyone dressed in Christmas best. "I saw you had a big case there a few years back," he says quietly. "On those serial murders."

I feel heat rise toward my face, every nerve ending in my body suddenly alert. I do the thing I do to stop the rush of adrenaline. I breathe. *Inonetwothreefour. Outfivesixseveneight.* The first breath slows the response, the second chases back the heat. "You Googled my cases, Roly?"

"Only I read about it on some law enforcement news thingy. I saw Long Island, like, and wondered if it was anything to do with you."

I take another breath, feel him hearing it. "Yeah. That was a crazy one. How did you and Laura meet, again?"

He glances over. "Ah, it was a couple years after . . . well, after you left, after everything. You might remember I always liked to keep my flat nice. I went along to this decorator's showhouse and there was a room that I loved. I just walked in and I thought to myself, I'd like to live here. A few months later, I started chatting to her at the pub, we started talking about our jobs, she said she was an interior designer and, trying to impress her, I told her all about the showhouse and the room I loved."

I interrupt him. "And she'd done the room?"

"Ah, you bollixed my story. That's right. That was it, but. I knew that night I was going to marry her. I didn't tell her for a couple days." He winks at me. "But I knew that night. Love at first sight, like."

"Aren't you going to ask me how my love life is going, Roly?" I grin at him from my reclining position.

"Since you bring it up, how's your love life going?"

"It isn't," I say. "Not so's you'd notice."

"No? You're not a whaddayacallit, cougar?"

I laugh. "I don't think so. The only guy I've dated seriously since the divorce was like fifteen years older than me."

"Really? An oul' fella?"

"He wasn't that old. I was thirty-five then. He was fifty."

"Sure, I'll be fifty in a few years," he says soberly. "There hasn't been anyone since then?"

"No," I say. "Not really. It's sad, isn't it?"

"Why'd you get divorced? If you don't mind me asking."

"We got married because I was pregnant. It was okay for a bit, but . . . there wasn't enough there to go the distance." It's the best way I can think to say it, but it doesn't quite capture the sadness of my last couple of years with Brian. "It's actually so much better now. We get along pretty well. Lilly's doing great."

Our conversation slows and I fall asleep for a bit. When I sit up we're already well south of Dublin, into green fields and sheep. I feel something wash over me, despite everything. Awe. It's so beautiful here, it fills me up with a kind of glorious recognition. *Ireland.*

"Good kip?"

"Mmmm." I take a long sip of the coffee Roly got me, rub my eyes and fix my seat.

"Okay," I tell him. "I'm awake now. What can you tell me about Niamh Horrigan without putting yourself in the shit?"

He looks over at me and winks. "The family rang up the local lads in Galway Monday morning. Niamh Horrigan, age twenty-five. She's a teacher at a school there. She had planned to walk part of the Wicklow Way at the weekend. She was staying at the youth hostel in Glendalough, and on Saturday morning she woke up and left early. They think she was going to try to walk to Glenmalure as she was booked at the hostel there for Saturday night. Then she was to take the bus from Roundwood back home. Her family expected her home Sunday evening, started ringing her mobile. She didn't answer. When she wasn't home by Monday morning, they got the Guards involved."

"Phone?" I ask.

"It's not pinging, wherever it is. Could be the battery died, could be someone switched it off. You know yourself. Anyway, so, they were out looking for her, with the dogs, and they found the scarf. I'll show you on the map when we get there. It's fairly far away from where you found the necklace, up in the trees. As I told you, one of the lads remembered the description and they rang me up. Techs started excavating the site yesterday." I try to figure out what he's not saying. My instinct tells me that Roly's urgency yesterday means there's something else.

"Bad luck about the phone. Anything else? Is the bed-and-breakfast still there?"

"Your woman's not running it as one anymore, but the local lads made sure Niamh hadn't been there. I've a bad feeling, D'arcy. As for the excavation around where they found the scarf, it may be a few days. They have to do it very carefully. If there are remains, they don't want to disturb the evidence. Ah, you know all that shite."

I look out the window for a long moment. "Remind me about McKenny and Talbot."

"All right. This has all been in the papers. My team had taken a look at the cases a couple years ago, even recommended to the local lads they interview some witnesses again. But there wasn't really anything to go on. Teresa McKenny, twenty-two when she disappeared while walking from Aughrim to her job at the golf course in Macreddin Village in June of 1998. Tiny little places, so they are. Normally her brother drove her but his car was knackered and so she set off walking. She never made it. Two weeks to the day after she was last seen, her body was found by a farmer in a streambed in some foothills about fifteen kilometers away. She'd only been dead a day, from blunt force trauma to her skull. She'd been raped. Repeatedly. But the fella who did it must have used a johnny. Condom. There was nothing for the techs to look at. The stream was full from recent rain and washed away any trace evidence.

"Then June Talbot in 2006. She was English, thirty when she disappeared. She'd been over here for a few years, living with her Irish boyfriend in Cork and working as an early childhood teacher at a crèche in Frankfield. Her friends said the relationship wasn't going too well. Maybe she had a fella on the side, but no one knew or would say for sure. She went on a bit of a walkabout, just to think things over. Boyfriend swore he didn't know she wasn't planning on coming home, but she checked herself into a guesthouse near Baltinglass for a couple of nights and told the woman who owned the guesthouse that she was going walking at Baltinglass Abbey.

"It took them a while to figure out she was actually missing, but two weeks after the last time she was seen, her body was found in the river Slaney by a woman walking her dog. Same details as McKenny. Blunt force trauma, sexual assault, no evidence to speak of. They looked at the boyfriend but he was well alibied and . . . that was it. As you know, since McKenny went missing in 1998 we've considered your . . . Erin's case a possible link with them, but the fact that her body was never found . . . Maybe now we'll have something. I'm awfully sorry to get you over here under these circumstances, D'arcy."

I push the emotion down. *Not now.* "I know. Tell me more about Niamh Horrigan."

"Lovely girl, everyone adored her. Excellent teacher, nice to her granny. Wasn't seeing any particular fella but she wasn't against the odd shag now and again, I'd say. That's the feeling I get. They're looking there, of course. She was an experienced mountaineer and hillwalker. One of her friends said she could take care of herself, had in fact once fought off a pervert when she was walking in Killarney. We'll get some more about that now. But that's it. Nothing to suggest she was going to take off." He looks over at me. "She bred Angora rabbits."

"Rabbits?"

"Rabbits."

"She went missing Saturday?"

"Yeah." Today's Thursday. *Five days.*

We drive in silence. The landscape is familiar but new, too, greener and fresher and wetter than I remember.

"Ah, it's a lovely day now," Roly says.

It is. The hills are purple and green, bright yellow gorse blooming all along the road. I open my window and breathe in the cool, fragrant air.

We're in Laragh by eleven and Roly turns left and then hangs right to stay on the old Military Road.

"It hasn't changed a bit," I say as we climb past little cottages and fields of white sheep, then start down the other side into the Glenmalure Valley.

"Some parts of Wicklow have," he says. "But you're right. It's a bit remote for commuting, I suppose. The trees have probably grown up." The plantations on either side of the road seem to have expanded. The hillsides are greeny black with conifers.

They've set up a staging area in a little parking area and clearing off the old Military Road. I can see the uniformed guards moving around in their reflective vests and the white vans that likely belong to the crime scene processors. "It's Coillte property," Roly says. *Queel-cha.* "The state forestry service. There's a track that goes up through the forest not far from where the scarf was found but they'll still be walking for a bit."

The detective in me recoils at the task they've got up here. From an evidence preservation standpoint, this is a nightmare. The wind, the weather, the inaccessibility. They may have to come in with helicopters if they find anything, depending on where they find it.

I walk back toward the road, away from the marked cars and crime scene vans, and stand there for a moment looking back across the valley. In my memories of this place, the hills are socked in, obscured by clouds, the air cold and heavy with rain. But today the sun is shining over the valley, the greens are brilliantly green, the purply browns rich and dark. It's beautiful and wild. The wind moves across the near-distant mountains. I think about the search for Niamh Horrigan. The search for Erin. It seems impossible you could find one woman in all this vastness.

Tell us, Erin. Tell us who. But the only sound is the wind through the trees. The long sweep of golden grass by the road, edged by the rows of conifers, the bright blue sky and smudgy clouds, everything is rich and strong and brilliant.

Ireland.

When Roly comes back, we stand there letting the sun warm our faces for a few minutes, and then we drive down to the crossroads.

7

THURSDAY, MAY 26,

2016

I remember the long, whitewashed hotel from before. It's close to the road, making its stand in the landscape. A few people are clustered around the door, and one of them, a big guy with a ponytail, calls out, "Detective Byrne!" Roly waves but ignores him and mutters, "Fuckin' reporters." The pub is exactly the same, warm and low-ceilinged, with lots of wood and stone and knickknacks on the walls.

The waitress takes our drink order and leaves us with menus. She's young, too young to be the girl I remember. They're playing a CD of traditional music, instrumental only, "Caledonia," then "Skibbereen," then "The Fields of Athenry."

"I'm glad they haven't changed it," I say. "I read an article about how all these Irish pubs are getting turned into fancy wine bars and bistros."

"Well, you know some of those old places could use a bit of up-dating," Roly says. "Better décor and that."

"I think they should keep them just the same. I love this kind of thing." I breathe in the peaty, smoky air, the delicious must of old pubs.

"Ah sure, Americans like all that old Ireland shite. I have a theory about it. Do you want to hear it?"

"I have a feeling I'm going to whether I want to or not."

"You want Ireland to stay the way it was so you can come over here and feel good that your piss-poor ancestors got out. You can indulge in a wee bit o' nostalgia for the mother country and then go home to your high-quality Italian marble countertops."

I burst out laughing. "You may have something there, Roly. But truthfully, I don't really like Italian marble. When I redid my kitchen I used wood."

"Ah, for your piss-poor ancestors, I bet."

I order leek and potato soup with a piece of brown bread and a pint of Guinness. Roly orders a half pint of Heineken and a ham sandwich. There's a nice wave of heat coming from the fireplace against the wall behind us. As I take my first sip of the Guinness, I sigh happily. "Why you drink that yellow crap when you have the best beer in the world, I'll never know," I tell him.

"Well, that's why you Americans are all so overweight," he says seriously. "Not you, like, but I hear it's a public health epidemic over there. Myself, see, I like to watch the figure." He pats his middle.

The soup is good, thick and a little sandy, with a strong taste of leeks and butter. I spread Kerrygold on my bread and dip the bread into the soup. *Ahhh.*

"All right," I say, once we've both finished eating. I can feel the emotion that started welling up at the scene starting to build again. I can push it down by doing my job. "I'm okay. I really am. What can you tell me about the review of Erin's case?"

"You know yourself, D'arcy, not a lot. The updates I've given you and your uncle over the years, I can go over those with you. As I said, I'll bring you in tomorrow and they can ask you some questions about Erin, about her mind-set and that. But I've to take care."

I wait a second, figuring out how to come at this. "Didn't you tell us at one point that you did some interviews a few years ago, someone who thought he had seen Erin at the bus station?"

"Yeah, there was a fella who rang us after RTÉ ran a special about cold cases. He said he wasn't sure, but he thought he remembered seeing someone who looked like Erin at Busáras on the eighteenth, the Saturday of that weekend after she went missing. He was taking the bus home to Galway for the weekend and he noticed her, thought she was nice-looking, etc. But he couldn't be sure."

"I imagine there have been reported sightings?"

"Sure, a good few over the years. They usually spike after RTÉ or one of the UK stations do something on outstanding missing persons cases. Nothing that's amounted to anything, though."

"Can you give me anything on Niall Deasey? He show up on your radar at all over the years?"

Roly sits back in his seat. I can see him thinking, sorting through what's public information and what's not. I'd do the same, but right now my job is to get him to tell me more than he wants to, and it makes me feel guilty all of a sudden, that I'm not on Roly's side.

"Niall Deasey has kept his nose clean," Roly says. "Now, that's not to say I haven't heard . . . rumors. My pals on the drugs squad mostly. But nothing that we could use. As you know, he moved to London in the late nineties. So he was out of the country when June Talbot went missing. His alibis checked out. He returned three years ago and he's kept his head down."

"Anyone else who wasn't one of the original persons of interest?"

He thinks for a minute. "Few fellas with sex charges who lived on Gordon Street or nearby, a few tips called in. That's all I can tell you." Roly takes a long sip of his lager and pushes his chair back. "Nothing good."

We're finishing our food when the waitress looks up suddenly, caution on her face, and Roly and I follow her gaze.

One of the uniformed gardaí from the site is standing in the door, and she crosses the room and gestures for Roly to stand up. I can see the reporters behind her, trying to sniff out why she's here.

"We tried to ring you on your mobile," she says. "But you must have the ringer off." Roly scrambles in his coat pocket as she looks at me and leans in to whisper something to him. She doesn't keep her voice low enough. I hear her say, "They found something."

My stomach tightens. *This is it.* I think of Uncle Danny first.

I have some news, Uncle Danny. I have something to tell you. Are you sitting down?

"Lads wanted you to know," she says, just loud enough for me to hear. "They've got a human skull. And that's not all. Whoever dug the grave and buried her threw his spade in after him."

◆　◆　◆

We spend a couple of hours back at the site. The skull and shovel— *spade*—are four feet under, not far from where they found the scarf. Roly goes up with the techs and I wait in the car. When he comes back he tells me they're doing another large-scale search for Niamh Horrigan tomorrow. The family will be coming back from Galway. Everyone's worried about coordination, jurisdiction. Roly, who they know is working the cold cases, is putting everyone on edge, now that they've found the remains.

"What do you want to do?" Roly asks me once we're back in the car. "I can drop you at the hotel. I can take you home to Laura. She'd love to make you a cup of tea and some toast and put you right. Sure, I don't like thinking of you in a hotel room."

I watch the orange vests, still moving up in the hills.

I imagine the excavation site suddenly, a dark hole, up among the trees. I push it away but something else comes to me, unbidden—Erin's face, alive, laughing, her blue eyes fixed on me, her brown curls falling across her face, running away from me on a beach. *Sun on the water. The smell of suntan lotion and salt. Erin's nose peeling from her sunburn.* I push that away, too.

I look over at Roly. "I know you have to be careful, Roly. I know you can't tell me everything. But I want to help you work this case, however I can. I know things about Erin no one else knows. I was here. I have a sense of her. I found the necklace."

I can see him getting ready to protest, to tell me that there are procedures and rules and protocols for a reason, that you have to keep a line between the family and the investigation, that you have to keep details back from the public.

I meet his eyes and stare him down. "If I can help you find the fucker who killed Erin, they might be able to find Niamh Horrigan before he kills her. I want to help you work this case, Roly. I want to do whatever I can."

8

I wake up at five a.m. in the hotel, disoriented, jet-lagged, a caffeine headache starting. Friday morning. I'm longing for Lilly. It's been years since she snuck into bed with me in the morning, curling her little warm body against mine, tangling her fingers in my hair. It was a habit she got into after Brian moved out and she kept it up until she was ten or eleven. I can distinctly remember a morning when she came in and lay down next to me but didn't snuggle herself around me.

I'm grieving for that Lilly now, wishing I could go back and have that small body next to mine one more time.

It's what people say when someone dies: "I'd kill for one more minute with him." I remember feeling that way about my mother after she died. Days after that last moment of stillness, it hit me that I'd never feel her hand on my head ever again. And because I've been thinking nonstop of Erin, I remember the feeling of her hand in mine. *Let's go, Maggie. Let's run!*

It's the middle of the night in Alexandria, but I can't stop myself. I call the house landline. Brian answers on the fourth ring, his voice full of sleep. "Yeah? Hello? Maggie?"

"Yeah, it's me. Everything's fine. I just missed her so much suddenly. I just wanted to make sure she's—you're both—okay."

"Yeah, we're fine. She's good. Are you okay?" I can hear him coming awake, remembering. "Do they know anything?"

"They did find remains, but there's a lot of work to do. And there's this other woman missing. I don't want to tell Danny yet, but can you keep an eye on him? If they get an ID, I'll call you before I tell him so you can be with him. I'm worried about his heart."

He takes a deep breath. He loves Danny. "Yeah, just let me know."

"So everything's good at school?"

"She got an A on her English paper. She was pretty happy about that. She let me read some of it and I could barely understand parts of it." I can hear the pride in his voice and I feel a surge of appreciation for it, that I have someone to share my joy in her accomplishments with. "She's a smart girl."

"Yes, she is. Is she helping out with dinner and dishes and everything?"

"She's been busy with school. I don't mind. I haven't had a lot of hours this week, so it's okay."

Good." There's a long silence, dead air across the wide, dark ocean. "Brian, thanks so much for this. I really appreciate it."

I can't tell if he's sad or just tired, but he sighs again and says, "Of course, Mags. Anytime."

I recognize the compulsion in my voice, figure he can hear it, too, but still I ask, "You're setting the alarm, right? And you remember the combination for the gun safe?"

"Yeah, don't worry. Everything's good."

"Okay, tell her I love her and I miss her a lot. Sorry to wake you. I'll call again tomorrow when she's up."

Breakfast at the hotel is coffee and lukewarm oatmeal sprinkled with dried cranberries and walnuts. I check my cell phone to make sure Roly hasn't called, and take a left out of the hotel, crossing College Street and walking under the main gate of Trinity College. I have the words memorized. *Dr. Conor Kearney, Associate Professor of History, Room 4000, Arts Building, Trinity College Dublin 2.*

I think about just finding the Arts Building and climbing the stairs to room 4000, but I don't have the nerve. So I get a cup of tea at the little student dining hall and sit there, my heart pounding, looking around me, waiting for him to walk through the door. But of course he doesn't. It's all students and it occurs to me that there must be a separate place for the professors to have lunch.

I search on my phone and find it. The staff common room is upstairs. Back outside, I find a spot to sit on a low concrete wall across from the steps. The *Book of Kells* is around the corner and the tourists have already started streaming in. They've still got students doing tours. The campus looks exactly the same, except for how the students are dressed, the girls in jeans and high boots instead of short skirts and Doc Martens. My stomach is tight with anxiety, the coffee and tea and oatmeal sloshing around, sending nauseous jitters through my veins.

Out in the courtyard, it's breezy. The air is cold but it carries the promise of sun and spring and a salty, peaty scent.

If this were a movie, I think, *if this were a movie, he'd come down those steps right now and I'd look up and he'd look up and . . .*

But it's not a movie, and I sit there for thirty minutes getting

thoroughly chilled, scrolling nervously through my phone and trying not to look at the door to the dining hall. Finally I decide to
get a cup of tea and wander the city until it's time to meet Roly and
the team. It's a city of new, translucent layers, I discover, as I walk
through the lanes behind Grafton Street, down Duke Street and
Lemon Street and around to Clarendon Street and across Dame
Street down to Temple Bar. It's the same and not the same, shinier,
newer, but filled with shops and pubs that seem familiar, too. I find
Essex Street and it takes me a few minutes to find the café. It's been
painted a tasteful gray and it's now the Bistro Le Mer. The pubs
seem the same, the bright red one and the yellow one and the blue
one basically as I remember them. I walk back to the hotel by the
quays. The Liffey is black and silver, the brick red faces of the buildings on the north side staring like a crowd of faces waiting in line.

◆ ◆ ◆

I'm carrying two coffees when I meet Roly in front of the Westin at
two.

"What is that, a latte? Lovely, lovely."

"Your tune seems to have changed, huh? I remember when you
thought fancy coffee was ridiculous."

He grins and takes the coffee. "I am a man who is open to new
experiences, D'arcy. Right, then, I'm going to introduce you to some
of the lads, but you're here to answer questions about Erin and help
us find any links between these cases so maybe we can get this guy
before he kills Niamh Horrigan. They know you're a cop but I have
to be very careful here. Capiche?"

"Capiche."

"You all right, then?"

"Yeah, mostly. I called home at midnight, US time, just to check on Lilly. I think I'm more anxious than I realize."

"Well, we should have something from the state pathologist's office by tomorrow."

Roly works out of a new extension on the back of the Pearse Street Garda Station, around the corner from the hotel. The offices are brand-new, modern, tastefully decorated. The chairs are even comfortable. Roly explains that members of the team spend some of their time here and some at local Garda stations, depending on which stage of a review they're in.

"This is nice," I say. "You should see the dump Suffolk County Homicide has to work out of."

"Ah, now, I'd have thought you'd have nothing but the best over there."

"We're a society in decline, Roly."

"Ah, you know I'd say you are, now. The girls like to watch this Kardashian thing on the telly. That's what made me realize."

The Serious Crime Review Team has a small suite of rooms full of desks and phones and filing cabinets that I get just a tiny glance at before Roly hustles me into a conference room, which smells of fresh paint and cake. I sit there alone for a few minutes before he comes back with a young guy.

"Joey. This is Detective Maggie D'arcy. Maggie, this is a young up-and-comer, Detective Garda Joey Brennan. He's going places."

"Ah, yeah. Today I'm after going to the Spar." He turns to me and makes an expert shift in tone. "You're very welcome to Dublin. Sorry it's under these circumstances." He's a wholesome-looking guy, maybe thirty, tall, with black hair, olive skin, and a country accent, softer than Roly's, more stereotypically Irish. I shake his hand and he sits down across from me, setting a laptop on the table and spreading out paper files.

"When's Griz getting here?" Roly asks.

"She texted she's on her way," Joey says. "Ah, there we are."

A slight young woman with light blue eyes and brown hair cut in a short-banged pageboy comes in, holding a paper cup that's leaking brown liquid from the top. She's wearing jeans and boots and a trendy-looking corduroy jacket. "Hiya," she says, grinning at us. "The Luas was packed." The thought pops into my head that she looks more like an artist than a police detective, and I tell myself to fuck off. I hate it when people tell me I don't "look like" a cop.

"This is Detective Garda Katya Grzeskiewicz," Roly says. "That's G-R-Z-E-S-K-I-E-W-I-C-Z. Most of us call her Griz because we're a fuckin' bunch of barbarians and we can say 'O'Coughlihulihan' but we can't say 'Grzeskiewicz.'"

"Apparently they can't say 'Katya,' either," she says, then grins. Her accent's Dublin like Roly's, but with a tiny bit of something else. "To be honest, now, I can barely say 'Grzeskiewicz' myself."

I shake hands with her and Roly tells her and Joey to get the rest of the team into the conference room. While he does the introductions, I make a little tree in my notebook. Roly is the detective inspector in charge of the team, and a stocky dark-haired guy my age or a little older named John White seems to be the next most senior member, with a rank of detective sergeant. I write him in. Then there are Joey and Griz, who both have the rank of detective garda, which would be a detective on my squad. I know that all of Ireland is policed by the Garda Síochána, with local and regional stations having jurisdiction and specialist teams like Roly's and technical bureaus and labs aiding in investigations as necessary. "The rest of the team is still out on other cases," Roly says. "We'll bring them in if we need to, but for now, you're stuck with this shower. They have some questions to ask you based on their review of Erin's case, if that's all right."

"Of course."

Roly looks around the table, makes eye contact with each of them. I can feel the energy coming off him; he's practically hovering over his chair at the head of the table, his right leg vibrating, his fingers making tiny, tight circles on the table in front of him.

He smiles briefly, then wipes it off his face and says, "Okay, Detective D'arcy is all yours. What are you going to ask her?"

9

I met Roly Byrne for the first time at the Irishtown Garda Station. When we got back from Glenmalure, Emer and Daisy and I went straight to the station to report Erin missing and hand over the necklace. It seems impossible now that I didn't even think about preserving it as evidence at the scene, but our only nod to procedure was to wrap it in Saran wrap—which Emer called "cling film"—when we got back to Dublin. It sat on the table in front of me while I gave all of Erin's vital statistics to the young guard they sent out to talk to me. They said they would get in touch with the station down in Wicklow and contact the American embassy for me. The next day, they called and said we should come back to speak with the detectives assigned to the case.

We had been waiting for twenty minutes when Roly Byrne exploded into the room. We heard him first, an Irish accent I was starting to recognize as Dublin, fast and loud out in the hallway.

The door slammed open and a young guy, only a few years older than me, with a thatch of blond hair and a sharp, hawky face, burst through it as though he'd been at a full run on the other side. He was wearing a dark suit that fit him well and he stopped in front of me. There was so much energy behind him that when he stopped, he swayed a bit on his black leather wingtips.

He thrust out a hand and said, "Detective Garda Roland Byrne."

A tall woman in a navy pantsuit entered the room behind him and shut the door. She had short, bowl-cut dark hair and very pale skin, delicate reddish freckles spattered haphazardly across her nose and cheeks. She was broad-shouldered, and her black blazer, with wide lapels and large brass buttons, looked uncomfortable, like she'd stuffed her arms into it. She didn't look happy to see me.

"This is my partner, Detective Garda Bernadette McNeely," Byrne said. "Now, tell us about your . . . cousin, is it?"

I gave them the basics, Erin's full name, age. I told them she had moved to Dublin in January, that she'd been working at the café and that it was the photographs in her room and my conversation with Conor Kearney that made me think she might have gone down to Glenmalure. Byrne nodded his head, but McNeely had a little scowl on her face, like she didn't quite believe me.

When I was done, they asked Emer and Daisy about how Erin had ended up living in their house.

They were friends from back home in somewhere called Ballyconnell and they'd come to Dublin for college, computers, they said, at someplace called DCU. The house belonged to Emer's aunt, an inheritance from her husband's side of the family. "Sure, she's got a house in Killashandra now, so she had no use of it," Emer said. "She said we could have it if we wanted. We put a sign up in the corner shop for a roommate and Erin rang up."

Erin had been living with them since January. Everything had seemed fine. She'd traveled without telling them before, and when they got home the evening of the sixteenth and realized that she was gone, they just figured she'd gone to Galway or something.

"So it wasn't out of the ordinary for her not to tell you where she was going?"

"No," Daisy said. "She's a lovely girl. But we're not in each other's pockets. She doesn't usually let us know where she is or what time she'll be home or anything. She sometimes . . . stays out for the night."

"So no one rang or anything that day?"

"Well, we were out all day. There weren't any messages on the answerphone, anyway."

McNeely looked at them and then at me. "She have a fella?"

They shook their heads and said there didn't seem to be anyone regular, and Byrne asked me, "Did your cousin tell you or her father about anyone she's seeing?"

"No. She told my uncle that she was having fun, but he said he didn't think she had a boyfriend or any really close friends here."

"Any fellas ring her up?" That was for Emer and Daisy.

"A few," Emer said. "An Irish fella named Donal rang her a couple times. He had sort of a Limerick accent. She said she met him at a pub and gave him her number and then wished she hadn't."

Byrne thought that was interesting. "Donal. Do you think he might have tried to contact her again?"

Emer shrugged. "It was back in January and he only rang twice. I wouldn't think so."

Daisy said, "There was another fella who rang a few times in the summer. He had sort of a funny accent. American or Canadian, but not really, a bit neither here nor there, if you know what I mean. I can't remember his name, but the last time he said to tell Erin he was meeting some friends at O'Brien's on Pearse Street if she wanted to join." McNeely wrote that down.

"Anyone ever stay the night at your place?" he asked Emer and Daisy. They said no, never.

"So, she left on, what day was it now?" McNeely got out a little paper date book and turned it to September.

"The sixteenth," Daisy said.

"What was the longest she'd been gone before when you didn't know where she was?" Byrne asked Daisy.

She looked up. "She went up to Belfast in April, I think it was. She was gone ten days, eleven days, something like that."

"And she hadn't said anything to you?" Byrne asked me again. "She didn't tell you or your uncle she was going on a holiday? She hadn't been depressed, in trouble, anything like that?" When he said "in trouble," Emer and Daisy both looked down at the ground.

"I haven't talked to her in a while," I said. *Since she left. I haven't talked to her since she left. The beach. Her face wet with rain.* "My uncle said she called him a few weeks ago and said she was having fun, but nothing about a trip."

I'd brought a photograph—Erin's high school graduation portrait—and I handed it over. Then he asked me for my full name, date of birth, address. "So, you're twenty-two years of age, then. Erin is twenty-three?" I nodded. "And there's nothing you can think of that might tell us what was on her mind?"

I shook my head. "Nothing specific."

They took some more information down and I told them I'd be staying in Erin's room until we knew more.

I thought we were finished, but McNeely turned to me. "Why did Miss Flaherty come over here? She's not a student. Does she know anyone in Dublin?" McNeely's accent was different from Byrne's and Emer's and Daisy's, Northern Irish, I was pretty sure. Her sentences headed toward Scotland, veering up at the ends, reminding me of a guy from Belfast I knew at Notre Dame.

"Erin is impulsive sometimes," I said. "I . . . I don't really know why she moved here. We're Irish, Irish American—Erin and I practically grew up in my uncle's bar. It's called Flaherty's. Maybe she wanted to . . . I don't know, live here for a bit. Learn about Ireland." My voice caught and I swallowed. "She . . . we'd had a hard year. My mother died a year ago last summer and Erin had a rough time. She just wanted to try something new, I guess."

I took a deep breath and proceeded. They were going to find out. "And her mother was Irish. She left right after Erin was born and they never had a relationship. We don't think she was looking for her or anything like that, but maybe she wanted to see where she . . . where she was from. I don't know."

"Do you know her mother's name?" McNeely looked interested all of a sudden. There was something there. They could feel it.

"Brenda Flaherty. I think her maiden name was Donaghy. But we really don't think she ever contacted Erin."

Emer and Daisy were staring at me. It was obvious Erin had never told them her mother was Irish.

"Had she been to Ireland before?" McNeely asked. Her eyes were a dark, navy blue. Her freckles swam together in front of my eyes for a moment.

"No. Neither have I," I said.

"We'll look into it and we'll be back to you, Miss D'arcy. We'll get on to the bus stations and that. The lads down in Wicklow. We'll check with her job." McNeely studied me thoughtfully and asked, "Could your cousin have wanted to harm herself?"

I froze. "I don't know. She was . . . She'd had problems before." I tried to keep my face neutral.

"What kind of problems?"

How to say it? "She got depressed sometimes and she would go off by herself when that happened. She dropped out of college a couple years ago and since then she's been pretty up and down."

"All right, all right," Byrne said finally. "They'll search the walking paths tomorrow." His light blue eyes swept across us. He was distracted, antsy, fiddling with the buttons on his suit. McNeely put a hand on his arm, as if he were a child and she was reminding him of his manners, and he stood and shook my hand and gave me a card with the station number on it.

"Don't worry yourself too much, now," he said. "I'll bet she'll turn up with a grand story." But the grim tone of his voice told me he didn't believe a word of it.

10

Things started moving quickly after that. Byrne and McNeely got back to me the next day to tell me that they had found the bus driver who had taken Erin down on the sixteenth. He drove the private bus to Glendalough, but he said the bus had been empty and she'd asked if he could drop her in Glenmalure. He blushed when he said it and finally admitted she'd offered him five pounds but he hadn't taken the money. Byrne told me that the guards in Wicklow were working with the Army Reserve to search the forest and mountains where I'd found the necklace, and would interview potential witnesses, including the bus driver.

I tried to settle in at Erin's, but it was strange sleeping in her bed while I waited for news. The sheets smelled faintly of her perfume. The next day I woke up and went to the corner store to get milk. I grabbed an *Irish Independent* and was reading a story about Erin when Emer and Daisy came into the kitchen.

"Is there news?" Emer asked, flipping the switch on the electric kettle.

I pushed the paper across the table to her. *Gardaí Searching for American in Wicklow.* Above a small reproduction of Erin's picture, the article read, "The Gardaí are looking for any information about the whereabouts of an American student, Erin Flaherty, 23, who has been living in Dublin for the past year. Flaherty was last seen in Glenmalure on the afternoon of September 16 and the Gardaí will search the area today. Anyone who may have seen her or who may have information about her movements on the sixteenth of September is asked to contact the Gardaí."

"It's awful, waiting," I told them. "You haven't thought of anything, have you? The names of any of the guys who called, anything like that? Any friends who visited the house?"

Daisy looked up. "I realized last night. Her school friends came for a few days back in the summer. I think they were going Interrailing and they stopped in Dublin to see her. She seemed to have a good laugh with them."

"Really? American friends? Jessica? Was that one of them?"

"Yeah, and two lads. Chris, I think, and Brian."

If Uncle Danny knew Erin's best friends from high school had visited Dublin, he hadn't said anything about it to me. Everything seemed to speed up for a moment. Maybe she was traveling around Europe with Jessica right now. "You don't think she might have been going to meet them or anything like that?"

Emer said, "She didn't say it to us anyway. And that was back in the summer."

"I'll check with my uncle and see if he's been in touch with Jess's parents."

Emer and Daisy said they were going to the shops and did I need anything? I asked them to get me more coffee and once they were gone, I shut Erin's door and lay down on the bed, my eyes closed.

They were back an hour later. From Erin's room, I could hear the front door open and close and their voices out in the living room. Something made me get up and tiptoe to the door, where I pressed my ear against the wood.

"Put it there," Emer called out. "We'll just be getting it out again in a bit." They must have been unpacking groceries.

"Did you . . . ?" Their voices were too low for me to make out what they were saying. I moved my ear to the crack between the door and the wall. There were a few minutes of silence.

One of them said something I didn't understand and it took me a minute to realize they were speaking Irish. I took two semesters at Notre Dame and got really into the idea that I was speaking the language of my ancestors. I even joined a little Irish society on campus my sophomore year. But then I let it go and I don't remember a lot—*Conas tá tu?* (*Cone is Taw Too?* How are you?) *Go raibh maith agat.* (*Go Rev Mahagut.* Thank you.)—I could only pick out words here and there. *An raibh Erin . . .* (*On Rev Erin . . .* Did Erin . . .*)

One phrase stood out, though.

Tabhair aire. Pronounced *Tur arah.*

I remember that, remember my teacher showing a slideshow with Irish phrases.

Tabhair aire.

A warning. *Take care. Be careful.*

Byrne called the next morning to say they had something: a woman named Eda Curran who said Erin had stayed at her bed-and-breakfast near the Drumgoff Crossroads.

"Here's the thing, though," Roly Byrne said. *Here's the ting.* I could hear the excitement coming down the phone line. "It was the sixteenth she stayed there."

"So . . ." I was trying to put it all together, what it meant. "So she . . ."

"So she didn't disappear up there on the sixteenth," he finished for me. "On the night of the sixteenth she was alive and well and sleeping at the Rivers Glen Bed and Breakfast. The woman who owns it said she was walking on the Wicklow Way. The next morning she said she was getting a bus. Didn't say where she was going."

"So she must have lost the necklace the day before?"

"Yeah." Roly shouted something to someone else in the room. "And that's not all." He told me they'd searched the bed-and-breakfast. At first they hadn't found anything, but as they were leaving, McNeely had asked if there was another toilet in the house.

"In the rubbish there was a little crumpled-up piece of paper," he told me, his voice fast and excited over the phone. "It had a bus departure time written on it. We think it's your cousin's handwriting, based on the guest book she signed. It's for the seventeenth, Miss D'arcy. From Dublin."

It took me a minute to understand what he was saying. After staying at the bed-and-breakfast, Erin had been planning to go back to Dublin? To take a bus?

"Did she take the bus? Where is she now?"

"It didn't say where, just the time and 'Busáras,' which is the central bus station. None of the drivers remember her but we're looking into it right now. I'll ring you if anything turns up. One other thing. Does the name Gary Curran mean anything?"

"No."

"He's the son of the woman at the bed-and-breakfast. He works for the forestry service sometimes. When he was at university he got a bit too enthusiastic about a young one who didn't return his enthusiasm. We're looking at that, too. In the meantime, see if there's anything else you can remember that could help us out, that could give us a sense of her state of mind. Sure, it always helps to have a nice, full picture of the subject." I could hear people talking in the background, phones ringing. I thought about those green-and-brown mountains, the clouds moving over them.

"Okay," I said.

But he'd already hung up.

Erin, where are you?

I tried to think about Erin. I tried to remember.

Erin.

    Erin.

    Erin is quick, a blur, always in motion. Maggie sits quietly and plays or looks through books. I am Maggie. Maggie is quiet. Erin is not. Erin is freckles and brown skin in the summer. She is hair in her face and quick smile and loud voice. Erin is always moving. Grown-ups have to watch her every second or she'll be off, over the fence, out into the road. Uncle Danny is tired all the time. He doesn't have the energy to do it. She gets away, over to the neighbors', out to the beach, into the water. Someone finds her playing alone in a neighbor's yard.

    She starts staying at our house more so my mom can watch her. I hear my mom say to my dad, "Sometimes I wish I had a leash for her."

    "Just like Brenda," my dad says.

    "You're terrible," my mom says, but she's laughing. I don't know what they mean.

    But I imagine Erin on a leash. She's a happy, loud, jumping dog, a golden retriever or a Labrador. She's always trying to get away.

    Erin's mother's name was Brenda. I ask my mother about it and she tells me. Brenda. She grew up in Ireland. She somehow ended up at Uncle Danny's pub and applied for a job as a waitress and "she and Uncle Danny liked each other a lot," my mom says. When I ask what happened to her, she says that Brenda "wasn't happy" and she "had some problems."

"What kind of problems?"

"She just . . . She had trouble staying put. Don't say anything to Erin."

I wouldn't. I've already figured out that Erin doesn't like to talk about it.

"Where did she go?"

"We don't know. She doesn't seem to want to be in touch with Uncle Danny."

"Or Erin?"

My mom sighs. "Or Erin."

Later that night, when she comes to put me to bed, my mom says in my ear, "You know I'm not going anywhere, right, sweetie? That was a different thing, what happened with Erin's mom."

"Yeah. But . . . why did she go away?"

"Like I said, she just . . . she couldn't stay put." She pushes my hair back from my forehead, kisses me. "So we have to be extra nice to Erin, right?" She lies down next to me for a little bit and I breathe in her scent, Alberto VO5 shampoo, cigarette smoke from the bar.

After that, I imagine Brenda as a helium balloon with its string tied to the roof of Uncle Danny's house.

I imagine the balloon tugging, trying to get away and finally breaking free, floating up into the air until it's just a tiny red dot high above us, among the clouds.

11

The faces around the table blur and I take a deep breath, feeling my brain click into vigilance. This is my chance to get a sense of the investigation. If I am very careful, I may be able to get them to tell me more than they want to. I need to answer their questions, and I need to do it in a way that invites more. The longer this goes on, the better my chances.

They go over the public details of the case for an hour, double-checking things with me, going over how I came to find the necklace. I tell them the story as clearly and concisely as I can.

"This isn't a judgment, like, but why didn't you ring the Guards when you realized she'd been to Glenmalure?" Joey asks me. "When you realized she'd been up to the woods?"

I meet his eyes. "I know it looks weird now, but I really thought she might be up there, just waiting for me. I know how that sounds. I do. But she'd done it so many times before. Disappeared, I mean."

"Everyone described her state of mind before her disappearance as fine, normal," John White says. "Your actions suggest otherwise."

"I know. Erin was . . . She could be erratic, unpredictable. At the time, no one thought it was more than teenage rebellion. She went through periods where she was drinking a lot, maybe more than that, not taking care of herself. I worried about her, I wanted to protect her. That's the only way I can explain my actions now." I'm telling him the truth and he knows it. He nods. When I meet his eyes, he looks away. I get a little ping of recognition from some drawer of the filing cabinet in my brain. He looks familiar, and I wonder if I met him on the original investigation.

"After we found the piece of paper at the bed-and-breakfast, the investigation shifted back to Dublin," Griz says. "I don't mean to call you out, Roly, but we're in the business of reviewing decisions made in past cases. Did you agree with that decision to shift the investigation?"

Roly pretends to stab himself in the back, but he's got a grin on his face and he nods at her to say, *good question.*

"It made perfect sense," I say. "They'd already searched the hills around the walking trails. She wasn't there. All of her actions suggested she was going back to Dublin that next day. It was an understandable shift." They can all hear my hesitation. "But I still thought there was something in Wicklow we didn't find. Maybe not . . . her. But something." I look up, decide to risk it. "I always wondered about the door-to-doors, whether there were any eyewitnesses who didn't want to come forward because their underwear drawers were filled with bags of pot. You know."

Nods around the table, but nothing else. If there were underwear drawers, they're not going to tell me.

"We haven't been able to find any links between Erin and June Talbot, Teresa McKenny, or Niamh Horrigan," Griz says, moving on. "There isn't anything you can think of there?"

"Well, there's the geographic link," I say. "Other than that, no. But there must be potential links there. Everyone Erin came into contact with on her trips to Glenmalure is a possible link. The guy at the B-and-B, right? Whatever happened with him? Or the bus driver?"

"We're on it," Roly says quickly, and I look up to find a tall man with gray hair standing in the doorway. I know I recognize *him* from before. Superintendent Wilcox. "What else would you like to ask Detective D'arcy?"

Griz exchanges a glance with him that I can't read. "Well, the romantic angle is the obvious one. We have all these men who she knew, who she may have been involved with, but nothing definite on any of them. You knew her well. Did you ever have an instinct about that?" They're right to be thinking this way. Murderers, even serial ones, have to identify their victims somehow. Truly random abductions and killings are remarkably rare.

I start to tell them that any one of the men who were original persons of interest could be our guy, that I wasn't satisfied by their alibis, that boys and then men had become obsessed with Erin before, but then I realize that's not what Griz is asking. "My instinct was that there was someone," I tell her. "Someone we didn't know about, someone who wasn't a main suspect in the original investigation. In the years since . . . I was over here, since she disappeared, I've come to think of him as this . . . this gray shadow. That's how I see him. I've had dreams and . . . All of her actions those last few days, they make me think she was meeting someone. That guy, whoever he is. That's who I think it is. And I think he must have a connection with Talbot and McKenny and Niamh Horrigan, too. Even if it's just the geographic one, even if he happened to come across them because he delivered vegetables or cement or drove to work a particular way every morning and his route took him by the roads where they all disappeared. It's something like that. You asked me about my instinct and that's my instinct."

Everyone's silent.

"We know about those serial murders on Long Island," Griz blurts out suddenly. "We know what you did there. You profiled that fella. You found him. The FBI couldn't do it and you did it. What's this fella's profile? Who is he?"

I force myself to wait. The panic starts, but I know this is my leverage. Carefully, I say, "I don't have all the data I'd need. I couldn't profile without that. But the infrequency, the span of the disappearances and killings. That's the thing that jumps out at me—1993, 1998, 2006, 2016. What's the pattern there? Your people are good. You've looked. But there must be something you're not seeing. Are there other crimes that haven't been included? It's a long time line. The infrequency makes me think you're missing something."

"Nothing else fits," Roly says. "Believe me, we've looked."

"So, what's happening in this guy's life that these were his opportunities?"

I can see on their faces that they've spent so much time thinking about this exact issue that my raising it feels like nails on a chalkboard. "That's the question, isn't it?" Roly mutters.

We go over a few more details and then John White says, "What about the political angle? What was your instinct on that?" He gives the word *instinct* a little stress that makes me pay attention. He thinks my instinct is bullshit.

I shake my head and say, "I've gone over and over that so many times I can't count. There's nothing specific. She wasn't ever overtly nationalist around me. But I mean, my uncle has a picture of Gerry Adams hanging in the bar."

"But sure, so does every Irish bar in America," Joey says.

"Yeah, you're right. And Erin just . . . She wasn't interested in any of that. At least she wasn't before she came over here."

"This case," John White says. "I keep going around with it. It's an odd one. No matter how many times I read the files, I don't feel like I have a sense of it, of her."

I don't say anything, though I agree with him. It feels like agreeing would be a betrayal of Erin.

When it's clear they won't get anything more useful out of me, Roly stands up, a little too quickly, and says, "Anything else, so? Thank you, Detective D'arcy. Everyone, back to your work."

When they've gone, Wilcox comes in and shakes my hand. He's thinner, grayer, but I remember the fine-boned face, the nice suit and careful blue eyes. He's the stern, upperclass dad in a romantic drama. "Thank you for your assistance, Miss D'arcy. Detective Inspector Byrne tells me you have made a career in law enforcement as well. Quite a successful one, it seems."

"Oh, well, thank you."

"It must be interesting to compare techniques," he says.

"It's mostly the same, actually. Your team is doing an excellent job."

He watches me for a minute. He was a handsome man, back then. He still is, elegant, all silver hair and blue eyes and shirt collar. "God willing, there'll be some progress to report," he says.

When he's gone, Roly announces, "Now then, I want you lot

working away like busy little beavers. Not a word until you've got something for me. The clock is ticking. If there's a connection between Niamh Horrigan, Teresa McKenny, June Talbot, and Erin Flaherty, we need to find it yesterday. McKenny's and Talbot's bodies were found two weeks after they went missing and all indications were that they'd been alive for most of those two weeks. Niamh went missing last Saturday. Tomorrow it will be a week. That means that time is of the essence here. If we've just found Erin Flaherty's remains in Wicklow, then that gives us a new opportunity for evidence. She's not in the water. If there is anything we can find that can help us get this bastard, we need to do it fast. I can't think too much about what Niamh Horrigan is going through, but if there's anything we can do to get her back, we're damned well going to do it."

He turns to me and I can see the frustration on his face.

"Get your clogs on, D'arcy. I'm taking you home for dinner."

12

"Laura won't mind you springing a guest on her?" I ask Roly once we're out of a traffic jam around College Green and heading toward Clontarf to the north.

"Not at all. She's been looking forward to meeting you."

I'm sorry I wasn't more helpful," I tell him. "I feel like they thought I was withholding something."

"They know you're not. It's just, this case. I've never had another one like it. But maybe . . ."

I know what he was going to say. "It's okay," I tell him. "I'm hoping we can get some evidence from Erin's remains, too." I catch myself. "If they're hers, I mean. I'm hoping we can find something that will help with the Niamh Horrigan case. It's okay to say it."

"If they're connected, D'arcy. That's what I need to keep telling myself. If they're connected."

We drive in silence for a bit and then I say, "Let me ask you something. How long has John White been a guard?"

"Long as I have. No, maybe a few years less. Why?"

"Just wondering. Would I have met him on the original investigation?"

"Wouldn't think so. I think he started out at some godforsaken country station, Donegal or somewhere. Why?"

"He looks familiar. I'm just trying to figure out where I've met him."

"Dublin's small like that," Roly says. "I'm always running into people I met on cases or from school. The other week now, I was having lunch at the Stag's Head and I looked over and there was this fella and we kept looking at each other, but I couldn't figure out where I knew him from. Finally, it hit me. We'd been standing in line for pints at my local the week before. Don't know why I remembered his face and all. Ah, here we are, then."

Roly and Laura have a big, semidetached house on a quiet cul-de-sac. I smell roasting meat and cinnamon when we come through the front door. It's out of a design magazine, lots of gray and cream and natural fibers. A handwoven blue-and-white rug hangs on one wall, a gleaming blue ceramic vase holds a single orchid. As we come in, a dog barks and two little blond boys run in with a miniature poodle and surround us. Roly introduces them as Diarmuid and Daragh and they say hello very politely and then run off to some other part of the house.

Laura is tall, blond, elegant. She makes me conscious of my makeup-free face, my scuffed boots. Roly kisses her and introduces us and she shakes my hand and says warmly that it's wonderful to meet me finally, after all this time. Roly hands me a glass of red wine and we sit in the living room. Roly and Laura's girls, Áine and

Cecelia, come in to say hi. Áine looks just like Laura, and Cecilia has Roly's angular face and pale blond hair.

"Do you live in New York?" Áine asks me.

"Nearby," I tell her. "Long Island."

"Áine's going to go to New York someday to be a fashion designer," Roly says.

"Dad, a fashion industry executive."

"Oh yeah, sorry. Only I thought you wanted to be a designer."

"Dad!"

"Does Dublin seem different to you?" Laura asks me once we're all at the table, digging into roast pork and potatoes and apples. "It's been, what, twenty years?"

"It does and it doesn't," I say. "I haven't really explored, but there are so many new buildings on the river. Everything seems . . . I don't know, fancier."

Laura laughs. "Wait until you see Ringsend. I was raised in Irishtown. When my mam told me they were making the gasworks into luxury flats, I nearly died. The gasworks! But sure we've all gotten used to it now."

"I have a cousin who works for Facebook," Roly says. "He's making three hundred thousand euros a year. Little bollix. He used to nick sips of my lager at Christmas. It's mad."

They tell me about the other changes, describe their neighbors who lost everything during the recession.

"It was the way we all went house mad," Laura says. "We did as well. We bought a rental property down the road, thinking we'd double our money. We're lucky. We can just about pay the mortgage with what we're getting for rent, but it's still a bit touch and go. A lot of people we know never recovered."

I help Laura clear and Roly and I stack the dishes.

"Have you been by that place Erin lived?" Roly asks me, a dish towel over his shoulder.

"Not yet. I checked it out on Google Earth, though." Laura hands me a glass of whiskey and we all sit in the living room. There's a gas fire and she turns it on and puts a plate of thin slices of fruitcake out on the coffee table. "It looks like someone's fixed it up. I should have bought it way back when."

I take a piece of fruitcake, crumbling it into pieces on my plate. It's good, dark and spicy and full of dates and raisins.

"Ah, that's the Dublin game these days. 'I should have bought this one, I should have bought that one.' We're all potential billionaires in our minds."

"The young ones she lived with have moved on," Roly tells me. "One of 'em works for one of these software yokes down by the canal."

"Yeah?" It's something I've been thinking about, the silences, the whispered conversation in Irish. "I always felt there was something they weren't telling us."

Laura stretches her feet out toward the fire. "You mean, like they knew something about what happened?"

"No, just . . . I don't know. Something they were holding back."

"Funny, Bernie thought so, too," Roly says. "She was convinced they knew something, but we never got anything out of them."

"How is she really?" I ask after a moment.

"She's at a place near Drogheda, a sort of nursing home." Roly looks away. "It's grim, I'm telling you, D'arcy."

"He visits every week or two," Laura says. "He drives up there and spends an hour or two with her. Everyone else has stopped going."

One of the boys shouts from the other end of the house.

"We'll know a lot more tomorrow, anyway," Roly tells me.

"It must have been awful for you and your uncle all these years," Laura says. "Not knowing."

"Yeah, that's the worst of it. He hasn't gotten over it, you know? He can never move past it." I think about how on some level, all of us have been stuck back there in the mountains—me, Roly, Uncle Danny, Jessica, Emer and Daisy, probably even Conor and Laura and Brian and Lilly.

Roly reaches over to pat Laura's knee. He looks at me and suddenly it's twenty-three years ago and he's walking ahead of me on the sidewalk, looking back over his shoulder, his blue eyes meeting mine. "I hope we'll have something soon," he says. "I'd like to do that for your family."

13

In the morning, I find myself a quiet table in the hotel's dining room and spread out my notes and laptop and a piece of paper on which I've written "Erin."

When I first joined Suffolk County Homicide, I worked under a guy named Len Giacomo. He was a legend in the Suffolk County P.D., and by the time I met him, he'd solved more cases and had more convictions under his belt than anyone who'd ever worked homicide on Long Island. Len was a true intellectual; he liked opera and modernist literature and wine and he and his wife traveled a ton, to Rome and Thailand and Guatemala, and any topic of conversation that came up, Len had something to say about it. But he wasn't showy, and when I look back at how he worked, it was the fact that he was completely unbiased that was probably his greatest asset. He'd go into a case with an absolutely open mind; he told me once that he had a strategy for this, a meditation technique he'd learned on an ashram in India. He would write the victim's name in the center of a piece of paper and as the case went on, he would slowly add pertinent information to the paper, with everyone he met surrounding the victim so he could see the relationships, the dynamics.

He taught me this technique when we were working a domestic homicide case together, and over the years I've refined it for my own purposes.

I start by writing in "Emer Nolan" and "Daisy Nugent" up at the top. I can't find anything on Daisy, but a few minutes of Googling Emer's name turns up the software company Roly mentioned. Under "About Us" there's a picture of Emer and a biography and email. I send her a message, saying that I'm in town and I'd love to see her, just to catch up. Then I go back to my diagram. I write in "Conor Kearney," "Hackman O'Hanrahan Jr.," and "Niall Deasey." Then I add in "other girls at the café," "neighbors," and "Jessica, Chris, Lisa, Brian," and, because Len taught me well, I write in my own name and Uncle Danny's and my dad's, too. Everyone in her orbit. We were all in her orbit.

I'm about to put the paper away when I think of another Len lesson. *Don't get ahead of yourself.* I make a little circle at the bottom of the paper and write "?" The unknown person, the man I've come to think of as the gray shadow. Who is he?

Back in my room, I turn on the television and catch the noon news. There's a short update on the Niamh Horrigan case. It sounds like they're still searching the hills and doing door-to-doors in the area. The Army Reserve is helping, along with various mountain rescue and hiking groups. Niamh's parents have offered a ten thousand–euro reward for information leading to her safe return. That's what they talk about on the television. What they don't talk about is everything else that's going on, the interviews that Galway police must be doing with anyone who ever knew Niamh, the frantic scouring of sex offender databases, the tearing apart of every social media account or electronic device Niamh's ever used.

"Niamh has been missing for a week now and her family and friends are starting to ask the Gardaí why there has been so little progress on finding her. The Gardaí say every measure is being taken to locate Niamh, but given the fates of the other women who have disappeared under similar circumstances, the family feels time is growing short to find Niamh safe and well," the announcer says.

"In a related development, the cousin of Erin Flaherty, the American student who disappeared in 1993 and is widely believed to be the first victim of the so-called Southeast Killer, has arrived in Dublin as the Gardaí examine the remains discovered in Wicklow this week to determine if they are Flaherty's."

My cell rings and I switch off the television. It's Roly. I can hear that there's something as soon as he says, "D'arcy? Where are you?"

"At the hotel. What? Have you identified her? Is it Erin?"

I know from the way he hesitates. I can feel the hotel room shrinking around me. My vision narrows. I take a deep breath.

"It's more complicated than that," he says. "It's not Erin. But they found something with the remains. Something of hers."

◆　◆　◆

What they found is a student ID card from the year Erin had spent as a student at C.W. Post. It's laminated, which is why it's held up all this time. Roly meets me in the hotel lobby and takes me into the bar to show me a photograph of the card.

Erin Mary Flaherty, it reads. *DOB 3/14/1970.* The photograph is a little cloudy, but I remember the frosted pink lipstick she liked to wear. She has on the leather jacket; I can just see the collar and top button in the photo. I nod. It's hers. As if there's any doubt.

"But who is it? Whose remains are they?" I'm practically shouting at him. "If it's not her, Roly, who the fuck is it? And how did the ID and the scarf get in there with her?"

He glances over at me. His eyes are lined. He looks about a hundred years old. "I'm heading over to talk to the state pathologist. We hope she'll be able to give us something more."

I walk him outside. He's parked in an illegal space around the corner from the hotel. I know I shouldn't, but I can't help myself, and I say, "Let me come with you. I may be able to help. You're going to have to review missing persons reports. You're going to have to figure out who that was who was buried up there, look for links to the other victims, to Erin. I can help with that. I know how to do it."

My voice is whining. I'm ashamed and yet I want in on this so much, I don't care what he thinks of me.

Roly rubs his eyes, watches a group of teenage boys cross the street in front of us. Finally he says, "D'arcy, I'm doing everything I can, but you are a civilian." He puts a hand up when I start to protest. "Yes, when you're here, you're a civilian. And I know that if it was you at the top of the investigation, you would be saying the same thing as well. You have a role to play here. You knew her better than any of us did and you were here twenty-three years ago and I know you're a fucking amazing detective. I read the stories." He fixes his gaze on me. His eyes are a pale ice blue in the direct sunlight. "I know what you did. But this is my show, and even more importantly, it's Wilcox's show, and if I let a civilian sit in on a briefing with the deputy state pathologist, Wilcox will have my head and we won't be any closer to figuring out what happened to Erin or to saving Niamh Horrigan from whatever psychopathic piece of shite plucked her out of the mountains."

Sirens scream outside, somewhere up near O'Connell Street.

"Okay," I say. "I know. You're right."

Roly's hair looks thinner somehow. I have that displaced feeling of déjà vu, except of course it actually *is* happening again. His words, his exhausted face and voice.

He reaches across me to open my door. "I'll ring you as soon as I've got anything to report."

He pulls out so fast he almost clips me before I can jump onto the curb, and I'm still startled, stumbling back toward the Westin's main lobby door, when a large man, his belly stretching his shirt beneath a voluminous tweed jacket, his eyes friendly behind round glasses, puts himself between me and the hotel. He has a straggly dirty-blond-and-gray ponytail. He was one of the reporters standing outside the pub in Glenmalure.

"Are you Detective Lieutenant Maggie D'arcy?" he asks.

"Yes." His face lights up in a smile and he sticks out a hand. I shake it, feeling vaguely manipulated.

"I'm Stephen Hines," he says. "I'm a reporter for the *Independent* and I'm wondering if I could ask you a few questions." He doesn't wait for an answer, just plows ahead before my training kicks in and I can shut him down. "Is that your cousin they found in Glenmalure? Is that Erin Flaherty? Do you think she was a victim of the Southeast Killer? Are you going to help them find Niamh Horrigan?"

"I'm not going to comment on that," I say, pushing past him.

"You're an excellent detective," he calls after me. "You got that psycho guy on Long Island. Shouldn't they be using you to find Niamh Horrigan?"

I keep walking until I'm through the hotel's revolving door and safe in the elevator heading up to my room. It's not until the elevator doors close that I realize I'm still holding my breath.

14

1993

While Roly Byrne and Bernie McNeely searched the bed-and-breakfast in Glenmalure and questioned neighbors and possible witnesses, Emer and Daisy went to classes, and at home Uncle Danny smoked too much and tried to get in touch with Jessica Friedman's mom, I walked the streets of Dublin.

Over the Grand Canal, past the building painted with the words *Bolands Flour Mills* as the chilled wind whipped my face, fast up Pearse Street, past gray shops and around the back of Trinity College on Westland Row and onto Nassau Street, where I could see boys in striped shirts running back and forth on green lawns, around the black gates to College Green, where it felt like all of Dublin opened up before me, a wide avenue reaching across the Liffey, and the big round fortress of the Bank of Ireland.

From this side, the pale gray facade of Trinity rose above the street, the blue clock and huge bronze statue of Edmund Burke. I had seen them before, on a poster and in a brochure in the Notre

Dame career counseling office. I had imagined myself walking beneath the archway, heading to classes.

I stood there in the forecourt, wondering where exactly Conor Kearney studied the history of Ireland in the twentieth century, and then I wandered the city some more, taking shortcuts down little side streets, finding my way back to Grafton Street, Dame Street, Nassau Street. Dublin was a city of lanes and alleys and gray cobbles, of pubs and old men and teenagers. Everywhere I looked, I saw them, boys in leather jackets, talking, smoking, watching people walk by, girls in jeans and sweatshirts or school uniforms, laughing and grabbing hands as they dashed across the street to bus stops.

By lunchtime I was back to Temple Bar, not far from the Garden of Eating, and I ducked into a little pub called the Raven, painted a bright yellow, and ordered a cup of coffee, enjoying the warmth and the cozy interior. I recognized the décor—if it wasn't exactly the same as Flaherty's, it was what Uncle Danny was going for: tin ceiling, stained glass, dark wood bar with bottle-lined mirrored shelves behind it, old photos of Dublin on the walls. It was a little touristy; there was a line of backpacks just inside the front door and I picked out Australian and American accents in the orders being shouted up to the bar.

I downed the coffee and ordered a Guinness, taking a long sip and sighing in pleasure. The bartender, an old guy with a gray moustache and a kind smile, grinned and said, "That's the best review I've had all week." *Tat's.*

I grinned back. "My uncle has a bar on Long Island. We have a sign up over the bar that says, 'Best Guinness Outside of Dublin.'"

He laughed. "Is it?"

"It might be, but it's not this good. Don't tell him I said so."

At the end of the bar, a tall guy with bright red hair in a thick ponytail was switching out a keg. He looked up and stared at me for a minute. I smiled, thinking that maybe he knew Erin, but he just looked confused and went back to switching the keg.

"I used to know a man had a bar on Long Island," the bartender said. "It was in a place called Smithtown. Do you know it?" We talked about Long Island geography and Irish bars for a bit and then he left me alone. I watched him unloading glasses from a tray and suddenly, with an intensity that surprised me, I missed Uncle Danny. When I left, I told the bartender goodbye and that I'd be back for another one of those pints.

I was crossing Essex Street when I looked up to find Conor Kearney walking toward me, his head down.

"Hey," I said. He started, the way he had when I'd walked into the café, and I could see his brain processing my face. *Not Erin.*

"Hiya."

"Maggie," I said.

"No, I knew. I just—Maggie."

We stared at each other awkwardly for a moment. Finally he said, "Is there anything new on Erin? The Guards were round to me. They told me they're looking down in Wicklow."

"No, nothing."

He was wearing a leather jacket and jeans. He had a manila folder under his arm. A woman holding the hand of a small child in a raincoat came up behind him and he stepped to the side, bumping my hip. "Pardon," he said, then, "It must be torture, waiting. Seemed like the Guards thought maybe she'd come back to Dublin."

"I think they don't know what to think." I pointed to the manila folder. "You look like you're on an important mission. Top-secret spy stuff?"

He grinned. "Ah, yeah. I've to stop the war with my important papers, like."

"Well then, I won't keep you. Go save the world."

He leaned forward. "I can reveal that it's actually a petition related to Temple Bar rubbish removal, but if it makes me seem more exciting, I'll go with top-secret papers."

"Good choice." I smiled back at him. "Good luck." He started to go, but I blurted out, "I . . . I'm sorry about . . . when I came into the café. I was tired and I thought Erin had just gone somewhere . . . It isn't the first time I've had to go looking for her like this and I kind of took it out on you."

"No worries," he said. We stared at each other. "Well then, stop by sometime." I nodded. "See ya." I didn't turn to watch him go, even though I wanted to.

I found a phone booth and called my dad at his office. He sounded tired and sad and when I told him about the bed-and-breakfast, he said, "Oh, sweetheart. I should have gone. What a mess for you to deal with." I told him I was fine and to take care of himself and when I hung up I leaned my face against the cold metal of the phone as the scent of his shaving cream rose in my sinuses and I missed him so much for a moment, it actually hurt. Then I wandered Dublin some more in a cold, gray mist that hovered just above the rooftops, taking the wide O'Connell Bridge across the Liffey. This was ground zero of the Easter Rebellion, I remembered from my Irish history seminar, where a small group of men and a few women holed up and tried to direct an assault on the British in the streets of Dublin.

It didn't work, but the execution of sixteen Irishmen turned once ambivalent Dubliners against the British.

A terrible beauty was born.

But it was that song about being too sexy for your shirt that was blaring out of a shop on O'Connell Street, and Yeats faded away as I walked the streets north of the river. They seemed smaller, tighter, leading to an outdoor market not far from the bridge, and I wandered for a bit, listening to old ladies shouting over their produce, browsing the vegetable sellers and used book stalls. I walked under a big clock hanging out over the sidewalk in front of a department store, then crossed the street and strolled past the gray columns of the General Post Office.

The day had run away from me. It was nearly dinnertime now.

A little fish-and-chips shop on O'Connell Street beckoned and I got mine to go, taking the greasy newspaper down to the quays. The fish was crispy and hot, the chips tender and with just the right amount of bite. The sky was full of gulls. They called across the river, flew back and forth from north to south. I was halfway through my dinner and full when a thin, wobbling old man stopped to look at the river.

"It's lovely this evening, isn't it?" he slurred.

"It really is." The sky was pale blue, washed with blurry gray clouds. A hint of pink crept in, crisping the edges of the clouds. A gull landed on the quay, looking up expectantly at me.

"Cheeky little bugger," the old man said. "He'd like your chips, so he would."

"Well, he can't have them."

"You tell him," the man said, stumbling. I looked at him again. His clothes were shabbier than I saw at first, his shirt yellowed and frayed. He was drunk, but only for maintenance. His eyes were yellow, too, his nose red with broken capillaries. We watched the sky for a few moments.

"You 'merican?" he asked. "Or Canadian?"

"American."

"I lived in New York for fifteen years. Worked as a crane operator. It was grand, New York, but it never felt like home. Never home." He was off somewhere in his head, thinking about New York and home. I could see that he had been handsome once.

"I'm all done," I told him. "There's a piece of fish I haven't touched and a lot of chips left. They'll go to waste otherwise. Or to the gulls. Sit down."

"Ah, now, I think I just might take you up on that." He sat down next to me on the bench and took the bag from me. When he bit into the fish, he sighed with pleasure. "That's lovely, so it is."

"I know."

He smiled at me. "Life's little pleasures, isn't that right."

I left him to the pleasure of the fish and chips.

Erin in her red bathing suit, her arms and legs tan, her nose burnt and peeling, her little body rushing into the waves. Her hair is hard at the ends where it touched her Popsicle. Her hands and arms are covered with a fine layer of sand that glitters in the sun. A summer Sunday at Jones Beach. The constant crashing of the waves. People shouting across the beach. Suntan lotion runs in my eyes and I cry. Erin and I play on the sand where the waves are breaking, digging holes, building walls. First the holes fill in and then the walls get swept away. Erin has her back to the ocean and when a wave creeps up and washes over her, she screeches and jumps up, running away into the sea of people on the beach. I look up. She was there and now she's gone. I squint into the sun. Everyone looks the same on the beach. Their faces stare at me. I get up and walk straight back, find my mom, who's lying on her towel and reading a magazine.

"Where's Erin?" she asks me. I point to where she was. My mom jumps up, runs to the sand, looks up and down the beach. Her bikini slips away from her skin. I can see a white line over her breasts. "Erin!" she shouts. "Erin, honey!"

Another mom hears her and comes to help us look. The two moms ask people if they've seen a little girl in a red bathing suit. People get up, help us look. Someone says we should find a policeman.

My mom's eyes are scared and wide. She ignores me when I try to take her hand.

And then someone's shouting. My mom is running toward the sound. I follow and I see her kneeling, holding Erin. Erin's crying. A man is gesturing with his hands to my mom. I wait there, watching them. My mom brushes Erin's hair out of her eyes, holds her against her body.

A seagull calls overhead. The sun seems to drop as we walk to the car. Little pools of water appear in the parking lot, between the shiny cars, then disappear as we get close. The asphalt burns my feet. My mom gets us strapped into the back and Erin reaches over and takes my hand, clinging tightly to it as we pull out and head for the North Shore and home, as though the waves that threatened to carry us away on the beach are coming for her now, even though we've left the beach behind.

15

....

Niamh Horrigan's parents have great faith in the Garda Síochána.

That's what they say on the news when the anchorwoman asks them if they believe the Gardaí are doing everything they can.

I've barely slept, waiting for Roly to call, and now I'm out of bed, showered, room-service oatmeal and coffee half-finished on a tray at the end of the bed. It's 7:10 a.m. and he still hasn't called, and my mind is going a thousand miles an hour trying to imagine what that means. Maybe there was a mistake and it *is* Erin up there. Maybe Roly doesn't know how to tell me. Maybe it's like he said, it wasn't Erin, but in the meantime, they've found her, buried nearby.

"We just want her home," Niamh's father says, looking into the camera in a way that I know means someone has coached him. He's a tall, good-looking older man, with graying hair and a beige outfit that was probably a recommendation of the coach, too. If the guy who has Niamh is watching, they don't want the dad to push any buttons for him. He needs to be neutral, loving, concerned, but not angry or challenging or possessive. The mom is pretty, blond, sub-dued, but I don't like the royal blue blazer they chose for her. It's too masculine, too businesslike, the color too strong. Her voice rises as she says, "Please contact the Gardaí if you know anything that could help bring our daughter home." I feel like swearing. They should have had her say "Niamh" to humanize the victim. I give them a five out of ten.

My cell phone buzzes on the bed and I scramble for it. "Roly?"

"Yeah, hiya, D'arcy. Sorry I'm just ringing you. It's been a long night. We don't know a lot about the remains yet, but I can tell you what we'll release to the press later today."

I mute the TV and say, "Hang on, Roly. You gotta tell whoever's advising Niamh's family that the mom needs to be softer. She needs to feel like an ally to our guy, you know?"

"They're on it, D'arcy. Don't worry. Here's what they've got so far on the excavation. We'll be making most of this public to try to get a match. Yesterday the techs recovered most of an intact skel-eton. Analysis of pubic symphysis indicates the victim was likely early twenties. We did not find parturition scars on the pelvis, but as you know some of that science has been questioned. Path said she's fairly confident saying female, early twenties, no parturition."

"Any cause of death?"

He doesn't say anything.

"Skull trauma?" It's one of the only things they'd be able to find this quickly. Strangulation, maybe, but not always. Drug overdose, or suffocation, you're not going to see it.

I can hear him hesitating. "Examination revealed two points of blunt impact on the right temporal bone. That part won't be public."

"Of course," I say. "And dental comparison says it's not Erin."

"That's right. They've excavated in a radius around the remains and there don't seem to be anymore. But of course we'll continue looking."

"Anything else?"

"Not at the moment." There's something else, but he won't tell me.

"So who is it?" I demand. "If it's not Erin, who is it?"

I can hear him hesitating. "We don't have an ID. Path dates the burial to 1992 or a few years later."

"Based on what?"

"Can't tell you."

I go to the window, look out over College Green. The city's waking up and I watch a young woman wearing a red jacket make her way along the sidewalk and through the Trinity gates. "Roly, if Erin's scarf was in the grave with her, then the victim must have died around the time Erin was there, right? How did the scarf end up with the body? Whose blood is it? Was there any evidence to suggest that someone else was with this woman, whoever she was?"

"We don't know." I can feel it again, whatever it is he's not telling me.

"Do you think Erin was there?"

"That's the question, isn't it?" There's an ugly little bubble of silence that almost makes me gasp.

I force myself to breathe. "I should call my uncle."

"Yeah. You do that. I'll be in touch. Okay?" He puts a soft little spin on it, reaching out, trying to soothe me. "I'm heading down to Wicklow so I may be out of touch. We've got some stuff going on in another case, too, so I'm going to be out straight. I'll let you know if anything comes up. Hopefully we'll know something soon, D'arcy."

He's gone before I can ask any more questions.

I tell Uncle Danny the news. "I'm so sorry, Uncle Danny. I'm having a hard time with this, too."

"Oh God, Mags, I didn't want it to be her, but I wanted to know, you know?"

"Yeah, it's totally normal."

"But why was her scarf with the . . . why was it there?" I can hear glasses clinking. He's unloading the dishwasher, keeping himself busy, trying to cope. "Is it this girl who's missing?"

"No. The remains have been there too long for that. We just don't know. There may have been some connection between Erin and whoever is there." I say it again: "We just don't know. I'll tell you as soon as I hear something. Are you okay? You know you can go over to the house and hang out with Lilly and Brian any time you want, right? They'd be happy to have you."

"Yeah, yeah. I don't know. I got stuff to do around here." He sounds awful. "What are you gonna do, baby? You gonna come home now we know it's not Erin?"

"No, I'll stay a bit, Uncle Danny. Her scarf was there, her I.D. She must have had something to do with this woman, whoever she was."

I hear a *clink* as he drops a glass in the dishwasher. "What do you mean? Like she had something to do with a murder? But don't they think she went back to Dublin after she was down there? Didn't they find that piece of paper?"

"No, no. But maybe she knew this woman. Maybe she gave her

the scarf. I don't know. Look, I'm going to try to do whatever I can to help them figure this out, Uncle Danny, okay? Don't worry."

I can hear the emotion in his voice. "Okay, baby. Take care now, right?"

Brian answers on the first ring and when he hears my voice he asks, "Are you okay? Did they find her?"

"No, it's not her, Bri." I give him the update. "Uncle Danny is a mess. Can you check on him?"

"Yeah, we'll go over tonight. Take him some dinner."

"Thanks. Give Lil a hug."

A low-slung but rising sun hides behind the buildings surrounding the Trinity forecourt. *Dr. Conor Kearney, Associate Professor of History, Room 4000, Arts Building, Trinity College Dublin 2.* I walk slowly across campus to the Nassau Street entrance, and then up Nassau Street toward St. Stephen's Green, where I find a coffee shop that has Wi-Fi. It's busy but I get a table at the back and start working the missing persons angle. The *Irish Times* has an online archive—I've already subscribed—and I start searching for stories about missing persons between 1992 and 1994. I come up with twenty-three involving women of the right age. Most have updated stories indicating the women were found safe, but there are eight that I save to my desktop.

There are four stories about Erin's disappearance from 1993. I vaguely remember reading the first two, which have a panicked tone. It's clear that the reporter covering the story, as well as the guards working the case, started out thinking that she would be found in the mountains. But the third story, which appeared after they found the piece of paper at the bed-and-breakfast, is a shift. The reporter writes that "the Gardaí are asking the public if they saw the American student, Miss Erin Flaherty, on or around September 17 or 18, either in Dublin or in any other location around Ireland." For some reason, the press referred to her as a student, as though that was the only reason an American would have moved to Dublin. Another story announced that the search in the Wicklow Mountains had been called off, "given new information." The fourth story appeared six months after Erin's initial disappearance and quotes Garda Sergeant Ruarí Wilcox as saying, "The Gardaí are still actively following up on leads. We are doing everything we can to find out where Miss Flaherty went after leaving Wicklow." *Where she went.*

When I expand the search perimeters over the years, I find more follow-up stories and then, after Teresa McKenny and June Talbot disappeared, a story about the formation of the task force. Roly's name starts appearing in the stories. I've read all these, but not for a while. There are a few things that jump out at me. The first is that even after the formation of the task force, the investigating officers—even Roly—talk about Erin in a slightly different way than they talk about the other victims. In 2009, a reporter asked Wilcox about the fact that Erin Flaherty's body was never found, and he made it clear that he also thought that was suspicious.

I go back to the other women who went missing in Ireland in 1993. There was a forty-year-old mother of six who disappeared from her home in Donegal, a couple of young girls who were reported missing but then found in County Cork. There's a German backpacker who may have visited the monastery at Glendalough and a twenty-three-year-old woman who took a bus to Galway from her home in Wexford and never contacted her family. The Wexford woman and the German backpacker are the ones that have my attention. I write the names down—Louise Dooley and Katerina Greiner—and finish my coffee.

I've spent hours at home Googling the list of persons of interest in the original investigation, checking Facebook and LinkedIn, with nothing much to report. I let myself search for Conor and come up with all the same pages I've seen before, department information on Trinity's website, announcements for his latest book about Ireland after World War II, a picture of him from the book jacket. The first time I saw it, late at night, a few Novembers ago, while Lilly slept inside and the water moved against the beach outside the windows, I almost gasped, seeing him after all these years, an older Conor, but recognizable.

I let myself stare at the photos from the launch party for the book at Trinity a couple of years ago. There's a picture of a beautiful blond woman, dressed in a flowing yellow dress, a huge smile on her face as she poses next to older Conor. *Dr. Kearney and Ms. Arpin*, the caption reads. I let the little knife edge of pain slide underneath my skin for a moment and then I slam the laptop closed and get up to go.

St. Stephen's Green is exactly as I remember it, flowering trees and hedges lining the walking paths, the pond placid and full of ducks. The park is only moderately full; I find a bench in the sun and I have it all to myself once a young woman with a stroller moves along, the toddler in the stroller shouting about the ducks as they go.

Every man who walks by could be Conor, but I get tired of the disappointment and I close my eyes and let the sun warm my face. I'm still jet-lagged and sleep deprived and for the first time since I arrived, I let myself relax a little, let go of the tension.

I must doze off for a minute but when I start awake, the voice is still clear in my mind. I was at the hotel in Glenmalure. Talking to the woman behind the bar. *The Guards were in a few months ago asking about a German girl. I think they found her, though. They didn't ask about your cousin.*

A German girl.

Griz answers on the first ring, like she was waiting for a call.

"It's Maggie D'arcy," I say. "Roly told me he'd be in Wicklow all day but I thought I'd better tell someone. I just remembered something. There was a German girl. Back in 1993. The first time I went down there, the woman at the hotel mentioned that someone had been asking about her. She said they found her, but maybe she knows something. Maybe there was a mistake." I don't say anything about my archive search.

But Griz already knows about her. I can tell by the way she hesitates. "Thank you, Detective D'arcy. I'll make sure we follow up. I'll ring you if we need to ask you any more about it."

"Okay," I say. "Thank you."

There's a shout in the background. She's not indoors. "I've to go," she says. I recognize something about the quality of the noise behind her. She's got a lot of people, a lot of cars around her.

"Has something happened?"

She hesitates. I can feel her wrestling with herself, trying to decide. I've been there. In the end, I'm a fellow cop.

"You'll see it later on the telly," she says, "if the number of cameras here is any indication. We found something." She hesitates again. "We found something of Niamh's."

16

After Bernie found the scrap of paper with the bus times at the bed-and-breakfast, Roly told me to sit tight and wait for word. "We're following all the leads," he said, distracted, "just making a courtesy call before heading off to Galway to check bus station security tapes. Don't worry if you don't hear anything. It may be a couple of days."

But I was still thinking about the bartender at the Raven. I went for a run in a little park further down Ringsend Road and then, wearing one of Erin's cotton fisherman sweaters against the cold afternoon, I walked into Temple Bar. The streets were busier now at the end of the working day, buses pulling up along St. Stephen's Green and commuters hurrying along to their homes, their faces cast down at the sidewalk. The air smelled deliciously of smoke and, though it wasn't raining, the gray, metallic tang of rain.

At five fifteen, the pub was about twenty times as full as it had been before. I pushed my way up to the bar and looked for the red-

headed barman. He wasn't on duty—the older man with the moustache was holding court instead—and I was just about to go when I
saw the redhead sitting at the end of the bar, a pint of Guinness in
front of him. He was chatting with a very pretty blond woman who
looked interested in whatever he was whispering in her ear, and he
didn't look like he wanted to be interrupted. I ordered a pint and
took it down to his end of the bar anyway.

"Hi," I said, leaning in and addressing him over the woman's
head. She looked up and smiled. My bartender friend didn't smile.
"I don't know if you remember. But I was in yesterday and I thought
that maybe you thought you recognized me. The thing is, it may
have been my cousin. Or you may have thought I was my cousin, I
mean. We look a lot alike. And I don't know if you heard, but she's
missing. The Guards are looking for her and I came over from the
States to help find her. If she came here a lot, you might have seen
something or heard something that could help us find her."

He stared at me for a minute and then muttered, "Jaysus."

The woman was staring at me, too, and she put a hand to her
chest. "Not the American girl who went missing down in Wicklow?
It was on RTÉ this morning. You're very like her, aren't you? Sean,
do you know her?"

"No, I don't know her," he said, in a resigned way. "Not really.
But she used to stop in quite a bit and your man Andy fancied her,
so sometimes I'd ring him up if she came in. It gave me a turn when
I saw you. I thought to myself, 'Oh, she's come back. That's grand,
so.' But then I realized you weren't her. You're very like her, but
you're . . . not her."

"No," I said. "Did she ever talk to you? Did you ever see her
with anyone in here?"

He hesitated and then he said, "We just chitchatted a bit, if you know what I mean. At the bar, like, with Andy." He pointed to a skinny, acne-plagued teenager behind the bar. "I knew she was American and all that. God, you look like her. I could have sworn it was her. Ah, yeah, we chatted sometimes, but not a lot."

"Was she ever in here with anyone? A man?"

"No, she always came by herself. She mentioned getting off work a couple times, like, that it had been a long day or whatever at the café. She'd usually have one pint and look at a newspaper or just have a chat with whoever was around."

"Did she ever meet anyone in here? Did guys bother her?"

He hesitated. "They always bothered her, but she didn't let them bother her, if you know what I mean. She knew how to smile and chat for a minute and then move on if she wasn't interested. Working as a barman, you see a lot of different sorts o' brush-offs. She was a pro, she was."

"So, no one ever made it past the brush-off?"

He hesitated again and I felt a little prickle at the base of my neck. This was it. Whatever he was going to tell me next was important. It was why he said "Jaysus" when I came over. He was afraid of something.

"What? Who was it?"

He thought about lying, then thought better of it.

"All right, look. I don't know if this is important at all. But back in, oh, I guess maybe August, end of the summer, she was in and these four fellas were talking to her and I noticed she didn't just brush them off. They were talking real intensely, like she was interested in whatever they were telling her. I heard one of them say he was staying at the Westbury and they were going to be there later and she should join them. I was listening because like I told you, your man Andy really fancied her and I was wondering would she go or stay, so I could tell Andy, like. He was gearing up to ask her out for a bite to eat. He had it all planned out, the sad bastard."

"Did she go?"

"I don't know. It got busy and when I looked up again, they were all gone."

"So . . . what? That's it?"

"Well." He hesitated again. "Two of 'em were Americans and the other two were Irish. One from the north. The Americans were older fellas, but the Irish two were a bit younger, like maybe thirties. That seemed weird, for one thing."

A group of guys at the back of the room were laughing loudly and shouting. I had to lean in to hear the barman's words.

"They were asking her where she was from," he said. "I heard them asking if she knew someone named Pete O'Connell and she said she did but I think she was just slagging 'em off, like, 'Yeah, do you know how big America is, you eejits?' and they were all laughing. Then, like I said, it got really busy and when I looked up again they were gone. She was, too."

"Is there any way to figure out who they are? They didn't pay with a credit card or anything, did they?"

"For pints? No. Maybe the Westbury would know."

"That's a good idea," I told him. "What about the other two?"

He hesitated again. "Like I said, one of them was from the north. One was from here. I heard him saying he was from Arklow, something about coming up to Dublin to get parts, like maybe he ran a garage." He took a deep breath. "I'm not a hundred percent, but I heard the other lad call him Niall."

"Where's Arklow?"

"Down in Wicklow."

I could feel my heart speed up a little.

"When you say the north, you mean north like Northern Ireland?"

"Yeah." There was more. I could tell.

He looked at the woman as though he was hoping for guidance. "The other fellas, the Americans. Like I said, they were a bit older. The Irish fellas didn't know them. Didn't know them *already*, like. They were meeting for the first time. The Irish two came in first and then the Americans came in and one of them kind of looked around and then he held up his newspaper—it was some kind of sign—and then they went over and shook hands and they started talking to each other. They seemed to have a lot to say."

I looked from him to the woman and back again. "So?" I was missing something.

"So they had a look about them. The Irish guys. If you want to know the truth, they looked like fucking Provos. Especially the guy from the north."

I must have look confused, because the woman explained, "Provos. Provisional IRA."

"Really? And Erin—my cousin—she was talking to them? To all four of them?"

"That's it," he said. "And it's right after that that she stopped coming in."

I waited, and finally he said, "There was something about them. I've been a barman a long time. You see all kinds, you know, you really do. Something about those fellas made me wonder what she was mixed up in and hope she was all right."

17

1993

It was nine, still not quite raining but almost, the moisture hanging there in the air as though it was just waiting to be pushed over the edge.

He had said, "Stop by the café." Had he meant it? Was he just being polite?

I turned down Eustace Street and wandered around Temple Bar. People poured out of the pubs and I had to dodge a kid vomiting against a brick wall on Temple Lane and a couple making out next to the youth hostel entrance on Fowne Street.

Conor was locking the door as I approached the café and I called his name so he wouldn't be surprised to find me standing there.

He looked surprised anyway. "You're not looking for salad, are you? Trust me, it's shite by this time of night."

"No. I was walking by so I thought I'd see if you were here."

He looked down at me. He was wearing a brown leather motorcycle jacket, boots. He put the keys in his pocket and then held his hands out at his sides. "I'm here," he said. "At least I think I am. I just had a load of seventeen-year-olds come in completely langered. One of them was sick in the bathroom. Another one had to run out to be sick."

"I think I saw him," I said. "I had to move fast to save myself."

He grinned, then caught himself and asked, "Is there, uh, news?"

There were still a lot of people on the street and it didn't seem like the right place to ask him about Erin. "Not exactly. Look, do you want to get a drink? I could use a pint, and it sounds like you could, too. There's something I want to ask you. About Erin."

He looked away and I thought he was going to give me an excuse, but then he forced a smile and said, "All right, then. It's going to be pissing rain in a few minutes."

We started walking and he said, more to himself than to me, "Where will we go? Ah, the Palace is all right," and we walked along Fleet Street for a couple of minutes before he held the door for me at the Palace Bar. It was small and crowded and old-fashioned inside, but we got our pints and found two stools at the back, up against a bar along the wall.

The stools were close together and when I slid mine in, my thigh came to rest alongside his. I could feel the heat from his body. He shrugged off his leather jacket and I caught a whiff of his deodorant, spicy, sharp, not something I recognized. He took a long sip of his Guinness. "Well, what is it you want to know?"

"The cops, the Guards, wanted to know if Erin had any boyfriends. They probably asked you, too." He nodded. I said, "I was just at the Raven and the barman said that Erin was in there talking to some older American guys. They were with an Irish guy and a guy from the north and he said he thought they were Provos." The word felt odd in my mouth.

He stared at me, shocked. "Provos? Fuckin' hell. He said that?"

"Yeah. Does that . . . Did she ever say anything to you about that?"

He still looked shocked. "That's . . . He can't be thinking . . ." But then something occurred to him. He met my eyes and looked away.

"What?"

"It's not . . . I just remembered it now. She left one night after her shift and came back a bit later. She said she thought someone was following her. I was finished my shift anyway, so I saw her home. She said maybe she'd imagined it, but she was a bit wobbly. Something scared her right enough."

"But she didn't say anything about any Americans or these . . . Provos? I don't even really know what he was saying."

Conor took a deep breath and leaned back against the wall. "That's . . . I'd say his implication was that the Americans were over as part of some kind of arms-smuggling arrangement. Or maybe just arranging financing."

I stared at him. "And Erin was somehow connected with these guys?"

"I don't know. Maybe he thought they were trying to recruit her."

"What? To the IRA?"

"One of the splinter groups, like. I know it sounds mental, but it's happened. Not recently, though. It feels like a bit of a relic of the seventies and eighties, if you know what I mean. But a clean passport, an American who can travel freely. I've heard stories, but it's probably pretty uncommon."

I say, "Erin, she . . . I never heard her talk about any of that stuff. I don't think she even, like, understood the Troubles. I tried to explain the demographics of Northern Ireland to her once when some guys got into an argument at the bar, and she didn't understand it. I mean, beyond singing 'The Foggy Dew' on Saint Patrick's Day, I never heard her talk about politics. I don't think she could have told you what 'home rule' meant." He was watching me, a little smile on his face. "What?"

"Nothing. I don't want to offend you."

"You were about to say that not understanding Northern Ireland has never stopped Americans getting involved before?"

He grinned. "Yeah, but." We stared at each other for a long moment.

A couple of guys at the front started playing traditional tunes, not a proper session, just the two guys, a guitar and a fiddle between them.

Now he was watching me. "You're a bit of an Irish history buff, are you?"

"I went to Notre Dame for English and focused on Irish Studies. I got a prize and everything."

"Really?" I liked the way he said *really*. He found vowels in it I didn't even know it had. "Erin never said. Are you in grad school?"

"No, I was planning on it. I was about to do my junior year here but then my mother got really sick. And then she died. And after all that was over . . . I don't know. It was all I could do to finish my undergrad degree." He didn't say anything for a minute, so I went on, babbling out of nervousness. "Maybe I'll still go. I really like it here, even with . . . I don't know what I'm doing, to be honest with you. I've been working at my uncle's bar. I think I sort of just felt like, what was the point, you know? Did I really want to spend the rest of my life reading and rereading one particular passage of Joyce and, like, writing about chickens in his work or something? I mean . . ."

He had an amused look on his face and I realized with horror what I'd done. "Oh God," I said, but I couldn't help laughing. "I just totally offended you, didn't I? Oh my God, you're studying chickens in twentieth-century Irish history, aren't you? What are you studying?" I covered my face with my hands. But I was laughing so hard I couldn't stop.

He was laughing, too. "Well, yes, it's true, I've devoted my entire academic career to . . . the role of chickens in late-twentieth-century Irish political history, but you know, you're right. It's totally pointless, so if you'll excuse me, I think I'll just go and off myself in the toilet." He pretended to get up, but I grabbed his arm and pulled him back onto his stool. He fell against me and I felt a charge of energy when he grabbed my arm to steady himself.

There was a raucous shout of laughter from the other end of the bar. The guys were playing a jig now and a drunk tourist was trying to dance.

"I'm so sorry. What are you really studying? I bet it's hugely important to the survival of the planet."

He put on a mock formal voice and said, "Irish neutrality during the Emergency and the development of European identity."

"Hmmm. Interesting." "The Emergency" was the term used to describe the World War II years in Ireland. "What are you writing about?"

"Right now I'm writing about the secret negotiations between Ireland and the US to buy arms during the war."

"Did we sell them to you?"

"No. You rejected us."

"I'm so sorry. I thought we had this special relationship, America and Ireland. I took a whole class about it."

"Ah, but you see, there was FDR, who was very pro-British. You also have a special relationship with Britain, a very, very special relationship. And see, that's always been the tough thing about *our* relationship."

I swallowed, ventured. "Is that right? That's the tough thing about our relationship?"

He laughed. "I don't know what the tough thing is about *our* relationship, mind you . . ." He grinned at me and I felt my heart shift. "But the tough thing about the Emergency was that Roosevelt wasn't going to do anything to go against Downing Street, even though there was the Irish and American relationship, fed and watered by Irish Americans in Boston and New York and—"

"And Long Island, probably."

"And Long Island."

"So what happened? We wouldn't sell you any guns?"

"No, you wouldn't. Though you made up for it later."

"Northern Ireland?"

He studied me for a minute. "You and Erin, you grew up around the bar, right?" I nodded. "Did your uncle have a bucket hanging on the wall? For the widows and orphans in the north?"

I hadn't thought about it in years, but suddenly I remembered it. It had disappeared at some point, but when I was little, it had been there. "Yeah. He did. Was that the IRA?"

"In the late sixties, when the civil rights protests started in Northern Ireland, things got really violent. Once internment of IRA members started, people started raising money for the internees' families and for the widows and orphans of hunger strikers. NORAID's the big one most people know. But loyalist groups and the British government have always claimed that NORAID was actually fund-raising for the Provisional IRA."

"Were they?"

"There was certainly some mission creep there. You have to remember that the Troubles started with the civil rights protests and the slaughter of protestors on Bloody Sunday. From there, different groups sort of used the struggle for their own purposes."

"That bucket. I never thought anything of it. But he took it down in the eighties when I was in high school."

"Yeah, the Provisional IRA leaders would go over and talk to the NORAID guys in New York. They'd do the rounds and rally the troops and raise some money. By the eighties, Reagan and Thatcher had such a romance going that the general American attitude toward Northern Ireland shifted. But there are bars in the Bronx and Boston that still pass the bucket."

"But Erin?" I was trying to think now, trying to remember. "She never said anything to you about being involved with anything like that?"

"No," he said. But there was something. His brown eyes narrowed and flashed. "I just thought of something, though. Not about that, but only . . ."

"Only what?"

He met my eyes. "She asked me once about mass rocks."

"What's that?" My pint was gone. His was too.

"During penal times, when the practice of Catholicism was prohibited by law, people would hold mass outdoors. There were rocks that were set up as altars. Sometimes caves were used. You can still find them sometimes, outside of Dublin, like."

"Did she want to go see one or something? Why was she asking you about it?"

"I don't know. She said she'd heard about them and did I know where any were? But it felt like she was just making conversation, not like she really wanted to see one, if you know what I mean. That's funny. I just thought of it."

I didn't know what to say. The pub was starting to clear out.

"It'll be last call soon," Conor said. "I should get going. I have an early lecture."

"Oh yeah, of course." We got our jackets on, spilled out onto the bright, wet street. It was barely raining. The air was so heavy I felt as though I could hold it in my hands.

18

We walked in silence for a little bit and then he said, "So, have they found anything? About Erin, I mean?" He was trying to sound casual, but his voice wavered, and he made a point of looking at the window of a shop we were passing. "Where do you think she is?"

"I just don't know. Erin and I used to be close when we were kids. But not anymore, really. I love her but I don't know her anymore, if that makes sense. She's done some crazy stuff the last couple years. She got a DUI, she dated this guy who was literally a criminal. She used to—I don't know what she'd do."

He sighed and picked up his pace. "Where are you staying?"

"Erin's."

"Ah, I'm not far then. Do you go Pearse Street or by the quays?"

"Pearse Street, I guess."

"I'll see you home. Let's go by the quays. All right with you?" He seemed happier now, more relaxed.

I nodded. The air was moist with just a faint hint of the smoky smell. We wound around by D'Olier Street and then along the quays, the Liffey to our left, flowing to the sea.

"What's that smell?" I asked him.

"Hmmm? Oh, the smoky sort of smell?"

"I love it."

He looked down at me. "So do I. I think it's peat fires some-where."

"They let people burn peat in the city?"

"Maybe. I don't know. Maybe it's fires out in the country, or . . ."

"You don't actually have any idea, do you?" I looked up at him. "You're just making that up."

"Well, it must be peat, right? It smells like peat." He stopped and put his hands out. "All right, all right. You're right. I don't know where it's coming from, but it's Dublin to me, you know? When I first came, for college, I had a flat in Rathmines and when I opened the window I smelled it and it made me think of home."

"Aw. What a nice story."

"Feck off, you." He gave me a little shove.

The lights blurred a little. I bumped against his arm, hoping he'd take my hand, but he kept his hands in his pockets and kept walking.

We were almost to the canal. There was a pub right on the river, a glossy red pub that said "O'Brien's" on one side of the door and "The Ferryman" on the other. It was after last call, but people were still going in and coming out.

"That's a dockworker's pub," Conor tells me. "It's good *craic* in there. You should walk over some time."

"Who's the Ferryman?"

"The . . Oh, there used to be ferries that ran on the Liffey. For the workers. They stopped running in the eighties. Have you not heard that song, 'The Ferryman'? It goes like, 'The little boats are gone on the breast of Anna Liffey, the ferryman is stranded on the quay, da, da, da. I love you today and I'll love you tomorrow, something, something. Sure the Dublin docks is dying . . .' Oh, Jaysus, I have a terrible voice, I know I do. I can't remember any more."

I was laughing, hard now. "You really do have a terrible voice, you know."

"Well, what about you?" On the next block, we took a right and walked along the canal. I could see the Bolands Flour Mills sign up ahead, just past the canal bridge. We were almost to Erin's flat.

"I can sing a little." I felt a small flush of triumph. I had a nice voice. Better than nice. I got it from my mother. She taught me a lot of Irish songs and I used to sing in college sometimes, when I'd had a few drinks, at a little Irish pub in South Bend.

"So, give us a song, Maggie D'arcy." He was still laughing. He thought it was going to be funny.

Instead I stopped and closed my eyes. I wanted to impress him. I was hopelessly attracted to Conor Kearney and I wanted to impress him.

At least I was honest with myself about this.

It was a classic one my mom loved, that I finally learned phonetically once I had a little Irish.

Trasna na dtonnta, dul siar,
Slán leis an uaigneas is slán leis an gcian
Geal é mo chroí, agus geal í an ghrian
Geal a bheith ag filleadh go hÉrinn.

I did the first chorus again and I ended on *hÉrinn* and something about the song, about saying her name, made tears come into my eyes and I turned away.

But he took me by the shoulders and turned me back and looked down at me. "I learned that in primary school. That was fucking brilliant. You've a lovely voice. Do you speak Irish? You never said."

"Níl ach beagán. Agus tú féin?" Not but a little. And you yourself? Then I laughed and said, "You'd better answer in English. That's about it."

He laughed too. "Not bad. Yeah, at school, you know. And we spoke Irish at home a bit. My mam was quite militant about us learning."

We were crossing over the canal.

"How many siblings do you have?" I asked. It suddenly seemed important to know.

"Just five of us. That'd be a small family, in most people's books, but my mam always had modern ideas about things. She's a poet and she had grand ideas of fame and fortune. Of course, she was married to a sheep farmer in County Clare so the chances of that were pretty long, but they have a good life." He hesitated, then said, "I've got three sisters and a brother—I'm the little one—and the sisters are all abroad, but doing well for themselves. One of them is a barrister in London, the other one is an art teacher in Denmark, married to a Danish guy, and my other sister's in America—she's a graphic designer in California."

"What about the brother?"

"He's a story for another day."

"Don't your parents miss your sisters?"

"Oh yeah, 'course they do, but it's kind of what you do. Do you have brothers and sisters?"

"Nope. Both Erin and I are only children, which is why we were so close. As kids, anyway."

He touched my arm and steered me around a pile of something dark on the sidewalk. I leaned into him. He didn't lean away. Suddenly we were holding hands, rounding the Irishtown shops and starting down Ringsend Road. We'd be back to the house soon. I was still half drunk. The air was full of the smoky smell and the glow of the streetlights.

"Do you miss it, where you grew up?" I asked him. He rubbed my hand with his thumb. "Dublin must be really different."

"Yeah, I miss it a lot," he said. "But I don't think I ever really thought I could stay there. When I think about going home for Christmas, the *craic*, my mam's brown bread and roast and potatoes and going out in the morning to help my da with the sheep, watching telly with my sisters. I don't know. I guess it's family, though it's the place, too. There's this little hill just out the back of the farm and I used to go out there to think when I was a kid. Whenever I'm home, I always go out there to watch the sunset. That's what I miss. Ah, I'm sad, amn't I? Do you feel like that about your place?"

"Yeah, well, the beach mostly. I grew up looking out at the harbor. The sunsets. The smell of it. The sound of the seagulls. Boats always moving on the water."

In the distance, a gull called, and we both laughed.

"You sure you don't want to devote your life to studying seagulls in Irish literature? There's a lot of textual evidence."

"So much better than chickens," I said.

After a minute of silence, I asked him, "Did Erin ever tell you her mother was Irish?"

"Yeah, I think maybe she mentioned it."

"Did she ever tell you she was looking for her?"

"I don't think so. Is that why she came over here?"

"I don't know," I told him. "I don't really know why she came over here."

We were at the flat. We stopped and he looked down at me, then glanced away. His eyes were liquid light on the dark street.

"Thanks for walking me home."

"Well, I should let you get inside," he said. "And I have a lot of studying to do tomorrow. You know, chickens."

"I'll see you?" I said, laughing.

"Yeah. Stop by and have lunch. Or stop by and don't have lunch. Our food's not very good."

"Okay. I will. Thanks, Conor."

"No worries." He hesitated again. I thought he was going to kiss me, but he didn't. He just turned, stopped, turned again, and then he was off walking down the street, his shoulders hunched down in his leather jacket, and I was left standing there, listening to the gulls calling over the canal and out toward Sandymount and the sea.

19

Whatever they found down in Wicklow has everyone excited. The news announcer doesn't know what it is, but that doesn't stop her from speculating. They've got shots of a cordoned-off area next to a narrow road, gardaí walking back and forth. I realize that Griz must have been standing not far from the spot when I called her.

They have a "former law enforcement professional" with an English accent piling on the speculation. He straightens his tie and looks sympathetically into the camera. "In these kinds of cases, you would be looking for clothing, perhaps a piece of physical evidence. It is entirely possible that they have found a piece of clothing with enough blood on it to indicate that Miss Horrigan has indeed met a violent end. It is also possible that they have located a piece of evidence that may lead them to Miss Horrigan's abductor."

The newscaster asks him why it would be kept confidential. "Well, if it is indeed a piece of evidence that could lead gardaí to the perpetrator, then they would want to keep that to themselves.

It might be something that only the person who took Niamh would know about. It might be a way to test a confession. Or they may not want the person in question to know that they are on his trail." The newscaster and the expert have an awkward little moment of silence where they both realize that their coverage means that the person in question definitely knows the police have found something.

Then the newscaster hands it over to a reporter in Wicklow, saying, "Aiofe Callahan, tell us about some new information we're just getting about the location of this search."

"Yes, Allison. The Gardaí hope that this development will help lead them to Niamh, who has now been missing for a week," says the young reporter in a concerned voice. She's standing close to the Wicklow Way trail marker. "We can report at this hour that the location where the item was found is very near to Drumkee and the former grave of Kevin Whelan, the Belfast teenager whose grave was identified by members of the Provisional IRA as part of the Good Friday peace agreement. As you know, Allison, Kevin was eighteen years old when he disappeared from his home in Armagh in 1981. There had been rumors in his community that he was an informant and his family assumed he'd been murdered. After the Good Friday Agreement, an IRA splinter group revealed the location of his grave, in a patch of boggy hillside in Drumkee, close to where Erin and now Niamh Horrigan were last seen. His remains were recovered and now the Gardaí wonder if there is any connection between Niamh's disappearance and the dark history of this place."

I scramble for my laptop and search for "Kevin Whelan" and "Drumkee." There are quite a few stories, mostly archived reports from the late '90s. As part of the Good Friday Agreement, which mostly brought the sectarian violence in Northern Ireland to an end, paramilitary groups on both sides of the conflict had to agree to put their arms beyond use. While some arms were buried in concrete or destroyed, others were illegally buried in secret locations, Wikipedia tells me, in case the violence started up again. The stories refer to anonymous sources that say it's widely believed that arms were brought over the border and buried in multiple locations in the Republic. The stories don't say it directly, but the implication seems to be that there are some arms caches in the Wicklow Mountains, in Drumkee, among other locations.

I call home to talk to Lilly but she doesn't answer her cell phone, and when I call the landline Brian tells me that she's gone out to Montauk for the day with her friend Cory's family. "She doing okay?" I ask him.

"Yeah, she's doing great. How are things there?"

I go to the window and look out at the street. It's quiet, late on Sunday. I remember this about Ireland, how quiet Sundays can be in public spaces. I wonder suddenly what Conor Kearney is doing right now. "They're no closer to finding Erin, and Roly has me completely sidelined," I say. "I mean, I know he has to, but I'm just sitting in this hotel room. They found something today, something belonging to the girl who's missing. Niamh. I could help them but I have no idea what it is and they won't even tell me anything." I'm unloading my frustration on him and I feel bad about it. "I'm sorry, Brian."

"No, it sounds awful."

"How's Danny?"

"Okay. You know. Lilly went over and took him some brownies she made last night. He's just . . . waiting. The bar's been busy, so that's good."

"And . . . everything else is okay?"

I don't want to have to say it and blessedly he picks up on my meaning. "Yeah, yeah. Nothing strange. I've been setting the alarm. Don't worry, Mags. There's nothing to worry about."

I feel relief stream down toward my legs. "Okay. I'm going to go out and find some dinner." I tell him to give Lilly a big hug and to tell her to call me when she can.

◆ ◆ ◆

I'm heading out of my hotel room, my bag slung over my shoulder, my key in my hand, when a man waiting in the hallway surprises me, clearing his throat and smiling sympathetically when I jump and whirl around.

"Oh, I'm so sorry. I didn't mean to give you a fright. I just thought I could see if you were here."

It's the reporter with the ponytail from the other day. In the dim hallway he seems freakishly large, his shoulders twice the width of me, his legs thick under his suit pants. His forehead is dotted with beads of moisture and I take in his sharp sweaty smell from two feet away. He's older than I thought, closer to my age.

"Stephen Hines?" he says. "We met the other day."

"How did you know where my room was?" I ask. I'm still holding my key in my hand and I point the sharp edge of it out.

"I didn't. I've been trying every floor." He shrugs and smiles. "I got very lucky."

"It's creepy," I tell him. "Please don't do it again."

He says, "Look, I'm sorry to bother you, but I just want to get your sense of the investigation. You're not just a family member, you're a highly skilled homicide detective, with apparent expertise in serial murder. What do you think about this find in Drumkee?"

"My sense is that the Garda Síochána is doing an excellent job," I say. I put my room key into my bag and zip up my jacket.

But he's still standing there, his body a barrier between me and the elevator. "A number of people have mentioned to me that they're not sure why the Guards aren't using you more, using your expertise. Would you like to be more involved in the investigation, Detective D'arcy?"

I look up at him. "The Guards are doing an excellent job," I say. "I have a lot of confidence in them."

"Have you been told that Niamh's family wants to meet you?"

Now I'm interested. "Are you making that up?"

"No, no," he says. "I wouldn't make up something like that. They want to talk to you. They want to meet you. Why are the Guards keeping that from you?"

I watch him for a moment. He's got an angle, but maybe I do, too. "Okay, what's your theory?" I ask him. "You seem to really want to talk to me. What's your theory on my cousin? On Niamh?"

He smiles kindly, a favorite college professor getting ready to answer a question. "I was just starting out when your cousin went missing," he says. "They had me writing stories about cattle auctions and traffic. I've only read my colleagues' stories in the archives. But I think whoever took your cousin never stopped taking women and I think he took Niamh Horrigan and I think whoever it is there in the trees at Glenmalure was taken by him, too. Don't you want to help find him? It must be driving you mad, with all your expertise. I mean, you bested the fecking *FBI*."

"Is that what you told the Horrigans?" I ask him.

He only appears a little embarrassed.

"I'm just looking for some information," he says. "I'm a journalist. This is quite a confusing situation, as you know. My editor, like, he thinks I'm not working hard enough on this."

I feel the rage build up inside me. "Don't do that. I know who you are. Are you kidding me? Do you know how many hours I've spent reading every fucking article about this case? I've read everything you've ever written, Stephen P. Hines, for the *Independent*. You're a good reporter, you're a dogged reporter. You're obsessed with these cases. I can tell. So don't pretend you don't know what you're doing."

"All right," he says. He's smiling. This is just what he wanted. "Thanks for that. Really, very flattering. I can show my appreciation by giving you a little scoop. It's not public. They're just about to arrest some guy down in Wicklow."

Everything stops for a minute. I can hear a low buzzing coming from the emergency exit light on the wall.

"Who?" I want to shake him and demand he tell me what he knows. Everything narrows down to his face, the dim hallway. Suddenly, I realize what he's saying, what he's doing. I take a deep breath. "I would be happy to meet with the Horrigans," I tell him. "Of course I would. And I would be happy to aid the investigation in any way I can. But it's delicate. I'm a civilian when I'm here." I keep laying it on. "They would have to believe that the Horrigans really want me involved. The Horrigans would have to *demand* that I help with the profiling, really. Perhaps they might threaten to go to the press if I didn't. I'd need access to a lot of case files and interviews.

That's not strictly legal. And it would have to be very clear that they were asking for this. That it's not me who's trying to get in on this."

Stephen Hines smiles angelically and spreads his hands at his sides.

"I think we all just want to find Niamh safe and sound," he says. "I think that's what we all want. I'm sure someone will be in touch, Detective D'arcy."

I stand there, breathless, for a few minutes after he walks away.

I've just played the only card I have.

I'm sorry, Roly.

I don't feel nearly as guilty as I should.

20

I caught up to Byrne and McNeely outside the Irishtown Garda Station that next morning to tell them about Erin and Niall from Arklow.

October 8. She had been missing for three weeks.

They didn't look happy to see me but they stopped and listened to me while I told them about the men at the Raven.

Byrne looked up at the sky for a minute, then pinched the bridge of his nose as if he had a headache. "That's interesting. He really said that?"

"Yeah. What does that mean? I know it's for Provisional IRA, but I don't really get it. Do they dress a particular way or something?"

"Well, it might mean that your man from the bar is a prejudiced git and he thinks anyone with a northern accent is a terrorist, but it also might mean that they're actually Provos. He's right. There's a sorta look, an energy. Can't really explain it."

Bernie sighed but didn't say anything.

I said, "The town where Erin and I grew up on Long Island? It's a regular suburb, but it's Long Island, and there are a few Mafia guys living there. They don't come into the bar a lot—I guess 'cause it's an Irish bar—but I always know when they do, even if I've never seen them before. Is that what you mean?"

"Yeah, I guess it is. Were they real Mafia guys? Like *The Godfather*? That sorta thing?"

"Yeah. They had these shirts they always wore. Silk. I've never seen any other man wear a shirt like that."

He grinned. "'I'm gonna make him an offer he can't refuse,'" he said, in what was supposed to be *The Godfather* but didn't quite hit the mark.

Bernie rolled her eyes.

"You sound more like Vincent Connelly than Vito Corleone," I said.

Roly and I grinned at each other. "Very funny," he said. *Foony.*

"So what are you going to do?" I asked.

He glanced at Bernie. "We're going to go down to the Westbury Hotel and we're going to try to figure out who they were."

"Can I come with you?"

"How did I know you were going to ask me that? No, you can't."

McNeely said, "I understand that you're worried about your cousin, but you going off and pretending to be an amateur detective isn't going to help us find her, and it's likely to hurt, if you want to know the truth."

"I didn't do it on purpose. I went in there and I could tell he recognized me. I figured he might know something and thought I should ask him. If you'd gone in there he wouldn't have told you."

"Fair enough," she said. She studied me for a couple of seconds.

We stood there for a moment in awkward silence and then I asked McNeely, "Are you from Northern Ireland?"

Something crossed her face, annoyance maybe, and she said, "That's right. I was raised in Armagh."

"That must have been intense, growing up there," I said, then immediately felt stupid when I saw her face.

"Ah, yeah, 'intense' is one word for it," she said, then studied me for a long moment before she said, "Well, we'd better leg it, Roly."

"We'll let you know if there's anything," he said.

I'd already turned around and was walking back down Charlemont Place when he called out, "Miss D'arcy!" and I stopped and turned around to find him jogging after me.

He stopped when he got to me and said, a little out of breath, "Let me ask ya something. She may or may not have come back to Dublin. She may or may not have known those fellas at the pub. I don't know what to think about this thing. Where do you think she is?"

I watched a couple walking by the canal. "When we were little, she used to run away all the time. She didn't do it to be cruel or to make people worry. She just . . . ran. But she always came back." There was a long silence. "Or I could always find her," I added.

Byrne didn't say anything and I kept talking. "I think something happened to her. If she came back to take a bus, it was because she was going to meet someone. And that someone knows where she is."

"Okay." He looked tired all of a sudden and I didn't believe him when he said, "Don't worry too much about Detective McNeely. She just doesn't like Americans much."

"Why?"

"That," he said, with a little grin that wasn't really a grin, "is a long story for another day."

* * *

I got back to the house just as Emer and Daisy were leaving for classes. They'd bought the *Irish Independent* and I asked if I could read it.

"'Course. I'm finished with it," Daisy told me, drinking a cup of tea while Emer packed up her books. "Actually, do you know, I was reading it and I think I remembered the name of your man who rang for Erin. The sort o' American-sounding one. It was that story that made me think of it. I can't believe I forgot it, actually."

"Really?"

"Hacky O'Hanrahan." She said it in a funny voice.

"What?" We both laughed. "It sounds like a cartoon character."

"I know. I wouldn't have remembered but there's a story about a fella named Hackman O'Hanrahan Sr. in the paper today and I thought, that was the same name as the one who called." She picked up the paper, turned it to an inside page, and handed it over.

IAI Chief O'Hanrahan Seeks Investors for New Sectors Fund

The Irish American banker Hackman O'Hanrahan Sr. announced today a new fund for investors in new sectors in the Republic. O'Hanrahan, a former director of Allied Irish Banks and the Green Island Fund, calls the new fund a rare opportunity for the manufacturing and computer sector . . .

"I'd say your man is his son," Emer said.

"That makes sense. That would make sense, right? If his father's been over here doing business, his accent might be a bit funny. And he could be a Trinity student, right?"

"Yeah," she said, with a look I couldn't quite read. "There are loads of Americans at Trinity."

After they'd gone, I reread the story and paced around the house a bit, thinking.

If Erin had been seeing this Hacky O'Hanrahan guy, he might know something about where she was and he might be able to tell us about her state of mind. He might know where she went when she left the bed-and-breakfast.

I was just about to leave the house when the phone rang.

"Maggie?" I didn't recognize the voice but she said, "It's Jess. Jess Friedman. My mom said you were trying to get in touch with us about Erin." I can hear the emotion in her voice. "I'm with Lisa and Chris and Brian. We're in Madrid at a youth hostel and my phone card might run out but she said you wanted to know when's the last time we saw Erin. It was when we left Dublin in August."

"So she didn't come over to travel with you or anything?"

"No," she said. "Is she okay? What's going on?"

I told her the basics. "The last place she was seen was at this bed-and-breakfast. She didn't tell you about a boyfriend or anything or any travel plans, did she? How long did you guys stay with her?"

"Three nights," Jess said. "We flew into Dublin and stayed with her for, yeah, three nights, then took the ferry over to London and then Lisa and I met up with Stacy and we went over to France and started Eurailing. Brian was in London with college friends. Chris visited his family in Ireland then went over to London. And then they came over to Paris and met us."

"How did Erin seem?"

"I guess good," Jessica said. "Like she liked it there. She was . . . I don't know. Different but happy."

"What do you mean different?"

"She was just . . . She kept trying to talk about like, the news. There was some riot or something. She wanted to talk about it, but I didn't really know anything about it. Here's Chris."

Chris Fallon was one of Erin's friends, too. "It's Chris. Yeah, she seemed pretty happy. What did you think, Bri?"

I heard Brian Lombardi's voice say, "Yeah, she seemed good. You know Erin." His voice called up his face. I'd had a huge crush on Brian in high school. He and his older brother, Frank, had both been popular, good-looking, and talented athletes.

Jessica got back on and said, "Well, yeah. The last night, though. She . . . we went out. We had a lot to drink. And then she took us to this, like, club. We were all dancing and having so much fun. It was weird, you could only order, like, red wine. And then she just disappeared. We were ready to go home and we couldn't find her. We searched for like an hour. We didn't know what to do so we figured out how to get back to her house and we had to knock on the door and wake up her roommates. Chris was really pissed."

"So what happened? Did she come back the next day?"

"Yeah. She came in and said she'd been to mass. It was weird. We were already up because we had to catch the ferry."

"Mass?"

"Yeah."

"Did she say she'd started going regularly?"

"No, but she said something about Father Anthony. You know, just that she still couldn't believe he was gone, that she really missed him. Anyway, she said she was sorry, she was really drunk and whatever, but she didn't say who she'd been with." I heard a beeping over the line. "Shit, Maggie, the card's about to run out. I'll try to—"

The phone cut out and I stood there for a moment listening to the silence coming across the line.

Erin has her Holy Communion first, when she's in second grade.

My mom gets her a white lacy dress with puffy sleeves and a white ribbon around the waist. She looks like a bride and I'm so jealous I think about spilling paint on the dress so she can't wear it.

I sit in the church next to my parents and watch Erin go up to kneel for the first time and take the wafer from Father Patrick. Father Anthony stands nearby and smiles at us. I feel guilty, thinking about how I wanted to spill paint on the dress, and I'm glad I don't have to confess, for I know that Father Anthony won't like me if I tell him how I feel.

I watch Erin as she goes, Jessica behind her. When she kneels, she turns her face up to Father Patrick and the sun shining in through the windows covers her in golden light. She smiles and she looks happier than I've ever seen her, as though she's smiling at Jesus. Later, I hear her tell Father Anthony that she felt Jesus there next to her, that she felt his presence, heard him telling her what to do.

When I make my communion a year later, the lace dress is scratchy against my neck and the wafer makes my mouth feel funny. I wait to hear Jesus's voice, but he never speaks to me.

21

There was no listing in the Dublin phone book for a Hackman O'Hanrahan, but there was a listing for the IAI group, with an address on Fitzwilliam Place, not far from St. Stephen's Green.

Fitzwilliam Place was a long avenue lined with huge Georgian houses, all of them with brightly painted doors and brass knockers and tiny signs indicating the businesses occupying each floor.

The air smelled of peat fires and I thought of Conor, a sudden thrilling image of his neck and face flashing into my mind. I shook my head and tried the door. It was locked, but a little sign next to it instructed me to press the bell, and once I did, the door clicked open and let me into a tastefully decorated reception area.

The woman behind the desk looked up curiously at me. She was perfect: long brown hair, a pale blue wool pantsuit and lavender silk scarf at her throat, and I was suddenly conscious of my jeans and sweater and backpack. "Can I help you?" she asked, studying me over the top of her reading spectacles.

"I don't know. I'm sorry to bother you, but I'm looking for a friend of mine. Hacky O'Hanrahan? I'm over here just traveling around and he said if I was ever in Dublin I should look him up. He gave me this address, but I didn't realize it was a business . . ."

The woman smiled. "His father owns the investment company," she said. "That must be why he gave you this address. Mr. O'Hanrahan Jr. has a flat in Merrion Square, I believe. I'll check on the number for you."

She disappeared through the door behind her desk and came back a few minutes later with a piece of expensive-looking blue paper with a tasteful "IAI Investment Fund" embossed at the top. She'd written *93 Merrion Square West, #3* on the paper. I thanked her and headed back out to find Hacky O'Hanrahan.

Merrion Square was a green rectangle surrounded by streets of brick Georgians. Some of the houses had freshly painted doors and neat black iron fences, but others looked a bit shabby. Hacky O'Hanrahan's address fell somewhere in between. I stood there for a minute, trying to get a feel for the building before I rang the bell. There were four floors and the little directory next to the door had a law firm listed for the first floor and then the name Murphy written in pencil but scratched out. There were no names by the other two.

I was about to ring the bell when the cobalt blue door flew open, nearly knocking me to the ground, and two boys came running out, backpacks flying behind them.

"I'm fucking *late*!" one said to the other.

"I am as well, Hoopers. Shite, shite, shite!" The taller of the two stopped to hunch down on the stairs to tie his bootlaces and I was about to ask if either of them knew Hacky O'Hanrahan when the taller, better-looking one, looked up and said, "Erin?"

I tried to remember later exactly what combination of emotions flashed across his face. The first was fear, the second confusion, and the third was actually something more hopeful, maybe even excitement.

My first thought was, *He's exactly Erin's type.* He had longish brown hair that curled around his ears and a conventionally handsome face. His clothes were shabbily expensive: worn cords, a gray cashmere sweater, leather boots.

I stuck out my hand. "I'm Erin's cousin Maggie, actually. I know I look like her. You're Hacky O'Hanrahan. Can I ask you a few questions?" I was flustered, not quite ready for this.

Suddenly he was guarded. His friend was still standing there. O'Hanrahan pushed his hair out of his face. "I'm really late, actually," he said. "I can't really talk now."

"Can I just walk with you? I'm heading that way, too."

"Uh, sure. All right." His accent was only very faintly Irish, the edges rounded and smoothed—American, with just the slightest hint of Dublin.

The friend said, "I've got to run. Sorry." He searched O'Hanrahan's face for a moment, and then took off, a small smile playing at the corners of his lips. I imagined the conversation that would come up later. *Cousins, huh? So she gave you a rave review and her cousin thought she'd give you a try.*

"I'm really late. Sorry." O'Hanrahan lengthened his stride and I matched it.

"I can keep up," I told him. "You know about Erin, that she's missing." It was a statement, not a question, and he hesitated before nodding.

"How did you know her?" I asked him.

"I didn't know her, not really," he said.

We turned onto Nassau Street. I saw him glance up at the college entrance and then glance at his watch. It was a fancy watch, big and metal and bulky and expensive-looking. I didn't have much time. At the pace we were walking, we'd be inside the walls of the college in five or six minutes.

"But you did know her?"

"We weren't—it wasn't like a *relationship*," he said.

"But you slept with her." Statement, not question. I was going by instinct and his expression told me I was right.

"Well—why are you asking all these questions? I don't know anything about what happened to her." He was blushing. He looked scared.

"I didn't say you did." I was practically running to keep up with him now. "I know you don't know where she is or anything, but I'm thinking maybe you could give me a sense of her state of mind before she disappeared. Did she say anything about going on a trip? Did she seem depressed?"

His upper lip curled in a smirk. "She definitely didn't seem depressed. In fact, she seemed pretty happy to me."

I stared him down. "You mean sexually? She seemed pretty happy sexually?"

"Uh, yeah." He blushed hard. "You asked if she was depressed."

"Okay, so she was so happy. Why didn't you go out with her again?"

That smirk again. "I rang her. Called her. I didn't really care. I wasn't going to beg her or anything. I'm not exactly hurting for, uh, a social life."

I was trying to think what to ask next when he blurted out, "She was a crazy girl, you know. I mean, I know you're her cousin, but I gotta tell you." He looked away, his face transforming into a small boy's for just a second. "She liked it rough, if you want to know the truth. Who knows who she was mixed up with. Some freak. I bet that's where she is."

"Rough? As in, rough sex?"

"Yeah." He blushed again.

"Are you American? Is that why you and Erin started talking?"

"I've lived here since I was ten, but yeah, maybe. I heard her accent. We talked about Long Island a little. My family summers in Bridgehampton."

I thought of something then. "How did you know she was missing?"

There was something there. I could see him looking for the words. "I saw it on the news. I have to go now."

He was gone before I could get another word out.

Erin had been missing for three weeks now and I was no closer to figuring out what had happened to her than I'd been the day I arrived. All I had were a bunch of dead ends.

I stood in the forecourt for a long time before I pulled the collar of my jacket up around my face and set off into the wind.

22

It's a cloudy morning, a wind from the east whipping paper and dust into small tornadoes on Grafton Street. Niamh Horrigan's been gone nine days. I can't get Roly on the phone and there's nothing on the news about an arrest in Wicklow. That makes me think it's something minor, someone in one of the door-to-doors who had a big pile of pot on his dining room table when the Guards knocked on his door, a guy on probation who wasn't where he was supposed to be. Every homicide investigation has a few of these arrests, collateral damage, the not-so-innocents who have nothing to do with the actual crime but get caught up in the nets we cast when we're looking for a killer.

But how did Stephen Hines know about it, and what's he doing trying to bring me onto the investigation?

I have generally good relationships with the press back on Long Island. I know when to throw them something and I know when to clam up and reveal nothing. There's something about Hines that puts me on edge.

I stop at a café on Lemon Street for an espresso and carry it through to Parliament Square in Trinity, standing under the Lecky statue for a moment and then walking over to the stairs to the library. I'm ridiculous, a forty-five-year-old woman stalking a grown man who probably hasn't thought about me once in twenty-three years. Finally, I stand right in front of the Arts Building, checking my phone.

No Conor.

When I finish my coffee, I head back to the hotel. I send some emails to my team so they'll have them when they get in. There's a message from Emer apologizing for the delay in getting back to me. She's been traveling in Singapore and Hong Kong but she suggests a time for coffee midweek. I lie on the bed watching CNN and looking through the old notebooks and files I brought from home. At nine a.m., I turn on RTÉ news. The announcer says that officials in Wicklow are searching a new area at this hour. There's nothing about Drumkee and that line of the investigation. Nothing about an arrest. Niamh's parents have offered an increased reward for any information about her disappearance. Her uncle asks the public to think hard about whether they saw anything that might help bring her home.

They interview a retired detective garda, looking for a theory on what's happened to Niamh. "Certainly, at this stage of an investigation, the concern is that she has been abducted," the white-haired man says. He's standing in front of an elaborate flower garden. "The location, sure it makes you think it could be connected to the American girl, Erin Flaherty, and Teresa McKenny and June Talbot. With every hour that goes by, the chances of her being found alive continue to decrease."

I shut it off.

At loose ends, I go for a run along the quays. It feels good to move my legs and I go out fast, full of ambition. I'm still amazed at all the changes on the riverfront. There are huge new buildings on the north side, a giant glass-and-steel structure that looks like a barrel tipped onto its side and new office buildings gleaming along the river. I'm running past the Ferryman when I remember walking past it with Conor. It's now surrounded by tall, gleaming office blocks. It feels like it's been moved to a completely different part of the city. When I turn onto Cardiff Lane, the facade of a sleek modern building with the Facebook logo comes into view. I can see what Laura was talking about. Erin's old neighborhood has gone ritzy.

The day is so beautiful, I don't want to be back in the hotel, so I try to remember the way to the strand. I run straight out past Irishtown along Sandymount Road and then along one of the pleasant little streets lined with prosperous-looking bungalows to the park right on the strand. It's just the way I remember it, the sand and the gleaming water in ripples across it, reaching so far out toward the sea I can't tell where it ends. I run hard on the path out to the nature preserve, thinking of Conor, and then turn around, all my limbs feeling loose and strong, my head clearer. On the way back, I take a few pictures of the harp bridge and the view down the Liffey toward the Four Courts and text them to Lilly. I write, *Miss you so much, Lillybean! Love you!* I can smell her all of a sudden, her hair and her skin.

I'm almost to the hotel when I look up and find Roly and Griz

coming my way on the sidewalk. I stop and watch them for a moment before they look up and see me. Roly looks exhausted, his hair
and clothes the most rumpled I've ever seen them, his eyes baggy
and bruised. Griz seems thinner, old mascara crusting in the corner
of her right eye. She's wearing a bright yellow wool coat and she's
the only colorful thing on the sidewalk.

"D'arcy," Roly says. "We need to talk to you."

"What did they find in Wicklow?" I ask them. "It must be a
piece of clothing, right? I was thinking phone, but the way they
covered it, it made me think it was a piece of clothing. I was trying
to read between the lines in the stories."

Roly sighs. Griz is trying not to smile.

"All right," Roly says finally. "They found a fucking button. Let's
go inside and sit down."

Of course. I should have known. A button, a medium-sized
wooden button from the neck of a fleece pullover like the one
Niamh Horrigan was wearing when she disappeared, and wrapped
around it are three brown hairs, similar in length and color to the
ones in a hairbrush obtained from her flat by her family. They have
a picture of Niamh, on a mountaintop somewhere, wearing a green
pullover fleece jacket with a hood and two wooden buttons at the
neck, exactly like the button that was found.

I can see how hopeful it's made them. Something as small as a
button, but it's significant. Instead of a vast mountainous area to
search, they now have a neat little pin to put in the center of the
map, a radius to draw. They can look for tire tracks, CCTV footage.

"What about the Drumkee angle?" I ask. "They made a lot of
that on the news. Do you think there's anything there?" I want to

ask about the arrest, but I can't. I can't let them know I've been talking to Hines.

"We're looking at it," Roly says in a resigned voice. "And we think we may have a lead on the remains. Griz?"

Griz says, "Katerina Greiner. There's a good chance it's her." She glances over at Roly and he nods for her to go on.

"In January of 1993, Katerina Greiner—she was twenty-three— left Germany to travel. Her family didn't hear much from her. They didn't have a close relationship. But they got a postcard from Galway and she said she was going to stay in Ireland for a few months and do some hillwalking in Wicklow and maybe go to Glendalough."

I ask them, "But there was never confirmation that she was actually there?"

"No. The postcard was it. Her family contacted the Guards in July, to see if there had been any word of her. They did a bit of asking around, but couldn't find anyone who'd seen her. Then, about a month before your cousin went missing, they spoke with the family and they seemed to be satisfied she wasn't in Ireland. A friend of hers had seen her in Berlin and they were pretty sure she'd gone home."

"Someone," Roly says. "Someone who will surely be getting a good tongue lashing, closed the file. But when we looked, it was pretty clear no one really knew where she was. Her parents are both dead. Her brother had his own troubles. She was eventually declared dead. Anyway, we're getting the dental records from Berlin." He looks down. There's probably more they're not telling me. "That's actually not why we needed to talk to you."

I take a long drink of the water the waitress has brought me.

"Niamh Horrigan's parents want to meet you," Griz says.

"Really?" I try to look surprised.

Roly says, "No one wants to allow it, but everyone's worried they'll go to the press if we don't let them. A day or two of blanket coverage of how shite we are at our jobs isn't going to do anything to help find Niamh. So, the decision has been made that you can meet with them, briefly, mind, with Griz and myself and Wilcox and Bill Regan, who's handling the search down in Wicklow. If you want to. What do you think?"

I make myself hesitate, act as though I'm thinking about it. "What do they want to talk to me about?"

"We don't know exactly. They said they want to ask you some questions."

Griz says, "They think you may be able to understand what they're going through. The other families, well . . . it's a different sort of thing."

I know what she means. With the other families, there were bodies. Meeting me allows them to keep hope alive.

"Of course I'll meet them," I say. "When?"

"Today," Griz says. "They're waiting for you at their hotel down in Wicklow."

Roly makes a face. "So go and take a fucking shower. You smell like a locker room."

23

The Americans Erin had been talking to at the Raven were William and Gerald Murphy from Boston and they had charged their stay to a credit card belonging to a company called Murphy Brothers Cement. The Irish guy was named Niall Deasey and he owned a garage in Arklow.

Roly Byrne and Bernie McNeely told me all this in a conference room at the garda station. I sat across the table from them and an older guy with gray hair and a fancy moustache who had been introduced to me as Sergeant Ruarí Wilcox. They seemed to be afraid of Wilcox, and I could understand why when he fixed me with an intense stare and asked me if I had ever known Erin to be interested in nationalist politics or political causes. I said no and they asked me if any of the names were at all familiar to me. Again, I said no, and they said that they wanted to search Erin's belongings again to make sure there wasn't anything there indicating a relationship with these guys.

"Have you ever heard of the IAFNI?"

"The what?"

"Your cousin never mentioned an organization called the IAFNI?"

I shook my head. There was something they weren't telling me; I was smart enough to know that, and whatever it was had gotten Wilcox into that room. I had the sense that this thing had been moved up some invisible ladder because of what the bartender at the Raven had told me.

"So, none of the names are ones you've heard before?" Wilcox asked again.

"No. Why? Have these guys done something? Do you think they know where Erin is?"

No one said anything.

Finally Wilcox said, "The men, the Americans, well, they are known to the RUC Special Branch. We're looking into this. That's all I can say."

I stared at him.

All my associations with the RUC, the Royal Ulster Constabulary, were from history, grainy black-and-white documentary footage of riots. The RUC was the police force of Northern Ireland, but I remembered reading that it had colluded with Unionist paramilitary groups—the ones that wanted Northern Ireland to remain part of the United Kingdom. I assumed Special Branch was responsible for investigating paramilitary organizations during the Troubles. I was thinking about what Conor had told me.

"Okay," I said.

Wilcox leveled a serious look at me, as though I wasn't taking it seriously enough, even though I'd barely breathed since he started speaking. "If your cousin was mixed up with these fellas, she was playing with fire."

• • •

I found a pay phone and used the rest of my phone card to call 617 information and then the main switchboard for Boston College and asked to speak to Ingrid Harbit in the English department. Ingrid had been the graduate teaching assistant for a class I'd taken at Notre Dame, and she'd helped me with my thesis. I knew she'd gotten a job as an assistant professor at Boston College and, most important, I knew she knew her way around a research library.

"Ingrid," I said once I had her on the phone, "I'm in Ireland and I don't have time to explain, but I'm looking for my cousin who's disappeared. It's kind of an emergency. I need to know if you've ever heard of two guys named William and Gerald Murphy in Boston. They have a company called Murphy Brothers Cement, and they may be connected with something called the IAFNI."

"Irish Americans for Northern Ireland," Ingrid said. "I can look around a little. I have a colleague who may be able to help. When do you need to know?"

"As soon as possible," I said. "We're worried something happened to her. I'll have to call you back, though. I'm not by a phone."

I could hear her hesitating. "Okay. Give me two hours and then call back at this number. I'll see what I can do."

"Thanks, Ingrid."

I wasted time looking at shampoo in a drugstore on Grafton Street and then browsing the books at Hodges Figgis on Dawson Street until it was time to call back. Ingrid answered on the second ring and as soon as I heard her voice, I knew she had something for me.

"Okay. Got lucky. My colleague remembered that there'd been something in the papers about them so I checked and, well, in 1989, they held a gala fundraiser for the organization you mentioned, IAFNI, Irish Americans for Northern Ireland. My colleague says it's a well-known front for the Provisional IRA. They raised fifty thousand dollars. The fundraiser sparked a protest. The microfilm printing thing was broken here, but I wrote it down in my notebook." She raised her voice an octave, so I'd know she was quoting. "One of the protesters was Kevin Mahoney, from Donegal, Ireland. Mahoney was holding a sign reading, 'IAFNI equals Terrorists.' Mahoney said he's lived in Boston for five years. 'I'm as patriotic as they come,' he said, as guests filed into the Boston Central Hotel for the fundraiser. 'But these fellas have no business meddling in things they don't understand. American money is as bad as British money. They're all the same.'"

Ingrid told me that according to the article, the IAFNI was founded in 1982, supposedly to raise money for the families of Republican prisoners in Northern Ireland. I thought about Uncle Danny's bucket and Conor's explanation.

My card was running out, so I thanked Ingrid and she said she would see what else she could find if I wanted to call back in a few days.

I got a coffee, finished it slowly, then bought another phone card and went back to the pay phone. There was now a guy about my age inside and I could just barely make out his words through the glass: "I'm tellin' ya. I'm tellin' ya I didn't get off with her. I swear I didn't. I missed the last bus, was all, and I slept in a chair." He stood there for a minute, holding the receiver in his hand, staring at it, and I guessed he'd been hung up on. I knocked on the glass and, dazed, he came out of the phone booth and sunk down onto the low brick wall, his head in his hands.

I squeezed past him into the phone booth. Roly Byrne answered on the first ring. It might have been my imagination, but I thought he was waiting for something.

"It's Maggie D'arcy," I said. "William and Gerald Murphy were definitely supporters of the IAFNI. They definitely fundraised for the Provisional IRA. Why would they be interested in Erin?"

"How the fuck did you get all that in the last couple hours?"

"What are you doing about it? What if they tried to recruit her or something and she said no and they were worried she'd tell someone so they"—I couldn't say it—"did something to her?"

"Jaysus. Look, get off the phone. I'll meet you in St. Stephen's Green in an hour. By the famine statues. Okay?"

"Okay. Did you get some of this, too?"

"Not on the phone." He slammed it down. I stood there for a minute, my heart pounding, listening to the beeping dial tone. The handset was cold on my face. It smelled metallic, faintly like blood.

He was already there when I reached the statues, thin gray figures, their suffering evident even from far away. As I got closer, I could see that one figure was feeding another from a round spoon, filled with rainwater.

Roly Byrne didn't see me coming along the path but he was alert, checking in all directions, looking suspiciously over his shoulder. I found myself following his lead, pausing and checking to make sure no one was tailing me before I came up behind him and tapped him on the shoulder.

"Christ!" His hand came up.

"What's going on?"

"Let's walk." He set off at a fast pace, but I matched him step for step, even though his legs were longer than mine. He was breathing hard before I was.

"Right. You can't be going around asking questions about this." His eyes were hard, ice blue. I suddenly had a sense of what it would have been like to be on the other side of an interview table from him.

"But what if they know where Erin is? What if they kidnapped her or something? Doesn't everyone understand that we might not have a lot of time if—"

"Look, I don't want to sound harsh here, but this is something bigger than your cousin. This is . . ." He trailed off as a man in a black leather jacket came along the path in front of us.

"What?" I whispered, once the man had passed.

"Politics. You have to let this go for a while."

I stared at him.

"Well, what else is going on? Did you go down to Glenmalure to talk to Gary Curran?"

"Yes. His mother swears he was there all morning, but I'd say there's something off about that fella. We're looking into it. We'll talk to the young one who made the complaint back when they were at university. You may see something on the telly tonight," he said. "We want to know if anyone saw her after she came back, if she came back. We'll be putting up posters and doing some canvassing in Ringsend and around Busáras and Connolly station."

"Okay, makes sense." I hesitated for a moment and then I said, "I talked to her friends, the ones who visited back in the summer. They said Erin was trying to talk to them about some riots or something. She seemed frustrated when they weren't interested."

"When was this? August?" I nodded. "There were riots for marching season earlier in the summer, up in Belfast. Jaysus. You really think she'd get herself wrapped up in all this shite?"

"I don't know. What does Detective McNeely think about all this?" I asked him.

"Ah, you can bet she's as bewildered as I am."

There was something else there, in his voice, something that made me ask, "You said it's a long story why she doesn't like Americans. What is it?"

He hesitated. "Look, Bernie was reared up in Armagh, in the north, right?" he said, and I nodded. "That's only 120, 130 kilometers from here, but when she was a kid, it might as well have been fucking Vietnam or something, a world away. One of her uncles was interned after a bombing near a police station. I don't remember when. It was a fucking jungle up there, D'arcy, snipers on street corners, shooting at the RUC on patrol. Loyalists killing people in the night. They brought the British Army in in helicopters. She grew up hating it, came here as soon as she could, joined the Gardaí. But, couple of years ago, one of her brothers got shot at a checkpoint by the Royal Marines. He was nineteen. Her favorite brother. They ambushed him." He was still whispering.

"So, why does she hate Americans so much? I understand she might hate the British, but . . ."

His eyes flashed. "She thinks they're paying for the fucking guns that keep the whole thing going up there? She hates the fucking violence. She hates the killing. We all do."

"I'm sorry," I said. "I didn't know."

"I'm sorry too. This shite has my head done in. I'd better get back."

"But you can't just let it go," I said. I could feel the panic starting. "She's out there and it's your job to find her."

"We're not fucking letting it go. Mind yourself, now. Ring me if anything seems weird to you."

The summer after Erin's seventh grade year. We're walking home from the beach when she starts crying. We're walking and talking about what we're going to do over the summer and then suddenly she makes a gasping noise and she's sobbing. I don't understand why.

"What's wrong?" I ask her.

"Nothing." But the tears are rolling down her face. She's wiping them away. "I don't know."

"Are you okay?" I whisper. You can't push too hard with Erin. I know this already. If you say the wrong thing, she just . . . disappears. She shuts down and she's not there anymore.

She turns away from me, her shoulders heaving and shaking.

I don't know what to do. I stand there, looking out to make sure no one comes along and sees her. The sun is hot. I can feel a thin layer of sweat on my forehead. Finally, when she doesn't stop, I go over and put an arm around her. Erin and I used to hug and touch each other all the time. We used to stroke each other's hair, we used to give each other back scratches. But for the last few years, she's only touched me once in a while. When I try to touch her hair, she pulls away. I've felt the loss of that touch so sharply that it hurts sometimes, a barely healed burn on my skin.

I wait for her to push me away, but she doesn't. She leans into me, crying, and I hug her, for a long, long time. We can hear kids shouting and laughing down at the beach. After a while, she stands up and walks ahead of me as though it never happened. I'm left watching her disappear up the road and into her and Uncle Danny's house.

24

The parents are camped out at the hotel with some extended family and family friends, Roly says, far enough from the search command post that it's not in their face all the time. He says it's a new place, built during the boom, and they were able to clear out most of the other guests so the Horrigans could be in peace.

"Thank God they've got some dosh, like," he says. "When the poor family's got no money you always think about how the week in the hotel is going to bankrupt them. And then if there's a funeral, too." He shakes his head.

"How are they holding up?" I ask him as we drive down.

"They're doing okay so far. The local lads have been the ones spending time with them. But we're getting to the point where desperation will start to set in. You've got to be careful not to get them upset, D'arcy."

He turns onto a narrow drive marked with gray stone pillars.

There's a fancy sign reading "Wicklow House Hotel and Spa Resort." "Ah, isn't this nice now?" Roly says, looking delighted.

The room is small, an events room off the main dining room. In addition to Roly and Griz from the Serious Crimes Review Team, there are a couple of other guards from the team that's trying to find Niamh. Roly introduces me to a compact older guy with a luxurious gray moustache. "Superintendent William Regan," he says, nodding at me. The room is tense but under control. It feels good, familiar to me from well-run investigations. Everyone's putting aside their egos to focus on the objective, for the moment anyway.

As we drove into the parking lot, I caught sight of Stephen Hines's lurking frame, hunched over his cell phone by the back door. There are other reporters outside, a few television cameras and more print reporters clustered by the front entrance to the hotel, and a hotel employee comes in and shuts all the drapes. The room is painted pale lavender, the walls covered with watercolors of irises.

Niamh's mother is thin, well-dressed, her face drawn in worry. She looks fit and prosperous, her short, frosted blond hair expertly cut but left unstyled, her athletic frame too thin for the navy blue pants and blouse that are hanging off her. I'm betting she's lost ten pounds over the past week.

Mr. Horrigan is tall, his hair still mostly brown, only peppered with gray. He's the first one to speak, to step forward to shake my hand and say, "Thank you so much for meeting with us, Miss D'arcy." His hand is large and warm and he reminds me of my father.

"Maggie," I say. "Please. I've been thinking about you so much, and about what you're going through. My uncle sends his best, too. We've been praying for Niamh."

"Thank you," Mrs. Horrigan says, stepping forward to take my hand. "It's the waiting, as you know. It's driving me mad. How do you stand it?" Tears fall out of her eyes. She's not even aware of them. Her husband rubs her shoulder.

"You keep hoping," I tell her. "But I know, it's awful. It's a place no one would ever want to go. I'm so sorry you have to spend time in this place."

She keeps patting my arm and then she says, "We don't have much time, if what they say about the other girls is true. We heard . . . we learned about your career in the States, about Andrea Delaurio, about what you did. Detective D'arcy, we don't have a lot of time." She sits back and now she's all strength. "What do we need to do to save my daughter?"

Everyone in the room turns at her words.

She isn't nervous. She isn't scared. I'm not a person to her—I'm a means to an end, and she's going to use me however she needs to to get what she wants. "You know what to do. If there is any chance you can help save her, you must do it. You know what this is like. You know how this feels. Detective D'arcy, how can we save my daughter?"

Regan stands up. "Mrs. Horrigan, it's much more complex a—"

She's just staring at me, not letting me out of her gaze. "How, Detective D'arcy? What do we need to do?"

I look up to find Roly watching me. He knows he's been played. He's just not sure if it's by me or Stephen Hines or the Horrigans. I ignore him and try to look humble and disinterested. Griz is pretending to inspect her nails, but she's hanging on every word. I have to do this right.

"Mrs. Horrigan," I say. "You have the best people working to find your daughter. I can tell you that with absolute confidence. They have done everything according to the absolute highest standards of best practice. They have run an exemplary investigation, both into your daughter's disappearance and also in the reviews of my cousin's case and the disappearances of the other women. Of Teresa and June."

"We know that," Mr. Horrigan says. He looks up at the guards standing around. "We are incredibly grateful. We know we have the best here. But we are desperate, Detective D'arcy. We are absolutely desperate. If there is anything that you can bring to the table, a new look, an outsider's eye. You found that girl, in the States. Andrea." He looks directly at me when he says it, when he says her name.

"Mr. Horrigan." I breathe through the flash of panic and surging adrenaline. "That was a very different set of—"

"The FBI couldn't find her and you found her! Please, Detective D'arcy." He's crying now, too. He looks up at one of the guards, a middle-aged guy in a red sweater. "What would you need, Detective D'arcy? What would you need to do a review?"

"Please, Mr. Horrigan."

"Just . . . What would you need? Just tell me that?"

A long silence. I start, "A review of the case files, a visit to the scene of Niamh's disappearance, would be the way I would start to create a picture. But, as I said—"

"Can she do that?" Mrs. Horrigan asks. She stands up, turning to Regan and Roly and Griz. "Can she look at the files? Can you take her up to Drumkee? When can she do it?"

Roly looks panicked. "Mrs. Horrigan," he says, "there are protocols, there is the Official Secrets Act. I don't even know how we would—"

"Detective Byrne," she says, in a strong, even voice. She is standing so still she could be a statue. There is not a trace of weakness or emotion in her voice. She will not be denied. "There is my daughter. There is her life. Next to my daughter's life, there is nothing. There is *nothing*."

We're all watching her. We can't look away.

"Give us a minute," Regan says finally, gesturing to Roly. "Everyone just stay right here."

Through the closed drapes, we can see the silhouettes of the reporters crossing back and forth outside the window.

◆　◆　◆

I have forty-eight hours.

"That's not what I wanted to happen," I tell Roly when we're in his car again, on our way back toward Glenmalure.

"Really?" He draws it out and raises his eyebrows at me. I try not to blush.

"Look, D'arcy." He sighs and runs a hand through his hair. "We've got Regan on board. We've got Wilcox on board. If you can help us find Niamh Horrigan, then it's grand. You've got two days—from tomorrow morning—to review the files. Griz will be with you at all times. You are not to be alone with them and you are not to discuss anything you read with any other person. That is absolutely non-negotiable. And nobody can know you're doing this. If there's even one fucking story about how we had to call in the Americans because we weren't up to the job, they'll have my head and Regan's head and Wilcox's, too."

"Of course, Roly."

He sighs again. "Mr. Horrigan's brother is best friends with a fucking TD and pressure was placed upon Wilcox. Don't make him sorry. Just mind yourself and work as quickly as you can, right?"

"Right. Thanks. I'll do anything I can, though as I told them, there may be nothing else to find."

He raises his eyebrows again. "There's always something else to find," he says ominously. "I know that better than anyone."

We park in the turnoff where he brought me the first day and start walking back along the road toward Laragh. We walk for thirty minutes before he says, "This is Drumkee." I'd been expecting a town, but it's nothing more than a stretch of land on either side of the road, a few outbuildings reaching up into the hills. A few driveways hint at cottages somewhere in the trees. "Right about there is where the button was found." He points to a spot on the other side of the stone wall. "Up there, into the trees."

"So she'd completed the walk and was walking back towards Laragh," I say. "And he drove up and pulled the car over. She must have realized something was wrong. Otherwise, the struggle would have been right here by the road. She must have started running back towards the trees, but he came after her." I climb over the wall. "Where is it? How far?"

Roly directs me to the spot. We walk for a couple of minutes into the trees.

"He's strong and able for the run," Roly says.

I look around. "It's not far from Glenmalure and Laragh, but it's pretty desolate here, isn't it? There hasn't been a car since we've been here. And those cottages are too far away to see anything. You wouldn't worry too much about being seen."

"But you wouldn't be sure," Roly says. "It's pretty brazen, taking her next to the road."

"What's on the CCTV?" I ask. "Anything?"

"You'll be looking at it soon enough," he says bitterly. "Ah, no, nothing good. Regular traffic on the lodge security camera and one on a house further up the road towards Laragh." We stand there for a few more minutes and then walk back toward the Wicklow Way signposts.

"I just want to walk up a bit," I tell Roly. "To remind myself where I found the necklace."

It doesn't take us long to reach the spot. "I think that's it," I say. "I recognize that tree." I suddenly remember drawing a little map that I handed over in the Irishtown Garda Station and I wonder if he ever saw it.

We stand there for a minute. I try to picture Erin, walking along: *The necklace snagging on a tree branch, falling silently to the ground, Erin walking on.* Or, another image: *Erin, running, someone chasing her, grabbing for her, the necklace torn, forgotten on the ground as Erin is lifted and carried . . .*

Except that's not what happened. So . . . *Someone pulling the necklace from Erin's throat, Erin looking down at the woman on the ground.*

I shake the image from my head. "Okay," I say. "I'm done here. Let's go back to the city."

25

It's eight a.m. before they can get all the files set up in the conference room at Pearse Street and get the necessary people to sign off on me looking at them.

I down an espresso and Griz and I wait while people scurry around, bringing in boxes and laptops. Roly made me come in a back door; there's a scrum of reporters along the narrow sidewalk by the main entrance. Looking out the second-story window, I can see Stephen Hines, the great bulk of him leaning casually against the wall. He's looking at his phone, waiting there as if he has all the time in the world.

"Where do you want to start?" Griz asks, once we're alone. It's a gorgeous day, the sun streaming in the windows. I move my chair into a beam of light flopping across the conference table.

"Explain the system," I tell her. She goes over the evolution of Garda investigation recordkeeping, typed and signed statements from interviews in the '90s, casebooks with all the relevant information included, files and files of paper. Then there are recorded and transcribed interviews and some digital records for more recent cases. It's a hodgepodge, like the records for any law enforcement investigation spanning twenty-three years. But I'm lucky—because of the task force and cold case review, almost everything I want to look at has been copied and is stored together in neatly labeled files.

"I can find things for you and bring you casebooks or any other files you might want," she says. She has on a bright yellow blouse and red pants. Her hair is glossy, tucked behind her ears, and her reading glasses are red and yellow plaid to match her outfit. My black sweater and jeans feel funereal next to her bright colors.

"I want to start with the initial missing person reports and the postmortems," I tell her. "I want to come up with a rough profile. Then I'm going to read through everything quick and see if anyone jumps out at me."

I think of Len Giacomo and try to clear my mind of all my preconceptions. I start reading, translating the initial Garda reports and the pathologist's jargon into my own shorthand so I'll have all the essential details at my fingertips.

After a couple of hours of reading and asking Griz to find details, I have five sheets of paper. I write each victim's name and a few details underneath each, then circle each name.

Katerina Greiner, 24, brown hair, brown eyes, German national. Date of disappearance not known. COD cranial blunt force trauma. Sexual assault unknown.

Erin Flaherty, 23, blue eyes, brown hair, average height and weight. American. No remains found. Last seen at bed-and-breakfast in Glenmalure Sept. 17, 1993. Evidence suggests she may have returned to Dublin. Remains not found.

Teresa McKenny, 19, brown hair, blue eyes, Irish national. Last seen June 18, 1998. Disappeared while walking along the R747. Body discovered July 5. Evidence suggests death occurred not more than two days prior. COD cranial blunt force trauma. Evidence of repeated sexual assault. Evidence of adhesive around mouth. Evidence of ligature marks on both wrists. No physical evidence due to submersion in water.

June Talbot, 30, blond hair, green eyes, English. Disappeared September 3, 2006 near Baltinglass Abbey. Body discovered September 17. Death not more than two days prior. COD cranial blunt force trauma. Evidence of repeated sexual assault. Evidence of adhesive around mouth. Evidence of ligature/ wrists. No physical evidence due to submersion in water.

Niamh Horrigan, 25, brown hair, blue eyes, Irish. Disappeared May 21, 2016, near Glenmalure, likely from road. Button from clothing found near road.

Then I start adding the persons of interest who orbited around each victim. Katerina Greiner doesn't have many. Erin's I've already done. Teresa McKenny had quite a lot: family, friends, the people she worked with at the golf course. June Talbot had fewer: her boyfriend, his family, her friends from work. For Niamh, Griz prints out the emailed list they're working with down in Wicklow. All of hers are in Galway: family, friends, former boyfriends, the kids she taught and their families. I spread my sheets of paper out and look them over.

"So, the adhesive," I say. "He kept them somewhere he was worried about being overheard. He had to duct tape their mouths. He has a place to bring them, but he can't risk them being overheard."

"Yeah, we had that, too," Griz says. "We told Regan's team. When they did the house-to-houses they had that in mind."

"At the same time, though," I say, thinking out loud, "the repeated sexual assaults. He had somewhere safe to keep them, somewhere he wasn't too worried about being caught. He was able to rape them whenever he wanted."

Griz doesn't say anything. I look up and meet her eyes. "I know," I say. "It's awful. He has a place. A place where he can keep them, where he can do what he wants. That's why we haven't had any sightings of Niamh. She's somewhere secure."

I think of the outbuildings that Roly and I saw when we visited Drumkee, but Griz says, "They've searched all around there. They've visited every house. Twice. Probably three times by now. But it could be further out, it could be halfway across the country."

"Yeah, but he's got a territory. See if you can get a sense of those house-to-houses. Anything they might have missed." I stare at the map they've brought me, with the locations of the abductions and the bodies, the places where Erin had visited and where Niamh was hiking. I draw a circle around the dots, Baltinglass to Aughrim to Glenmalure to Glendalough and back to Baltinglass. It's a neat triangle, with the long green shape of the mountains in the center. "There's some pattern here, some routine, that we're just not seeing."

Griz looks skeptical. They've spent years looking for patterns. "I know," I say. "If there was one, someone would have found it. It's just . . . his vehicle. He's got some way of getting them into his vehicle. When Roly and I visited the spot, I felt like I could see it. A woman walking on a desolate road. A vehicle pulls over, she approaches it. For some reason she trusts him. Suddenly she realizes, but it's too late."

"We checked gardaí, mail deliverers, ambulance drivers. We've been over and over it."

"Yeah. I know." I don't tell her what I'm thinking. *What if they trusted the vehicle because there was a woman in the passenger seat?*

"All right," I say. "I'm going to take a look at all the persons of interest, see if anyone gets my Spidey sense going. Could you make a list of any eyewitness statements or surveillance video from all of the abduction sites? Try to keep the window fairly narrow—say, the day of the abductions? I know you guys probably tracked down anyone you saw, but I just want to see if there's anything that jumps out."

"Of course," Griz says. "Good luck with the Spidey sense."

◆ ◆ ◆

We work all afternoon, Griz diligently going back and forth between the files and her computer, searching for the dates of the abductions and listing any witness statements from those days, then collating them with all the vehicles and pedestrians caught on video on the days of the abductions.

I start reading through interviews with persons of interest who were interviewed by the Guards. The ones for Niamh Horrigan aren't all transcribed and filed yet, but I read about all of the people interviewed right after Teresa McKenny went missing and then everyone they spoke with after her body was found. Most of the interviews are straightforward, everyone saying that she never would have taken off, that something must have happened to her, then an interview with an ex-boyfriend who seems to have a strong alibi for the day she disappeared.

There's an interview with a groundskeeper at the golf course where she worked that I read twice. When asked if he knew Teresa McKenny and how she seemed before the disappearance, he said, "She was a little minx. If she got into trouble, it were her own fault."

"Griz," I say. "Can we look for anything in the system on the groundskeeper at the golf course where Teresa McKenny worked? Robert Herricks. Anything at all. I don't like how he describes her. It's not in keeping with the other descriptions of her and it just gets my back up for some reason."

"Sure. I'll get going on it."

I have the rest of the Teresa McKenny statements and then June Talbot and then all of Erin's to review. I flip through the files of transcribed Garda interviews. *Emer Nolan. Daisy Nugent. Conor Kearney. Maggie D'arcy.* I can feel my brain starting to slow. When I look at my phone, it's almost eight. "Find anything?" I ask Griz.

"Not really. I got everything in order, though. Do you want to take a look?"

"A quick one. I'm getting tired." I skim the list. "Is this the list of vehicles?"

"Yeah. That's Teresa McKenny. So June eighteenth, 1998. No CCTV there on the R747 at that point, but there was one camera, a homeowner's private security job, a bit further along the road, closer to Woodenbridge. I guess the guards down in Wicklow thought to get that and they tried tracing all of the vehicles that passed the camera that day. They didn't get all of them; the angle was weird and they couldn't see all the number plates. And obviously, they didn't know if those cars continued along the road to Aughrim. But this is the list."

I scan the descriptions: *gray Ford, white delivery van, blue Mercedes.* The words swim together, their meaning not making its way to my brain.

"Okay," I say. "What else?"

"Niamh Horrigan. We've got loads of CCTV footage from Saturday the twenty-first. We have her leaving the hostel in Glendalough. We have her passing a camera at the visitor's center and walking towards the trails. A couple of walkers saw her on the paths, here and here." She points to a spot on the map of the Wicklow Way. "So according to the statements from the walkers, she made it all the way to Mullacor. Then of course the button suggests she made it off the trails and onto the road.

"They did an analysis of all the CCTV around Glenmalure and on the main roads leading to and from the crossroads and in the other direction, to Laragh. There are about twenty vehicles that are in the right time frame. There aren't any matches with the McKenny CCTV footage. Nobody who raised any red flags on the registrations. Here they are." She hands over a typed list. I start scanning it: *Red 2015 Ford Fiesta. 2008 Gray Skoda. White Citroën Dispatch. Skoda panel van. Blue Volkswagen.* It looks typical for a Saturday.

"One of them must be it, though, right?"

"Well, maybe. Someone could have approached from a driveway between the site and where the cameras are. Some of them only drove to the crossroads. Some didn't go as far as Glenmalure from the other direction. Or so they say. They were able to track down some of the drivers. Here they are. Everyone checked out okay." I scan the statements. *I was driving to see my mother in Templerainey. Our drivers make regular deliveries on that route every Saturday. I only drove to Greenane and back.*

I look through similar searches that were done during Roly's original review of the disappearances. They'd tried to get a sense of the cars that had passed nearby on the days Teresa and June went missing, but nothing had come of the query.

Someone even did a search of traffic or parking tickets given to anyone remotely connected with any of the investigations, just in case it threw something up. In fact, it threw up a lot. I scan the list of persons of interest or witnesses. Eda Curran got a parking ticket in Wicklow in 1998. Bláithín Arpin got a ticket for speeding in Glendalough in October, 1993, and another in 1997. A truck that was still registered to Niall Deasey's garage got a ticket for illegal parking near where June Talbot was taken in 2006, but it turned out Deasey had given the truck to a nephew. In 1999 and again in 2004, Conor Kearney got parking tickets on Morehampton Road, in Donnybrook.

Conor Kearney.

I stare at the black forms of the words on the page. "I'm packing it in," I tell Griz. "I need to sleep for a few hours. Let's come back in the morning."

26

If Roly Byrne and Bernie McNeely had found anything on Niall Deasey or the American guys, they weren't telling me about it.

It got colder. Uncle Danny's mental health was deteriorating. My dad said he'd started bursting into tears behind the bar. I tried to stay busy while I waited for word. One afternoon, I ran all the way out Ringsend Road, where there was a park and walking trails heading out toward a lighthouse along the coast in the distance, and the two red-and-white-striped smokestacks I'd been spotting from afar since I'd arrived in Dublin. In front of me was the sea. The tide was out and the sand stretched forever, wet, dark ripples reaching for the water. Sandymount Strand. I walked fast in the sand, out into the indeterminate nothingness. There were several people walking out here, a couple with a dog, a few single figures against the milky white sky. I kept walking.

Am I walking into eternity along Sandymount Strand?

The ground was gentle folds, pocked with shells. I picked

them up, salmon pink cockles and little scallops, tucking them into the pocket of my running shorts. I felt better, peaceful, suddenly and inexpressibly full of joy. There was something about the sight of the two candy-striped smokestacks against the sky that cheered me. The landscape was familiar. It was like I'd been here before, not just once, but thousands of times. I raised my arms to the sky and turned around, my eyes closed, feeling the wet wind against my face. My skin felt extra sensitive, my nerves taking in every little bit of stimuli: the breeze, changes in temperature, the sound of cars and buses shifting, a voice shouting to my right. I touched the back of my hand, where Conor's thumb had rubbed small circles.

Conor.

And then, as though I'd willed him into being, when I opened my eyes he was walking toward me, a huge grin on his face. He was wearing his blue sweater and dark jeans and leather boots. His hair was damp, curling around his ears.

He stopped ten feet away. We stared at each other.

"Are you all right, then? Is this what Americans do, come to the beach and like, I don't even know what you're doing there, modern dance?"

I laughed. "I went for a run and then I was just—let's say I was communing with Sandymount Strand. Into eternity."

"Ah, communing. That sounds suspicious." He glanced down along my body and I was conscious suddenly of my bare legs, my arms and shoulders under my sleeveless shirt.

We began walking back toward the park and when he started around the path toward the Poolbeg Lighthouse, I fell in next to him, my whole body floating with joy. I tried not to smile, to giggle.

He's here. I thought of him and now he's here! And he's walking with me. He could have said he needed to go. But he didn't. It means something. It must mean something.

"I didn't realize it was so warm today," he said. "Or did you actually exert yourself so hard you sweat? That's very un-Irish, you know. You should be careful jogging around here. Someone might think you robbed a bank."

"I did get some funny looks. I should be careful. The Guards may be on their way."

A gull called, very near, and we glanced at each other, and then we started as a cloud of small black birds rose and swooped over the sand, then settled down again.

"I'm—"

"What—"

We laughed and he said, "Pardon?"

"What are those birds called?" I asked him. "The little ones."

"Sandpipers, I think," he said.

"You don't sound very certain."

"Sandpipers!"

"That's right, own it."

He laughed. We walked in silence for a minute, then he started to say something, turning to me and opening his mouth and then swallowing and turning away. He looked miserable.

"What were you going to say?"

"Oh, just that—" He stopped walking. "Look, I'm sorry about the other night. I . . . had a great time with you. I like . . . talking to you. A lot. But I—The thing—" Finally, he stammered it out. "I'm—I have a girlfriend and I shouldn't have—well, I guess that's the thing. I have a girlfriend."

"Oh." I looked up at him. "So, you and Erin, there was nothing going on between you?"

He blushed. "No. That's not . . . We were . . . just friends. That's all." He looked away. He was so uncomfortable I could feel it hanging in the air between us.

"What's her name? Your girlfriend?"

He hesitated. "Bláithín." *Blah-heen.*

"Did Erin meet her?"

He rolled his eyes a little. "Yeah, that didn't go so well. Bláithín got really stroppy about it."

"Is it serious?"

"Yes." He looked away.

"Shit." I said it without thinking. "I think I really like you. I couldn't stop thinking about you. I was thinking about you when I opened my eyes and saw you. That has to mean something, right?" His eyes were wide, shocked.

It was desperate. And honest. I had never said anything like it to anyone before. But there was something about him, and the place, and the air on my bare skin, and the little dark birds whirling in the sky, and Erin missing, too, I guess. I felt stripped down, incapable of pretending. The wind whipped at my skin, tiny drops of rain like needles on my cheek. I was completely exposed. It felt like the wind could carry me away.

"I—" He met my eyes and looked away. For a moment I thought he was going to kiss me, but he didn't.

"I'm sorry," he said. "God, I love talking to you. And I—Well, I'm just sorry."

Talking to you. That's it. That's all he likes.

I started walking again and he followed.

The silence was better now, not exactly comfortable, but not so charged as it had been just a few minutes ago. I felt light-headed and fragile and somehow clean.

"Do you know what that is?" he asked after a few minutes, pointing at a spot on the path.

"What?"

"It's where Gerty MacDowell flashed your man Leopold Bloom in *Ulysses*."

"Oh God, really?" I was laughing. "Right here?"

He was laughing too, and then he wasn't. He looked down at me and he made a little gesture with his hands, pulling me in, and I leaned in, smelling the damp smokiness of his jacket, feeling the strength of his chest beneath it.

"Aw, fuck," he said "Can I just hold you, like?" His hands went around my back and I pressed myself against him. He hugged me fiercely, stroking my hair, my back, but we didn't kiss, and when we stopped I was breathing hard, turned on, bereft.

We walked a little ways holding hands and then we let them drop as someone came toward us, and he said, "I'm sorry. I'll see you," and I watched him go, disappearing into the gray-white sky above Sandymount Strand.

•   •   •

"Maggie, maybe you should come on home," my dad said on the phone. "You've done everything you could. No one could have asked for more. Danny knows that."

Panic set in. "I just need to keep looking, Dad. The police have given up. They think she took off."

"Mags, maybe she did take off, you know? Even Danny has started wondering about that."

"I know, Dad. But there are some strange things going on here, and even if she took off, I'm worried maybe she isn't . . . thinking straight."

"Maybe I should come over," he said. "I shouldn't have let you handle this on your own. I've been so . . . tired, since your mom. But I'm doing better. Want me to come over?"

I could feel the temptation of it. He'd come over, he'd talk to Roly. He'd make lots of noise. But then I thought of his face the day I left, thin, drawn, his shoulders slumped in his baggy suit. "Let's give it another week," I told him. "The police may find something by then."

"What do you think? Do you think she just took off? Danny asked me if I thought she had it in her, to do that, and I said no, though it's so much better than the alternative."

"I don't know, Dad. I don't think so, but there's just nothing to go on. I don't like to tell Uncle Danny, but I think we may not know. I think she may just have disappeared into thin air."

"Oh, darlin'. I'm so sorry." His voice was quiet, tired, and I was suddenly overcome with the most intense wave of homesickness I'd ever felt. I wanted to be home, instantly, magically. I wanted to walk through the door and find him sitting in his chair reading the papers, a glass of gin by his foot. I wanted to tell him everything but I didn't want him to worry.

"Love you," I told him. "Don't worry."

I thought about Niall Deasey and Arklow. I even went so far as to go to the bus station and look at the schedule. There were four buses a day. *11:30.* It only took an hour.

When I talked to Uncle Danny, I didn't know what to say anymore, so I lied and said that the police were following lots of leads and that I was making sure that they kept Erin on the front burner. My dad asked again if I wanted him to come over and I put him off for another week.

I barely slept that night, the room closing in on me from all sides, the loneliness and sadness crushing my chest. I cried, really cried, for the first time since I had arrived in Dublin, sobbing, raggedy crying I'm sure Emer and Daisy could hear through the walls, and I woke up groggy, frustrated, and homesick, and decided I was going to demand some answers from Roly and Bernie.

I was walking down Irishtown Road toward the Garda station when I saw Bernie McNeely walking toward me. She stopped, trying to figure out if she could get away before I saw her. When she realized the game was up, she waved and came to meet me.

"Hi, D'arcy," she said. "I know we've been a bit hard to pin down."

"What's going on?"

She looked up and down the sidewalk. "Let's go for a coffee. I can tell you a bit."

"Everybody's nervous about Deasey," she told me, once we were settled into a coffee shop far enough away from the station. "He's got a lot of paper associated with himself.

"Apparently, he's been on everyone's radar for a while now. His father was a fella named Petey Deasey. He was an old republican from way back. Petey's da fought in the civil war; as a lad, he probably served as a messenger. Grew up in it, ya know. We know Petey ran guns for the IRA in the fifties. He had two families, one in Ireland and one over in London. Two wives, two houses. He went back and forth for years, one step ahead of whoever was looking for him. I once heard a story about a shootout down in Wicklow in 1967.

He holed up in some cottage down there with a load of guns from America. The Guards had a standoff with him for nearly twenty-four hours. Right rebels, that family.

"Petey Deasey is a bit old to make trouble now, but his boy Niall is involved in various criminal enterprises in Wicklow and Wexford. He definitely has some Republican connections up north. He was suspected in an arms running ring in eighty-nine, and though they never got the evidence, my friend swears Deasey did it and is probably still doing it. He's got a half-brother in London who they think was somehow connected to it over there." She gestured vaguely at the Irish Sea.

"What about Erin?"

"Someone asked him about meeting her at the Raven. He claims those fellas with him were in town for a dog conference."

"A what?"

"Like a get-together of breeders of those real jumpy dogs, boxers. That's what he claims. He says they chitchatted to Erin but that was all."

"But what if he's lying? What if he's holding Erin or knows where she is—" I was trying to keep my voice down, but Bernie's face told me I hadn't done a very good job.

She didn't say anything.

"If I go down to Arklow," I told her, "I could just see how he reacts when he sees me." She didn't say anything.

Her hands were fidgeting around her coffee mug, and when the bell over the door jangled, she started and looked up to watch two older women, laden with shopping bags, coming through the door.

"No, it's too dangerous," she said finally. "You'd need to be miked, we'd want backup. There's a way to do something like that, and they're never going to agree to it. I'll keep looking and we'll let you know. Roly feels badly about cutting you out, but his job might be on the line. I'm telling you, Wilcox shut us down when we even mentioned going to talk to Deasey. I'll give you a ring in a couple of days and give you an update. By the way, Roly and I interviewed Gary Curran last week. There was nothing definite there, but the pair of us, we didn't like him. We're trying to find something more than the stalking charge in college. But I'd say we'll be looking for a warrant in the next couple of days."

"Good, that's progress, at least."

"So it is." But she didn't look very sure of herself. "Don't blame Roly. He's just following orders."

"Okay, thanks, Bernie." She nodded and left me alone.

Outside, I hunched my face and neck down into my coat and walked slowly into the city center, down Grafton Street, trying to will Conor into existence again. The shop windows were bright. The warm mouth of Bewley's beckoned to me, the fragrant air wafting out whenever someone pushed through the doors. I sat in a corner with my coffee, watching an elderly couple sitting silently, holding hands, and a teenage girl laughing with her mother, their feet surrounded by shopping bags.

When I was done, I walked back out onto Grafton Street and let myself get absorbed by the crowds. *It must be almost Thanksgiving*, I realized with a start. Pretty soon it would be Christmas.

Christmas.

Erin had been gone two months.

Where are you?

September. Long Island in September is summer and fall together: hot days, sweat running down the back of my school-picture-day blouse with the lacy neck, and nights that smell like cold ocean flowing in the windows.

Erin's at junior high now; she rides a different bus. I only see her at Irish Dance. My mom takes me but Erin walks over from Jessica's house.

That summer, Erin starts sleeping over at Jessica's the night before class. They walk over to Brian Lombardi's or one of the other boys' in her class and they watch movies. Brian has an older brother—Frank—who's in high school and his friends are always over, too. Erin tells me that Jessica has a crush on Frank but he never remembers her name. Frank has a girlfriend named Melissa and Erin and Jessica save their money to get blue hooded sweatshirts just like the one Melissa wears.

In October, I smell cigarette smoke on Erin's jacket when I move it in the changing room at dance class. When I see Erin at class, she always seems distant, older now. She starts wearing lots of black eyeliner and mascara, and I get the idea she wears it for Chris. I'm shy around her now. She can barely look at me, as though my very existence embarrasses her.

Uncle Danny starts dating a woman named Gloria when Erin is in ninth grade. Erin hates her and Uncle Danny can't even bring her into their house. So he starts going out to Montauk with her for the weekend sometimes, and Erin stays at our house.

One of those weekends, I wake up to darkness and the sound of rustling and open my eyes to see Erin dressing by the window. My clock glows red—10:34 p.m.—and I sit up, confused. "What's going on?"

"Shhhh. Nothing. Go back to sleep," Erin whispers back.

"What are you . . . ?"

"Nothing." She waits there for a moment. Even in my half-asleep state, I know what to do. I lie down and close my eyes, breathing heavily so she thinks I've gone back to sleep. I can hear her hesitating and then she moves and I open my eyes, just a tiny bit, and watch as she bends to tie the laces of her sneakers, then slowly stands up and lifts the screen of my bedroom window. My bedroom is on the second floor but because the house is built into the hill above the water, my window opens onto our back deck. I watch her slip through the window and hear her drop onto the deck. She leaves the window open.

I count to one hundred in my head and then get out of bed. I open my bedroom door and go across the hall to the upstairs bathroom. When I get to the window, I can just see the disappearing taillights of a car.

I don't think of getting my parents. I don't know why. I get back in bed and I must fall asleep because the next thing I know my mom is waking us up and I look over and see Erin in the other bed and I wonder if I dreamed it.

But then, when I come back to my room after brushing my teeth, I see a line of gray at the bottom of the window, the deck through the bottom of the screen, which is still open just a crack.

27

Griz and I are back at Pearse Street by seven a.m., ready to go. As soon as I see her, I know there's been a development.

"We got the ID," she tells me first thing. "The remains are Katerina Greiner's. Dentals confirm it."

"Good," I say. "What's the story?"

"It's a fucking odd one. After they reported her missing, the brother ran into a friend of Katerina's and the friend said he'd seen her in Berlin. They called off the search in Ireland. But the brother told me that he now questions whether that was true. The guy was also into drugs, he said, and he thinks maybe he was mistaken, or lying for some other reason. The family had sort of broken up at that point. The mother had died. The father had moved to Luxembourg, and it had been so long the brother just assumed that either she didn't want to be found or that something had happened to her. After more years went by, he assumed it was the latter. There were the drugs, and she'd had a couple of suicide attempts, too.

When the father died, the brother needed to have her declared dead so he could inherit the estate outright, so he went to court and got the paperwork completed. They must have done some sort of investigation but it didn't turn up anything. It had been the right number of years."

"Did she spend time in Dublin?" I asked Griz. "How did she and Erin meet each other?"

"The brother thought she must have spent a night or two in Dublin when she got here, but he doesn't think she'd lived here."

"So, why the ID card? Did she steal it? Did Erin give it to her?" I ask.

Griz knows what I'm thinking. *Was Erin there when she was killed?*

"We need more on her," Griz says. "Joey's going to go down and organize the door-to-doors. Roly said for me to keep at it here."

I know what she's saying. We have today and tomorrow morning. This is it.

"I guess we'd better get to it," I tell her. I've brought my files and I put them on the table in front of Griz. "Take a look at all of this. It's the stuff from Erin's room at the Ringsend house. I've had it in my basement and I've looked at it a thousand times, but I was thinking about Katerina Greiner and, I don't know, whether there's something in there I didn't know to look for before? Also, can you take a look at the missing persons lists so I can review them? I want to finish reading these files and then I'll take a look at what your profilers have put together over the years."

"Sure." She takes the files from me.

"Thanks, Griz."

We get to work. It's a bright day, the sun angling in the conference room windows, and for the next few hours, everything narrows to the words in front of me and what they might mean.

*   *   *

I put June Talbot's file and Erin's file on the table in front of me.

June Talbot's is fairly thin. They had been completely focused on the boyfriend for the first couple of days. Once they realized he had an alibi, they seemed to lose their momentum. Without a body, they hadn't connected the disappearance to Teresa's yet. There were a few interviews with possible eyewitnesses and men with records in Baltinglass, but by the time they'd realized that June's disappearance might be related to Erin's and Teresa's, they'd lost some advantage.

Griz looks up. "I've got something else on Robert Herricks. An interview that wasn't filed with all the rest. One of the girls who worked as a cleaner at the golf course with Teresa McKenny thought he was a little creepy. Something about him spying on them in the bathroom."

"Anything else on him? Any harassment or sexual assault charges unrelated to Teresa?"

"I'm waiting on that. I'll let you know as soon as I get it."

I think for a minute. "Can you check in the system for any mention, not just charges?"

She wiggles her eyebrows. "They're transitioning the database over or some shite like that. I'll try."

I turn to Erin.

It's all here, a record of those two months of my life. The initial interview that Emer and Daisy and I gave at the Irishtown Garda

Station, the interviews with neighbors and the other workers at the café.

The first thing I notice is how much of it there is. They were working it all along. What felt like inaction was just withholding of information. As soon as the report was made, the Gardaí in Wicklow had started canvassing, interviewing bus drivers, checking all the bed-and-breakfasts in Glendalough and Glenmalure. They'd discovered Mrs. Curran almost immediately.

The first interview with Conor Kearney took place the same day I reported Erin missing. They seemed to be looking at him fairly seriously—a couple of subsequent interviews with him, interviews with his known associates—until they interviewed Bláithín Arpin and she told them that he'd been with her at her parents' holiday house in someplace called Brittas Bay the weekend of the sixteenth. Additionally, every single friend of his said he had never shown any signs of violence or aggression, that he was one of the kindest people they knew. A friend from his graduate program said he knew that Bláithín hadn't liked Conor's friendship with Erin, but that he didn't think there was anything more in it than Conor feeling protective of Erin. "I always thought it was more a little sister sort of relationship than anything," he'd told Roly and Bernie. "He seemed to worry about her."

Back then, no one had told me Conor had a solid alibi for that weekend, and it makes sense all of a sudden that they turned away from him, especially once they knew Erin had gone back to Dublin. They'd clearly started looking elsewhere.

The other surprising thing to me is how seriously they seemed to be considering Gary Curran as a suspect. As they'd mentioned, he'd been cautioned for stalking a fellow UCD student a few years before Erin's disappearance. The picture I get, though, is of a socially inept teenager with a desperate crush on a girl who became increasingly alarmed by his behavior. In their interview with him, he said he hadn't met Erin because he'd been doing errands in Wicklow when she arrived at the bed-and-breakfast and then was off to work again by the time she left the next morning.

"Did you all look at Gary Curran again as part of the review?" I ask Griz.

"Yeah, but he's been out of the country for most of the last twenty years," she says. "It seems like they were looking at him for Erin initially, but not once their focus shifted back to Dublin, and he wasn't really in the picture for any of the other disappearances. That's my sense of it, like."

Still, he and his mother were perhaps nearly the last people to see Erin, and they're right there in Glenmalure. If I were in charge, I'd want to talk to him again.

After I told them about Hacky O'Hanrahan, they had gone and interviewed him at his parents' house. The report lists the house name and address: Bridgehampton, Killiney Hill Road, Killiney.

The parents seem to have controlled the interview fairly tightly but Hacky O'Hanrahan had told Roly and Bernie the same things he'd told me, that he and Erin had met at a club and gone back to his flat in Merrion Square. She'd left in the morning and he'd never seen her again. That must have been before they started recording interviews, because instead of a transcript it's a signed statement.

She seemed like a girl who wanted to have a good time. She was a nice girl. But she was the one who said she wanted to come home with me. She seemed pretty happy, if you want

*to know the truth. She said to ring her so I did. But she
didn't ring back and I left it. I didn't even think of her again
until I saw the thing on the SixOne.*

Reading between the lines, I can tell that they thought he was an asshole. But there isn't anything more incriminating than that.

I turn to Niall Deasey.

Roly and Bernie had gotten the Murphy brothers' names from the Westbury and run them through the system. I remember the conference room, Wilcox's gaze on me as I said I'd never heard their names. He'd probably thought I was in on whatever it was Erin had been involved with. I read the detectives' statements, laying out an incomplete profile of the brothers.

They had been born in 1940 and 1945, respectively, and after a middle-class Irish American childhood with four other siblings in Somerville, Massachusetts, they'd started a cement company that had been very successful, mostly by obtaining contracts with the city of Boston and other municipalities in the suburbs. The Murphys had been active in raising money for IAFNI, the Northern Ireland aid organization I'd learned about from Ingrid, in the '80s and early '90s, and there was a note that the US Department of Justice knew about them because of it. Whatever they were up to then, they're both dead now, one from lymphoma and the other from a classic widowmaker heart attack while eating at a Boston steakhouse.

It still isn't clear, though, exactly why they were flagged in the system.

And it leaves unanswered another question: Who was the guy from the North?

On to Niall Deasey. It's all the stuff Bernie and Roly told me.

He owned a local auto garage in Arklow and, the Arklow cop told them, he probably dealt drugs and, in his younger years, did a little armed robbery here and there. His father, Petey Deasey, had been a known republican but Niall Deasey, in the '80s and '90s, was known to have associations in criminal enterprises in Wicklow and Dublin that had connections to dissident republican groups claiming to be fighting the drugs trade. But after 1998, he seemed to fall off the radar a bit, and at some point there was a note that he'd moved to London to run a garage with his half-brother. He seemed to have stayed out of trouble since then, and in 2013, when his mother became ill, he moved back to Arklow and reopened the garage. Back in 1993, a local cop had a chat with him and asked him about the Americans. He claimed that the American men were over as part of some conference for breeders of boxers. He'd corresponded with them before the conference and taken them out for pints when they'd arrived. It didn't seem like anyone had believed that story, though.

That's it. I Google Drumkee and read some more *Irish Times* stories about arms dumps in Wicklow and Carlow and about Kevin Whelan and the graves of other victims of the loyalist and republican paramilitary organizations. There's something knocking around in my head, something about Katerina Greiner and Erin and what they were doing in the forest in Wicklow, but I can't find it: It's like a marble that keeps rolling just out of reach.

Griz is still working the missing persons cases, to see if she can identify any other possible victims. Now that we know he buried Katerina Greiner, it opens up the possibility that there are undiscovered victims.

She shows me a huge stack of sheets printed from the database: missing men and women of all ages. Before 1990 the names are mostly Irish ones, but starting around 2000 there are Polish and Bulgarian names and then, more recently, Chinese and Nigerian ones.

"A lot of these probably went home, but it's a lot," Griz says. "What I wanted to ask you, though, is if you have any ideas about Brenda Donaghy. I've started looking a bit but I can't find any evidence she returned to Ireland. I talked to all the Donaghys in Dublin, which is a lot, but no one's missing a daughter of the right age."

"I've done as much nosing around as I could over the years," I tell her. "After she left my uncle, she didn't leave any tracks. I checked Social Security, DMV, marriage and death certificates. I couldn't find anything. A few years after Erin went missing, my uncle had to admit to me that they'd never actually gotten married, so I wondered if she had a different name. He told me that she loved shrimp—she always ordered it when they went out to dinner—and that she used to tell him about going to the beach in somewhere called Sherries or Serries. My instinct is that Erin never found her, but obviously I can't be sure."

"Skerries. It's a beach town north of the city. I'd say that's what it was. I was wondering if maybe there was someone connected to Brenda Donaghy," Griz says. "A brother or a friend or . . . I don't know. Maybe it was when Erin went looking for her mother that she met the fella who . . . who killed her or who she's with. Maybe he's the same guy who killed Katerina Greiner. Maybe he's our suspect for the others, too. I don't know. We know who the rest of our suspects are. Like you said, maybe there's someone here who we don't know about yet."

"It's a good theory, Griz." I can feel my pulse speed up a little. She's right. If Erin made contact with Brenda or with her family in

Ireland, then there's a whole pool of known associates we haven't identified yet.

"All right," she says. "I'm going to put together something we can post up near Skerries. It's worth a try, sure. Here's the other thing you asked for—as part of the last review, we checked homicides and missing persons files in the Republic and up north, looking for patterns. There were a couple of disappearances near Newry that were being looked at as part of a pattern around 2006, but two of the women turned up years later and one was killed by her husband. He'd taken the body to a friend's garage and they buried it at a junkyard."

She lays the papers down on the desk and I flip through them: There's a printout of unsolved homicides in Ireland and the UK: two teenage girls who went missing in Donegal in the '70s, an unsolved murder of a forty-three-year-old woman in Cork. A woman raped and murdered in Limerick. Another woman raped and murdered in Limerick. A teenage boy in Tuam.

On the UK lists, Griz has highlighted the ones up north, the Newry ones and some unsolved murders of women in Belfast and Antrim. She's crossed out some of the murders, ones she's labeled "sectarian" and then ones in England, Scotland, or Wales. These are endless, lists of geographically linked murders or disappearances— five disappeared and then murdered women in East London, three teenagers murdered in a car in Manchester, four young women who'd gone missing in Croydon over ten years, their bodies found a couple of weeks after they'd disappeared; the murders of three women hiking near Snowdon Mountain in Wales; on and on and on. It strikes me that Ireland really is a lot safer than most other places in the British Isles. It seems important somehow.

It's usually someone known to the victim.

Griz turns on the television for the news at one. Someone brings in ham sandwiches for us and we eat while we watch. They're expanding the search in Glenmalure, around where they found the button, and the newspapers are full of pictures of Niamh Horrigan's family, her mother tearfully pleading for anyone with any information to come forward. She's been missing for eleven days.

We get back to work.

◆ ◆ ◆

"Hang on," Griz says. I look up from my files, my eyes throbbing from the focused effort over so many hours.

She has my accordion file emptied out on the table and she's sorting pieces of paper into individual folders. "What have you got?" I ask her.

"Well, look. I was going through all these receipts and things and there's one that I . . . well, look." She pushes over an AIB bank receipt. I read it carefully. It looks like Erin changed $100 worth of traveler's checks and got back 70 Irish punts. It shows the exchange rate on the day she changed them. It looks just like the other receipts that I found with Erin's things at the house. As far as I remembered, she'd had them in the zippered pouch she'd used to hold all her financial documents. I'd looked through a lot of it when I was in Dublin and then I'd looked through them again when the boxes Emer and Daisy had packed had arrived in the US. I'd kept all the receipts together, but there hadn't been anything very interesting there.

But I see why Griz picked this one out.

"The date is the eighteenth of September, 1993," she says. "In Dublin."

"You're right. I didn't notice it before because they all looked the same. Griz, this is a good catch." I stare at the receipt. "You know what this means, right?"

Griz's eyes are wide. "She came back to Dublin. She came back, she changed money, and she went back to the flat and left this there," she says. "Why? To get something? To meet someone?"

"Yeah." My mind is going a hundred miles an hour. This could explain why it seemed like she took a lot of clothes for a day or two. She didn't, but she came back to the house to get more clothes because she knew she was going to be gone for a while.

"But why didn't the roommates tell us that?" Griz asks.

"Because they weren't there. They were mostly out during the day. They hadn't checked her room so they wouldn't have known if anything was missing. They would have had no way of knowing she came back. Can you find me the statements for Daisy and Emer?"

She finds the file. "Here." Daisy and Emer both signed statements saying that they were out all day on the sixteenth. They came home that evening and found Erin gone. They were around the house on the seventeenth, but she didn't come home. Then, my memory is right. Daisy and Emer said they were out all day on the eighteenth. They'd gone shopping on Grafton Street and then met some friends at a pub and hadn't gotten home until late Saturday night.

I say, "So she was in Glenmalure on the sixteenth and the morning of the seventeenth. And she was still in Dublin on the eighteenth."

"But what about the bus time on the piece of paper?" Griz asks.

"Why did she have the bus time if she wasn't going somewhere on the seventeenth?"

It hits me. "What if she was meeting someone at the bus station? It wasn't so she could take a bus, it was so she could pick someone up?"

"That's good," Griz says. "That's really good."

"But who was she meeting and where did she sleep the night of the seventeenth?"

"I don't know," Griz says. "We should ask Roly. They must have interviewed the neighbors. Did anyone see her on the eighteenth?"

"Let's check." We find the interview reports and read through the door-to-doors on Somerset Road. It looks like Bernie did most of them, and her notes indicate that they talked to all the residents of the street, as well as the surrounding streets. No one saw anything on the seventeenth or eighteenth.

"I'll see if I can find clerks who worked at the bank then who might remember her," Griz says. We both know it's a long shot.

"Are the phone records in there?" I ask, pointing to the file. "I always wondered who called the house on the sixteenth and if there was anything interesting there."

"Not really," Griz says. "There was a call from a pay phone on O'Connell Street that morning, but I think the roommates thought it was one of their friends." She leafs through the papers in the file. "Yeah, it's in Emer's statement. She figured it was a friend of hers calling about homework."

"They never talked to the friend, though?"

"Doesn't look like it." She looks up at me and raises her eyebrows. "Was there anything else in those boxes?" she asks. "I checked our

files and I didn't see anything, but your uncle ended up with everything from her room, right?"

"Actually, I have them in my basement. I'll call my ex-husband
later and see if he can look. But I'm pretty sure I went through
everything." I look at the receipt. "Wow. Nice work, Griz. We figured she'd come back to Dublin but we didn't have proof. But what
was she up to?"

Griz doesn't say anything.

"I'll say it if you won't," I say. "It looks like she was getting ready
to run."

♦ ♦ ♦

We gather everything together and Griz starts putting things back
in the files. We have two main points for further follow-up: Robert
Herricks and Erin's AIB receipt. There's likely nothing in either
of them that can help Niamh, but it feels good to have something,
scraps, even if they lead nowhere.

When we're done, I tell Griz I'm taking her for a pint. We walk
down to the Palace Bar, blinking at the late evening sunlight. Everything looks throbbing with color and light after our conference
room prison. It's Wednesday night, early summer on the air, and the
streets are filling with early drinkers and shoppers.

"Did you always know you wanted to be a guard?" I ask her
once we're settled in against a wall with our pints.

She laughs. "It was about the last thing I thought I'd be."

"So, what happened?" I'm curious about how her family ended
up in Ireland, curious about how she became a guard.

"We came here when I was eleven," she says. "There were a lot of Poles, lots of Czechs coming over then. The EU, you know. There were jobs. Everyone thought it would be easy since Ireland's a Catholic country. It wasn't easy. My father couldn't find work and went back. My mother had lots of cleaning work but she hated it. I did well at school but I never felt Irish, even though I worked my arse off to get rid of my accent. There was a nun who was pushing me to apply to university. There was some scheme to get recent immigrants to take the leaving cert and go for university places and they held an information night. The Guards were there, too. I'd always loved detective novels and shows. My mam and I used to watch *Law and Order*." She grins. "I imagined myself as the detectives, not the solicitors. So I guess there was something there. But joining the Guards, it was totally impulsive. I didn't even know you could be one if you weren't a huge big blondy lad from the country with an Irish name. But I signed up that night. Best decision I ever made."

"You're good," I tell her. "You're really good. I'd hire you to my team in about two seconds. But Roly would kill me."

She grins. "I don't know, America might be fun. Thanks."

"What's it like being . . . not Irish? Not originally Irish."

"Ah, better than it used to be. Ireland's changed. You wouldn't know it looking at that lot." She points back toward Pearse Street. "Though Joey's ma is from Pakistan and there was a guy who was born in Nigeria in my class at Templemore. It's getting better. I think it's harder being a woman, honestly. What about you?"

I take a nice long sip of my Guinness, starting to relax, just a little. "Before . . . Erin, I had thought I was going to get my graduate degree in literature. But there was something about all of that, about the frustration of not finding her. I wanted to know, you know? And it drove me crazy that we didn't know. There were these two cops, detectives on the organized crime squad, and they came into my uncle's bar all the time and I loved listening to them discussing their cases. I asked them how someone could become a detective, and it turned out that the academy was giving the test that summer. Like you, I just . . . jumped. It was hard when I was in uniform, when I had a baby. The fucking sexism. It's better now, though. Too." I smile. "The homicide squad is my place. I love it there."

Griz gets another round. When she's back, she looks at me seriously and says, "Can I ask you a question? When you found Anthony Pugh, did you know? Was it a feeling, an instinct? How did you do it?"

I feel the panic start. His name makes it especially bad, I think because it must bring back the aftermath, the days and weeks when his name was in the paper every day, every time I turned on the radio. I take a deep breath. "I just worked it. That's all I can say. The FBI thought he was a doctor or a nurse, someone with a healthcare background, because of the drugs they found in his victims' blood. But I wondered about him being a veterinarian instead. I caught his last victim. I went out and saw the scene; he dumped them on the beach. Her name was Maria. Anyway, I stuck with the vet angle, mostly because no one else was and it was a place I could get some space, you know? I made lists of all the vets on Long Island, figured out where they lived."

She's watching me with wide eyes, completely focused on my story. This happens a lot, with other cops; people hear my name, make the connection with the Anthony Pugh case, and they want to hear the story. I hate it.

"I started mapping it out, like, 'This guy lives here, that guy lives there, this is his route to work. This is where he drives every day.' And I looked at where the women had been picked up, where they'd been dumped, and I started to see it, on the map. Dr. Anthony Pugh. He had a vet practice in a town called Northport and he lived about ten miles away, and it just . . . it just made sense. I asked some other vets about him. Most of them said they'd heard he was good, but this one young woman, just out of vet school, she said she'd treated a dog, the owner said she'd taken him to Pugh for a stomach problem but the dog had ended up with a broken leg. The vet told me that she'd heard a rumor about him operating on animals without anesthesia."

Griz looks horrified.

"I started driving by his office on my way home. It was out of the way. He liked to drive around kind of aimlessly, you know, and that made me wonder. Anyway, a call came in that a woman was missing. Her friend didn't want to give her name—they were both working as escorts—but she said that her friend Andrea had been picked up by this guy and hadn't come back when she was supposed to. I knew. I just knew. I put his plates out, a description of his car. A uniform in King's Park called it in. He was behind the car and the guy was driving erratically."

I have the line memorized for times I have to tell the story, and now I say it even though all I want to do is jump up off my stool and run out into the street and keep running until I can't remember the stale smoke smell of his car, the way he never looked at me or the guys arresting him, the way the drugs made her look frozen: "I got there just as they were cuffing him. She was in the trunk, in bad shape, but still alive. He was heading for the beach."

I stand up before she can ask anything else. My head hurts, my mouth feels dry, my breath tinny. "I don't know about you, but I'm wrecked all of a sudden. You ready to go?"

"Yeah, of course." She's startled and she drops her purse, bends to pick it up. I take a deep breath, force my heart rate down.

Out on the sidewalk, I say, "Griz, I can't tell you what a pleasure it's been working with you. Thank you for everything." I give her a hug.

"You too," she says. She watches me for a minute. "And listen, Maggie, I'm going to find out, about Erin, for you. I want you to know that. I'd like it to be now, so we can find Niamh. But even if it takes another twenty years, I'm going to do it for you. I'm going to work this case." She smiles, gives me a little salute, and takes off.

28

....

1993

By late October, there was nothing more on Erin, and I had become all too used to the rhythm of the Dublin pubs. At four o'clock, it was old men, exhausted-looking tourists, and students going for a pint after class, depending on the pub. By six, it was a respectable crowd of workers, couples meeting up. The really touristy pubs served a lot of food between five and seven, the rest handed out sandwiches to drinkers to line their stomachs, but things tended to clear out between seven and eight for a bit and then filled in again with after-dinner drinkers and students out for pints or, on the weekends, a night on the town.

Then you settled in.

I had come to love Dublin at night. It wasn't romantic, exactly, not Paris or even New York. When I think of Dublin now, I think of empty stretches of sidewalk, skittering leaves at dusk, sideways rain. Lights on the Liffey. The looming darkness of the Dublin mountains on one side and the wide emptiness of the sea on the other. The sudden burst of sharp yeasty warmth that hit you when you got inside the door of a pub.

I spent a lot of time sitting in warm pubs, thinking, counting hours, talking to people I'd never talk to again, old men and girls made up to look old enough to order pints, and married couples out for a treat. I listened to a lot of sessions, the circular rhythms of traditional tunes taking me out and back again, letting me out, reeling me in.

But the waiting was getting to me.

The phone rang one night at the house and when I answered it, there was only silence on the other end.

"Hello?" I couldn't hear anything but static.

"Who's there?" I shouted. "Erin? Erin?"

When I turned around, Daisy had come out of her room and she was standing there with a terrified expression on her face.

"Are you all right?" Her eyes were wide. "Was that . . . ?"

"I don't think so. I thought . . ."

She went back to her room.

One night, I drank at Brogan's on Dame Street and then walked around Temple Bar, tipsy and sad, hoping I'd see Conor, but he never materialized from the darkness, never stepped out of the café. I went home, fell into a drunken, dreamless sleep that left me with a headache and a healthy dose of self-disdain the next morning.

Emer and Daisy watched me warily that week. When they asked how the investigation was going, I answered with platitudes about the long game and having patience.

I kept looking for Brenda's family in the phone book.

I was walking home from the pubs one evening when I got the feeling that I was being followed. It was still pretty early, people heading for home after work, and I slowed down right around Bo-lands Mills and bent down to tie my shoe. When I turned my head, I saw someone walking quickly on the other side of the street.

I turned onto Barrow Street and walked straight along to the house. It was dark; Emer and Daisy were out. I went inside and, leaving the lights off, I looked out the narrow panes of glass next to the door.

He didn't come onto Gordon Street, but I saw him stop at the corner of Barrow and find a doorway to turn into. He stood there, his back pressed against the door, and casually lit a cigarette. He didn't look in the direction of the house.

I rummaged in the drawer next to the kitchen sink and took out a Phillips-head screwdriver. I tucked it into my coat pocket. Out-side, I stopped in front of the house for a minute and buttoned my jacket up around my neck, to give him time to see me, and then I set out again, walking east on Gordon Street.

There weren't many people out and about now, and when I turned left, I saw him walking slowly, the cigarette a distant red glow. He was keeping his distance.

I was scared now and I thought of finding a phone booth and calling Roly to come meet me. But I was worried he'd take off if he saw me make a call and it felt like this might be my only chance to figure out who he was and why he was following me.

I turned onto Irishtown Road, wanting to stay where there was more traffic for a little bit so I could think. Finally I decided to try to draw him out. I turned down one of the little streets just off Irishtown Road and waited to make sure he was behind me before I made another turn and then sprinted to the end of the street and darted into one of the lanes. There was a knee-high cement wall and I hid behind it, waiting to see what he'd do.

He wasn't stupid. He didn't sprint after me and stand on the corner looking in both directions. He just came down the street, walking very quickly, still smoking the cigarette. He looked the opposite way down the street, toward a little shrine to the Virgin Mary, and then reversed direction and walked past my lane. I looked up at the windows above me. The lights were blazing in most of the houses. I was pretty sure someone would come out if I screamed.

I waited until he was almost to me and then I swung out of my hiding place holding the screwdriver in front of me. "Why are you following me? Did you know Erin?" I asked him.

He barely started. He was young, close to my age, with thick dark hair and a pudgy face. He was wearing a dark overcoat and underneath I could see a light shirt collar peeking out.

He watched me for a long moment, his body relaxed.

"I think you've got it wrong, miss," he said in a quiet, controlled voice. Dublin accent. "I'm not following you. I'm just walking home from the office. Taking a stroll, like."

"You've been following me. I recognize you," I told him. "Who are you? Why are you following me? Did you know Erin?"

"Don't know what you're talking about. I'd take care with that, if I were you." He nodded to the screwdriver, then he winked at me and walked off, slowly and deliberately, in the direction of Irishtown Road.

··

When I start high school, I think Erin and I are going to get close again. We're riding the same bus and I assume we'll sit together the way we did the year we were in junior high with each other.

But when I get to the bus stop, she's already there and she's already talking to Jessica. She says hi and asks me if I'm ready, but when we get on the bus she and Jessica sit together and immediately start whispering.

I walk into the building alone.

The first couple of weeks are fine. Once in a while, Erin and Jessica talk to me on the bus. They sit in a group with the boys in our neighborhood, Brian and Chris and Devin and Derek. They make fun of each other and talk about our teachers, about how they dress and how lame they are.

Devin O'Brien is telling a story about a party his older brother, Greg, had at their house, about how out of hand it got. Brian tells about how his older brother, Frank, lied to their parents about where he was and then his dad took the dog for a walk on the beach and found him passed out in a dinghy by the club pavilion. They're all laughing.

"How about you, Maggie?" Devin says suddenly. "You like to party?"

I look up from my book, terrified. It feels like a trap. If I say yes, they'll laugh. I can't say no. I stare at him for a minute.

Then Erin says, "Maggie doesn't party, guys. She thinks we're all just so ridiculous. She'd rather stay in and study."

There's a moment of utter quiet. She meant it as a joke, but something in her voice tells us all that it's not. I flush and look back down at my book, tears springing into my eyes.

"You're such a bitch," Jessica says.

"I'm totally kidding," Erin says, too loud.

When the bus gets to the high school, I get off first and walk straight inside. I ask my mom to drive me the next few days, without telling her why. She doesn't ask, but after a week she says she has a doctor's appointment and I'll have to ride the bus.

When I show up at the bus stop, Erin's head is bent over something in her hands. Jessica's not there.

"Hey, Maggie," Erin says, too brightly. "Hey, you know I was just kidding, right?" She watches me. "That time. Totally joking around."

"Yeah." I can't look at her. If I do, I'll start crying.

I can hear Devin and Derek joking around as they walk down to the bus stop. They're almost here.

"Hey," she says. "Look at this."

She's holding a piece of paper out to me. I look down. It's a photocopy of a phone book page. I'm confused until I read down the names and find "Flaherty, Brenda M."

"Where is this?"

"The city," she says. "She lives in the city."

29

The morning after I was followed, I woke up to a note by the phone in Emer's writing: *Erin's da rang. Talked to Detective Byrne. Ring him when you can.* When I went out to the corner shop for eggs and coffee, I picked up an *Irish Times* as well, and I was sitting at the table in the kitchen, eating scrambled eggs, when I read the small headline on an inside page: "Gardaí Say No Indication of Foul Play in Erin Flaherty Case: Active Search Suspended."

> The Gardaí say they have moved on from the initial stage of their investigation into the disappearance of American student Erin Flaherty and will suspend active searches. Detective Superintendent Ruarí Wilcox says that the working theory is that Flaherty is traveling and hasn't been in touch with family and friends, and that there's no evidence of foul play. Nonetheless, the Gardaí have been unable to definitively rule out an abduction in the Wicklow Mountains. Wilcox says that any members of the public with informa-

tion about Miss Flaherty should call the Gardaí Helpline on 1-3045672.

The receptionist at the Irishtown Garda Station saw me coming and stood up as though she was going to physically prevent me from getting through.

"I need to talk to Detective Byrne and Detective McNeely," I said. "I know they're here." The look on her face told me I'd gambled right.

"I'll just check now," she said. "I believe they may be in a meeting, however."

"I'll wait," I said. I sat down and picked up an *Irish Independent*. It had a longer version of the same story, with a quote from a criminologist at Queen's University Belfast saying that, with no evidence of foul play, the case does seem to be that of a "young woman who has decided to disappear of her own accord."

It was Roly who came down to talk to me, sheepishly opening the door and coming to sit next to me in one of the hard plastic chairs.

"You called my uncle and told him you're stopping the investigation." He was staring straight ahead, not looking at me. "Why didn't you tell me?"

"Now, we're not stopping the investigation, D'arcy. We're—One phase has been suspended, pending further developments, now, and then we'll see where we are. We've thoroughly investigated every lead there is, and if new ones emerge we'll investigate those, too, but—"

"What about Niall Deasey? Have you thoroughly investigated him?" I said, too loudly. Roly winced. "And why didn't you tell me?

I've just been waiting for someone to call me back, like an idiot. What about her mother?" My head was pounding and my stomach actually hurt. I felt like I was going to throw up.

"D'arcy, you've been a bit erratic. There's a feeling that you're too involved. Now, I know that may be my fault, but for the good of the investigation, we need you to be patient and wait a little. Maybe you could go home for a bit and then check back with us when—"

"Erratic? You think I'm being erratic? Do you know what happened to me last night? Some guy followed me. He was there all the way home and when I got back to the house, he waited for me. I went and got a screwdriver because I thought if he tried to attack me I could—"

"D'arcy, please tell me you didn't fight with some fella on the street."

"No, but I waited and sure enough he followed me. I asked him if he knew anything about Erin and I swear he did. He had this *look* in his eyes."

Roly ran a hand through his hair and said, "D'arcy, you're making this very difficult for me. If there really was someone following you, you'd no right to confront him. It's mad. He might have been a mentaller and he might have attacked you."

"He might know something about Erin. I wrote down a description."

"D'arcy." He leaned in, his voice very low. He glanced up at the receptionist and said, "My job is on the line here. I've been told to keep you away from the investigation. I need you to stay away."

"But—"

"I'm sorry, D'arcy. I'll be in touch if there's anything new."

He stood up and started to walk away, but before he opened the door, he turned around again. His eyes were shadowed and I could see the strain on his face. He looked years older than the Roly Byrne I had met when I reported Erin missing. He said, "I really am sorry, D'arcy," and then he was gone.

* * *

I went for a long run, nearly six miles, and took a hot shower in the empty flat when I was back. I had that light, anxious, hollowed-out feeling you have when you've just recovered from a hangover. I knew I should drink lots of water and have a quiet night in.

Instead I went to the Raven. The red-headed barman was behind the bar, and I sat on a stool and chatted with him while I drank cider and got the update on his girlfriend and told him about Uncle Danny and the bar.

A couple of older guys joined us and we all shot the shit for a while, until I was good and tipsy and the sun was gone and the streets of Temple Bar were full of people. I walked for a bit, feeling the hard elbow of my loneliness in my side. And then I took a right onto Eustace Street.

He was there, locking up, and when he saw me, he didn't say a word. He just put the keys in his pocket. It was a dark night and his face was in shadow. I stood in front of him on the empty street. I was suddenly sober, the chilled wind coming off the river a jolt of adrenaline.

"Let's walk," he whispered.

We started walking, along the quays, and we didn't touch until we were past the DART station. On City Quay, he took my hand. The sky was dark gray above the river. We could see our breath on the air.

Once we got to Gordon Street, I let us in and we stood for a minute in Erin's silent room, staring at each other in the low light coming in the window, breathing, before he reached for me.

For years, I would remember almost everything about that night, the way the light came through onto the bed, the way his lips brushed my shoulders, the blur of his face above me, the feel of the corded muscles along his back, and the way he smelled—sweat and smoke and the cold metal tang of the outside air still on his cheeks and hands.

We talked in hushed voices all through the dark night, murmuring into each other's bodies, skin on skin, lying tangled under the sheet. I memorized the shape of his neck, his shoulders, his stomach.

He said, "I can feel your heart beating."

I put his wrist to my lips and said, "I can feel your pulse."

"Why are you crying?"

"I don't know."

When the sky began to lighten, I asked him, "What's the worst thing you've ever done?"

He was silent for a long time. Finally he said, "I can't."

I traced the line of his jaw with my index finger.

I said, "One time, when I was ten, I had to go looking for Erin. My uncle woke up and she was gone and he called us. My mom went door to door and she told me to go down and check the beach. Erin loved the beach. I walked for a long time and then I saw her. She was sitting on a log and when I got to her, she didn't even look up, she just said, 'Leave me alone. I don't want to go back.' I told her everyone was worried about her and she didn't say anything. She was stacking these rocks on the log and she kept stacking them, making little piles. I didn't know what to do. I just sat there. Finally she got up and started walking. I just followed behind her, until we got home."

He stroked my hair away from my temples.

"Did you ever ask her? Did you ever ask her why?"

"She would never say. I always thought it was . . . my fault somehow. Because I had a mother and she didn't. Because . . . I just thought it was my fault."

"You can't think that," he said. "Where do you think she is?" His body was warm against my cheek.

"I don't know. I keep thinking if I could just remember more about the last time I saw her, then I would know."

"What was the last time?" he asked quietly.

"She told me she was moving over here and I accused her of doing it just because I was supposed to come here, because I was supposed to come and then I couldn't because my mother got sick. And I . . . I said some awful things to her about my mother and how Erin made her last weeks worse." My voice caught and he rolled over and pulled me in closer.

"You have to forgive yourself," he said after a long moment. "You have to forgive yourself for everything."

We slept until a thin cold light came in through the windows. I opened my eyes to find him dressing. He wouldn't even look at me.

"I'm sorry," he said. "I shouldn't have. I can't do this again."

I went back to sleep and when I woke up I was crying.

I'm taking the trash out when I see Erin standing in front of our house.

"Hey," she says. "Can I ask you something?" She looks smaller, hunched down into her blue flannel shirt, her hair tucked into the collar.

I nod. I'm in tenth grade now, Erin's in eleventh. I haven't been alone with her in nearly six months. She gets rides to school now and we've only seen each other a few times in the last year, when she and Uncle Danny come over for dinner or in the hallways at school.

"What?"

"Will you lie to your mom and come into the city with me on the train after school tomorrow?" She waits a minute and then her face breaks into a wide grin. "I know that sounds super weird."

I just look at her.

"Why are you asking me?"

"Because I want to go look for Brenda Flaherty and you're the only one I can ask. But your mom can't know because, like, my dad can't know." She's holding the photocopy of the phone book page.

She's beautiful. She's tan from the summer and her hair has bright blond highlights. She has it in a ponytail but it's falling down around her face. Her flannel shirt is soft, worn, the blue pulling out the blue of her eyes. She's thin, her jeans loose around her waist.

She looks tired, but the bruises under her eyes and her

messy hair only make her seem more romantic, wild. I've seen how boys at school are drawn to her, tried to figure out why I don't have the same effect.

I don't want to go, but something about her makes it impossible.

"Yeah," I say. "Okay."

Erin has money for a taxi and we meet up after school and she calls from the pay phone. When the taxi pulls up, it's Aaron, this guy in his twenties who buys beer for high school kids if you throw in an extra ten dollars. "Hey, Erin," he says. He's a little flirty with her but she just gets in the back and looks out the window as we drive to the station.

We're on the train before she says, "I just want to know if she's there, you know? If we can find her."

"How do you know it's her?" I ask.

"I don't, but it's the only one I could find. I asked my dad and he won't tell me anything. He literally won't even talk about her. Your mom hasn't said anything to you, has she?"

"She doesn't know anything," I say.

"I know. So at least . . . Maybe this is her."

The address is on East Thirteenth Street and Avenue A. We take the subway to Union Square and then walk over. It gets grittier the further east we go. I've only been to the city with my parents or on school trips. I know Erin and Jessica come in sometimes to go to bars so I tell myself she knows what she's doing, but after we cross Second Avenue, Erin says, "Put your wallet in your shirt in case we get mugged."

I do what she says.

Brenda Flaherty's address is a rundown-looking build-ing squeezed between two bigger rundown-looking build-ings. Erin stares at the door for a minute. I don't say anything. There are a couple of bells next to the door, with numbers, not names. She rings the one next to apartment 7 and waits a minute. Nothing happens. She tries again. Nothing.

"I just realized," I tell her. "If she works, she might not get home until six or seven." It's five. I told my mom I had to stay at school late to build the homecoming float. I told her I'd get a ride when we were done.

We sit down on the front stoop to wait. People come and go, but no Brenda Flaherty. A tall black guy wearing a pink sweatshirt puts his key in the lock and then turns to look at us. "You okay?"

"Yeah, we're just . . . we're looking for Brenda Flaherty. She lives in apartment seven. Do you know her?"

He watches Erin for a moment. "I live in apartment seven, and I can guarantee you there's no one named Brenda Flaherty in there with me."

"Oh." Erin looks stricken.

I jump in. "How long have you lived there?"

"Like five years."

I look at Erin. "Okay. Thank you."

The guy goes inside and I try to put my arm around her. "It must have been an old listing or something," I tell her.

"God, I was so stupid." She's staring at the door as

though someone is going to come out of it. "It's like she tricked me again."

"You should ask your dad," I tell her as we walk back to Union Square. "He should at least tell you everything he knows."

"It makes him too sad," she says. "I can't do it."

"Erin, maybe she . . . maybe she doesn't want you to find her. Maybe she wanted to disappear."

She looks up at me. "But she didn't even know me. I was a baby. Even if she wanted to leave Danny. Why would she just disappear?"

I don't have any answer for her.

On the train, I look over and see her staring out the window, tears in her eyes. The sleeve of her flannel shirt pulls away from her arm and I can see scars and scabs, lines up and down her lower arm. I don't say anything. It feels like there's a question I'm supposed to ask but I don't know what it is.

30

I have a text from Lilly when I wake up in the morning, a selfie of her on the beach, with her hand outstretched, a gull snatching a piece of bread from her palm, that she must have sent last night. *Me and the seagullies miss you*, it reads. "Seagullies" was her name for them when she was little. I resist the urge to write back, *The seagullies and I* and instead write, *I miss you soooooooo much. Call you later. Love you more than all the seagullies in the universe.*

Roly and Wilcox and Regan are waiting for us at Pearse Street. No reporters today. Griz is late but when she comes rushing in, clutching her phone, I know she has something. "Robert Herricks," she whispers to me. "I've got something on him. He was living in Baltinglass when June Talbot went missing."

"Are you shitting me?" She waves the paper at me but I don't have time to read it. "Here, you can tell them now."

Griz and I lay out copies of the files we've prepared, everything narrowed down to just a couple of sheets. Roly nods at me to begin. Everyone's tense, in a hurry.

I start. "The first thing I want to say is that the Garda Síochána, at every turn, to my mind, has run an absolutely exemplary investigation into my cousin's disappearance and into the deaths of Teresa McKenny and June Talbot." I meet Roly's eyes and he gives me a tiny nod. "Detective Garda Grzeskiewicz and I reviewed a huge amount of information and found only two small areas of interest for follow-up related to these cases. They may have a bearing on the search for Niamh, and they may not. I'll talk about the profiling I did and then we'll detail those for you.

"As you know, psychological profiling is an inexact science. Take everything with a grain of salt. But when I look at these crimes, I see a couple of different things. Like your profiler, I'd put this guy's age somewhere between forty and sixty. That's based on him being involved in Katerina Greiner's murder and then the disappearances in 1998 and 2006 and in Niamh Horrigan's disappearance. But I'd put him somewhere around fifty now. Obviously that changes if he's good for some of them and not others. It's rare for seventeen-year-olds to commit these kinds of abductions and murders and get away with them.

"So, forty to sixty. He's from Wicklow or was once. He knows the roads, knows when they're busy and when they aren't. He has a place to take the women. It could be close by. It could be far away, but then he's bringing them back to dump their bodies. He's of the area in some fundamental way. He's spent time there. It has associations for him.

"Your profiler thinks he's married. I'm not sure. If he is, then he has a job that gives him a lot of flexibility. He's got time and space. No one's bugging him about where he is. Could be a very submissive wife or partner. I'd bet on that anyway. But he also might be single.

"He's angry. He feels that women have treated him badly in some way. He dehumanizes them. He controls them. He may have a history of domestic abuse or he may only act out in this specific way. He is probably a respectable member of society. People would be very surprised to know that he has committed these crimes."

I pause for a minute. It's warm in the room and I can feel the drag of not enough sleep the past couple of days.

"Okay," I say. "He's able to get them into his car without too much of a struggle. If I was just coming in on this, I would say you need to consider the possibility that he's a current or former police officer, or an ambulance driver, or someone else in a position of authority and trust. But I know you've done that. I'd keep working that angle.

"Your profiler was good. I think you're on the right track. I wish I had something more to add but . . . I really don't." Wilcox smiles, just a little, a self-satisfied little smirk. Regan and Roly nod.

"The final thing I would say is something that sounds a little out there," I tell them. "When I look at this map, I see a triangle with the mountains in the center. The mountains, I don't know. It's like they mean something to him. Like he's keeping them in sight. I wonder about that. It's a feeling, really. Nothing concrete. Maybe there's a trauma, an early experience that established some psychosexual pattern. I don't know. But . . ."

Roly nods and Regan makes a note on a piece of paper.

"Okay, now on to the two things we found. The first is a groundskeeper interviewed by gardaí after Teresa McKenny's disappearance in 1998. His name is Robert Herricks and he didn't set off any alarm bells when he was interviewed. He had an alibi for the day of Teresa's disappearance, but it was provided by his brother and, well . . . it would be worth checking it out again. I didn't like the way he described Teresa. It was dehumanizing, sexualizing. All things I'd expect of our guy. I was going to tell you to take a second look at him. But there's something better than that." I nod to Griz. "Detective Garda Grzeskiewicz just got it. It's good. Really good."

"Robert Herricks was raised in Baltinglass," she says, standing up and passing copies of the report around the table. "He moved back there in 2005, when the golf course went under. He was living in his sister's house when June Talbot disappeared. We know this because there was a string of burglaries earlier that year and he was interviewed about whether he'd seen anything."

"Shite," Roly says. "How did we miss it?"

"It's about the only thing you missed," I tell him. "Anyway, someone will want to go and talk with him."

Regan excuses himself to put it in the works. When he's back, I get going again.

"I'm also going to let Detective Garda Grzeskiewicz do this one. It was her find. It's also a good one," I tell them. "But it casts suspicion on my cousin's actions before she disappeared."

Griz shows them a photocopy of the receipt and explains how it must have been overlooked in the original search of Erin's room. "I've already put in a call to AIB," she says. "They're trying to track down the employees who might have been working that day to see if they'll recognize a picture. As you know, after twenty-three years, it's a long shot. But it raises some interesting possibilities. If Erin Flaherty came back to Dublin and changed traveler's checks and then disappeared, it could have been because she was told to do it by someone who was controlling her. It could have been because she was getting ready to flee. There may be some other reason we're not thinking of. But I think it bears looking into immediately, just in case there's a connection with Niamh Horrigan's abductor."

Griz says, "Someone made a phone call to the house the morning Erin Flaherty left for Glenmalure. The roommates said it *could* have been a friend of theirs, but that was never confirmed in any way. I'd love to know who made that call. Also, Detective D'arcy raised a possibility that I think is very interesting. What if she wasn't coming back to Dublin to *take* a bus somewhere, but to *meet* someone who was coming in on a bus?"

"So she came back to Dublin, met someone at the bus station, they went to change traveler's checks, and then she fled?" Roly says.

"Why would she have been fleeing?" Regan asks. "Is there a possibility she was involved in Katerina Greiner's death?"

"Of course," I say. "The question is—and has always been, really—why did she go down to Glenmalure? Was it just to go walking or was she meeting someone? And if she returned to Dublin, why? If she was killed by the same person who killed Katerina Greiner, Teresa McKenny, and June Talbot, and who took Niamh Horrigan, then figuring out where she met him, how he convinced her to go down there, how he convinced her to come back, well, that's how we'll find Niamh."

Regan nods, then looks up at me. "Thank you, Detective D'arcy. We appreciate your efforts and I know the Horrigans do as well."

Outside, Roly pats me on back and says, "Well done, D'arcy."

"Well, there wasn't much to do. You've done everything right, all along."

"Now, you know that's not true, but thanks for the vote of confidence. We'll be in touch." I can already see him switching gears. They'll start working on Robert Herricks, on the receipt angle. They'll go down and badger the folks at the bank until they get something there. Regan's already got things in motion. "Not a word," he reminds me.

"Of course," I say. "Not a word."

"Thanks, D'arcy." He's gone, back into the bowels of the building, while I step out into the glorious sunshine outside on Pearse Street.

I don't know what to do now, so I start walking, down Pearse Street, past all the new buildings at Grand Canal Dock, past the church at the turn of Irishtown Road, all the way out to Sandymount.

A warm breeze is coming from the east and I take off my jacket and tuck it into my bag. The sun comes through the clouds. It feels good on my face and arms. There's a great little bookstore right on the Sandymount green and I stop and browse for thirty minutes, picking out a novel for Lilly and a mug for Brian with a picture of the Poolbeg Lighthouse and one for Uncle Danny with a picture of the smokestacks.

The strand pulls at me and I hop over the concrete wall and onto the sand and start walking. The wind whips at my hair, plucking it from my ponytail, and the sand beneath me bubbles with water just under the surface, revealing tiny holes and shells. I remember them from before, their pale pink insides like the pads of kittens' paws.

I stoop to pick some up, tucking them into a pocket, and then I venture out to the edge of the water.

The wind moves through my body. I can feel it all, feel time fall away. It's in my lungs, my chest, my belly. I put a hand over the place where Lilly grew. I remember the feeling of Conor Kearney's body against my belly, his voice in my ear, the way he held my face that night in Erin's room. I'm aching for him, or for something. Overcome with a sense of timelessness, I feel suddenly that these twenty-three years are both in me and not in me, that I am twenty-two and forty-five, all at the same time, a mother and not a mother. I close my eyes and let the wind rush all around me.

I had stood here, right here, and opened my eyes to find Conor in front of me.

I count to ten and open my eyes, but the strand is empty in front of me, the water coming in, washing across the little mountains and valleys in the sand.

It's early afternoon now, the day slipping away. I start walking away from the water, just wandering, turning right and left on winding little streets lined with neat stucco and brick houses, the sun catching windows and bits of quartz in the pavement.

Across the street a dog barks and I have a sudden image of Lilly and me living in one of these houses, walking along these little streets, sitting on a bench looking out over the gray-blue water, the clouds rolling in above Dublin Bay.

I don't know where I'm going and I don't care. I choose turns, one after another, until I'm by the Dodder and I follow the gray snake of it, swans floating here and there like litter, like I'm following a line on a map.

It dumps me out in Ballsbridge, on a busy main road lined with shops and restaurants and I make my way across the intersection to a green patch of park. It's suddenly quiet, the path I'm on lined with fruit trees still hanging on to a few final blossoms. The grass is strewn with browning petals.

I come around a corner and I'm startled by a corgi that comes running out from behind a tree. A teenage boy calls out, "Beanie, Beanie." The dog barely looks up at him and it's running toward the gate so I bend down to pick up the trailing leash. When I stand up again, the boy is right in front of me looking panicked and I'm about to say that everything's okay, that I've got him, when a man comes around the corner, calling out, "Don't let him go through the gate," and I look up and it's Conor.

Finally, Conor.

31

The morning after Conor walked out of the Gordon Street house, winter came for real. On Sandymount Strand, the cold air made little shells of ice on the rocks in the frigid mornings. The seaweed sparkled with hoarfrost. The Dublin Mountains were a bank of darkness in the distance. From the endless expanse of sand and water on Sandymount Strand, they sat there, waiting.

At first, Daisy didn't want to let me borrow the car. "He doesn't like to lend it out," she said lamely. "My brother, he's very particular about his things."

"I'd happily pay him, like, rent," I told her. "I just need it for a day or two, to go down to Wicklow. I want to talk to the woman at the bed-and-breakfast." Something in Emer's face made Daisy relent, say she would ask him. Later I realized they were relieved I was going.

• • •

I drove slowly, hunched over the steering wheel, trying to stay on the left-hand side of the road. It took me an hour and a half to get to Glenmalure but I found the bed-and-breakfast easily; it was the first one you came to as you walked along the lane branching off from the main road, a long two-story cottage with window boxes and a deep flower garden, mostly gone to brown, around the house.

I knocked and waited while footsteps inside approached the door. When it opened, the tall, white-haired woman on the other side looked shocked until I said, "Hi, I'm Maggie D'arcy. My cousin Erin is the girl who is missing and I was wondering if I could just ask you a few questions."

"Ah, you put a fright in me," she said, before stepping aside to invite me in. "You're so like her. Is there . . . is there any news? The guards told me they think she went back to Dublin after leaving here." She was wearing a pale blue handknit sweater with little silver buttons in the shape of thistles. Her eyes were pale blue, lost in her pale face.

"That's one thing they're looking at," I said. "But I was just wondering if you've remembered anything that might point us in the right direction. Did she say anything to you about her plans?" I can hear how desperate my voice sounds.

"Come in and sit down," she said. "It's terribly cold today."

She put me in a chair by a peat fire in a cozy room at the back of the house. Through the windows I could see the hills rising behind us, the sky darkening as the afternoon came on.

"Is there anything you remember?" I asked again. "What did she say when she left that morning?"

She smoothed her white hair and leaned forward. "As I told the guards, she told me she had to get going early. She seemed in a bit of a hurry. I assumed she had to get back to Dublin for one reason or another. She didn't say."

"Did she actually say to you that she had to get back to Dublin?" I asked.

"No . . . I suppose I assumed, since she'd said she lives there."

"Did she say she might be going walking again?"

"I don't think so. She said she'd had enough the day before. And she wasn't dressed for walking. She did seem anxious to leave. I offered her breakfast but she didn't have the time. My breakfast is very good, I'm told." A hurt expression flashed across her face. "She left and I waved and watched her walk down the drive and . . . that was all. I went back inside to clean."

"Mrs. Curran, what about your son? Did he talk to my cousin? Could she have said anything to him?"

"I told the guards this," she said. "He never met her. He was working and he had to leave very early. He never saw her."

"Are you sure? If there's anything that could help us . . ."

"No, I'm so sorry. And I really should get started on my cleaning." She stood up and led me back to the front door. The air between us was awkward now. "I'm praying for her," she said. "I hope you find out where she went."

Outside, I stood on the road for a moment, imagining I was Erin leaving the bed-and-breakfast. It would have been morning, warmer, with clouds overhead and the mountains rising behind her as she walked down the drive. There were only a few houses this way and it was so narrow that she would have had to jump off the road if a car came by. There were stretches where you weren't in sight of a house, and she could easily have been abducted by a car. She'd walked past the lodge and then . . . what?

Where are you, Erin?

• ◆ •

It was a tedious drive over to Arklow on tiny roads that demanded all my concentration, but it only took half an hour. I was exhausted by the time I parked at the tourist office and I stood for a minute in the parking lot and breathed the river bottom–scented air. The night was still and humid, uneasy. I could feel a headache starting and my stomach felt like it was full of gears grinding against each other. I hadn't eaten anything since a piece of Emer's bread with butter at seven a.m.

Arklow was a seaside town, a river snaking from the sea into the interior of Wicklow. The main drag was festive, Christmas lights already up in some of the shops and pubs.

I asked about the best pubs and the young guy behind the desk pointed out two on the little map he gave me. The Old Ship and the Harbour. "Oh," I said, trying to make it sound like an afterthought. "One of my distant cousins supposedly lives here. Deasey? Niall Deasey?"

The guy's eyes widened a bit. Apparently he knew about Niall Deasey. "Ah, yeah, he has a garage down Coolgreaney Road. Now, you'd be more likely to find him at the pub this time of the day, mind. Try the Old Ship first."

The Old Ship was a busy, low-ceilinged pub, with a band setting up and a teenage barman who barely acknowledged me when I asked for a pint of Guinness. But he slid it across, perfectly pulled, five minutes later and ignored the pounds I left on the bar until I turned away.

Frank Sinatra was playing, "New York, New York," and an old guy pulled up to the bar was singing along, too loud, but in a lovely, on-pitch tenor. Everyone ignored him.

I drank the Guinness then got myself a whiskey and tried not to gulp it as I watched the patrons of the bar and willed Niall Deasey to appear.

There were a couple of groups of older men, laughing and telling stories, ribbing each other and buying each other rounds. I missed my dad suddenly, missed his easy humor, his smirky grin. A group of teenage girls at the next table over were talking about the young guy working behind the bar. "He was looking down your top, I'm telling you!"

"Sure, everyone in the place was looking down her top!" said another, and they dissolved in laughter.

And then the energy in the room changed. It was subtle, but every person in that room was aware that the door had opened and a big group of men had entered the pub. I heard shouted greetings and laughter but I didn't turn around immediately. Instead, I pretended to drop my sweater on the floor and stooped to pick it up, glancing quickly at the men coming in the door. There was a tall brown-haired guy, powerfully built, not handsome, and a shorter black-haired guy, both of them in their late twenties or early thirties. An older guy came in behind them, white-haired and barrel-chested, and a few younger guys trailed behind. They were mostly dressed alike in black jeans, leather jackets, short haircuts.

There was something about them, an encircling energy. They

walked in like they owned the bar, their bodies challenging the space, their eyes wary and darting. I knew what Sean saw in them at the Raven.

I was betting that the tall brown-haired guy was Niall Deasey. There was something about him that told me he was the boss. Everything was revolving around him. He was the center. The shorter black-haired guy resembled him in some undefinable way, the eyes maybe, or the shape of their foreheads. The older-looking guy and the younger guys all stood around for a minute waiting for their pints and chatting with the barman.

I tried to stay calm, sipping my whiskey and then turning slowly in my seat so I could get a view of them. One of the younger guys had blond hair flopping over his forehead and innocent blue eyes. *That's my guy*, I said to myself. *I can get that guy to talk to me.*

I caught his eye and he lingered for a moment before blushing and moving on. A few minutes later I caught him looking again. I played with my hair and met his stare before arching my back a bit and draining my whiskey. I was betting that if I could get him to want to buy me a drink, I'd get myself within spitting distance of Niall Deasey.

Frank moved on to "It Was a Very Good Year" and I waited a few minutes, then got up and headed for the ladies' room. It was a tiny closet at the back, the toilet and sink crammed in against the wall. I didn't actually have to go, but I sat on the toilet and counted to sixty, then got up, washed my hands, and slipped out into the dark and narrow hallway.

Bingo. He was coming out of the men's room and it was easy to bump into him as I went by and then turn, smiling, apologetic.

"I'm so sorry."

"No, you're fine. No worries." He gave me a smile and put a hand on the small of my back to steer me out of the way of an older woman coming through toward the restrooms. I stumbled a little. I'd had a few drinks now on my empty stomach.

"I like your jacket," I said. He was cute. I smiled up at him.

"You American?"

"Yeah. You can tell from the accent, huh?"

"You over on holiday?"

"Well, I have a lot of family here. In Dublin, but our grand-mother was from Wicklow and so I wanted to see what it was like."

"And what da ya think of it?" he asked politely. He was nervous; his right hand kept going up to tug his earlobe.

"I like it so far, but we'll have to see." I tried to say it flirty, with a little innuendo in it, but he just blushed and looked away again.

"I need another drink," I said, gesturing to the bar. "Do you . . . ?"

"Ah, sure, of course," he stammered. "What are you drinking? I'll get it for you."

"Guinness, please." A Guinness might help slow things down.

He nodded and I followed him up to the bar, where his friends had been watching us. Deasey wasn't there, though. He must have gone somewhere while I was in the bathroom. I gave them polite smiles, but I knew this depended on them egging him on a bit, so I looked back up at the blond guy in what I hoped was an adoring way.

"I'm Maggie, by the way," I told him when he handed me a fresh pint, the bubbles still rising from the bottom toward the head.

"John," he said quietly.

"You American?" the guy with the black hair asked.

"Yeah," I told him. "This is my first time in Arklow."

"What do you think of it? Bit of a tip, eh?" He had an English accent, not an Irish one, and I remembered Bernie saying something about Niall Deasey's father and London. I nodded and he looked back at John.

"That's my uncle Cathal," John said.

"Are you English?" I asked Uncle Cathal.

The question seemed to piss him off, but he forced a grin on. "I'm Irish as these fuckers. I just talk like the Queen of England on account of being raised there," he said. "Where are you from?" He checked me out and I feigned nervousness, looking away and then down at the floor. I wanted him to think that I had an innocent schoolgirl crush on John. "New York?" he guessed.

"Outside New York, Long Island."

"One of the lads went out to East Islip, now," the other young guy told me. "That's Long Island, right?"

"Yeah, that's not far from where I am."

There was a television mounted above the bar and a soccer game was playing. They all kept glancing up at it and John groaned when a goal was scored. "You like football?"

"Yeah." I had a long drink of my pint and he did, too, as though taking his cue from me.

Niall Deasey—if my instinct was right and that's who he was—still hadn't come back, and I was just about to order another beer for John when I felt the energy in the pub shift again.

It was fear that entered the room. Not abject fear, but the subtle undercurrent of the possibility of danger. Niall Deasey sauntered in and came up to us and said, "Who's this, then?"

"This is Maggie," Cathal said. "She's from New York. She and Johnny have been making friends."

"Is that so?" He smiled and shook my hand. "Niall Deasey." He was nearly six feet and he had a body that held power. His brown hair was cut short, showing off his broad skull and thick neck. His eyes were pale blue, intense. He searched my face for a moment, a quizzical look on it. He was confused. And that meant something. Because there was no reason to be confused here. He'd just met me. Unless he hadn't just met me. Unless he wasn't sure.

His eyes narrowed a little bit, still perplexed, and then he wiped the look right off his face, just erased it like it had never been there. And that told me something else. That told me he'd done this before—recognized someone, but pretended not to. It told me what kind of person he was and what kind of people he was involved with. I remembered Uncle Danny once telling me that there are two kinds of people: people who live in their own skin and people who wear their skin like a costume. He told me and Erin that we should always look out for people who didn't live in their own skin.

As I got older, I figured out what he meant. There were people who had an agenda. You felt it as soon as they looked you in the eye. It was a wariness, a way of keeping part of themselves protected.

Niall Deasey had it.

I finished my drink and immediately there was another one there. The men told stories. They laughed and kidded each other. I tried to go slow, but Uncle Cathal said, "Isn't your pint all right?" and winked at me as John kept nudging it closer. The pints snuck up on me and suddenly I realized that I was good and drunk. I didn't care, though. This was it. This was my chance.

"Do you follow the football?" one of the other young guys was asking. He swam in front of my eyes, his head splitting in two and then coming back together.

I heard the door of the pub open, was aware of the cold air sweeping in.

"Football?" I could hear myself slurring a bit. "Sorry, yeah."

"You okay there?" John asked. "You want to sit down somewhere?"

"No. No. I'm good." I took a deep breath, trying to get myself together.

I turned to John and tried to enunciate. "I'm going to Dublin next. Where should I go there?"

Suddenly, Niall Deasey was in front of me. He was studying me, looking me up and down. "What did you say your name was again?"

"Maggie."

"Have I met ya before?"

"Do I look familiar?"

"A bit." He stared at me some more.

I became aware that the band had started warming up. There were Christmas lights strung above them and each one looked incredibly bright, with a little halo of light around it. "Oh, they call it puppy love," someone was singing. John looked so embarrassed, I was worried he was going to run away, so I leaned in a little bit closer and said, "What's your favorite movie?" I carefully enunciated each word so I wouldn't slur.

"I liked *A Few Good Men*. Did you see that?" He seemed happy to have a topic of conversation. "Jack Nicholson's brilliant."

"Yeah, it was great."

"'You can't handle the truth!'" he said in what I thought was supposed to be an American accent, though it sounded more Australian.

"That's good," I told him. "You're good at that."

"Johnny wants to be a movie star, don't you, Johnny?" one of his friends called back and he put his arm around me and ignored them.

"He wants to go to America," someone else said.

"Well, you should call me if you come to America," I said, but he was looking at me strangely. I stumbled back. The room was turning slowly, like a strobe light. I could feel a wave of nausea rising up through my throat.

"I'm getting some air," I said. I rushed out the front of the pub and stood on the sidewalk for a minute. A couple of deep breaths helped. Everything stopped spinning for a minute.

The door opened.

I leaned against the outside wall of the pub. It was rough and cold. I closed my eyes to make everything stop spinning. But someone was standing in front of me.

Niall Deasey.

"I'd like to know who the fuck you are."

I opened my eyes slowly, forcing them to focus on him.

"What?"

"I'd like to know who the fuck you are?" Niall Deasey said.

"Uh, Maggie. I'm from New York."

He leaned in and studied my face and I knew what was happening. He was seeing the differences between me and Erin. And that told me he knew Erin.

"This is fuckin' mad, but . . . I think I've—" He stared at me again, then said, "What are you playing at?"

We stared at each other for a long moment and I realized that this might be my only chance. I had to know, so I looked him in the eye and I said, very slowly and deliberately, "I have a cousin who looks like me. Her name is Erin. Maybe you're thinking of her. Maybe you met her in Dublin? At the Raven?"

Something came over his face.

This is it, I told myself. *He knows.*

"Where is she?" I asked him in a low whisper.

"Why are you here? What the fuck do you want from me?" Niall Deasey said. Lights spun over his head. I could smell the whiskey on his breath. When he grabbed me by the arm and pushed me into the bricks, I felt a flash of pain in my shoulder.

"Where's Erin?" I asked him again, shouting now.

"I don't know what you're fuckin' talking about, but—" Everything was spinning. He let go of my arm and I stumbled away. I was drunk, but coherent enough to know that I had one chance to get it out of him. I swung at him and my fist made contact with his jaw. It took a second for me to realize what I'd done.

"What the fuck?" He went for me, getting me by the shoulders, and I could see and feel his anger. He was about to lose it. He narrowed his eyes and said, "You little bitch—"

Music came through an open door. The streetlights spun. *Erin. Is this what it was like? Is this what it was like to look up and see violence in someone's eyes? When did you know?*

Erin?

Erin?

Suddenly, someone was pulling him off me and I looked up to see Roly and Bernie standing there. "Let's leave it," Roly was saying in a low voice I could barely hear. "We're the Guards and we're willing to let you go back inside that pub if you just walk away right now."

Niall Deasey looked up at Roly, surprised, but he nodded and stepped back, turning and heading back into the pub.

"Don't let him go," I yelled at them. "What are you doing? Where is she?" I screamed after Niall Deasey as he disappeared inside, and Roly and Bernie led me away into the night.

Early fall.

We're sitting at the kitchen table when Uncle Danny calls. My mom answers the phone, tucking it under her chin while she brings a plate of chicken cutlets over from the stove, the long curly cord snaking across the linoleum.

"No, she's not here. I'll ask Maggie. Hang on, Danny." She puts the plate down in front of my dad and holds the phone at her side. "You see Erin today, sweetie? Danny says he just got a call from her guidance counselor that she wasn't at school, but he hasn't seen her."

My dad looks up. He's holding his gin and tonic and I can smell the clean silvery smell of the gin from across the table.

I shake my head. "I haven't seen her all day."

"And she didn't say anything to you?" My mom presses the phone against her leg so Uncle Danny can't hear.

"She doesn't talk to me," I whisper. My mom does something with her eyebrows.

"Hey, Dan," she says. "Maggie says she didn't see her today. Did you see her this morning?" She nods, murmurs something into the phone. My dad and I both have our heads up, listening. "Okay. Yeah, do that. Maybe Maggie can call around. Let us know if you want me to come down, okay?" She hangs up the phone, coiling the cord back in its spot in the corner.

She sits down and pushes the cutlets over to me. "She told him she was sleeping at Jessica's last night, but he just called Jessica's house and her mom said Erin hadn't been there."

My dad raises his eyebrows and serves the chicken.

"Can you call some of her friends?" my mom asks me. "Who else does she hang around with?"

"I don't know. Lisa? Jessica?"

"Should I call them?" My mom already has the phone book down and is flipping to the T's, looking for "Tyler."

"No, I'll do it." My mom calling them is worse than me doing it.

Lisa's mom answers and when I ask if I can talk to her, Lisa comes to the phone and tells me she hasn't seen Erin at all. Same with Jess.

Uncle Danny waits a long time to call the police. He thinks she's just going to come strolling in, full of apologies and kisses. But finally my mom makes him. They come to the house, interview all of us, ask for her friends' names.

The next day I don't go to school. I wait with my mom and Uncle Danny at our house. My mom makes tomato soup and grilled cheese and we wait by the phone until Uncle Danny says he might as well go to the bar.

Around eight that night, I hear a horn outside and go to the door to find Chris Fallon and Brian Lombardi in Chris's Chevy Blazer.

"Uh, can you help us out with something?" Chris asks when I go to the door. "Don't tell your parents."

"What is it?" I try to keep my voice neutral.

"I think I know where Erin is, but I need help. I can't find

Jess. Can you come with us?" I've never heard Chris Fallon sound so serious. Brian Lombardi doesn't look at me.

"Hang on. Let me get my coat."

I poke my head in the kitchen.

"Chris thinks he knows where she is," I tell my mom. "You can't tell Uncle Danny, though. I'm going with him. I'll call you if I need you."

"Oh thank God. Why don't I come, too?" my mom says, but my dad takes a long sip of his drink and says, "Let her go, Mo. She'll call if she needs us."

I don't ask any questions when I get into the Blazer. Chris gets on New York Avenue, heading toward the station. He's got Robert Palmer on the tape player.

Past the train station, he takes a left on a little side street off New York Avenue and pulls up in front of a low ranch house. There are three old cars out front, and kids' toys littered around.

"Who lives here?" I ask him.

He doesn't say anything.

"Why didn't you call the cops?"

He just raises his eyebrows at me and opens his door.

Inside, there are too many people. Two older guys, their arms covered in tattoos, are sitting around a low coffee table, smoking. One of them is completely bald. Lisa's in there, looking exhausted and sick and about twelve years old. "Hey, Maggie," she says when she sees me. "Can you talk to her?"

"Erin," I call out through the door. There's a crocheted doily hanging on the door with a little purple stone in the middle. "It's Maggie. Are you okay?" I can hear crying through the door. I try the handle, but it's locked.

"Mags," she whispers. I can hear her, but just barely. "I'm so sorry, Mags. I'm so sorry."

"It's okay," I tell her. "If you come out we'll take you home. Chris has a car."

"Mags," she whispers again.

But she won't open the door.

"I'm going to call the cops," I tell Brian and Chris. "What if she took something?"

"No way, man, no cops," one of the older guys says.

"Well, then you better break that door down right now."

"I'm not breaking the door. This is my mom's house."

"Give me the phone," Brian says.

"Don't call the cops, man." The bald guy looks terrified.

"I'm not. Give me the phone. I've got someone who can get her out of there."

Brian takes the phone into the kitchen.

We wait forever. I keep trying to talk to her through the door. And then headlights sweep across the windows.

Father Anthony comes in, wearing jeans and a black shirt. "It's okay, Maggie," he tells me. "We'll take care of her." I've never been so glad to see someone in my life.

He knocks on the door. "Erin, can you hear me? It's Father Anthony. I'm here to help you, to pray with you if you want."

There's a huge waiting silence in the house. And then the door opens. And as Father Anthony goes in, I can see Erin's hair and tearstained face for just a second before the door closes again.

32

1993

It was early morning by the time Roly parked Daisy's brother's car on Gordon Street and half carried me out. I had slept on the drive back, but I was still drunk when I woke up and I stood for a minute in front of the house and looked around. "Where's Bernie?"

"She drove my car back. Come on, now, let's get you inside. Where are your keys?"

"In my pocket." He got them out and opened the door.

"I don't think anyone's home. Here now, leave your coat. Which is yours?"

"Erin's," I told him. "That one is Erin's room. It's not mine at all."

"Okay." He got me into the room. "Now, you get into bed. I'm going to get you some water. You'll definitely want to drink some water."

When he came in, I was curled up under the comforter in my clothes. The room was spinning a bit, but not as badly as before.

"I'm sorry, Roly," I said. "I know I shouldn't have done that. It's just that I thought he could tell us where she is. I thought if he saw me, he'd tell me what happened."

"I know. But look here, we don't have any information that says she came to harm, D'arcy. You need to take a step back from this. You do."

"I know. I just . . . He recognized me, Roly. I know he did. I think he knows something."

"We'll keep an eye on him. Don't worry about that. There may be a way for us to do some discreet poking around now."

"I'm sorry," I said again. "How did you know where I was?"

"Bernie got worried after her conversation with you. We checked in with the roommates and they said you'd gone to visit a family friend." He smiled. "I figured out where you'd gone. We tried another pub before that one. Do you know what could have happened? Those fellas? At the very least you could have gotten into a fight outside a pub and been arrested."

"I know. I'm sorry. I'm not . . . My head's all messed up right now, Roly. I'm sorry."

"It's all right now, D'arcy." He sat down on the bed.

"Can you stay until I fall asleep?"

"Sure." He stretched out on the bed and I curled against him. There was something comforting about the solidity of his body. His heart beat beneath the soft fabric of his shirt. After a few minutes I heard his breathing slow and then the faint whistle of air through his nose.

The room darkened and I was aware of fewer and fewer sounds. Kids playing out in the street, a car horn somewhere, a dog barking far away. And then I was in Wicklow, striding across a stretch of boggy field. Gorse bushes were blooming and the sun was shining overhead in a cloudless blue sky, but in the distance I could see a bank of dark clouds threatening.

I was walking fast, as though I knew where I was going, but then I saw someone up ahead walking toward me. As I got closer, I realized it was Erin. She walked toward me, but she didn't seem to know I was there, even when I called her name. There was someone else walking behind her, a tall man with dark hair, in a dark jacket, but he was too far away for me to see his face. I tried to warn her, to get her to turn around and see that he was following, but she couldn't hear me, or pretended not to.

As she strode past me, I reached out to grab her arm, but she shook me off and kept going. I followed and suddenly we were at a church, stone outside, with beautiful stained-glass windows and red carpeting inside. The church was empty except for a priest kneeling at the altar, but I couldn't see his face. Erin went to him and knelt down next to him. I called her name again, but suddenly the church filled with colored light. "Erin!" I called out. "Erin!"

I was coming awake. I heard a key in the front door and then a voice saying, "Sorry, how long have you been waiting?" I was still half in the dream, my body heavy, paralyzed.

A phone rang. It was Emer talking. My head was pounding. It took me a minute to wake up. The phone rang again. Someone was opening the bedroom door. "I don't think she's here," Emer was saying. "She's been away. You're welcome to check if you want—Oh!" And then she gasped and I opened my eyes to find Emer standing there with Conor. The phone was still ringing.

Sit up. My body responded slowly. Roly's arm was under my shoulder.

Conor's eyes were wide. He looked away. He murmured an apology and turned to the door.

"Conor," I started to say. "There's nothing—" But he was turning and running out of the house, out through the open door and before I could get out of bed to get him, the answering machine clicked on and we were all listening as Uncle Danny's voice filled the flat.

"Maggie, baby. I'm so sorry." He was stammering, nervous, upset. I pushed Roly out of the way, jumping up, going for the phone, but I didn't make it before we all heard his voice, raspy and devastated. "I wish I didn't have to do this, but you got to call me, baby. Your dad, he—Maggie, sweetie. He had a heart attack, baby. I'm so sorry. God, I'm sorry. He's gone, baby. You gotta give me a call."

My mom's bed has been in the den for the last four months, spring air coming in the open windows. We fill the room with flowers but it still smells like a hospital. My dad can't take it for long. He sits with her at night, drinking gin and tonics, one right after the other, and watching her sleep. During the day, he goes into the city. I sit with her, read, deal with the nurses, check in every night with my boyfriend back at Notre Dame, a sweet younger guy from Minneapolis named Josh who I will tell not to come out for the funeral and who will be perplexed and hurt when I break up with him over the phone and don't come back to school.

The lilacs bloom in May and I am so grateful for that, for the smell of lilacs in the windows. Erin comes a month before my mom dies, on a red eye from LA paid for by Uncle Danny. She comes home with a lot of stuff and I suspect she's not going back.

She hugs me when she arrives, and goes to sit with my mom. My mom perks up for a few days after Erin gets home, and Uncle Danny brings her baked ziti from D'Allesandro's and she eats a little. She asks us to ease off the pain meds and for a few days it's okay. She sits up and we even take her down to the beach in a wheelchair to sit on the sand.

One night, I go to take a shower and come back to hear Erin murmuring and my mom's weak voice answering back. I am washed by a wave of envy that horrifies me. When Erin comes out of the den, she's crying. She goes out and doesn't come back that night.

Uncle Danny is the one to tell my dad he should stay home, that we're getting close. I don't know how he knows it, but I am grateful. My dad rises to the occasion, starts sleeping in the hospital bed with her, holds her when she's afraid. He stops drinking.

My mom says to me, "I love him like crazy. I always have. It's so, so clear to me. Your dad. Your dad."

But Erin disappears. She comes to the house high, pretending she's not. Uncle Danny takes her in the other room and I hear them fighting in low voices. Then I hear the front door slam and he's gone.

One night, I'm singing to my mom—"Red Is the Rose"—I sang it sometimes in a bar in South Bend and I've always loved the tune. She sings along as best she can, her voice weak.

Come over the hills, my bonnie Irish lass
Come over the hills to your darling
You choose the road, love, and I'll make a vow
And I'll be your true love forever.

My dad is stroking my mom's hand. His eyes are closed. I know he's trying to fix this moment in his mind.

The phone rings and it's someone from the bar, looking for Uncle Danny. I hear him talking on the kitchen phone. "Where?" he asks. "Is she okay?"

When he comes back to the den, he whispers to us that Erin's been arrested for DUI. He's had a few whiskeys, "to cope," he says. He doesn't think he can drive.

I tell my dad I'll take Danny. I kiss my mom and then Danny and I drive to Suffolk County Police headquarters on the County Road. They bring Erin out. Her face is dirty and there's mascara under her eyes. Her arms are covered with scratches, one of them red and bleeding. She reeks of beer.

"Thank you, Daddy. I'm so sorry. Sorry, Maggie." She starts crying again, her shoulders heaving. I'm so angry I can't even look at her. I wait while Uncle Danny signs the papers he needs to sign, while they explain about how Erin will have to appear in court. We drive home in complete silence and drop Erin at Uncle Danny's house before going back to sit with my mom.

At the funeral, Erin's friends sit together in a middle pew. I hug Jessica and Lisa and Brian and ask questions about college and their families. When everyone comes back to our house afterwards, Erin stands off to the side and slips out early.

The sea is wild that spring. There are strange, unseasonable storms that batter the house and I start going down to stand on the beach, feeling the sting of the rain on my face, the wind whipping my hair. I start running once my dad goes back to work, pounding down the beach at low tide, then heading up into the streets above the beach, running until my muscles shake.

All that summer and fall, Erin is hardly around. I don't know where she goes. I start picking up shifts at the bar. She comes in sometimes but we hardly speak to each other.

My dad is a mess. I don't go back to college in September, make arrangements to finish my coursework from home.

I want to ask Erin what my mom said to her. I want to ask her if she's sorry. I want to ask her if she's given up on finding Brenda. I never do.

In November she announces she's moving to Ireland.

Ireland.

Ireland.

33

THURSDAY, JUNE 2,
2016

The wind is whipping dead leaves all around the park. Conor and I stand there just staring at each other for a moment and then he seems to remember the boy and he says, "Adrien, you take Mr. Bean," and he looks back at me and says, "Maggie?"

I don't know what to do. I can't hug him. I nod and say, "Conor . . ."

"I'm surprised to see—" he starts. "It's good to see you. I don't quite know what to say. You look just the same. I would have known you anywhere."

"It's good to see you, too."

His hair has thinned back toward his crown and it's half gray, but his eyes are the same and his grin is, too, and the stooping lean of his shoulders and his thin face. His voice.

"I . . . Look, my son is . . . Let me walk him home and maybe we can . . . Do you have time for a cup of tea?" He's very flustered now. The boy is holding the dog's leash and Conor looks at him and says, "Adrien, this is an old friend of mine. Maggie, this is my son, Adrien." His voice is practically shaking. The boy shakes my hand. He's tall and thin, but he doesn't look much like Conor. He's fairer and his face is rounder, his eyes blue. *Bláithín Arpin.*

"I'll walk home with you and Beanie and then Maggie and I will go and have a chat," he says.

The boy nods and we all walk out of the park together and toward the main road. I can't resist looking at Adrien. *Conor's son.* "Why don't I meet you there?" He points to a bakery and coffee shop on the other side of the road and I nod. "Ten minutes," he says. "The house is just up there." I watch him go, my heart pounding, a strange metallic taste suddenly filling my mouth.

I order a coffee and ask to use the bakery's bathroom.

In the mirror over the sink my eyes look lined, bruised. My hair is crazy from the wind and I comb it as best I can. I soak a paper towel with cold water and wet my face, then dry it. I chew some gum and spit it out and put on lipstick, then rub most of it off. It's a little better, not much. With my coffee, I stake out a table by the window. It's five minutes before he's back. I see him coming down the street and I feel my whole body seize up, adrenaline running through my veins. I pretend to be looking at a newspaper someone left on the counter so he won't see me watching him.

And then the door is jingling and he's there. "Hello," he says. He's wearing a black wool overcoat, a green-and-brown tartan scarf.

"Hi."

"Will I get you a tea?"

"I've got coffee."

"Okay. Hang on, then." I stare down at the newspaper while he's gone. The one time I look up, he's leaning over the counter, ordering, handing the money over.

And then he's here, sitting down and shrugging off his overcoat and I can smell him, soap and deodorant and the outdoors.

"You look exactly the same. I'm just . . . It's very strange seeing you again," he says. "I've seen the stories the last week or so. About the remains in Wicklow. Are you here as part of the investigation?"

"I am. As you probably saw, it's not Erin, but there may be some developments in her case, too."

"I'm so sorry. I heard about the search in Wicklow and it brought it . . . it brought that time back." He looks away and drinks his coffee, then sets it down and looks back at me. We're staring at each other. We can't look away.

"When did you get here?" he asks.

"What? Last Thursday, I guess. It's so strange to be back. My old . . . Erin's old neighborhood. It's all so different."

"It is. I forget sometimes. But it must look so different to you. All the new buildings. It's grand, I think, lots of different languages, different people, different countries. Half of my son's schoolmates come from somewhere else. We're a better country for it, that part is grand. It was the end of something, you know, when you were here, the nineties. I sound like a proper oul' fella, don't I? How are you?"

"Good. I'm a detective with a big police department on Long Island. Suffolk County. I investigate homicides across the county."

He looks away, waits, then grins sheepishly. "I knew that, actually. I saw a story a few years ago, about that case. About what you did. I recognized your name and I wondered. There was a picture, so . . ." He shrugs. I feel a little thrill. *I wondered.*

But I don't want to go there. I change the subject. "What about you?"

"I'm a professor at Trinity. I teach history and write. I'm just off a sabbatical but it's nice to be back." I could admit that I know, too, but I don't. I don't want him to bring up Bláithín Arpin.

Quick, before I second-guess myself, I say, "To work on your opus on chickens in Irish history, I imagine. I've been waiting for it, you know. Checking the bookstores every year."

He laughs. "There are just so many of them. It's taking me an awfully long time."

"What are you really working on?"

"Twentieth-century Irish political history, mostly."

"Is Adrien your only child?"

"Yes, he is. What about you?"

"I have an only, too. Lilly. She's fifteen. She's amazing."

"I'm sure she is." He smiles and I remember everything about his face, the way his upper lip is thinner than his lower lip, the way his nose is an elegant line running uninterrupted from his forehead, the lines from the sides of his nose to his mouth when he smiles.

I've finished my coffee and so has he. We stare at each other. We don't say anything. Outside the plate-glass window, I can see the wind whipping the trees. "I have so many things I want to ask you," he says finally. "But I need to get back to Adrien. Might we . . . Might I take you to dinner? Tomorrow evening, maybe?"

"Yeah, yes," I say. "Here, I'll give you my number." He hands over his phone and I put myself in his contacts. "I think you have to dial something first."

Outside, we stand on the sidewalk for a long moment, just staring at each other. "I'll see you," I say finally.

"Yeah, I'll ring you," he says. Something crosses his face, distress, sadness. I wonder if he's thinking about Erin. We walk off in opposite directions. I get back to the hotel and don't remember anything about the walk back.

34

On the morning news, they report that gardaí are continuing the search for Niamh Horrigan in Wicklow.

Thirteen days.

She's been gone thirteen days.

I eke out a slow five miles around the city, running alongside the Grand Canal all the way to Dolphin's Barn, then taking the little residential streets as they come, all the way back to the hotel. The run helps to get rid of my nerves, my anxiety at being displaced from the investigation. I know everyone down in Wicklow, as well as Roly and his team and everyone else working to find Niamh, are chipping away at the case, but after two days of total immersion, I don't like not knowing what they're up to.

Later, dressed in jeans and a black silk top I bought at a store on Grafton Street, I look at my eyes in the mirror. They're lined, tired. Still me. I remember his face from the park yesterday, older Conor. Still Conor.

Bláithín Arpin.

He's just being polite. An old friend. He knows about the investigation. He feels sorry for you. Of course he wants to take you to dinner. It doesn't mean anything. I put on lipstick and mascara, send Lilly an *I love you* text, and walk up toward St. Stephen's Green, through the early evening sun and after-work crowds.

He's waiting when I get there. "Can we walk a little?" he asks, and I nod. It's Friday night. The air is warm, the park is full of people, strolling, talking, celebrating the end of the week. Griz told me that down in Wicklow, people won't let their daughters go out alone. But here, it's like nothing's happened.

Walking next to Conor, I keep stealing glances. His graying hair. The way the angled light shows the lines next to his eyes. He's just a middle-aged man. I might not look twice at him if I passed him on the street.

But then he looks over at me and smiles and I remember his mouth, his skin, his back. I must blush. "I don't even know where to start," he says. "I have so many questions." A hesitation. "Are you, are you married?"

"Divorced," I say, too quickly.

"I am as well." I feel my heart leap when he says it. *Bláithín Arpin.* "Well, just about. We've been separated for quite a long time."

"I'm sorry. Is your son okay with it?"

"It's been tricky. You?"

"Yeah, I think she's happier this way. We get along well. But . . . tell me about your sheep farm. Are your parents still alive?"

"Ah, yeah. My da still does all the chores. My mam helps him. They're still going strong. Adrien and I are going home to see them in a couple weeks." He touches my shoulder to steer me out of the way of a group of teenagers, laughing and taking up the walkway.

"Do you still go and stand on the edge of the field and watch the sunset?"

He turns to look at me, his eyes wide. "I'd forgotten I told you that. I did, didn't I?"

"When I think about you, that's how I think about you," I tell him.

"I do still stand there. Every time I'm home. It's changed. Someone put up a holiday house. Someone else let a field grow up. But I can still see the hills."

We've stopped walking. We're just standing there, in the middle of the walkway, staring at each other.

Finally, he says, "I was thinking about you, all day. I couldn't sit down. I couldn't do anything else. Adrien asked me what was wrong and I didn't know what to say. I hope that's all right to say."

"I couldn't stop thinking about you, either."

He looks down at me. Then his hands are on my shoulders. "There's something I have to say."

"Yeah?" I'm holding my breath.

"I was completely fucking in love with you." He breathes out, as though he can't believe he said it. "It's terrible of me to say it. I was with Bláithín but I, right from the beginning, I was drawn to you. It felt like—"

I'm tripping over myself. "I was completely fucking in love with you, too. It was twenty-three years ago. But I can remember it exactly. It's—That first time, at the café—" I want to say that I can still feel it, this thing, like some kind of exotic animal. I can feel it hovering between us, levitating on invisible wings.

"Shite." He grins.

"Yeah, shite." I grin back. "Was that what you were going to tell me, that night when you came to the house?"

"I guess so. I was ready to tell Bláithín we were through and I went for pints with some friends from college and I guess I'd had a few and I just wanted to tell you. I wanted to say it."

"And then you came in and Roly and I were in bed." I hide my head in my hands. "I did something really stupid that night. I got really drunk. He brought me home and he was tired. There was absolutely nothing there. Just the friendship. A really good friendship. I replayed that moment over and over in my head. I wrote you letters, a few of them, to the café, to explain, and I thought after I wrote you and I didn't hear back that you'd come for some other reason, that it had to do with Erin or something. And then . . ." I tell him about my dad, about everything. In the sliver of light coming from a streetlight, I see something flash across his face. A quick grimace of pain.

"I never went back to the café," he says. "I . . . We moved to Paris for a year."

We stop walking. We're holding each other's hands suddenly, our fingers rubbing circles on each other's skin, and then we're kissing. Time folds in on itself. We're on the beach at Sandymount. The wind is blowing. He's holding my face. We're in Erin's bedroom. He's looking at me. He's stroking my face. We're kissing again. Harder. Hungrier. The air smells of apple blossoms.

When we break apart, we laugh and start walking again, hand in hand now. "We'd better get to the restaurant," he says. "I know you're a cop and all, but a charge for public indecency isn't going to help my career any."

* * *

It's dark, cozy, a second-story place off Dawson Street decorated with black-and-white photographs of 1950s and '60s Dublin. We order gin and tonics and salmon for dinner. He tells me he had to take Adrien to Bláithín's parents' house in Brittas Bay and it took longer than he thought.

"I'm not going to complain about my soon-to-be-ex-wife on a date," he says. "But it's not an easy situation."

"I don't think it ever is," I tell him. "I know a woman who was so angry at her ex that she hid opened cans of tuna all over his house. She was a completely normal woman, but she broke into his house and hid them in, like, really impossible places so that he would never find them."

"Tuna?"

"It started to rot and his house smelled terrible. He couldn't figure out what it was and he tried everything but it just kept getting worse and worse."

"That's awful. Did he deserve it?"

"I don't even know. He always seemed like a perfectly nice guy to me. According to her, he did."

"Do you and your ex get on, then?"

"Now we do. But it took a while. He was really angry for a long time. I didn't feel much of anything. I kept hoping he'd find someone else so I wouldn't have to feel sorry for him. I was so guilty for so long. We didn't really have much in common, but after Erin, and my dad, Brian was very kind to us, to me and Uncle Danny, and I guess I mistook that for . . . well, for the real thing." I can't help flashing back to the night Brian came into the bar, how I surprised myself by being happy to see him, by laughing, by having fun for the first time in a very, very long time. "We got pregnant and got married and . . . a few years in, he still loved me and I didn't love him and there was nothing I could do. It would have been better if I'd cheated on him. But now things are pretty good. He's staying at my house with Lilly right now."

"Did he ever find anyone?"

"He's had a few girlfriends. Nothing serious."

"And you?"

"Nothing very serious. There was this man in Ireland, you see, who I kept thinking about."

"Is that right? Tell me about him."

"Mmmmm. Well, I actually don't know him all that well. That's the thing."

"That is the thing, isn't it?"

We stare at each other for a long moment. Then our food comes and without talking about it, we sort of start again, talking about work, about our kids. I tell him about Lilly. He tells me about Adrien.

"He's been to so many therapists and doctors and I think what it comes down to is that he's got anxiety. Things at home were bad until Bláithín moved down to Wicklow and then he hit puberty and it's just been . . . fucking rough, actually . . . But he's better now. He seems to have evened out a bit. He likes his school."

We have another drink each when we're done with dinner and then we walk down Dawson Street and through Trinity. He takes my hand in Parliament Square and we stop to kiss underneath the statue of Lecky.

"Do you think we're horrifying the young ones?" he murmurs. "Old people kissing in public?"

"Probably." Kissing him feels both familiar and strange. *Cold air. Apples. Conor's sweater.*

"Maybe you'd better come up to the hotel, so we don't horrify these poor young people."

He smiles and tucks my hand under his arm. "It really is the least we can do."

I wake up at three, the feel of another body in my bed unfamiliar. Streetlights shine through the open curtains and I get up to close them, then snuggle up against Conor's back under the covers, finding the curve of his back again, the weight of his arms, the dip of his stomach.

"You're not going anywhere, are you?" he murmurs.

"Uh-uh," I whisper. "I'm not going anywhere."

"Okay," he whispers. "Okay."

....

My junior year of high school, I can't stop thinking about Brian Lombardi. When I see him at school, I feel anxious, unsettled, exhilarated. He always says hi, giving me a shy smile that I replay over and over and over again throughout the day.

One day in early spring, Brian and I walk to the corner store to get a snack before taking the late bus home. Erin and another senior named Alex Tsakos are smoking outside and when she sees us, something crosses her face. I can't read it. But later, I'm doing homework on our deck and she comes out and sits next to me.

"I had to give your mom money from my dad," she says. "So, what's up with you and Brian Lombardi? Do you like him?"

I can't lie to Erin. "I guess," I say.

"I think he likes you, too. He was asking me if you like anyone."

"Really?" I can't help the soaring hope that rips through me. Erin gets up and goes to the edge of the deck, looking out across the Sound. She's wearing shorts and I can see the strong lines of her legs, the delicate curve of her feet in flip-flops. I wish she'd look at me, tell me she misses me, come over and put a hand on my shoulder. Anything.

"Well, see ya," she says. And she's gone. It's the way she always goes from anywhere, slipping quietly out of view, leaving a hole where she'd been standing.

A summer night, a couple of weeks later. There's a party

on the beach. Someone's parents are away, is all I know. My friend Helen and I walk down from my house, find the light from a fire, try to identify the featureless figures in the dark. We're juniors now and we don't feel as stupid at these parties. The seniors have stopped caring about who's popular and who's not. They'll talk to anyone now.

By the firelight, I find Brian on the sand. He's got two beers and he hands me one. We drink in awkward silence. We both know that there's something here. I wonder if Erin's said anything to him. I imagine her saying, "My little cousin has the hots for you, Lombardi." It makes me feel ashamed to think of it.

"What are you doing this summer?" I ask him. "Before college?"

"Working for my dad," he says. "Hanging out. You going to be around?"

"Yeah, working at the beach probably."

"Well, we'll have to hang out a lot." He turns so he's standing next to me and I feel his hand snake around to the small of my back. He rests it there.

"Hey, little cuz," Erin shouts at me. Brian takes his hand back and we both look up at her. She's drunk, really drunk, and she's stumbling on the sand, coming toward us. "How are you guys doing?"

"Okay," I say. "You all right?"

"I'm fine." She's slurring a little, but she's not so drunk that she doesn't pick up on the tension between us. She gets a little grin on her face and then she reaches up to touch Brian's face. "You okay, Brian? You doing okay?"

"Yeah." He laughs nervously.

She looks at me then and she lets me see that she's putting an arm around Brian, squeezing his butt.

"You should go home," she says to me. "It's late. Too late for little girls."

Her words are a slap.

I look at Brian, but he refuses to meet my eyes.

"Come on, you should go home," she says. "Shouldn't she, Brian? Stuff happens late at night." She's running her fingers through his hair now.

Brian keeps his eyes down. He doesn't look at either of us.

There's a long silence.

Someone shouts at the other end of the beach.

Erin's looking up at Brian now, rubbing his cheek. He looks embarrassed. He still won't meet my eyes.

I feel tears welling and I mumble something at them, then turn and run all the way home.

35

Conor and I stay in bed all morning, fortified by room service coffee and scones.

We watch the news, our legs entangled under the covers. The newscasters remind viewers that Niamh Horrigan has been gone for fourteen days now. They're trying not to say it, to say that Teresa McKenny was held for fourteen or fifteen days before she was killed, June Talbot for sixteen or seventeen. Instead they say, "The Gardaí are concerned about the length of time Niamh has been missing. In Wicklow, surrounded by family and friends, her parents wait for news. And pray for her safe return." I imagine Roly and Griz and Joey and Regan and everyone, following up on the Herricks lead, getting CCTV footage, checking whatever alibi he might have given them.

We walk out to Sandymount Strand and have lunch at a little café on the green. Conor buys papers and I read the *Independent* while he looks through the *Irish Times*. Stephen Hines has a story with some good scoops in it in the *Independent*. He knows about

Robert Herricks and though he doesn't name Herricks, he writes that "gardaí are also searching the home of a Baltinglass man said to be a person of interest in the Horrigan disappearance."

Conor drops me at Grand Canal Dock and I sit on a bench in the sun, returning emails from home. I'm meeting Emer at her office at two.

The Triventa building is huge, the front made up of windows. There's a coffee shop next door and outside, a small group of young people stand around, speaking English with different accents, drinking coffee from paper cups.

I stand near the entrance and a few minutes later I hear a voice calling, "Maggie!"

It's Emer, her blond hair short now, her face thinner. She's wearing a black blazer and jeans. She gives me a quick hug and stands back. "You look just the same. Let's get coffee. I've been working today to catch up from my trip but it's always like this on the weekend. This lot have no lives to speak of."

We get lattes and find a table. I say, "That's your office next door? It's amazing."

"I know. I've been here a couple of years and I still have to pinch myself sometimes. I'm seriously one of the oldest people here." We sit down and she waves at someone across the room.

Finally she says, "So . . . ?"

"Sorry, as you probably know, I'm over because they've found some new evidence in Erin's case," I say.

"I saw. Do they think it's connected to this other woman who's missing?"

"They don't know. I assume the Guards have gotten in touch with you a few times over the years?"

"Yes. Not as recently, though. Detective, uh, McNeely, I think her name is. She rang me up a few times, to ask me if I'd ever heard a name or of a restaurant or pub. I assumed they were following up on tips."

"And you never did?"

"No."

"What about Daisy? Did they ask her?"

She hesitates, frowns, then says, "I think they did, yeah. They must have done."

"And you didn't think of anything or remember anything more that could have helped? It's funny. Over the years, I've thought a lot about Erin's decision to go down to Glenmalure. It just seemed so . . . sudden, as though someone must have called her and told her to meet them down there or as though she met someone. But in your statement, you said there weren't any messages. So why did she go down there?"

"I don't know, Maggie. I can't tell you the number of times I've given out to myself about not ringing her da earlier. I just keep thinking that if we'd rung him up the first night she didn't come home, then . . ."

"I didn't mean that at all," I tell her. "She'd done it before, so it didn't seem strange to you. She was an adult. She wasn't in the habit of telling you where she was going."

She smiles gratefully. "As my friends have had kids, and the kids have become teenagers, I just keep thinking about how the parents know where they are every second, with mobiles and social media, like. I don't even know if you could disappear like that again. If she'd gone traveling, she would have been posting pictures of her trip on Instagram and we would have been liking them and telling her to have a pint for us."

"It's true. You can't imagine how social media, camera phones, all that have changed police work." I take a sip of my coffee. "There isn't anything else you've thought of over the years, is there? We're a bit desperate. If we can figure out what happened to Erin, we may be able to help find Niamh Horrigan."

"So they think she . . ." Emer's eyes dart away, troubled.

"It's the logical assumption. Erin didn't ever talk about being afraid or thinking someone was following her, did she?"

I can see Emer thinking. "I . . . don't think so, but . . . you might want to check with Daisy. I have this memory of her saying something to Daisy, but I can't think what it was. It must not have been anything very important or Daisy would have said at the time."

"Maybe it was about Hacky O'Hanrahan? It was Daisy who spoke to him when he called, right?"

"Maybe." She doesn't sound convinced, though. "It's funny about him. I was in a meeting with him a few years ago and I remembered that he'd maybe been seeing Erin. He was putting together some deal with an American technology company and I was brought in to talk about the developers."

"Did you say anything?" I was curious how he'd reacted if she'd asked about Erin.

"No. It would have seemed mad. It wasn't my meeting."

"But you never met him, right? He never came to the house?"

"I don't think so. But I remembered the name. It was funny to be sitting across from him."

She tells me about her job as a programmer and I tell her about

Lilly and my job. We're like two old friends, catching up. For a little bit, we forget why we're talking.

"How *is* Daisy?"

Emer drains her coffee cup. "She lives in Germany now. Her wife is German and they have a lovely little boy. I get cards from them, but we haven't talked in years."

It's the way she says "wife"—a little hesitant, a little challenging—that makes me search her face. There's something there that makes me realize what I'd missed twenty-three years ago.

"Hang on, were you and Daisy a couple?" I ask her. "You were."

She laughs. "Oh God, it must have seemed so odd to you. I'm sure it did to Erin, too. Yeah, we were in love. Or lust, I suppose. No, love." She smiles a little. "We came to Dublin and got the place together because we wanted to be together for school. But neither of us was ready to be out yet, so we snuck around. Poor Erin. I think we made her really uncomfortable. She must have picked up on something, but we were so closeted—I was terrified my mam and dad would find out—and I think we gave her the idea we didn't want her around. I've felt badly about that, that we weren't friendlier."

I'm surprised, but it instantly makes sense. The silences, the way I always felt like I was intruding when I was at the flat. I *had been* intruding. They just wanted to be alone.

"Oh God, I'm so sorry," I say. "It's terrible, but I had no idea. I overheard you whispering once. You spoke in Irish and I understood a few words. Something about a secret and wondering if Erin knew."

"We couldn't tell if Erin knew," she says. "Or if she'd told you. We didn't know what to do. I didn't come out for a good five years after that. I think Daisy was longer. Her parents are really conservative. But they're fine now. She fell in love with a German woman at her first job out of college. They got married a few years ago and live in Aachen. They have a little boy. He's darling. Her mam and dad love him."

"And how about you? I was happy to see the news on marriage equality."

"Yeah, it was fantastic, wasn't it? My girlfriend and I have been together ages but we haven't taken the plunge yet. We'll see. It's amazing to me to think how far this country's come in twenty years. Are you married? You didn't say."

"Divorced. I got Lilly out of it, though. My ex and I get along well, so it's okay." I almost tell her about Conor.

And then she says, "I've wondered over the years how you were, whether there was anything new. I wonder and I . . . like to think she did just take a ferry or a plane somewhere and that she's happy. Really happy. I hope you don't mind."

"I like to think that, too," I say. "Erin could be so . . . You never knew what to expect. But when she was happy, she was like a beautiful kite on a perfect day, you know? She could be filled up with joy."

"I saw that once," she says. "Not long after she moved in. She'd been out for a walk and she came back, her cheeks pink, her hair all blown by the wind. She was laughing and she said, 'Emer, I love Ireland! I love it here!' It was so American, you know? That's what I thought at the time. But that's how I like to think of her. That happy and all."

She walks me to the main door and tells me goodbye. When I turn around to wave, she's smiling sadly.

36

SUNDAY, JUNE 5,
2016

Stephen Hines is in front of the hotel when I walk Conor down.
We've been holed up in my room since last night and I look up from
kissing him goodbye to find Hines standing in front of the main
hotel entrance, pretending to check his phone but watching us with
a small smile on his face.

"Detective D'arcy," he says, once Conor's gone. "Good morning.
Can I ask what you think about the search of a house in Baltinglass
yesterday? Is it related to your meeting with the Horrigans?"

"No comment." I push past him and take a right on Fleet Street.

He follows me, keeping a respectful distance, but calling after
me, "Did you find out anything during your review? Was that you
who identified Robert Herricks?"

People on the sidewalk are starting to turn to look at us. I stop
and spin around. "No comment," I say. "I'm sure you can appreciate
that Garda investigations have to be kept confidential."

Something flashes behind his eyes. They narrow a little, angry.

"Surely there's something you can tell me. I helped to get you involved, after all, Detective D'arcy."

"The Horrigans got me involved."

"Why are they looking at Robert Herricks? He's never been on anyone's radar before. It must have something to do with you."

I meet his eyes. "No comment," I say. But I don't like what I see there. He had a plan for me. He got me into the investigation and I was supposed to give him information. I didn't go along with it and he doesn't like that one bit.

◆　◆　◆

Later, after Conor's checked in with Adrien, we drive up to Howth to walk on Howth Head. It's overcast but not raining and the gorse along the cliffs is dark yellow, the greens rich and saturated. It feels good to get my heart rate going, and we walk through a residential neighborhood and then up along the cliffs, with the sea below us.

"Where are the rhododendrons?" I ask him as we kiss on the edge of the path. "I was led to believe there would be rhododendrons."

He pretends to look around. "No, no, no, no. Don't see any."

"No, I said. No!"

We laugh. The sky is huge above us.

"I'm so happy," I whisper into his chest. I'm not sure he hears me, but he pulls me in closer and holds my head against him. We have Irish coffees at a pub by the water and then we drive back down along the coast, the sea to our left, the sun streaming in the window. I close my eyes, let it warm me. Conor holds my right hand as he drives, rubbing little circles on the top of my hand.

"How's the investigation going?" he asks me later. We're lying in bed at his house, listening to Miles Davis and eating fried eggs and beans on toast. I'm wearing one of his shirts. He's wearing a pair of trousers and nothing else. I reach out to touch his chest. *Conor.*

"Slow. They have a few leads. But time is passing. It's horrifying, what her parents are going through."

"But the body they found. It's not Erin, right?"

"No. It's a German woman who we're now trying to trace."

He looks down at me. "A German woman? What does that have to do with Erin?"

"We don't know."

Now he's tracing my C-section scar with his finger. "Lilly?" he asks. There's something strange and delicious about hearing him say her name.

"Yeah. It was an emergency one. I'd been in labor for hours and hours and her heart rate started dropping and they finally just said she had to come out right away. Her cord was wrapped around her neck."

"Did you ever think about having another?"

"Not really. I think I knew the marriage wasn't going to survive. And it was a bitch, trying to work homicide squad and parent in those early days."

"I bet."

"How about you?"

"I think we might have. But Bláithín hemorrhaged with Adrien and we felt lucky they both survived. And I think I'd started to have doubts, too." He says it carefully.

I want to ask more about that, but I'm not ready.

"Tell me about being a professor. Do you like it?"

"I do." He puts his plate on the bedside table and pulls me over and into his arms. "There's politics and all that, but I love teaching and I love researching and writing and I get to do those things at least some of the time."

"What are you researching right now?"

"I'm working on a book about the Arms Crisis."

"When was that?"

"Nineteen seventy."

"I don't know about it. What happened?"

"Well, ministers in the government of Taoiseach Jack Lynch were sacked when it was discovered that they were helping to smuggle arms to the north. It set off a power struggle and split Lynch's political party. One of them was Charlie Haughey, who went on to become taoiseach later. But it kind of showed up this split in opinion in the Republic about how involved we should be in the north."

He turns out the light and we settle in under the covers. His arms feel good around me. He's warm and clean-smelling, and he holds my arms tight against him.

"I missed you all day," he whispers. "I don't want you to go anywhere."

I fall asleep curled against him, the length of me against the long, naked length of him, and sometime later I wake to darkness, my phone in the pocket of my jeans ringing and buzzing as though it's having a personal crisis. I jump out of bed, the cold air hitting my body like a bucket of water.

"Hello?"

"Mom?"

"Hi, Lil," I whisper. "Is everything okay?" I check Conor's bedside clock: 4:11.

"Yeah. You didn't call last night."

"I was so busy. I'm sorry. I meant to and then I knew you wouldn't be home yet. And then I was really tired so I went to bed early." I sneak out into the hallway, trying to navigate the unfamiliar surroundings. I pad down the stairs, whispering, so I won't wake up Conor, and I sit in the dark at the bottom of the long flight of stairs, smiling when my eyes light on the spot where we tore each other's clothes off when I first came in.

"How's school going?"

"Good," she says. "Play tryouts are next week and I've been practicing a monologue from *Twelfth Night* to do."

"What's the play?"

"*Little Shop of Horrors,* but Mr. Anderson looooves Shake-speare."

"Maybe you could do it with a big plant on the stage or some-thing."

"Mom."

I laugh, trying to keep it down. "I miss you so much, Lil." I do. I want to tell her about Conor. Tell her I'm in love. But of course I don't.

"Dad had a job interview today," she says. "At Shaver's market. To be a manager or something." I can hear the hope and pity in her voice. She loves him so much. She wants him to be happy.

"That's great."

We chat about school, a movie she saw with her friend Ava.

"I love you, Lil," I tell her. "Is your dad still awake? I want to just ask him a quick question." She hands the phone over. "Bri?"

"Yup. Everything okay?"

"Yeah. How's Danny?"

"He's holding up. Lilly made some cookies for him and we'll drop them off tomorrow."

I take a breath. "Everything's good? You're setting the alarm and everything?"

"Yeah. Everything's quiet."

"Thanks, Bri. Take care. I'll talk to you soon, okay?"

I check emails on my phone. There's one from Emer. She says she called Daisy after our conversation. *It was nice to chat, actually,* she writes. *I asked her if she remembered saying something to me once about Erin thinking someone was following her or after her. I didn't have it exactly right. She said that she got home and Erin was on the phone with someone. When Daisy came in, Erin got off the phone with whoever it was and Daisy asked her if she was okay—she said she looked annoyed. Erin just said something like, "Oh, some people just don't know when to stop pushing." She didn't seemed scared or anything so Daisy didn't think she needed to tell anyone. She had kind of forgotten about it. I wish I had more information. I'm sorry. I know it could be important. Anyway, it was lovely to see you again. Please stay in touch. We'd be happy to have you over for a meal!*

I sit there on the stairs for a minute. *Some people just don't know when to stop pushing.*

I'm scrolling through the rest of my emails when I hear a key in the lock on the front door. I'm about to call out for Conor but then I remember his son and I start to get up to run back upstairs when the lights come on and the door flies open and a woman is standing there, dressed all in yellow, scarves and skirts and a long silk coat and long yellow hair.

For a long moment, she just stares at me and then she says, "Who are you?"

I don't know what to say and I'm contemplating running past her out the front door when Conor comes flying down the stairs, bare-chested and flustered. "Bláithín, it's four a.m."

"He needs the inhaler," she says. "You forgot to pack it. You didn't pick up your phone." Her accent is funny. French, I realize, with a little bit of Irish. She's gorgeous. There's no way of denying that. She could be a model.

"Okay. Jaysus. I thought someone was breaking in. Bláithín, this is, uh, this is Maggie D'arcy. Maggie, this is Bláithín Arpin."

"Hello." There's something on her face that makes me think she's finding this amusing.

"I'm going to go," I say, looking from one to the other. I wrap the shirt more tightly around my body. I feel exposed, ugly in the harsh light, every line showing, every bit of cellulite on my thighs.

"You don't have to," Conor tells me. But I just keep going past him. They're silent as I head up the stairs. I find my clothes, put them on, quickly splash my face and rinse out my mouth in the bathroom. I can still smell him in my hair, on my clothes. I fold his shirt and lay it over the bottom of the bed just as he comes into the room.

"I'm so sorry," he whispers. "I'm going to tell her to go. Just wait up here."

"No, I'm going to go. You do what you need to do." I don't have any reason to be mad, but I am.

I put on my coat.

"Maggie," he says. But he's not trying that hard.

"Call me later." I put a hand on his arm, but I don't kiss him.

I just want to get out of there, but when I get downstairs, she's still standing in front of the door. She watches me. "You look familiar," she says. "Have we met before?"

"I don't think so."

Something clicks when she hears my accent and suddenly she looks confused. Then she says, "Oh God, you're the American. Erin's cousin." There's something in the way she says "Erin" that puts me on edge. She watches me for a moment and then something crosses her face. Wariness. Excitement.

"That's right. I'm so sorry. I'm going now." I try to brush past her, but she won't move.

She's looking at me with something I can only describe as fascination.

"Bláithín." Conor doesn't move, though. He's frozen on the top step.

"Did you know about him and your cousin?" she asks, quietly, still watching me.

I feel it like a blow. My vision blurs, my stomach contracts.

She meets my eyes. She's surprised that she's said the words and she looks down. She's not going to tell me.

"Maggie—" Conor starts to say.

"I'm going." I push past her, my head light all of a sudden. "Goodbye," I mumble as I shut the door behind me. The air outside is damp and cold. I button up my coat and start walking as fast as I can, out to Pembroke Road, then up Baggot Street toward the canal. There aren't any cabs on the road. The streets are deserted.

I don't realize I'm shaking until I get to the canal. I want to sit on a bench for a minute and calm myself down, but it doesn't seem safe. Suddenly the dark streets seem newly sinister. I force myself to breathe and keep walking, pushing her words out of my head. *Tomorrow*, I tell myself. *Tomorrow. Just get back to the hotel.*

My phone starts buzzing as I'm walking. *So sorry. She just left. Can we talk?* They keep coming, but I ignore them and walk faster.

Why am I so upset? So what if there was something between them? I'm an adult now. So is he.

It's that he lied. I asked him and he lied.

Did you know?

Did you know?

Did you know?

I walk all the way up Baggot Street, skirting the green, then down Grafton Street to the Westin. The woman behind the desk in the lobby doesn't look a bit surprised to see a middle-aged woman stumbling home at nearly five a.m. I'm sure she's seen stranger things. I take a hot shower, turn my phone off, and get into bed. I don't fall asleep until it's starting to get light.

··

When I'm ten and Erin's eleven, my parents take us to Disney World. It's the first time Erin's ever been on a plane and my mom says she should have the window seat.

"Look at that," she keeps saying. "Look at that. We're above the clouds. It's like we're in heaven."

"I think we are in heaven," I tell her. I lean across her body, feeling the warmth and weight of her. "I'm going to live on that cloud over there."

"I want that one." She points. "Imagine how soft and peaceful it would be to fall asleep in a cloud."

"All your furniture would be made of them."

"All your clothes and food."

We hold hands almost the whole flight, so excited we can't nap.

37

When I finally wake up, the sun is a bright knife through the gap in the curtains. I sit up for a minute. It's eleven already.

Monday. Niamh's been gone for sixteen days.

Sixteen. June Talbot was killed between days twelve and fourteen. On day sixteen, Teresa McKenny was already dead too.

I remember last night in a rush of pain. When I turn on my phone, there are three missed calls from Conor.

I shower and dress and start walking toward Ringsend and the canal. I check my phone again, almost call, then don't.

Did you know about him and your cousin?

I try to think of explanations.

Why didn't he tell me? I asked him, straight out. He said no.

Did you know?

I walk down Erne Street to Lime Street and then I'm on the quays.

I'm nauseous, sick. I think I'm going to throw up and I put my head down just in case. The Liffey runs dark and silent, swirling around unseen obstacles beneath the surface.

A few minutes later I stand up and look out over the river. Then I dial. He answers after one ring.

"Maggie? I'm so sorry about last night. Can we chat? Where are you right now?"

"I'm around the corner from the Ferryman," I tell him.

There's a longish silence and then he says, "I'll be there in a few minutes. Don't go anywhere."

I order myself a Guinness and I'm sitting at a corner table when he comes rushing in. I can't look at him but I can't not look at him. He looks terrible, his eyes lined, his shirt wrinkled. He smells like cigarette smoke.

"Maggie," he says. "Look at me. Bláithín was angry."

"What was she talking about? Was there something between you and Erin? I don't care if there was." *Liar.* "But you lied to the Guards. You're going to have to talk to them."

He runs a hand through his hair. "I know it, but let me tell you first."

I take a long drink of my Guinness. The pub is quiet, chilled. It still smells of cleaning stuff. I know this moment of the day, when you're still on top of things, when the bar's fresh and new and under control. The familiarity steadies me. "Okay."

He puts his face in his hands for a moment and then he looks up at me. "It's hard to explain. It's so long ago and some of it I only know now, but here's what happened. I had class all day. Bláithín had slept at my flat the night before so I guess she was there when, well . . . I guess I should back up and . . . I came home around four or five and Bláithín was there. I knew something was wrong immediately. She has this way of . . . She just goes absolutely silent and cold when she's mad and I knew she was mad. But we were . . Jaysus, we were just kids. Our communication skills were pretty shite." He breaks off and smiles at me. I don't smile back and he keeps going. "She wouldn't say a word. I sort of hovered around her for a bit, asking what was wrong and she just kept saying, 'You know. You know what's wrong.' It was fucking madness. I look back now and I wish I could say, 'Run for your life, lad!' But there were . . . I felt like it was my fault and to be fair, I could be right moody myself. So I left her alone.

"I was getting ready for work and I went to get my coat out of the press in the hall and then I knew why she was mad. Erin's leather jacket was hanging there. I recognized it immediately. I didn't know how long it had been there because I hadn't gone in the press for a while. But I saw it. I knew it was hers immediately. I didn't say a word."

I watch him for a moment, waiting for him to say it. He doesn't.

"You thought she'd left it there when she was at your flat another time."

"Yeah. It's . . . Bláithín was in France one weekend visiting her family and a group of us from the café went out and Erin got langered. I was worried about her and I brought her home with me. She slept on the couch. There was nothing . . . nothing happened. But given the way Bláithín had gone crazy the night Erin went out dancing with us, I just decided not to tell her. When I saw the jacket, I assumed that Erin had left it that night."

"When was that? When she stayed over?"

"A couple of weeks before she went missing."

"So, what happened?" I watch him. He's not meeting my eyes and he's tearing a napkin into tiny pieces while he talks.

"She didn't say anything. Neither did I. We were going down to her parents' holiday house that weekend and we did and we just . . . went back to the way things had been. And then Erin didn't show up for work and I went to the flat and, well, you know the rest."

"What happened to the jacket?"

He sighs. He still can't look at me. "I panicked. The first interview with the Guards was really scary. They thought I knew something. They were sure I had a romantic interest in her. If they searched my flat and found the jacket . . . I shoved it in my rucksack and took it into college. I stayed at the library late one night and then I went into the bathroom and put it down in the bottom of the bin."

I stare at him for a second. I think I believe him, but I don't know what to say.

He finally meets my eyes. "I'm sorry. I know it's . . ."

"You're going to have to tell the Guards," I tell him. "They'll have to bring you in and interview you and everything. That was evidence. Conor, this is . . ."

"I know, I know." There's something more, though. I wait. "The thing is . . . I always wondered if she *had* left it. The more I thought about it, the more I became sure that it *hadn't* been in the press. I wondered if . . . I don't know. It was a little thing that was between me and Bláithín, all those years. Sometimes I wondered about Bláithín, if she'd actually stolen it or if she knew something . . .

"A couple years ago, things were really bad. It wasn't too long before we split up, maybe a year. We had been going to a counselor and it just shook all kinds of things loose. In a good way, I suppose, but we were fighting all the time. And one night she said, 'You've never loved me. You've always loved that American girl. She even came here. She sat right on your couch and she pretended there was nothing between the two of you. She left her jacket and you never said a word!'"

He looks down at the table for a long moment before he goes on. "And I saw it. How the jacket got there. Bláithín told me that Erin had come to the flat, looking for me. She said she was upset and she came in and asked to use the toilet and that was when she must have taken off her jacket and left it in the bathroom."

"When did she come to the flat?" I demand. "What day did she come to the flat?"

He hesitates. "As far as I can figure out, it was the day she went down to Glenmalure."

"Did she say anything to Bláithín?" Her name feels strange in my mouth, like glue. "Did she tell her why she was upset?"

"I don't think so. Bláithín said Erin was a bit vague, like she was thinking. She asked if I was there. When Bláithín said no, Erin asked could she use the toilet. She came out, still sorta . . . spacey, Bláithín said, picked up her rucksack, and took off. Bláithín noticed that she'd left her jacket and she hung it in the press so I'd see it. I think that's it."

"She'll have to talk to the Guards, too," I tell him. "She should have told them. You should have told them."

"I know it." He looks awful, his face pulled down in worry.

There's something that still isn't making sense here. I hesitate. "Were you in love with her?"

He looks up. He looks so sad I have to look away.

"No," he says. "No, it wasn't that."

But I don't think I believe him.

"Can I ring you later?" he asks when I get up.

"I don't know yet."

"I'm sorry," he says. His face is crumpled in shame and disappointment. My last glimpse is of his dark eyes, pleading with me. Outside, the river is choppy. The wind has come up and it looks like rain. I hunch into my jacket and head west again, following the Liffey.

38

I call Roly and tell him I need to talk to him.

"D'arcy. We're right in the middle of—"

"Now," I say. "It's important."

Something in my voice convinces him. "I'll come to the hotel," he says. "There are fucking reporters everywhere."

⋄ ⋄ ⋄

"You need to interview Conor Kearney and his ex-wife," I say as soon as he's closed the door behind him.

"Why?" His eyes are lined with exhaustion, his suit is wrinkled, and there's a stain on his white dress shirt. For Roly, this is as bad as wearing his pajamas to the office.

"I ran into him a few days ago. I've been . . . spending time with him," I say. "A lot of time." I tell him about what Bláithín said, about Conor's story. "I'm sorry, Roly."

He just stares at me for a minute, as though he can't believe this is happening.

"Fuck. This looks bad, D'arcy. You were seeing someone who's a person of interest and we let you get close to the investigation. He fuckin' lied to us. We let you in the files." He stands up and starts pacing. "Did you say anything to him about the investigation?"

"No, Roly . . . No. He knows the body isn't Erin, but . . ." Suddenly I remember Conor asking me about the case, about whether the body was Erin's. "I didn't say anything about evidence. You don't have to worry about that." But now I'm thinking back. What did I actually say to him? "But it shows that Erin was . . . that she was upset about something, right? It's new information, you know? Right, Roly? She was upset about something. I think there's something more there." I take a deep breath. "More than he told me." I have to say it. "Roly, what if the reason she was so upset when she went to Conor's was that she had just killed Katerina Greiner? We've been trying to explain how the scarf and the necklace got there."

He looks over at me. "So, she went down to Wicklow, killed Katerina Greiner for some unknown reason, came back, went to Conor's all upset, then went back to Glenmalure and stayed at Mrs. Curran's overnight, then came back to Dublin, met someone at the bus station, slept somewhere that night, got a bit of cash, and . . . disappeared into thin air?"

"Let's just say she did." But it's nuts, a fucked-up, missing-pieces puzzle of a theory, and I know it.

"You're saying she fled the country and she's been in hiding all this time? Where is she? It doesn't make sense."

"Or she was with someone," I say. "And whoever it was killed her, too."

We're both quiet, thinking about that.

"We'll get them in," he says finally. "You need to just stay put. You need to—" His phone rings and he looks at it.

"I know, Roly. I'm sorry." I sit down on the bed.

"Hang on. I should take this. Yeah?" He turns away, going to the window and moving the sheer curtain aside to look out at the street.

He's listening to whoever is on the other end.

Then he says, "Jaysus!" and he's gesturing wildly at me, pointing at my laptop. I open it. "Look at the *Independent*," he mouths. "Open it up." He's agitated.

"What is it?" I'm scrambling to type it into the browser and as soon as the front page loads my stomach seizes up and I slam my fist into the bedspread. "Fuck!"

The headline is huge. Stephen Hines's byline looks huge, too.

HORRIGAN INVESTIGATION:

Gardaí Reveal Confidential Information to American Detective in Secret Relationship with Person of Interest in Southeast Killer Investigation.

Family Concerned Investigation Has Been Compromised.

It's a mess. I don't need Roly to tell me that. I know exactly how much of a mess it is. I've dealt with messes like this. I've dealt with the aftermath of messes like this.

"I swear to you, Roly. I swear I didn't say anything to Hines. He's tried to approach me a few times. He set up the thing with the Horrigans. But I swear to you, whoever leaked that to him about me reviewing the cases, it wasn't me."

I can't tell if he believes me or not. He looks tired, just absolutely exhausted, worn down to the most basic level of a human being: walking, breathing, not much else. He's lost weight just since I've been in Dublin.

"The hotel's under siege," he says. "Don't go out. Order room service if you get hungry. Don't contact your man Conor. We'll be talking to him and his ex-wife today and you can't have any contact with him. None at all. Okay?"

"I'm sorry, Roly." He just nods and goes out. The door shuts behind him and then I'm alone.

The story isn't as bad as it could have been. Stephen Hines doesn't name Conor, but he's got my name all over it and he quotes the Horrigans as saying that they had hoped bringing me in would lend an expert outside view of the case but that they had no idea I was having a romantic relationship with a person who had been interviewed by the Guards in my cousin's disappearance.

"We just pray that this doesn't affect the operation to find our daughter," Mrs. Horrigan said. "We just pray that this hasn't set us back."

Sixteen days.

I call home, hoping for some comfort from Lilly, but she's subdued. I can tell she wants to get off the phone so I ask her to put Brian on.

"Everything okay?" I ask when he gets on. "She sounded down."

"Yeah, hang on. I'm just going outside." I can hear him push through the swinging door out onto the deck. I imagine him standing there, looking out across the bay, at the dusky water and clouds, meeting at the horizon, the shadowy line of Connecticut imagined in the distance. I feel a pang of homesickness so strong, I sink onto the bed. I want to shove everything in my bag, get on a plane, run into Lilly's room, and hug her until she won't let me anymore. And Brian. I want Brian to stand there quietly, to make me feel like everything's going to be okay. "Sorry," he says after a minute. "She's in the living room. I think something happened with a . . . well, with a guy. Hannah dropped her off and after Lilly got out, Hannah yelled out the window, 'He's an asshole anyway, Lil! You're like a thousand times prettier!' I had to pretend I didn't hear. But she's been in a massive funk, slamming doors. I'm just going to stay out of her way."

"Probably the right thing to do. Poor Lil."

"How are you? You sound tired."

"I am. I am tired. I don't know, Brian. I may be coming home soon. They haven't found anything. This poor girl is probably dead."

I hear him hesitate. "I saw the . . . story, online. Are you okay?"

"No, I . . . I'm just worried I fucked everything up. It was a massive screwup. I—" My voice catches. If I start crying, I won't stop.

I imagine him looking out across the bay. It's early there, the pinky sky slowly turning gray and blue, a Boston Whaler chugging out as the day begins. I can smell the beach and the sand, can hear the play of the waves around the rocks at the point.

His breath catches. "I'm so sorry, Maggie. I know Danny appreciates that you're over there."

"Yeah. Well, thanks. Give Lil a hug for me. Tell her I'm coming home soon."

◆　◆　◆

I sleep fitfully that night, thinking about Niamh Horrigan, thinking about Conor, thinking about Erin. At some point, I get out of
bed and take out all of my notes, everything I've collected about
the case.

I keep coming back to the question I asked Emer: *Why did Erin
go down to Glenmalure? What was she looking for?*

And then I remember something. Conor. When we were sitting at the Palace the night he walked me home. He said that Erin
had asked him about mass rocks, where Catholics celebrated mass
in secret during the period of Irish history when the practice of
Catholicism was outlawed. Was that what she was looking for in
Glenmalure? That might explain why she'd gone down twice. She
hadn't been able to find them the first time. But why?

Had she been meeting someone there?

I search for "mass rocks Glenmalure." I don't come up with a
specific location, but I do find a reference to a local story about a
group of worshippers celebrating mass at a rock near Glenmalure
and being slaughtered by Oliver Cromwell's soldiers. It seems to
be a spot of significance for hiking and history groups from Glenmalure, and there's something about a celebration of the preservation of the spot.

A map on the hiking group's Facebook page tells me that it's
very close to Drumkee.

I go round and round with it, all night, trying to make it all fit.

Why would Erin have gone down there? What would the mass
rock mean to her? Who had she been meeting?

I text Brian: *You told me that Erin was trying to talk to you guys
about riots up in Northern Ireland when you visited. Do you remember that? Anything more? Did she say how she got interested?*

It's an hour before he texts back: *I remember her saying it but nothing more. I can ask Jess. Sorry.*

I look at the map again. There's something there, some pattern I'm not seeing. All night, I scan my notes, trying to arrange them into some order that will make sense.

When I sleep, I dream of Erin, Erin running through the woods, someone after her. I am her; I can feel the cool damp of the air in the trees and then I'm falling, tripping, and when I turn, I see someone looming over me and his face is familiar, his name almost on my lips, but then I'm rising up through sleep and wheezing to wakefulness again in my bed in the hotel and I've forgotten his face, forgotten the name.

39

Roly calls at seven. I'm still in bed, staring at the ceiling, and I jump up and scramble for the phone. "Roly? What is it? What did Wilcox say? Did you interview Conor?"

I hear traffic noise on the other end, the echo of his car phone system. "Hang on," he says. "Can you be downstairs in thirty minutes? Around the corner by Morelands?"

"Yeah, I guess, but what's going on? Won't the reporters be there?"

"They've moved on. There's a lot happening. Be outside in thirty minutes, D'arcy."

I'm dressed in jeans and a sweater and boots, standing on the sidewalk around the corner from the Westin and holding two lattes when he pulls up to the curb.

He waits until we're heading north on O'Connell Street to take a sip and say, "They arrested Robert Herricks this morning. Your tip was a good one. They went to talk to him in Baltinglass last night." Before I ask he says, "Yeah, they let Griz in on it. I'm not sure what it was that tipped them off, but he had some very disturbing videos on his computer and they talked to the young one who used to work at the golf course. She said he raped her, right around the time Teresa McKenny went missing. She was embarrassed back then, ashamed to tell us what happened, so she tried to point us in the right direction by saying he'd been spying in the loos. But we fucking missed it. We didn't ask the right questions."

He looks over at me. "I'm suspended until further notice. Wilcox told me to stay home and cut my grass for the foreseeable future. He ordered Griz and Joey and John White to go back to the reviews they were working on before all this started."

"Roly, I'm so sorry. It's all my fault."

"Yeah, well. I accept your apology." He doesn't look mad, just resigned. And tired. But there's something else there, too. Something to the set of his jaw, the way he's gripping the steering wheel as he drives in and out of rush hour traffic.

"So where are we going?"

"We're going to visit Bernie."

* * *

The nursing home is in Drogheda, up by the border with Northern Ireland, an hour or so from Dublin. The drive is boring, motorway and fields. Roly seems to want to be quiet so I listen to the Top 40 radio he puts on and look out the window at the flashing green pasture, the distant spires and gray roofs of towns off the motorway.

Finally I say, "Why do you want to see Bernie?"

"I haven't visited in a while," he says. "It's been too busy."

"Why else?"

He takes a deep breath. "I tell her everything about my cases. I go up and I tell her about what's going on and she gives me . . . not advice, exactly. But it helps to tell her. I haven't gone since before we found Erin's scarf. I want to ask her what she thinks about the receipt, about Katerina Greiner." He looks over at me. "It's seventeen days, D'arcy. If Niamh's not already dead, then she's about to be. It feels like we're getting there, like something's going to break. I'm off the case, but I'm not giving up. I want to talk to Bernie."

"Will she be able to tell us anything?"

"She's got this breathing thing," he says. "It makes it really hard for her to talk, so I try to ask questions she can answer with a nod or a simple yes or no."

"Is her mind okay? Can she remember things?"

"Oh, she can remember things. That's what makes it so fucking tragic. Her mind is basically fine, but her body's falling apart. She gets pneumonia because she can't clear her airways. She almost died last year."

"What happened, Roly? You only told me she was shot as part of an operation that went wrong."

"She was on the drugs squad. You know that. And they were going after some fella who had been bringing heroin from Spain and dealing out of some businesses in Crumlin. Bernie was convinced someone was passing information to him. He kept managing to stay just out of their way. She tried to figure out who it was and wasn't able to. Anyway, they knew there was a shipment coming in and they went to one of the businesses and got ambushed. She got shot in the back. Bullet tore into her spinal column. For quite a long time, they didn't think she was going to survive."

"Did they ever figure out who was leaking?"

"No." His hands are gripping the steering wheel. The veins in his neck stand out against his pale skin. I let him be for a bit.

"So this receipt," he says finally. "Griz thinks it shows that something happened when Erin was down in Wicklow. She came back to Dublin and got money and then she took off again. Who was she meeting? Who was she going with?"

"Niall Deasey?" I say. "You know what I thought back then. He definitely recognized me, or thought he did. He didn't say, 'Oh, didn't we meet at a pub once?' That would be the normal thing to say, right? And he didn't."

"Yeah, but he's a professional gangster, like. They don't give anything away, D'arcy. We checked him out. He has a great alibi: He was in hospital in London when June Talbot was killed, getting his appendix out."

"What about Teresa McKenny? He was still living here and operating the garage when she was killed."

"The ex-wife was pretty sure there was nothing funny going on. You could tell how much she hated him, so I think she might have been only too happy to give him up if she'd had something on him. But she didn't."

I watch the fields flash by outside the window. "Okay, but let's say he had something to do with Erin's disappearance. Let's say he recruited her to transport something, drugs, money, guns, whatever, between Ireland and the US. Let's say something happened and he killed her. Then what's the connection to Katerina Greiner?"

"She'd been missing for a while. Maybe she'd been with him. Maybe she got wrapped up in something dangerous, too."

I look over at Roly. "Drugs stuff? Prostitution? Arms smuggling?"

"Maybe," he says. "We didn't find any evidence of that, but . . ."

"But what about Niamh Horrigan and the other two? If he was recruiting Erin or something, if it was something related to Northern Ireland, then what about now? Does that stuff go on anymore? After ninety-eight? The location where Katerina Greiner was found has to be significant, right?"

"I don't know, D'arcy. It's hard to explain to ya. This thing, it's different now. There's peace. Yeah, there are fellas who still get up to it. Up north, yeah, there's always the politics. But especially down here, it's more drugs, organized crime these days." Roly slows the car. There's a sign up ahead for the exit to Drogheda and Donore. The M1 continues on to Belfast. "Will we?" he says quietly to himself.

"Will we what?"

"Ah sure, we're only thirty minutes at this point. We're too early for Bernie anyway."

"What?"

"I'm going to take you to the border." He speeds up and passes the exit and we drive north, past green fields dotted with sheep, stretching out toward low brown hills in every direction. In less than thirty minutes, we're there; the fields are flashing by when he says, "That's it. We're in the north now."

The only way I know is there's a sign announcing that all distances will be in miles. "I remember driving up here once when I was a boy," he says. "My ma had a school friend living in Newry and we came up to visit her at Easter. There was a border checkpoint, a low building, manned by British Army soldiers. The cars were lined up to get through and my da, he was a real joker, like, he said, 'Ah, I hope we don't get blown to smithereens, now.' My ma, she walloped him and said not to scare the children. But the whole time we sat in that long line, an hour or more, I thought about it, about what it would feel like to get blown to smithereens."

He pulls off the motorway, turns around, and gets us going south again. "We're back in the Republic now," he says after a few minutes. "The border's still there, D'arcy. Who knows, it might come back someday. They've been talking on the telly about this vote for Britain to leave the EU coming up. Some fella said maybe that'd bring back the border. And then maybe it all begins again. For now, it's quiet. For now, there's peace. Now let's go see Bernie."

* * *

We park in the visitor's lot and go in. The nursing home is a sprawling single-story building in the middle of an industrial park. It's barely decorated inside, a few Virgin Marys and landscape paintings on the stark white walls, a strong smell of antiseptic everywhere.

"Hey, Bernie. Look who I've got to see you," Roly calls out when we get to the room. He peeks around the doorway and motions me in. "A blast from the past, sure. Now, how's herself this morning?" A nurse nods and smiles, leaves us alone.

Bernie is sitting in a complicated-looking wheelchair, a blanket folded over her legs. A television set suspended from the ceiling is on and Roly shuts it off and gives her a little pat on the shoulder. Her hair is shorter and she seems much smaller than I remember, thinner, frailer, but when she turns her eyes to me, I remember them.

"Hi, Bernie," I say, my voice wavering now that I'm here. "It's so good to see you."

She tries to smile, but it comes out more like a grimace.

"D'ar . . . cy. How you?" The words come out slowly, with breaks for breath in between, but I can understand her. Roly adjusts her chair and talks in a nonstop torrent of words, telling her about the investigation. He gives her everything, every twist and turn, finding Erin's scarf, the stuff about Katerina Greiner, updates on the Niamh Horrigan search, the things Griz and I found in the files. Robert Herricks. Then, with a glance at me, he tells her about Conor and Bláithín and Erin's visit to their apartment. She nods, listening, and I can feel that this is a routine for them, that Roly talks so she doesn't have to.

"Why did . . . your cousin go down there?" she asks after a minute. "To the mountains?"

"I know," I say. "That's what we've been trying to figure out. Someone called the house that day, from a pay phone, then she left and went to Conor's house, then she went down to Glenmalure, went walking and lost her necklace, and then she stayed at the Currans' bed-and-breakfast and, we think, took a bus back to Dublin, met up with someone, changed some traveler's checks, and disappeared."

"No," Bernie says, with a lot of effort. "No . . . why mountains?"

"Why did she go to the mountains?" I ask.

"Yes." But there's something more she's trying to say. I can see her struggle with how to express it and give up. "What . . . about O'Hanrahan?" she asks finally.

"O'Hanrahan? There hasn't been much on him. He was connected to Erin Flaherty, but we haven't found any connection to the other women. You think we should look at him again?" Roly asks. Bernie nods.

"Back in 1993, when I confronted him," I say, "it was clear he had something to hide. Seeing me, he was freaked out."

Roly says, "Remember that day we went up there, Bernie? That fuckin' house? They had a solicitor there and everything, to make sure we didn't frighten their poor little lad. Remember?" She's nodding vigorously. "The father. I had the feeling he'd take my head off if I put a foot wrong. And he had a couple of bodyguards hanging around, real criminal types. Butter wouldn't melt in his mouth, like, but he had badness in him. You could see it."

She tries to say something, but can't get it out. It's excruciating, watching her get agitated trying to speak. "It's okay, Bernie," Roly says. "We're going to let you get some rest now. I'll be in touch." The nurse comes back in and we say our goodbyes.

Back in the car, we're quiet as Roly turns us around and gets us back on the motorway. "It's awful," I say. "It's like she's trapped."

"I know. It depresses me for days, coming up to see her."

"But you still do it," I say.

He keeps driving.

◆ ◆ ◆

We take the M1 as far as Dublin and then hug the coast down to Killiney.

"You really think we should be doing this?" I ask him when he tells me we're close. "How will Wilcox feel about you contacting a person of interest?"

"He's not a person of interest in Niamh Horrigan's disappearance," Roly says. "Besides, I've nothing to lose at this point, D'arcy. If Wilcox is determined to sack me, he'll sack me whether I speak to O'Hanrahan or not."

"Okay. It's your funeral." We grin at each other. It's a gorgeous day, all sun and water and blue sky, the big homes along the hills in front of us like white flowers on a vine.

"You'll love this," Roly says. "This is where the posh fellas live. All the celebrities are down here." The hills are dotted with the fancy houses and gardens, all of them oriented toward the view the way plants grow toward the sun. The O'Hanrahan house—inherited from his parents after their deaths a decade or so ago, Roly tells me—is halfway up the winding road, a small sign alerting me that we've reached "Bridgehampton." The drive is shaded by mature trees, but as we come out into the rectangular gravel parking area in front of the large stucco house, the sun breaks through and the view is all gardens cascading down the slope and, in the near distance, the glittering Irish Sea. A heavily made-up woman in tight pink jeans opens the door when we ring the bell. She barely acknowledges us, but opens the door wide. The house matches the view, blues and silvers and lots of metal and white furniture. A chrome-and-glass chandelier looms low overhead. It's very modern, with shards of glass and metal poking out in every direction. There's something threatening about it, the way the shards jut aggressively out into the room.

"We were hoping to speak to Mr. O'Hanrahan?" Roly says, showing his warrant card.

"If you want." She rolls her eyes, goes to the bottom of the wide, metal staircase, and calls up, "There's some guards here to see you!"

She turns around and stares at me, barely disguised resentment on her face.

We look up to find him coming down to meet us. Hacky O'Hanrahan has put on weight in twenty-three years, too much of it in his face. He's jowly and pink, his eyes bloodshot and shifty.

When he sees me, he stops, looking startled.

"Hello, Mr. O'Hanrahan," Roly says. "I don't know if you

remember me, but I spoke to you when we were investigating the disappearance of Erin Flaherty, back in the nineties."

"Yes, yes, I . . . do remember." His eyes keep darting over to me.

Roly says, "Could we sit down and chat for a bit?"

The woman, who I assume is Mrs. O'Hanrahan, looks positively gleeful. "Of course," she says. "Come in and sit down."

O'Hanrahan glares at her, but he leads the way into a pale, elegantly decorated room at the front of the house. The view of the Irish Sea through the huge windows is distracting. It's like there's a beautiful woman sitting in the room and no one can look away.

He sits forward in his chair, ready to jump up.

"This is Detective Maggie D'arcy," Roly says finally. "You may remember her as well."

"Yes, yes. Of course." He crosses his legs, then uncrosses them and leans back in his chair.

"We're going back over our investigation," Roly says, "and we just wanted to confirm a few things with you. You told us you met Miss Flaherty just the once and that you had no further contact with her after that. Is that correct?"

"Yes, yes, that's right."

I pick up the questions. "Though you did call her . . . ring her, I mean. To see if she wanted to join you and your friends for a drink."

"Well, maybe. I really don't remember. It was so long ago now." His wife coughs and he starts.

"Did my cousin say anything to you that could have indicated she was in trouble, that she was afraid of someone?"

"I hardly knew her. We didn't do a lot of talking."

"Just think. It could be very important."

"No, nothing like that. It was just . . . I did that a thousand times when I was that age. Meeting someone out at a club. You like the look of each other. You go home. That's it."

"Except that wasn't it. You called her. Rang her. You asked if she wanted to meet you and your friends at O'Brien's."

He hesitates, then says, "She didn't seem scared of anyone. As far as I remember, she seemed pretty fucking confident." He fiddles with the hem of his pants. "But then later, I don't know, she seemed sad. She was crying and . . . it was weird. I thought we'd been having fun and then she kind of freaked out. She was sobbing and trying to hurt herself. I didn't know what to do."

Roly and I look at each other. "Trying to hurt herself?"

"She was like, pulling at her hair, like she was trying to pull it out."

Suddenly, I remember Erin crying, pulling at her hair. *I'm sorry, Mags. I'm sorry. If I can just*—When was that? Why was she crying? The memory unnerves me. I have no context for it. It just comes out of nowhere.

Roly says, "Why didn't you tell the Guards that?"

O'Hanrahan's wife is pacing around the room, picking things up and putting them back down. He carefully places his hands on his thighs, then turns and snaps, "Would you stop walking around? Go get me a Bushmills, if you would."

"Get your own fucking Bushmills," she says. We listen to her clatter up the staircase in her high heels.

"Sorry," O'Hanrahan says. "I was . . . I didn't think it mattered. I guess I was embarrassed. I didn't want people to think it was, you know, because of me." He's lying, but he's embarrassed too, I think.

"What else?" Roly asks.

"My family thought . . . Well, I received legal advice that it might make it look like something had happened when we were together.

I was counseled not to say anything about it. My father was . . . his businesses. He was concerned about his reputation. Our reputation." He's very nervous now, his hands tapping out a fast rhythm on his knee.

"Is that why your father had me followed?" I ask him. "Because he was concerned about his reputation?"

I can feel Roly's surprise. He didn't know I was going to ask that. When O'Hanrahan looks up, there's genuine surprise on his face, too. "Did he?"

"That day that I waited for you outside your apartment. After that, you told him my name and you told him I'd been asking questions. He had me trailed."

"He thought you were going to try to get me up on charges or something," he says. "I didn't know he had you followed. He was probably just protecting me." He stands up. "I don't know anything more than what I've told you," he says. When I look up at him, he's pale in the sunlight coming through the windows. "If you need more information, you'll have to speak to my solicitor."

"Okay, Mr. O'Hanrahan. We'll leave you alone now. You'll be hearing from us if there's anything else."

I see the wife watching from an upstairs window when we leave the house.

We stop and look at the view one more time before we get into the car. The sea reflects the sun; the water is full of diamonds. "That's the thing about Ireland," Roly says finally. "One minute it seems like the arse-ugliest spot on the earth, and the next it's the most beautiful fucking thing you've ever seen."

40

In a coffee shop in Bray, Roly and I check the online sites for the *Irish Times* and the *Independent*. There's no real news about Robert Herricks, but Stephen Hines and the other reporters stretch it out as much as they can. The Guards are searching properties in Wicklow that Herricks has been associated with over the years. I imagine them approaching sheds and barns and basements, hesitating every time. This could be it. This could be the one.

Niamh.

She's been gone seventeen days.

"What was that about the fella following you?" Roly asks.

"I told you that, back then. I confronted him with a screwdriver."

"Ah, yeah. I thought you were mad, you know. I thought you were making that up."

"Well, I *was* a bit mad by then. But listen, I just realized. Something about O'Hanrahan made me think of it. Remember I told you that John White looked familiar to me when I first met him? I was asking you about him? Well, I'm ninety-nine percent sure he's the guy who followed me."

He'd ordered himself a fancy-looking pastry with lots of frosting and a cherry on the top. He stops demolishing it for a minute and looks up at me. "Are you saying O'Hanrahan hired Johnny White before Johnny White was a guard?"

"I don't know, but I'd swear in court it was him."

He thinks for a minute. "Ah, shite. I knew he worked private security before he went to Templemore. You think he was working for O'Hanrahan?"

"I don't know, but someone leaked to Stephen Hines to put me in the shit, and I'm the only one who can ID him from back then."

"Ah, fuck." He covers his face with his hands. It's the worst-case scenario, a trusted colleague, a suspicion, no evidence of corruption, though. He'll have to go to internal affairs. Or not. Either way, it's bad. "I can't even think about that now, D'arcy. Just fucking keep it to yourself, like, okay?"

"Of course. What do we do now, Roly?"

"I don't know." When he looks up at me he has a dollop of white on his nose. "But I've been thinking about something. That receipt. It shows she was in Dublin on the eighteenth. But it doesn't show she was in Dublin on the seventeenth. Other than your woman at the bed-and-breakfast's word that she was getting a bus back, we don't actually have anything. The son was kind of a dodgy fella, but we couldn't find anything on him. What do you say we head down to Wicklow and try to talk to her? Before the shit hit the fan, Joey gave me the address of the woman who remembered Katerina Greiner staying at the Glendalough Youth Hostel. Her name is Alice O'Murchú. We could talk to her as well."

He seems better now, more himself, as though the conversation with O'Hanrahan had reminded him of the battle.

"Okay," I say. "But you'd better wash your face first."

"Why?"

"You've got frosting on your nose."

"Ah," Roly says happily, running a hand over his face. "Fuckin' disgrace I am. But I think we've got something, D'arcy. I'm not sure what it is yet, but I think we've got something."

* * *

It looks only vaguely familiar to me, a long whitewashed cottage with an addition, the dark forested hills rising behind it.

A woman with white hair answers the door and I search her face for a moment to find Eda Curran in it. Failing, I stick my hand out, introduce myself and Roly, and say, "Is Mrs. Curran here?"

"I'm sorry, she's not well enough for visitors." Only then do I notice the woman's pale yellow uniform and white leather nursing shoes.

"It's very important that we talk to her. It's related to a police case. We're detectives." It's not a lie. Not really.

"Is this about the girl who went missing?" the nurse asks. Her accent's not Irish. Eastern European, maybe.

Roly and I glance at each other. "The girl who went missing?" I prompt her. I can't tell if she's talking about Niamh Horrigan or Erin. I want her to tell me.

"It was long time ago, I think, but she talks about it all the time."

"Could we just come in and speak with her?" I say. "I would really appreciate it if you could let her know that I'm here and would like to speak with her."

"Wait here."

The sun is bright and climbing in the sky. Roly and I wait in silence.

"She isn't very good today," the nurse tells us. "You can come in, but just for a short time."

The house seems shabbier, slightly darker, as if time has left a coating of dust on everything. Mrs. Curran is on the couch in the sitting room, wrapped in blankets despite the sun streaming in through the windows behind her.

A look of alarm spreads across her face when she sees us.

"I'm Maggie, Maggie D'arcy, Mrs. Curran," I tell her. "My cousin Erin was the girl who went missing twenty-three years ago. I came to talk to you then. Do you remember me? This is Detective Inspector Byrne. You would have talked to him as well."

"Of course I remember you." She tries to smile a little and I can see how sick and how old she is. Her face is pale and she's so thin I can see the shape of her skull. "Hello, I'm sorry I can't get up to meet you. I'm not well." She shifts on the couch and winces a bit. The nurse steps forward to put a pillow behind her.

"We won't take up very much of your time, Mrs. Curran," Roly says. "But we were wondering about something. Erin Flaherty stayed overnight with you on September the sixteenth, 1993. I know it may be difficult to remember, but you told us that she was taking a bus back to Dublin that next morning. Did she tell you that directly?"

"I think so." She closes her eyes, because she's thinking or because of the pain, I can't tell. "She said she had to go. The bus was going to leave, she said."

Roly and I look at each other. That seems pretty definitive. "And you said she didn't seem upset about anything. She didn't tell you she was scared of anyone, did she?"

"No, no, I don't—" She winces.

The nurse steps forward, giving us disapproving looks.

"We'll leave you," I say. "There's just one more thing. Do you have any memories of a young German woman who may have been hillwalking near here, right around the time that my cousin Erin disappeared? All those years ago."

"A German woman . . ." She thinks for a moment. "I don't know . . . I've had lots of tourists stay with me over the years, Germans, Japanese. But that was before . . ."

"I don't think she stayed with you," I say gently. "They would have checked all that in your guest log. We're wondering more about whether you might have seen her around, walking on the road or the trails."

"I don't know. Have they, have they found your cousin?"

"No, Mrs. Curran, but we think there may be a link between her and the German woman we're interested in."

"I don't . . . She was a lovely girl. I didn't know. I said so. That's what I told you, isn't that right?"

"I'm sorry, Mrs. Curran, told me what?"

"Oh, I didn't know. Isn't that right, dear?"

The nurse is running out of patience. She starts to say something so I jump in. "Mrs. Curran, your son. Gary. He was there when Erin stayed with you, wasn't he?"

She looks confused. "He helped me. With the bed-and-breakfast. Didn't he? I had so many visitors then. People from all over the world. Lovely . . . He's ill, you know. Gary." She trails off and I look up to find the nurse has come back.

"Is he here now?" I ask her. "Could we talk to him?"

"He went into Rathdrum," the nurse says. "To the clinic."

"When will he be back?" Roly asks her. "We'd really like to have a chat with him."

"By five. He said he will be back by five."

Roly checks his watch and nods at me. "Okay, we'll be back then. Thank you for your time, Mrs. Curran."

41

....

Roly finds the address Joey gave him and calls ahead so Alice O'Murchú knows we're coming.

She lives near Roundwood, in a huge, old stone house that we find at the end of a narrow country lane. When she answers the door, she's holding a toddler, who's naked except for a diaper and a purple ski hat. A little girl of about six is coloring at a small table behind her.

"Come in, come in," she says. "I've just got home from getting this lot at the crèche. My partner's not home yet and it's a mess. Sorry. But I can tell you what I remember. As long as you don't mind the chaos. Do you want a cup of tea? I've just put the kettle on."

She tells us that she teaches at an Irish-speaking school in Wicklow. "I love it there. It's been fifteen years now and the kids are really lovely."

"We were told that you were working at the hostel in Glendalough in 1993," Roly says.

"That's right. I'd just done my leaving cert and I worked there for about a year before going to university." The toddler makes a run for it into the kitchen and she goes after him, calling out, "I'll be right back. I'll just get him something to eat. And come with the tea."

She's back in a few minutes, the toddler under one arm and a plate of chicken and vegetables in the other. She drops him into a booster seat at the table and puts the plate in front of him, then gives the little girl a bowl of apple slices and goes to get our tea. "There, that should keep him busy for a bit. He loves his food, so he does."

She's done it properly, a teapot under a cozy and cups on a tray. When she's poured it out she says, "Now, right, I was working at the hostel and there was this German girl who arrived. Her name was Katerina. I don't remember her checking in or anything but a couple of days after she arrived, another guest came and told me that she was talking to herself in the dorm and the other girls in there were scared. I went up to the dorm and she was sitting on her bed and just, you know, talking to herself. She wasn't hurting anyone, but it was kind of aggressive and just, odd, like. I moved the other women into a different dorm and let her stay in there by herself and I thought that was the end of it. But a couple of days later, I was on overnight and I heard shouting down in the kitchen. I went down and there were a couple of English guys who had been out drinking at the pub and had come back to make a big fry-up. From what I could tell, she'd wandered into the kitchen and they'd tried to talk to her and she just lost it. She tried to hit one of the guys with a spatula. They were laughing at her and that made it worse. I think she was really mentally ill. It was very sad. But I couldn't have her hitting other guests so I told her she'd have to leave if she couldn't calm down and stay away from them. She was angry at me, but early the next morning she packed up all her stuff and she asked me how to get to the Wicklow Way. She said she was going to walk to Glenmalure."

We ask some more questions. She doesn't remember the date exactly, but she thinks it was early September. Joey had already tried to find a record of Katerina's stay at the hostel, but it had been before computerized registrations and they had thrown out the log books from the '90s.

We thank her and head back out to the car.

"So she left Glendalough and started hiking to Glenmalure. It's a two-hour hike, right, something like that. And along the way, when she was almost to Glenmalure, she met her killer."

"And she made contact with Erin. Or with Erin's scarf and necklace," I say. "Somehow." I open up a map on my phone. "Roly, we're not too far from Arklow now."

"Niall Deasey?" I nod. He slows the car and pulls over on the side of the road. "What do you think he's going to tell us?"

"I don't know," I say. "I just want to get a look at him. I feel like he's got something to say, you know? You did a search for parking tickets, back during your first review. Griz showed me. A whole bunch of people connected with the investigation had them. Conor. Bláithín. Eda Curran. Niall Deasey's truck had one too, right around the time June Talbot disappeared. He was out of the country, supposedly, but . . . what if he wasn't? What if he borrowed the truck from his nephew?"

"That's right." He thinks for a moment. "You think there's anything in the politics angle? That thing about her talking to her friends from home about marching season and the riots?"

"Brian said he remembered her talking about it. She was mad at them for not being more interested." I check my texts but there's nothing more from him.

"All right," Roly says. He pulls out again, heading east toward the sea. The sun is setting in the west. There are streaks of yellow behind the mountains on the horizon. The trees are swaying in a stiff wind. "It feels like we're getting close to something, D'arcy. Do you feel that?"

"Yeah," I say. I don't tell him it's accompanied by a feeling of danger.

You're getting close.

Don't get too close.

42

Arklow looks the same to me. More coffee shops maybe, but the Old Ship is still there. It's four thirty by the time we find Deasey's garage, on a little residential street backing up to a vacant lot and field. A "Closed" sign hangs in a window and there's an emergency number stenciled on the glass, but no signs of life. We go around the back of the garage.

The yard is neatly kept, car parts and scrap metal in orderly piles, the windows freshly washed. We knock on the office door and then, after a few minutes, go around and through the big open doors into the garage bays. There's a guy bent over, working in the wheel well of a Jeep, and when Roly clears his throat, he says, without turning around, "Hang on a mo."

I look around. The inside of the garage is as well-organized as the outside, with tools arranged neatly on the walls and shelves holding boxed parts and manuals.

"Right, then." The guy stands up and it's not Niall Deasey. This guy is stout, barrel-chested, with gray hair and a weather-beaten face. There's something familiar about him but he doesn't seem to recognize me at all. In fact, he looks past me to Roly.

"Pardon me," Roly says. "You are . . . ?"

"Cathal Deasey." The guy looks suspicious now.

Roly takes out his warrant card and flashes it. "Detective Roland Byrne with the Garda Síochána. We were hoping to speak with Niall Deasey. Is he in?"

"I'll get 'im." Cathal wipes his hands on his pants and goes through a door at the back of the garage. His accent's English, not Irish, I think, and suddenly I remember John introducing him to me as "Uncle Cathal."

"I think he was there that night," I whisper to Roly. "At the pub. I remember he had an English accent. He's Niall's brother."

"Half-brother, actually. They co-own the garage. He was definitely out of the country when Erin went missing. He's been living in London and came over to help Niall run the garage a year or so ago. We looked at him but there wasn't anything there. He wasn't even involved in the criminal stuff like his brother, though a fella I know on undercover said we shouldn't be too quick to count him out for a little drugs action here and there."

We look up to see a familiar, swaggering form coming through into the garage. Cathal Deasey stands behind his brother, protective, a little subservient.

"Can I help you?" Niall Deasey is older, but he's still handsome, his hair salt-and-pepper now and his blue eyes lined, alive, curious. He gives us a broad, welcoming smile, an absolute fake. "Problem with your car?"

"No, nothing like that," Roly says with a smile. "I'm Detective Inspector Roland Byrne, with the Guards in Dublin. I don't know if you remember, but I had a chat with you a good few years back now—twenty-three, actually—about an American girl named Erin Flaherty. We had a witness who saw you talking to her in the Raven in Dublin not long before she went missing."

Deasey doesn't say a word.

"Do you remember meeting her?"

"That was twenty-three years ago. I've chatted to a lot of people, men and women, in the last twenty-three years."

He's been looking at Roly, but suddenly he shifts his eyes to me and I can see him start. It's very subtle, but I think he's recognized me. He looks away quickly and says, to cover the awkwardness of the moment, "Can you give me a date at least? Perhaps I could check my calendar."

"This would have been in the summer of 1993," Roly says.

Deasey pretends to think, tapping an index finger against his forehead in a way that makes me want to haul off and punch him. "I don't think so. Nope, I don't remember that."

"What about a German woman named Katerina Greiner?" Roly says it quietly, trying to catch him off guard.

He looks confused. "What?"

"Do you have any memory of meeting a German woman named Katerina Greiner, around 1992 or 1993?"

"No. I wouldn't think so." He looks confused. "You remember who you met twenty-three years ago, detective?"

"When was it you moved back to Arklow?"

"Three years ago. My ma was sick."

"I'm sorry about your mother. That must have been tough," I

say. That gets him. He gulps and looks me right in the eyes, but doesn't say anything.

"Where were you on May twenty-first and twenty-second?" Roly blurts out. I look over at him. He's not supposed to be asking about Niamh.

"What, last week, like? Or back in 1993?"

"Last week?"

"Saturday? I was here, working on cars or out on calls. We'll often get called out on Saturdays, tourists with car trouble, like. And then I was probably at the pub with my brother, Cathal. That's where you'll often find me." He calls through to the back of the garage. "Cathal, come on out. We were at the pub, yeah? Saturday night last weekend?"

Cathal Deasey comes through, wiping his hands on a rag. "Yeah," he says. "It was Petey's daughter's twenty-first, wasn't it? We were all there most of the night. Anyone at the pub would tell you."

Niall Deasey grins triumphantly.

"You finished?" he asks us. "Because if you are, I'd like you to get the fuck out of my garage."

Roly walks right up to him, doesn't touch him, but looks right into his eyes. "If you know anything that could help us find out what happened to Erin Flaherty, you better tell me, Niall lad. Because there is no shortage of paperwork on you back at my office and I can pull out any one of the fifty things I think you've done and I can work those cases until I get something that will stick. You hear me?"

Deasey draws himself up and I know he's about an inch away from hitting Roly. I start to move forward but so does the brother.

"Niall," Cathal says quietly.

Niall Deasey turns and holds his gaze for a minute and then shrugs. "Lookit. We met her at the Raven like you said. Wasn't anything to it, really. Just a chat at the bar. She was a lovely girl. Had a bit of a flirt. Bought her a drink. We left and we never saw her again or heard anything about her until that one"—he doesn't look over at me—"chatted up my little cousin John down the pub. I didn't put it together, the resemblance, until she'd already been chatting with us for a bit. I remembered her, your cousin, because of the accent and because a few months later I saw the bit about her on the SixOne. But I don't know anything about her. Okay?"

Roly stares at him for another long moment. I can smell the tension in the air, sweat and gasoline and metal.

"All right, then. You take care, Niall. We'll be back to you soon."

"That's it? You're not going to arrest me for doing fuck-all?"

"Not today. See ya."

◆　◆　◆

Roly waits until we're in the car. "So?"

"Either he doesn't know anything about Erin or he's so sure we don't have anything that he wasn't thrown by us showing up unannounced."

"Yeah, I thought so, too," Roly says. "Something about him bothers me."

"He recognized me, all right. I could see it immediately. So his pretending he didn't at first was just posturing. He was keeping something from us, I'm just not sure what."

Roly puts on the radio in the car and we listen to a breathless story about the searches ongoing at Robert Herricks's house in

Baltinglass. "The family of missing woman Niamh Horrigan waits as the searches continue," the radio announcer says. I can tell it's driving Roly crazy not to be there as things heat up.

"I can check that alibi anyway," he says suddenly. "At the pub."

"Yeah. He sounded pretty confident though. But he said he was out on calls during the day. Maybe he had a window in there?"

We're back in Glenmalure by five. As we get out of the car, we can hear the distant chop-chop of a helicopter overhead. "Aerial searches," Roly says.

Mrs. Curran's house looks strangely desolate as we approach it in the dusky twilight. There's a light on somewhere in the back, and the yellow glow of it illuminates the house in the darkness.

A small, pudgy man is standing in the doorway. He's wearing sweatpants and a black T-shirt with purple writing on it. His hair is long and thin, gathered in a little ponytail that hangs over one shoulder.

We introduce ourselves and follow him into the house. It's not until he's under the light in the living room that I can see he's dying, too. His skin is yellow, his eyes bloodshot, and what I took for pudginess is actually bloat. Liver? Kidneys? Hepatitis? Whatever it is, it's bad.

I say, "Mr. Curran, you spoke to the police around the time of my cousin's disappearance. You said you didn't meet her and you didn't know anything about what happened to her."

He shuffles a bit farther into the room. "I guess. It was a long time ago. There's another one now, in't there? I saw it on the telly."

"Here, can we go inside?" Roly asks.

We get settled in the sitting room. Mrs. Curran is on the couch and I can't tell if she remembers us.

Roly asks Gary Curran, "Does the name Katerina Greiner mean anything to you?"

He shakes his head. "No, don't think so."

"Do you remember a German woman, a woman who had an accent, anything like that, around the time Erin Flaherty went missing."

"No," he says. But his eyes widen suddenly.

"What does the German woman have to do with it all?" Mrs. Curran asks. "What did she . . . ?" She gasps then, and I see pain flash across her face.

"She needs to rest," the nurse says, glaring at us. "I can give you something, Mrs. Curran."

I stand up and take my coat off the arm of the chair to show her I'm going. But I watch Gary Curran's face and I'm aware of Roly next to me. "Mr. Curran, is there anything you can tell us that might help us? You worked for the forestry service, for Coillte, in 1993, is that right?"

"That's right."

"Did you use a spade? In your work?" I hold my breath.

"Yeah." He shifts his weight from foot to foot and I can see that standing is making him uncomfortable. "That was my job, digging holes."

The nurse moves toward me and I glance at Roly. He nods. *Go for it.* "Mr. Curran, if there is anything you can tell us, we would really appreciate it."

"Sorry. My mother is tired." He turns and walks out of the room.

I can hear his footsteps disappear into the front of the house. His mother looks up at us, confused.

"Mrs. Curran," I say, "we're going now. It was lovely to see you again. I'm so sorry you're not well."

She tries to smile, but waves instead. I can see in her eyes that the pain's got her. "Yes," she says. "Nice."

Gary Curran is waiting for us in the hallway.

"I'm sorry about your illness, too," I tell him.

He frowns. "It's hepatitis. I got it from a needle in Thailand."

Roly's uncomfortable. I can feel it, but I force myself to stay calm.

I gamble. "Your mother knew something about my cousin's disappearance. Something she didn't tell me. Can you tell me what it was? It might be very important. They can't do anything to you now, the Guards." I glance at Roly. "They won't do anything to you. You know that. I'm so sorry you're ill, but you could help us solve this. I don't know if I can describe how much it would mean to my uncle, and to me, to know what happened."

The nurse makes a cluck-clucking sound behind me. There's a mechanical humming somewhere in the house. Raindrops are pinging on the roof.

He looks up at me and I can see his impulse to lie overridden by something else. He shrugs, as if to say, *What does it matter now?* And he starts to talk.

"I followed her. I used to do that, when I was younger. I got in trouble for it and my mother knew. She was very . . . She tried to stop me from doing it, but she couldn't always. The girl, your . . . cousin. She left the house pretty early and I watched her out the window."

He takes a deep breath. Just that much has worn him out.

"She walked down towards the lodge and I thought that I had to go to work anyway, so I would just walk that way and I could follow her. I could . . . watch her through my binoculars. I liked to do that, I had a whole . . . If I tried to explain, you wouldn't understand."

"So you followed her?" I can feel it, the knowledge that what's coming next is important.

"Yes. She walked down by the lodge and the bus came in. I thought she was going to get on it, but she didn't. She kept walking up the Military Road. Fast. I followed her. I had my spade and everything so if anyone came I could pretend that I was working. And I watched, I watched her walking toward the walking paths, like. And—" He breaks off and lets out a terrible rattling cough. When he picks up again, his voice is hoarse. "I kept following her. She kept going up the path, like she was looking for someone or something.

"I knew a place where I could sit and watch her, away from the path. And when I got up there, I saw her walking away from the path, off into the trees. But then there was a man. I think he must have followed her up, too, and I watched him coming towards her on the path, waving like he knew her. They talked for a little bit."

"And then?" I'm holding my breath. This could be it.

"I don't know because I stopped looking."

"Why did you stop looking?"

He takes a deep breath.

"Because someone was coming."

Something clicks in my brain. *Someone was coming.*

He sits back on the couch and runs a hand through his hair. There's a thin film of sweat on his face.

We're all silent. I can feel Roly and me waiting.

"It was a girl. She was talking to herself. In some other language. At first I thought there were two people and I put the binoculars away and started digging but she came up the path and it was just her. There was something wrong with her. When she saw me, she gave me a really weird look and muttered something and kept walking. I waited until she was gone and then I dropped my tools and tried to find your . . . your cousin. And I couldn't, so I went up a bit higher but I still couldn't find her."

Roly says, "Was she German? This girl you saw?"

"Might be. Yeah, I think that was the language. I don't know for sure."

"When did you hear that Erin was missing?" I ask him.

"I don't remember. Mam said the Guards came to see her and she asked if I had seen anything. I couldn't tell her, could I, because then she'd know I followed her. But I think she knew I had seen something. The Guards interviewed me." He looks up at Roly. "You interviewed me, but I couldn't tell you because then I would have to tell you I followed her. That would have gotten me in trouble."

The nurse steps forward and hands him a glass of water. He looks exhausted, spent. We don't have any more time with him.

But we need to push him a bit further. "What did the man look like, Mr. Curran?" Roly asks. "Had you seen him before? What did he look like?"

"I'd never seen him before. At least, I don't think so. I never really got a look at his face." I feel my stomach drop. "He had dark hair. He was pretty tall, and he was wearing something brown, like a brown tweed jacket, or maybe leather. That's all I could see."

I lean forward and try to meet his eyes, but he keeps looking down at the ground. "Mr. Curran, when you went back, was your spade still there?"

"No," he says. "It was gone. I had to pay for a new one out of my wages."

43

Roly and I find a pub on the road back toward the coast. The fire is burning, it's warm and welcoming inside, but the two of us just sit there dazed for a few minutes.

The television is on over the bar and the announcer is talking about a banking scandal involving the trading of mortgages. They run a clip of a gray-haired man leaving court and then the newscaster says, "As gardaí search properties in and around Baltinglass, County Wicklow, the family of missing Galway woman Niamh Horrigan is calling on Wicklow residents to try to remember anything that might help to find their daughter and bring her home safe and sound."

Niamh's parents are shown talking to a reporter, who asks them: "Do you feel the authorities are doing enough to find Niamh? There have been some problems with the investigation that you have found worrying, isn't that correct?"

"We do thank them for all they're doing, but it's been seventeen days now and Niamh is still missing." The mother begins to cry and the father finishes for her: "If there's anyone out there who knows where Niamh is, we just want to say that we don't care what might have happened, we just want our daughter back. She is such a kind and good person. All of the children she teaches love her so much. If you talk to her, you will see that—" Now the father's crying, too.

The screen cuts to a shot of the reporter standing in front of a small house that I assume belongs to Robert Herricks. "Gardaí will continue to search for Niamh, and her family will continue to wait and hope."

Who?

Who was the man on the trail?

Who?

"Whoever the man was, he must have killed Katerina Greiner," Roly says. "Do you realize how close Gary Curran was to witnessing the murder?"

"And he may have killed Erin, too," I say. "It was someone she knew, and it sounds like she wasn't expecting to see him on the trail."

"Except she was back in Dublin on the eighteenth," he says.

He's right. I'd forgotten. I can feel everything in me resisting the thought. *She was back in Dublin on the eighteenth.*

Roly's looking at me, not quite meeting my eyes.

"Let's start with who the man was. Who knew she was going down to Glenmalure?"

I say it before he can. "Conor, if she told him."

"But we don't know if she did."

I keep going. "Emer said she didn't tell her and Daisy." I tell him about my coffee with Emer. "I don't think they were hiding anything else. If she was in touch with Niall Deasey, then Deasey knew. And if she was in touch with Hacky O'Hanrahan, then he knew. Really, anyone who she might have told. The bus driver knew where she was going, obviously."

"Okay," Roly says slowly. "Okay. Let's think this through. According to Gary Curran, she left the bed-and-breakfast and she walked toward the lodge. The bus came in but she didn't get on it. Instead, she kept walking up the Military Road and onto the Wicklow Way."

I drain the hot whiskey I ordered and let it seep in, slowing my heart rate. There's something banging at my memory, something I missed; it's there, but not quite there. I close my eyes. When I open them, Roly's watching me. "That sounds like she was meeting this guy, whoever he is, doesn't it?"

"Yeah." Roly drains his drink.

"Roly, let's say something happened on the trail. The guy kills Katerina Greiner and then he forces Erin to go back to Dublin with him and get money and they flee . . . somewhere."

"But then it's some guy we don't know anything about. Because there's no missing guy." He's antsy, snapping at me. I can feel the weight of the days on us. *Seventeen days.*

Our food comes—fish and chips for Roly and potato-leek soup with salmon and brown bread for me.

"What are you going to do about Conor?" he asks me while we eat quickly, barely tasting the food.

"I don't know. He lied to me. All this time he was lying."

Roly takes a long drink, avoiding my eyes. Then he says, "You don't . . . you don't think it was him, do you? Does that mean anything to ya? The brown jacket, like?"

"The man on the trail? I don't know. Conor had a motorcycle jacket, brown leather. Back . . . then. But he had an alibi."

Roly doesn't say anything.

I say, "His girlfriend, the woman he married was his alibi. She may have lied to protect him."

"Yeah, but."

"Right," I say. I get up to use the restroom and on the way back, I stop to look at the walls in the hotel's lounge area. The red-and-white wallpaper is covered with historical memorabilia and information about important Wicklow sites in the 1798 rebellion. There's something about Cullen's Rock, near Glenmalure, where there was a famous battle and where the rebels holed up in the mountains in 1798 and were later hanged.

"Roly," I say when I get back to the table, "I was just thinking about what Bernie asked us. Why did Erin go to the mountains? The mountains. I was thinking. Bernie once told me a story about Petey Deasey holing up in a cottage near Glenmalure or something? Am I making that up?"

Roly looks surprised. "Petey Deasey . . . Yeah. That's ringing the old bell. What was it? They were using a cottage down here as a place to stash arms. There was some kind of standoff. Bernie found out about it. What are you thinking?"

"I don't know," I say. "If he has a house down here we don't know about and they never searched it . . . Maybe Erin was staying there, maybe they were somewhere else and then came back and . . ." I can't make the pieces fit, though. "Maybe the other women . . . I don't know. When Griz and I were looking over everything, that was the thing that struck me. The mountains. They're important to this guy somehow."

Roly's eyes are alive. His brain is already moving on this. "I don't know where the place is. I need to get someone to look it up for me," he says quietly.

"What about Wilcox?"

"Fuck Wilcox." He thinks for a minute and then he takes out his phone and presses something. "Griz?" he says. "I need to ask you to do something for me. Fair warning, Wilcox won't like it." He listens for a minute and then he says, "Yeah, I need the location and anything you've got on a cottage down here where there was a standoff between Petey Deasey and the Guards. This would have been in 1967. Okay, thanks, Griz. Yeah, ring me back."

We finish eating and get coffee while we wait for Griz. It takes twenty minutes for Roly's phone to buzz on the table.

"Yeah, you got it, Griz? Go ahead." He listens and then says, "Whose name is on it? Oh, yeah? All right, then. Yeah, text if you find anything else."

He looks at me. "In 1967 Petey Deasey holed up in a cottage in a townland called Ballyclash, the other side of Askanagap, she says. The Guards had been looking for him and he held them at bay for twenty-four hours before they arrested him. He served two years for various crimes. The cottage was packed with guns and TNT."

"Does Niall Deasey own the cottage?" I ask in a quiet voice.

Roly shakes his head. "Nope. He must have sold it. Some woman's name on it. Not Deasey."

"Oh." I'd been so sure. "Where is it? Did Griz have an address?" I'm already putting it into my phone.

"Just Ballyclash. Ah sure, we'll be able to find it. It's just a little place anyway. Let's just go take a look." Roly puts a twenty-euro note down on the table, jumps up from his chair. "Maybe this is it, D'arcy."

◆ ◆ ◆

It takes us nearly forty minutes on the tiny roads. The house is on the side of a narrow country lane stretching west from the signpost for Askanagap, pointing away from the mountains. It's desolate out here, the stone walls alongside the road overrun with yellow gorse and scrubby brush. We wouldn't know we were there if the GPS hadn't told us we'd arrived.

It's a low gray stucco cottage, completely out of sight of any other house and shielded by an overgrown stand of pines that's come up all around it, crowding it against the slope of the mountain.

We pull into the driveway and get out. It looks utterly abandoned, as if no one's been here in years. The roof is covered with green moss, the blue paint on the front door is peeling, and there aren't any patio chairs or newspapers or flower pots or anything to indicate human habitation. We try the front door and find it locked, then knock. We don't really wait for an answer before going around back.

There's nothing but overgrown gorse behind the house. When I put my face to a window, I just see a bare floor, dirty walls.

"It looks fairly abandoned," I say, peering through the window. "I don't think anyone's been here for years."

Roly nudges me over and peers through the window, too. "Yeah, you're right. It was probably a bit far out for the door-to-doors."

"We could ask someone at one of those houses back there. See if anyone knows."

Twenty-three years.

It's started raining now, but the air is warm. It feels like spring. Something's blooming up in the hills and the scent drifts down to us. I can hear water trickling somewhere, snowmelt and gravity creating little streams running to the sea. There's a half-moon casting a little light on the hills. I turn around and look back east toward the mountains. Something tugs at my brain. *Erin on the trail. She looks up. She sees him.*

"There's no one here," I tell Roly. "I don't think this is it."

"Ah, sure. D'arcy, there's something there that we're missing. Something obvious."

44

We sit in the car in the dark, trying to decide where to go next.

"What are you thinking?" Roly asks me. "About Niall Deasey?"

"If Erin was back in Dublin by the eighteenth, he could have met her then and . . ." Roly knows what I'm thinking. *And brought her here to the house in Ballyclash, where they could have hidden out until the searches for her were over.*

And then . . . ?

And then . . . ?

"I guess you should be getting back home," I say. "Laura's probably wondering what happened to you."

"Ah, she's all right. She knows by now that if she's not getting a visit from the uniforms, everything's grand. The house got me thinking. Somehow he got them back to wherever he got them back to. His vehicle. If it was one of those cars on the CCTV, then why—" He stops talking.

"What?"

"D'arcy," he says slowly. "Do you remember any of the names of the people whose cars were captured on the CCTV? You take any notes?"

"You mean the day Teresa McKenny was taken?"

"Yeah. And June Talbot."

"No. You told me not to copy any files."

He makes a funny face at me. "I'm an eejit." He dials Griz's number, puts her on speaker.

When she answers she says, "Jaysus, Roly. It hasn't been an hour. I'm not a fuckin' mind reader. Give me a few—"

"It's not that, Griz. I need you to see if you can find the contacts for the vehicles caught on CCTV for the McKenny and Talbot disappearances. Horrigan, too. Names, numbers if you have them. I know what I'm asking. You'll have to go into the files."

She doesn't hesitate. "Okay. I'll be back to you as soon as I can."

"Let's get out of this car while we wait," he says. He's pulled over into a little verge. We get out and walk over to the edge of a field.

"I'm not going to tell you what I'm thinking yet," he says. "I'll tell ya in a minute."

"Okay." I take a pack of gum out of my coat pocket and hand him a piece. "Moments like these, I wish I was a smoker, you know?"

"Ah, no," he says. "It's a nasty habit. Fucking ruins your clothes."

I laugh. "You and your clothes."

"Let me ask you something, D'arcy. Your big case. When did you know he was the one? That Pugh sicko?" I take a deep breath. Roly looks over at me. "You don't have to."

"No. I have this . . . It's okay." I take another breath. I lean against the hood of the car. "I didn't know for sure until we arrested him, but it was like a . . . dawning sense of the patterns, I'd say. You know the basics?" He nods. "The detail in the medical examiner's report had been bugging me. The victims had powerful tranquilizers in their systems and we'd looked at doctors, nurses. Someone mentioned they might be something a vet would have on hand. I just started looking at it, making lists, dropping pins on maps, thinking, putting it together. The way it was reported, that the FBI didn't believe me—it wasn't like that. They were just following up on other leads and I started on this thing. I just started working it. It took a year. I just kept picking at it, like a loose thread. I kept working at it until I had a sense of him. When Andrea Delaurio went missing, I knew, I just fucking knew, Roly. That was when I was sure it was him. I knew him by then, you see. I had a feel for his brain. When they got him, he had her in the trunk. He'd had her for hours and hours. He was going to the beach, to kill her and dump her. She was drugged up so he could . . ." I can't breathe now. I can feel my lungs seizing up. I wheeze, slow it down, get ahold of myself.

"It's okay, you don't have to tell me." I can hear the alarm in his voice. He puts an arm around me and pulls me in. I lean into him for a second and then I say, "We got him. She was in bad shape but we got her to the hospital. We got him, Roly."

There's a long silence and then I say, "She got out of the hospital, she went home, not to her house, to her parents' place. I went and saw her. We interviewed her a few times. I was spending all my days with him, in interrogation rooms, trying to get him to talk. He claimed she'd asked him to do it, to give her the drugs and everything. She was working as an escort. He said he'd been about to take her home."

I don't want to go on. This is the part that makes me freeze up, that takes my breath and paralyzes me.

"Yeah?" Roly knows there's something coming.

The clouds part for a moment and the moon washes the field with pure, pearly light. I whisper, "Her mother called me to tell me. Because I'd saved her life, she said. I still can't believe she had it in her to do that. They found her in the bathtub. She'd cut herself, taken aspirin, warm water. She knew what she was doing."

"Ah shit, D'arcy. I didn't know, like. That wasn't in the stories. Ah, D'arcy. No."

We're silent for a long time.

Finally I say, "They got him for the kidnapping, but that was all they could do. Without her to testify. There was no physical evidence to link him to the other women, even though we knew. He served two years and then he got out, last year, right around the time the leaves turned. I thought, right after, that maybe it was meant to be, you know? If Erin hadn't gone missing, maybe I wouldn't have become a cop. Maybe I wouldn't have saved Andrea. It gave it a purpose. But then . . . Anyway, I keep tabs on him, I have a couple guys in Suffolk County PD who help me, but he's out there. He's fucking out there, Roly, and there's not much I can do."

Roly doesn't say anything. He just pulls me in and lets me rest against him.

And then, we both see it, something moving at the other end of the field. "Shhh. Look," Roly says, touching my shoulder. He's pointing at something long and low, moving slowly against the darkness of the trees, and then it turns and we can see the flash of moonlight in its eyes.

Roly's phone buzzes and the animal, whatever it was, bounds away into the trees.

• • •

Griz has texted him five names, two from vehicles caught on CCTV around the time Teresa McKenny went missing and three from June Talbot. It's all she can find. He writes them down on a little sheet of paper from his glove compartment and hands the McKenny ones to me. "Ring 'em up," he says. "Ask them some basic questions about the car, when they got it, has it ever been stolen, where is it serviced?"

"Are you . . . ?"

"Just do it." He stands on one side of the car. I stand on the other. I call the first guy. He answers and when I tell him what I want, he sounds suspicious. Maybe it's my accent, but it takes some convincing before he gives me what I need. I call the second one. He's not home but his wife gives me everything I need.

When Roly's done, we get back in the car. "Well?" he asks me.

"The cars have never been stolen. They've both been fairly dependable. The Skoda is serviced at Lewis Motors in Bray and the Ford at, uh, Ryan's in Wicklow. What about you?"

"Nothing good."

"You thought we were going to get a hit on Deasey's garage."

"Yeah but. It fits, D'arcy. I was thinking, how could the same fella take different women without the same car showing up each time? I was thinking, who might have easy access to different cars, with different number plates? Fella who runs a garage."

"It was a good thought," I say. "You need more IDs. You need them all."

"I know."

"Besides," I say, "you told me that Niall Deasey had a solid alibi for Teresa McKenny and June Talbot. He'd left Ireland at that point, right? Moved to London."

"Croydon," Roly says.

Croydon.

Croydon.

"Call Griz," I say quickly. "Put her on speakerphone."

"What?"

"Do it."

When she answers she says, "For fuck's sake, Roly."

"Griz," I cut in. "That file you had. Of the serial murders in Ireland and the UK. Can you find it?"

"Right here. Why?"

"Can you read something to me? It had something about a series of murders in Croydon. What were the years?"

She reads it out: "1999, 2000, 2007, 2011."

"Thanks, Griz. Hang on the phone, will you?" I can hear her breath over the speaker system.

I turn to Roly, talk to his profile in the dark car. "Croydon, Roly. *Croydon.* We were trying to find the pattern in Ireland, the disappearances here. But it doesn't fit."

"What are you talking about?"

"Listen. He was here, Niall Deasey. He was here when Erin disappeared, 1993. And Katerina Greiner. And then . . . Teresa McKenny in 1998. Then he moves to London. To Croydon, Roly. And it didn't seem like a pattern, because it wasn't. Not here, anyway. It wasn't a pattern here."

"What do you mean?"

"He was living in Croydon! After everything that happened, he moved to Croydon, where his half-brother had a garage, for almost twenty years. And when Griz and I were looking at murders and disappearances in Ireland—unsolved ones—she pulled the UK ones, because of the north, and I looked and there were four women who disappeared in Croydon. Four women picked up off the street or in parks. They disappeared and then their bodies were found in local parks around two weeks later, submerged in water. All four died of blunt head trauma."

"Jaysus."

"Look at it, Roly! Erin and Katerina Greiner, 1993. Teresa McKenny in 1998. Then he moves to Croydon and the first Croydon one was 1999. The second, 2000. The third, 2007. The fourth, 2011. And then in 2016, Niamh Horrigan goes missing." But as I say it, I realize.

"But what about June Talbot?" Roly says. "He was living in Croydon in 2006. And he was in hospital, remember."

"You're right. Maybe she was . . . ah, shit."

We sit there in silence. On the other end, Griz is rustling papers. We can hear her. And then she calls out, "Guess what 2006 was? Guess what it was? Petey Deasey, Niall Deasey's father, there's all this stuff about him in the file. It has his birth date, too. September sixteenth, 1926. It was his eightieth birthday. How much do you want to bet the family had a big old party for him? Maybe they got him out of hospital to go or the dates are off or something?"

"Griz, go check on it. See if you can find out when he was actually, definitely in hospital," Roly says.

"Yeah—Wait. Roly, Maggie. I just got a text from my friend at the tax office. He got the records on that house in Ballyclash. It is owned by a woman. Her name is Mary Sheehan. She's dead now. But listen, he looked her up and guess what her maiden name was?"

"What?"

"Deasey! She was Petey Deasey's sister, Niall Deasey's aunt."

"Are ya serious?" Roly is hunched forward in his seat. "Griz, listen. Thank you. We'll be in touch. We gotta figure out what to do here."

Roly starts up the car but doesn't start driving. "Are you going to call Regan?" I ask him.

He looks over at me. "I don't know. There's no one at that cottage now. Maybe there's some evidence there that they can use to go nab him in Arklow. But if I call out everyone to go to an empty house . . . I'm not supposed to be looking at this."

"What we've got is pretty good," I tell him. But even as I say it, I know he's right. We've got a few circumstantial coincidences. And we've got an empty house owned by Niall Deasey's aunt.

"What do you want to do?" I ask Roly. "Check it out? We'd have to break and enter."

"Nah, we'd better not." He starts up the car, pulls off the verge without even looking. "Let's head back. We need to think about this, D'arcy. Griz is going to get on to the hospital. Regan might be able to get a search warrant for the garage." We drive in silence for a good twenty minutes, back toward Kilmacurragh and the M11. The car is full of our frustration, like a bad smell. We're almost to the motorway when he slows, slams his hand down on the steering wheel, and says, "Fuck it, I'm going back."

I grin at him. "Like I said, it's your funeral."

45

The cottage looks different now, the trees casting long shadows, the sound of our tires on the gravel driveway somehow louder.

Roly has a flashlight and he gets it out and shines it on the front door and in through the front windows. He knocks half-heartedly and then he stares at the window next to the door for a minute.

"Did you hear a dog whining?" Roly asks me. "I could swear I heard a dog whining inside."

"Yeah, you'd better check. It could be trapped in there."

"Yes," Roly says in a fake voice. "You are correct. It could be trapped in there."

I take the flashlight from him and shine it on the lock. "Roly, look." We hadn't noticed before, but it's new, the wood freshly chipped where the screws went in.

"Yeah. Here, shine it on the window." I shift the beam and he fools around with the sash. It doesn't budge. "Shine it here," he says. I do and he finds a good-sized rock, which he hands to me. Then he takes off his coat, wraps it around his arm, takes the rock back, and punches it through the window, then punches around the edges to break all the glass.

"Roly!"

"We were driving by and we noticed that someone had broken a window in this house," he says. "As law enforcement officers, we felt it necessary to investigate."

"Great. Now I suppose you want me to climb in there?"

He finishes clearing the shards of glass away and then he says, "I'm too big to fit through there."

"All right." I lay his jacket out on the sill and climb through into the silent dark house.

The sound of my feet on the wood floor surprises me and I take a deep breath to try to calm my heart. It smells of old paper and cloth, dust, mildew, earth. I turn the lock and open the door to let Roly in, then lock it again behind us.

"I don't like it," I say. "It's fucking creepy in here." I turn on the flashlight on my phone and shine it around. We check each room to make sure there's no one there.

"It looks like it was once some kind of hunting lodge," I say. "Look." There's a gun cabinet on one wall in the sitting room and someone's hung a mounted deer head above the fireplace. But everything's old and dusty. I'm holding my phone up when the flashlight dims. "Shit, my phone is dying. Roly, shine the light up here." There's a calendar hanging on the wall, a picture of a tractor above "June 1993" and the name of a farm supply store in Arklow.

"Well, someone was here in 1993, anyway," he says. "Let's see if there's any more evidence."

We check the bedrooms more carefully, but they've been emptied of anything personal. One has a stained mattress lying on the floor, but it's also covered with a layer of grime. We're about to leave when I see a closet against one wall in the back hallway. I motion to Roly to shine the light on it and I open the door. It's full of coats, old waxed-canvas hunting jackets, tweed blazers, rain slickers. Everything smells like it's been in here for fifty years. The floor is littered with Wellington boots and lace-up leather shoes. I'm about to turn around when I catch sight of a round, metal object on the floor. I cover my hand with the hem of my jacket and stoop to pick it up. It's a button. It reads, "Sustainable Galway."

And then I look up and see a door at the back of the closet with a padlock on it, also shiny and new.

"Roly!"

He shines the light on the door. My eyes are playing tricks on me now. I think I see something move, a mouse or an insect, but I'm not sure.

I knock on the door. Silence.

"What is it?"

"I don't know. Some sort of crawl space?"

And that's when I hear a faint thump, like someone hitting his or her body against the floor or a wall. It's coming from behind the door.

"Roly! Help me with the padlock!" We pull at it but it holds fast.

"Is there someone in there?" I call out. "Is there someone in there?"

"It's the Guards," Roly calls. "You're safe now. My name is Detective Inspector Roland Byrne." We're both silent, listening, and then it comes again, a faint thumping.

"Christ." Roly kicks the door. "I'm going to go get a crowbar out of the boot. Stay here, D'arcy. I'll radio the station in Roundwood and get some backup. Just sit tight for a moment."

He takes the light with him so he can see where he's going.

I hear his footsteps go out through the main room and then the soft catch of the lock as he goes out the door.

My heart is thudding in my chest. The house settles down around me, I say my name, pressing my lips against the wall, shouting as loudly as I can. "Are you in there? Can you knock twice if your name is Niamh Horrigan?"

A faint knocking comes from the other side of the wall. "Lots of people are looking for you, Niamh. Lots of people want to get you to safety. We're here now. Your parents are nearby. They'll be here soon. You're safe now." I press my hand against the wall.

It's completely dark in the closet. "Hang on," I say. "Hang on. He's coming."

I count to sixty, then count again, and again. It's been five minutes, too long. My hand goes instinctively to my left waistband. My service weapon is at home in Alexandria, locked in the gun safe in my bedroom. I have never wished for it quite as much as I do right now.

Seven minutes.

Eight minutes.

Too long.

"Roly?" I whisper into the darkness. "Roly?"

The house is absolutely silent. Then footsteps, very quiet.

I know. I feel him rather than hear him. I'm trapped in the closet. I need to get out into the open, where I might be able to fight. I slide along the wall and around the corner, into the living room. I remember seeing a fire poker leaning next to the fire. If I can get to it, I might have a chance.

But he's on me before I can do anything. He puts his hand over my mouth and locks a leg around my waist, wrestling me to the floor. I hear his voice and I know who it is.

"Shut up. Don't make any noise," he whispers hoarsely. "Is anyone else coming?"

"Yes." I gasp. "Backup. He called for backup. You better go. They'll be here any minute."

"I got him before he rang," he says seriously and it's only then that I see the knife.

Roly.

I feel myself start to panic, my breathing becoming shallow and inefficient. *Calm down. Make a plan.* I can smell his sweat, his breath.

"How did you know we were here?" I ask, as loud as I can make my voice, which is barely above a whisper.

"I have a camera on the driveway. The footage streamed to my computer when you came earlier."

"Did you kill my cousin?" I whisper.

He doesn't say anything. He's busy. He has my arms behind me now and I hear a ripping noise; when I feel him wrapping my wrists, I know what it is: duct tape.

I'm virtually incapacitated now. When you get someone's hands secured like this it's not just that they can't use them, it's that you take away their balance. Standing, I won't have much of a chance, but if I can stay on the ground, I can use my legs.

I roll over onto my side, bringing my knees up to my chest. I wait until he rolls back onto his knees, until his head is in the strike zone in front of me.

And then I slam my feet against the side of his head.

I hear him grunt. I got him, but not hard enough. He swears and grabs my shoulders, pulling me up to standing.

And then he starts pushing me toward the closet.

"No!" I'm thrashing around, trying to get us away from the doorway. If he puts me in there, that's it. For me, for Niamh Horrigan.

Erin.

"Shut up, you fucking bitch. Shut up!" And he raises the knife high above his head and I close my eyes.

Lilly.

And then I hear glass breaking and a second later what sounds like a shot and Cathal Deasey is rolling off me as the sirens scream and suddenly the room is full of light. There's one more gunshot, an explosion in the center of the chaos.

"Maggie, stay down," Griz yells and I look up to see her in shooting stance, looming over Cathal Deasey, who's clutching his leg and screaming. The lights from the cars stream in the windows. The room is full of people.

"It's okay!" she shouts to me. "It's okay now. We're here."

"She's in there!" I shout to them, pointing to the closet. "At the back! Get her out."

And it's only a minute before they're pulling her out, Niamh Horrigan, her hands and mouth duct-taped, her eyes wild and terrified. And I think, *Erin? Erin?*

But they go in and search the crawl space and there's no one—*nothing*—else there and I'm up and running and out the front door and it's then I see Roly on the ground. They're working on him but the blood is everywhere and when I look at his face, I can't see anything there to tell me he's alive.

I'm two days over my due date when the doctors tell me they're worried about Lilly. "Her fluid's low," a nurse says. "We want to get her out." I call Brian at work, and Uncle Danny. Brian meets me at the hospital, carrying my bag. He looks scared, so young I almost laugh, but I've never been so glad to see someone in my life. He grins and says, "Here we go, Mags. She'll be here soon." In that moment, I love him more than I have ever loved him. He's safety. He's home. He's mine.

The Pitocin hits me like a wrecking ball. I start to feel a few small contractions and then the next one feels like someone's got me in a vise and is whipping my body back and forth. It goes on for what feels like forever, a powerful contraction gripping me and rising to an unbearable peak, then easing off for a minute or two only to rise again, worse than before.

Brian keeps me going. He counts for me, tells me it's going to be over soon. And then suddenly they're pushing me down on the bed. Someone's talking to Brian. The bed is moving. They tell me they're going to get the baby out.

Something on my face. Pain. I don't remember anything after that.

I wake up to a blurry ceiling, thirst, more pain.

Brian is standing there, holding Lilly.

"Here she is," he says, smiling and holding her out to me. "Here she is, Mags. What's her name?"

"Lillian Erin," I say. "Lillian Erin Lombardi."

I whisper her name to her. She's tiny, wriggling a little as she gets close to me. "You should see her, Erin," I whisper into her soft hair. "You should see her."

46

It's touch and go all the way to the hospital, but then they get Roly stabilized and by the time they get him to St. Vincent's, they can tell us they think he's going to make it.

I sit with Laura until they tell her he's awake and that she can go in, and when she asks if I want to come, too, I tell her I'll catch up with her tomorrow. When she hugs me, I can smell her perfume and feel the tears on her cheek. She says, "A good few times now, I've had to sit with the wife at the hospital when her husband doesn't come home. One of my best friends, like. She was widowed at thirty-six. Bernie. We sat here for days. But I never thought we'd be here. I never thought it would be him."

"He's going to be okay, though," I tell her. "You're going to feel guilty about that, in the coming days, but don't let it take away from how grateful you are. I'm grateful, too."

She smiles and I watch the nurses let her into his room.

◆ ◆ ◆

When I come out of the hospital to hail a cab, Stephen Hines is up at the front of the clot of reporters. There are a couple of guards keeping them away from the entrance and they nod to me as I walk past. The reporters feel him watch me and they all converge, shouting questions to me: "Is your cousin's body in Ballyclash, Detective D'arcy?" "What is Niamh Horrigan's condition?" "Who kidnapped her?" I ignore them and keep walking.

But Hines breaks away and follows me. "Any comment, Detective D'arcy?" he asks. His hair is loose on his shoulders and he's wearing a dirty T-shirt under his jacket, as though he leapt out of bed to come here.

"No, I don't have any fucking comment," I say, but good-naturedly. I smile at him.

"Come on, give me something. You saved Niamh Horrigan's life." He's holding his phone out, recording whatever I'm about to say.

I talk to the phone. "No, I didn't. Detective Inspector Byrne and Detective Garda Grzeskiewicz saved her life. They're the heroes here. I just happened to be there."

"Does it give you any peace, knowing what happened to your cousin?"

I stop walking and meet his eyes. "No, it doesn't give me any fucking peace. What do you think?" For a second I wonder if he's going to keep badgering me, but instead he nods, as if to say *okay*, and lets me pass.

When I look up, past the reporters, Conor's standing there waiting for me.

"I called your phone," he says. "And the woman who answered it said you were here."

"My . . . ?" I realize my phone must still be in Roly's car. Griz.

"Can I drive you home?"

"I guess so." I look up at him for a long moment. His face is in shadow, his eyes dark and liquid. The car is warm. I wince putting on my seat belt and he touches my shoulder and then he pulls out into traffic and starts driving.

"I heard about what happened on the news," he says. "I saw you. They had a shot of the house and there you were in the background and I felt like my guts had been ripped out. You saved that woman. You saved her life. They said Detective Byrne is stable. I'm glad."

We're completely silent. I feel the weight of him, the inevitability of something. He drives smoothly. The road is clear and empty this time of night. "You haven't been honest with me," I say finally, into the emptiness. "There's something you haven't told me. I don't know what it is, but there's something. Will you tell me now?"

He turns the wheel, slowly, getting off onto a side street. He shuts the car off and puts both hands on the wheel. I wait.

A man walking a dog crosses in front of us. The car makes a settling sound, a fan shutting off somewhere beneath the hood.

He doesn't look at me. "You know when you meet someone and you recognize something in them? You think, 'Ah. I know you'? I felt like that when I first met Erin. She walked into the café and it was like I recognized her. I think she felt the same way. We just liked each other. We liked talking and I started walking her home sometimes."

I feel it as a physical pain. He loved her. I had known all along. I just hadn't wanted to see it.

"The gang of us from the café went out drinking one night. There'd been some conversation about a case that was in the courts then. It was in all the papers. She must have seen something on my face. I was walking her home and she said, 'How old were you? When it happened. How old were you?' and without even thinking, I said, 'Twelve,' and she said, 'It happened to me too. I was fourteen.'"

I turn to look at him but he has his eyes on the road ahead. I have the sense of something out there, something shimmering and dangerous, like an animal under the surface of the water.

"'Who was it?' she asked me. I couldn't say it. I'd never said it to anyone. I couldn't say it. I just . . . I asked her the same question and she started to cry. She said she'd never told anyone either. That she'd been . . . raped." There's a long, heavy silence. "That's what we were talking about."

Silence.

"I didn't know," I say.

"She said she'd never told anyone. I hadn't either. We . . . We were friends after that. Everyone at the café thought I fancied her. Bláithín thought I fancied her. It was terribly cruel, when I think of it now. Here was Erin, who knew the most intimate, secret thing about me, something I hadn't even told Bláithín. And I invited her out with us, let Bláithín see that there was this thing between us. In some ways, I don't think we ever recovered from that."

"Who was it?" I ask into the quiet car.

"Erin never told me," he says. "But me? A neighbor. I went round to feed his cows sometimes, make a little dosh. I learned, in therapy—there's been a lot of therapy—that I have it better than a lot of victims. I stopped it. I put my foot down after it . . . after it happened once. I made excuses not to be alone with him and it never happened again. I never told anyone, until I told the therapist. I'm okay now, but it took a long time. Splitting with Bláithín, it was . . . I could only see the marriage clearly once I'd reckoned with . . . it."

He starts the car up. I reach out and put a hand on his arm. I leave it there, rubbing little circles on his skin.

We're almost to the hotel. We pass the big AIB building. I take a deep breath.

"Why didn't you tell me?"

"It's embarrassing. There's a certain amount of shame. Erin told me never to tell anyone. I had the feeling it was someone close to her, that if it got out, it would be disastrous for her. She said something about how everyone would be mad at her if she ever told. Once she was gone, I couldn't ask permission. I'm sorry," he says. I turn to look at him.

"I'm so sorry," I say. "I had no idea. About Erin. About you. I'm so sorry."

He looks down at me. "It's okay. It really is. I'm okay."

"Erin didn't say anything . . ." I'm thinking horrible thoughts suddenly. Uncle Danny. My dad. *No.* "She didn't tell you who it was?"

"No. Not a word. It seemed raw, especially as the summer went on. It felt like she was starting to deal with it. I recognized the signs. I knew she hadn't, well, gotten past it, you know? Because I hadn't, either."

"Oh my God." I'm staring straight ahead at the houses along the little side street. He turns the car on again and pulls out, turns back onto the Main Road. We're silent as we drive up Baggot Street.

I reach for his free hand and he takes mine gratefully.

"I wanted to tell you," he says. "But I didn't know how to start. I almost did once."

"What stopped you?"

"I think I was pretty sure I was in love with you. I thought it might make you not love me back, I guess. That you'd think something was wrong with me."

"I don't," I say, rubbing my thumb along his. "I could never."

"She told me once that she had hurt you. She didn't tell me what it was, but she felt guilty about it. She said that it . . . the rape . . . made her do bad things. Made her hurt people. Do you know what she meant?"

I nod.

We're almost to the hotel when I say, "I don't want to go up there. Can we go to your house?"

"Yeah," he says. "Bláithín's bringing Adrien back, but I don't care. I just want you there."

We ride through the quiet streets of Dublin in silence.

Christmas. A grim, gray December day. My mother's been dead for six months. We're barely functioning, barely able to acknowledge the day. Father Anthony visits Christmas Eve and prayed with my dad but I can't bring myself to say the words with them. I stay in the kitchen, baking my mother's soda bread, trying to do it right. I can't get through it without crying.

On Christmas morning, we go down to Uncle Danny's and have breakfast, open a few presents. I give Erin a velvet scarf, decorated with butterflies. She puts it on, wears it all day. She's quiet, thoughtful, and we watch The Sound of Music, which is our Christmas tradition. Around three we head over to the bar. Uncle Danny opens it for a few friends, more than a few usually. This is our other Christmas tradition, and Jessica and a bunch of Erin's high school friends come out and so does my friend Helen, who lives in Portland, Oregon, now.

It's late when Uncle Danny asks me to take Erin home. "She had a few too many, I think," he says. "Get her into bed if you can."

By the time we're in the car, heading for the bay, she's not too bad, babbling about Jessica's new boyfriend and smoking out the window of my car.

"Can you put that out?" I ask her. But she ignores me, telling me about how Jessica met the guy at the supermarket.

"I was thinking, Mags," she says. "About moving to Ireland. Wouldn't that be awesome? Patrick's cousin is from

Dublin and he said they always need people to work in pubs. He said I'd be great at it because I know everything already, from the bar. I think I'm going to do it. You can come visit me. Weren't you supposed to spend the year over there before you left school? Maybe you can come and live with me."

I don't say anything, but she can feel the energy shift in the car. I just drive, focusing on the feel of my foot on the gas pedal, the way my back presses into the seat of my mom's Honda.

"What?" she asks after a minute, challenging, hurt.

"Nothing." I keep driving.

"Say it. I know you want to."

"Erin, you can do whatever you want. This is probably not the craziest thing you've ever done, even."

"You think it's crazy?"

"I think it's pretty par for the course, if you want to know the truth. This is what you do when things don't work out for you one place. You run away. I should have seen it coming, actually, after you broke up with whatshisname Patchogue guy."

"Fuck you, I'm not running away."

"Okay. Whatever you say." We're on Ocean Avenue now and I turn down Bay toward our houses. It's dark and cold outside. She pushes her cigarette butt out the slit at the top of the window and rolls it up. I just want her out of the car.

"Fuck you, Maggie. What if this is what I'm supposed to do? What if things work out for me over there?"

I don't mean to, but I must make a sound, a little Ha! *because she screams and says, "See! You don't think I can do it. You think I'm a fuck-up."*

"You are *a fuck-up. Why should this be any different?" I'm furious, the rage filling me up and exploding out of me. "Do you know how awful you make everything for everybody? Uncle Danny? He never knows if you're going to be alive or dead when he gets home. My dad? All your friends? Everyone thinks you're a fuck-up. Everyone's tired of your bullshit. Don't you know that by now?"*

I'm practically screaming. We're at the end of the road and I pull over, manage to get the parking brake on.

She stares at me for a long moment, her eyes spheres of reflected streetlight in the dark car. She smells like cigarette smoke and rum.

"You don't understand anything," she says finally. "You don't know anything at all."

There's a moment where she waits for me to ask, waits for me to say something else. I stare out into the dark night, pushing the tears down, pushing the words down. I focus on a tiny crack in the windshield, a crack my mom must have gotten at some point. The tiny sliver of streetlight reflects and bounces around inside the crack, a little mirrored hall of light.

"Maggie." She says it like the start of something. She's waiting for me to answer.

I keep staring at the little crack in the windshield. I don't say anything.

And she's gone, the door slamming, running toward Uncle Danny's house, the water below us black and yellow in the moonlight, and I don't even care, don't even check to make sure she gets home. I just drive away, trying to shake off my rage and shame.

47

Conor's house is dark and quiet. He turns lights on and makes tea. He puts Miles Davis on and we lie on the couch with a blanket over us and drink tea and listen to Miles. I tell him about Cathal Deasey, about Niamh Horrigan, about how when she saw him as they brought her out, she broke down, screaming and crying, how I hugged her hard, told her she was okay, stroked her hair, how her parents came to the hospital, how they wouldn't let go of her, wouldn't leave her room for a second.

They haven't found any remains, but today they'll search the grounds.

Conor asks, "Do they know if he was responsible . . . if he, if Erin was one of his victims?" He tries to figure out how to say it. "Were they able to link the scarf and necklace to him?"

I tell him we don't know. Before I left the hospital, they told me they found some things of Teresa McKenny's and June Talbot's in the house and they think he must have killed Erin and Katerina Greiner, too. They're searching his things, the house he lived in in Croydon. Niall Deasey's in custody, too, but they don't think he knew.

We listen to music. Conor rubs my feet.

I feel, for the first time in a long time, like I can stop paying attention.

And yet I notice the way Miles's trumpet wavers on high notes. I notice the framed black-and-white photograph of a peat digger hanging over the dining room table. I notice the way Conor's hair sweeps over his ears, the graying whiskers he missed shaving.

I like it here.

Then headlights sweep across the front window.

"Bláithín and Adrien," Conor says. We get up and go to the door. Bláithín's wearing a tweed cape in brilliant red. Adrien's hair is wet and he's shy when Conor reintroduces me. He comes in and goes straight to the kitchen and then upstairs. I stand back so Bláithín and Conor can talk but Bláithín just says she'll come and get him Thursday for his dentist appointment.

She's out the door already when I say, "I'll be right back," and follow her out. I close the door behind me and call out, "I'm sorry. Bláithín, can I . . . can I ask you a question?"

She turns, her keys already in her hand. She doesn't say anything. The streetlight is illuminating her cape. She looks on fire.

"I'm sorry about the way we first met," I tell her.

She hesitates. "I am as well. It was awkward and I behaved very badly. I saw . . . what happened, on the news. Are you okay?"

I dip my head, just a little. I don't know. I say, "I want to ask you something."

She looks up, on edge suddenly. The keys dangle from her hand. "Yes?"

"Did Erin leave anything else behind? At the flat that day? Anything besides the jacket?"

She puts the keys back in her pocket. She comes a little closer. Now she's standing in shadow and I can barely see her eyes. But her voice comes out of the dark, strong but low.

"I guess it can't hurt now. There was a letter in the pocket. It was part of one, like she'd started writing it but hadn't finished it. It was a letter to Conor. She said she'd been thinking about everything and she couldn't be quiet anymore. There was something about how she didn't care anymore what people thought, she had to tell the truth."

"It was a letter to Conor?"

"I wasn't sure—she hadn't written his name—but then she wrote something about something that happened at O'Brien's. 'I've been thinking so much about what happened at O'Brien's,' she wrote. I figured it out. It was a night I was away in Wicklow. He'd told me he'd been at O'Brien's that night. A pub. He'd said he was there with friends from college."

"This was in the summer?"

"Yes. I . . . I read the letter and then I ripped it up and flushed it down the loo. It was like if I could destroy it, it wouldn't exist and maybe she'd never tell him. Maybe he'd never know and then he'd forget about it and things could just go back to the . . . to the way they were before she arrived."

She looks up at me and smiles. "It was magical thinking. I was so young. I didn't know anything about relationships. I didn't know that you can't just erase things, you can't just pretend they were never there. They have to be brought out into the open or else they just fester and grow. That's what happened. All those years, it just sat there. We never talked about it until . . . well, recently."

I watch her for a moment. "I'm so sorry," I say. "I'm sorry for everything."

"I am as well." She smiles. "I hope they figure out what happened to her. I never thought . . . Until I had Adrien, I couldn't imagine what it must have been like for you, for her parents."

She gets in the car and she drives off. I watch her taillights heading south, back to Wicklow. I think of the mountains, the clouds gathering in the dark over the rusty brown and green valleys. Something's stirring in my brain, but it's not fully formed. An idea, a word, a name. *O'Brien's. O'Brien's.*

Conor is doing dishes in the kitchen and when I come back in he turns around and looks worried. "Is everything okay? Was Bláithín all right? She's okay, really. She just—"

"No, she was fine," I interrupt him. "Conor, did Erin ever tell you she had feelings for you?"

"Maggie, there was nothing like that between us. I thought you understood that."

His eyes are dark, troubled. I watch him.

I think of what he asked me.

Do they know if the guy in Wicklow was responsible . . . if he, if Erin was one of his victims? Were they able to link the scarf and necklace to him?

The scarf and necklace.

The scarf and necklace.

The water rushes from the faucet, eerily loud. My perceptions slide and blur. The lights are too bright over the sink, over Conor's face.

"I have to go," I say. I turn too quickly. My shoulder flashes pain at me, but I barely notice it.

"What's wrong?" he asks.

"Nothing, nothing's wrong. I have to go," I tell him. "Something's come up. An emergency. I need to go right now. I'm really sorry." I can't look at him. I need to get away from him. I need to think.

"What? With your family? What's going on?"

"I'll explain later but I have to go. I'm really sorry."

I grab my coat and I'm out the door, running, running north, across the canal and up to Baggot Street.

I don't stop until I get to the hotel.

I leave Roly a message while I pack. I don't tell him anything specific, just that I have a lead but I need to go back to the States for a couple of days to follow up on it. I say I'll tell him as much as I can when I know something definite.

My phone keeps ringing. Conor. I silence it and ignore his calls and texts.

I keep packing. I think about going to the airport, but when I call, I can't get a seat until the eleven a.m. flight the next day, so I put my bags by the door and I try to sleep.

....

Erin, crying.

When?

She's in my bed, curled into herself, her body.

The window, open just a little.

Outside. Summer.

Morning.

Her shoulder moves, up and down, up and down, but she keeps the sobs inside.

I only hear her breathing, uneven, her breath too sharp.

I start to reach out to touch her, to ask her what's wrong, but my hand won't move.

Reach.

I try to reach.

I don't move.

48

Later, I'll barely remember the hours in the airport, the flight, the drive east, home, toward Lilly and Brian. I just keep going over it in my mind, trying to put everything together.

Erin, on the trail.

She sees him. She doesn't know, not yet. She doesn't know something's wrong.

Her face as she realizes.

Alexandria is quiet, Main Street deserted, New York Avenue dark and silent. I drive slowly past the bar. Uncle Danny's car is there and the lights are on. It's nearly midnight. I head toward the ocean. *Back toward Ireland*, I tell myself. I think of Erin, looking across the Sound, wondering what it's like over there.

Erin.

Ireland.

When I pull up in front of the house, I sit there for a minute, the car windows open. The air is still and warm. I can smell the ocean as I walk the 542 steps to my house. I don't want to wake Brian and Lilly up, so I put the code into the alarm system, let myself in the back door, and head down the basement stairs.

I think I know what happened to Erin, but I need proof. And the proof is here.

It's cold down here, but I barely feel it. The boxes of Erin's things are over on the right side, stacked against the wall, exactly as they were when I looked through them before I left two weeks ago. I get all the boxes down and I start going through them, taking everything out and laying it all on the floor.

The box that held her claddagh necklace is still in the plastic tub I'd reorganized just before leaving for Dublin and I take it out and sit down on the hard floor. My legs and arms are shaky, as though I've just finished a long run.

The satin lining comes away easily, once I've untucked the edges. I wait a minute before taking the paper out of the box and carefully unfolding it.

It's been here all this time.

The handwriting is beautiful cursive, the date at the top clear and easy to read. November 3, 1988. The signature at the bottom is more flowery than I would have expected. *Father Anthony Meehan.*

It doesn't take long to read, and when I'm done, I refold it, holding it by the edges, and put it back in the box. Frantically, I search the basement, looking for a hiding spot. Finally I pick an old box over in one corner and tuck the box into that.

I know there has to be something else here, something that will prove it.

I'm sorting through papers and receipts, checking dates and locations, when I hear footsteps on the stairs and I turn to find Brian coming down.

"You're back."

He stops on the fifth stair up and stands there in sweatpants and a sweatshirt. In the harsh light from the hanging bulb, he looks as though he hasn't slept in weeks. His eyes are bloodshot, his skin gray. He watches me going through the boxes.

"Yeah, how's Lilly?" I ask him.

"She's great," he says. "She's still asleep."

"Good."

We stare at each other and I have a sudden flashback to our wedding, to his face, bathed in sunlight from the windows.

"What are you looking for?" he asks me.

"I'm looking through your boxes of things from your parents' house. There was a lot of your traveling stuff in there, an old passport, some old traveler's checks. Lilly went all through the change and took out the Italian and Greek coins and everything. She liked all the postcards and souvenirs and things. It got all mixed up. Your papers and the other stuff. When I put it back, I did it wrong, I . . . mixed it up. The chain of evidence is a nightmare of course. I could never use it, but . . ." I'm babbling.

He doesn't say anything. He just watches me,

"I'm looking for more receipts," I say. "From Dublin. For after you were supposed to have left. Well, you did leave."

He waits. I'm still trying to get all the details straight in my head.

"But then you went back." I pause, then start again.

"When I was over there, the last week, I found a receipt among Erin's things—someone had saved it after changing traveler's checks in Dublin on September eighteenth, 1993. I hadn't seen it before and it made us think that Erin had gone back to Dublin after being in Wicklow. It made us think it was more likely that she'd disappeared on purpose.

"But there was something else that made me wonder, what if she hadn't come back to Dublin? What if the receipt had gotten in among my stuff some other way? There was really only one way that could have happened." I point to the boxes. "Lilly went through all this stuff. She got it all mixed up. I thought it was from Erin's boxes, but it was from yours.

"I didn't know until yesterday—day before yesterday, now—that Erin had started writing a letter to someone. She referenced something that happened at O'Brien's and she said she was tired of keeping it a secret. There's a pub, in Dublin, called O'Brien's. She used to go there. The person who found the letter thought that's what she meant. But that's not what she was talking about. She was talking about the O'Briens' house. You guys used to go there a lot, didn't you? They used to have a lot of parties."

He sits down on one of the boxes and he leans back against the wall. He looks so tired.

I don't say anything. There's nothing to say. It's all up to him now. It's his story to tell. Finally, after a long silence, he says, "I think that for a long time I hoped someone would figure it out. But then, after Lilly, I was glad they hadn't. I was glad I was free and that was the first time I began to be glad that it seemed to have just gone away, that everyone seemed to have decided that it was the guy in Ireland."

"What happened at the O'Briens'?" I ask him. "What happened to Erin at Derek O'Brien's house?"

"Christ." He puts his head down. "That night."

"Tell me."

"We were at Devin and Derek's. Their parents were in Colorado or something. I don't know if you remember, but they always used to go away all the time.

"Anyway, there were a ton of people on the beach and the party was just like, really good. I don't know. It was a nice night. Almost summer. You know. Then the cops came and broke it up but some of us went back to the house. We were smoking pot, I guess, still drinking, and then Frank and Greg O'Brien showed up."

I try to picture Greg O'Brien. Like Brian's brother, Frank, he was older enough that he seemed like an adult to me when I was in high school. Tall. Greg hadn't been as good-looking as the twins, whereas Frank Lombardi had been the kind of good-looking that distracted people. Girls he'd never met knew who he was, talked about how he was home from college and that they'd seen him downtown.

"They'd been out at the bars and they came in and we were all hanging out. I guess Jessica and Chris went home but Erin was still there and she was wasted. She was having fun but I could tell she was pretty out of her mind."

He's doing something with his hands, pulling at his fingers as though he's trying to pull them off. He doesn't meet my eyes, just keeps talking.

"She and Greg O'Brien were kind of making out and then Frank was like, trying to make out with her, too. It was . . ." He's crying now and I feel tears on my own face. "We were so drunk. I didn't even know what he and Greg were doing until they were already in the den with her. They . . ."

He has his head in his hands. He doesn't say anything.

"They raped her," I whisper. I need to say the word. I need him to hear me say the word.

"It wasn't. I didn't realize. Devin and I watched. We . . . I wanted to stop them, but you know Frank. He . . . You can't talk to him. I was so drunk, Mags, I was just like, paralyzed."

I stare at him. "Derek, too? Three of them?"

It takes him a minute. "Yeah, I guess. And when they were done, they put her in a spare bedroom—she was crying, but then she fell asleep—and I took her home the next morning in Frank's car. He made me. I didn't even have my license."

"What did you say to her?" I'm standing now, moving toward him. I'm not sure when I stood up and I can feel my hands itching at my sides. If I had my gun, it'd be up against his head. I know that. I'm glad I don't have it.

"Nothing. Just, you know. 'Oh, we were all so drunk. You were so drunk.' I told her she'd been flirting with them and I didn't know what happened, but things had gotten crazy."

"What did she say?"

"She was just really quiet, looking out the car window."

Her face pressed against the window of the train.

"You fucking asshole," I say. "You told her not to say anything. You were warning her against saying anything about what happened."

"They didn't mean to hurt her," he says.

I'm still standing. Now I want my gun. I want it so bad I can taste it.

I lock eyes with him. We're almost there.

"Okay, Brian. So what happened in Dublin?"

49

He comes all the way down the stairs and, without looking at me, he walks a tight loop around the basement, his hands behind him. I can't see what he's holding, but I start paying attention.

"Mags," he says. His voice is different now, matter-of-fact. Everything before was a confession. This is different. "It doesn't matter anymore, exactly what happened. It was an accident and it . . . It can't bring her back."

I want to scream at him, curse him, tell him he owes me the truth. But I'm a cop, even now. And I know that won't get me what I want. Which is the whole story.

"I know, Brian. I know. It must have been awful. I assume it was an accident."

He looks up gratefully and sits down again on the bottom step.

"We . . Chris and Jess and I and Lisa, we were traveling that whole summer. You know that, right? We used our college graduation money and we were backpacking, Eurailing mostly. We started off in Dublin, staying with Erin. Then I went to London, to stay with this girl I knew from college. She was some kind of fucking genius. She was like in medical school or something but she was also like a total hash dealer and she was gone a lot and I stayed at her place for a bit."

I wait.

"Dublin," he says finally. "At first it was okay. We'd ended up being pretty good friends, me and Erin, over the years. I thought she'd forgotten about it. It was like we had a secret and that was okay. But when we got to Dublin, I could tell that she was pissed at me. She was just sort of cold. One night we were out at a pub and I'd had a lot of Guinness or whatever and I asked her why she was mad.

"Chris and Jess were off making out in the bathroom or something. It was just us. She said, 'You know why I'm mad. You know.' I had to think about it and I said, 'Oh that thing that happened at the O'Briens'? We never talked about that.'"

Floorboards creak upstairs. He stops talking and we both wait.

No more footsteps. *Lilly*.

"What did she say?" I ask him.

"She said, 'Yeah, that's what I mean, Brian. When your brother, Frank, and Greg and fucking Derek O'Brien raped me and you scared me out of telling anyone and it fucking ruined my life.'

"I felt like she'd punched me in the stomach, just like ripped me open." He looks up at me with wide, wounded eyes. I'm so close to lashing out at him, hitting him, scratching his face, *getting out my gun*, it scares me, but I manage to stay calm and wait for him to go on.

"I said that it was a long time ago and they'd been drunk, she'd been drunk. That if I were them I would have thought she was up for it. She wouldn't let it go, though. She said she'd decided she was going to tell everyone, that it wasn't right they should get away with it. That Father Anthony had known. She was going on about God in the mountains and some rock and she was acting crazy, saying that Frank was getting married and his fiancée deserved to know he was a fucking monster, all this kind of shit. Then she stormed out of the pub."

"That was the night she disappeared and you guys had to wake up her roommates," I say. I'm starting to fit it all on the time line.

"Yeah. We . . . I left the next day and went back to London. I didn't know what to do, though. Frank had just gotten the job at Goldman, he was getting married. My parents were so happy. She was going to freaking blow everything up. I didn't know if there was a statute of limitations or whatever, but I was pretty sure it wasn't up yet."

"What happened once you got back to London?"

"I couldn't sleep. I was really worried about it. I called her and tried to convince her to let it go. But she . . . she was just . . . calm, in a weird way."

I remember Emer's email, Daisy coming home as Erin was getting off the phone. *Some people just don't know when to stop pushing.*

"So you went back to Dublin."

"Yeah. I took the ferry over. There were so many people, all these long lines. They didn't even stamp my passport, just looked at it. I thought about that later, what if they had? It sucked. I got so sick on the way over, just like puking the whole time. I got there and I . . . I wasn't sure what to do. I took the bus to the city, you know, I was . . . I was sick still and so tired. I remembered where she lived."

I force myself to say, "You must have been really confused about what to do."

"Yeah, it was like, if she was going to tell people, it would . . . Frank couldn't have that happen. And it was my fault. If I'd just talked to her. I thought I could talk to her." He looks at the boxes, the piles of his stuff, Erin's stuff, my stuff. "She was my friend."

"What about Father Anthony?"

He looks at me. Something flickers in his eyes. I think maybe I've overplayed my hand, but he waits a minute and his shoulders slump and he says, "Yeah. There was that. I told him in confession one time. Then I regretted it, but I couldn't take it back. When he died, I was sort of relieved, but then something Erin said that night she took off . . . I wondered if she had a statement or something." He looks up at me, his eyes stricken.

"So what did you do?"

"I called her house from a pay phone I found on the way. She answered and when she heard it was me, I could tell she hadn't changed her mind. She was sort of calm, like she'd already decided. That was what freaked me out. Erin was always such a lunatic. Well, you know. But that calmness. It was like she was a different person."

I wait. He rubs a hand over his face, keeps the other one behind him.

"I thought it would freak her out if I told her that I was already in Dublin, so I . . I didn't know what to do. I looked up and there was a bus getting in at eleven thirty and I just said, 'I'm getting into the bus station tomorrow, the seventeenth, and can you meet me and we can talk and figure this out, Erin. Write down the bus time. Come on. We've been friends for a long time.' He's looking right at me now, talking directly to me. The basement feels cold, as though someone just opened a window.

The piece of paper. I picture Erin jotting it down, tearing it off, sticking it in her pocket. She wasn't writing it down so she could meet him—she was writing it down so she could be sure *not* to be in Dublin when he arrived.

Oh, Erin.

"But she said she wouldn't meet me. She said she was writing me a letter and I should just wait for it."

"What did you do?" I know, most of it at least, but I need him to tell me.

"I went to her house. I remembered where it was. I was almost there when I saw her come out with her backpack. She was wearing her leather jacket. I hung back and I followed her. She went to an apartment somewhere but she didn't stay long. When she came out, she walked for a bit and then she stopped and got her fleece out of her backpack. She almost saw me then. I had to jump behind a wall."

We hear the floorboards creaking again and he stops and gets up to go to the bottom of the stairs.

"Cat," he says finally.

"Keep going," I say. He almost looks relieved. I know that look. Once suspects have told you enough of their story that they know you've got them, they start to find relief in the telling. They start to enjoy the release.

"She walked up to that big park, near Grafton Street."

"St. Stephen's Green?" I say.

"Yeah, there were all these buses on the far side. She walked up to one of them and I saw her talking to the driver. Then I saw her get off and head toward another one. I was worried she was going to get on and I'd lose her, so I ran up and I said, 'Erin!' and she turned around and she looked shocked to see me. Like, really shocked. I told her I just wanted to talk, about what we'd talked about before, about Frank, and how he hadn't meant anything by what he did. She just looked at me and she said, 'Leave me alone, Brian,' and I heard her ask the bus driver if he could drop her in Glenmalure, after he took everyone to Glendalough. I guess he said yes, because she got on and the doors closed."

He hesitates. What he's about to say holds some kind of power for him. He's gearing up for it. "I came so close to going back to London, Mags. I did. I went to a pub and had a drink and I figured I'd go back and call Frank and warn him. I drank too much that night. I kept meeting people and finally I fell asleep in some park somewhere and when I woke up the sky was, it was, it was just getting light. And I thought, for some reason, I went back to the buses and there was one leaving and I said, 'Can you drop me in Glenmalure?' and the driver said sure, he was going to stop there anyway because someone had arranged for it ahead of time. So I got on."

I know why he's stuttering now, struggling with it. This is the hinge. It's where the whole thing could have turned out differently.

"We pulled up in front of this hotel and, I couldn't believe it, I saw her. She was walking down the road. I don't think she saw me. I got off the bus and I saw her walking up the road and I just, I followed her. Into the woods."

He takes a deep breath. He's staring at the ground. He barely knows I'm in the room. I almost tell him to stop, but I know I need to hear him say it. Without the next part I've got nothing.

"She realized you'd followed her all the way down there," I say quietly. "She was scared."

"Yeah, she freaked out. When she saw me, she accused me of following her to try to convince her not to tell and she started running away and I was chasing her and I grabbed her by the leg and I just . . . She wouldn't stop screaming and I needed to make her be quiet. That was all I wanted, to quiet her down so we could talk and I could explain to her about Frank and about how she couldn't say anything but maybe he could apologize, maybe I could get him to apologize." He's crying hard now, tears running down his cheeks.

"Her fleece, her, her jacket came up over her face. We were on the ground and I was . . . I didn't mean to hurt her. I just pressed it against her, her mouth, so she'd be quiet, but then she . . ." He takes a huge, shuddering breath. "Then she was quiet."

We're both silent for a long time. I don't want to keep going but I need what's next. "Where was the shovel?" I prompt him.

"I'd seen it along the trail. I think that was a lot later. I waited . . . all day, I guess. It all kind of blurs together. At one point, I heard people talking and I lay down next to her in the, like, the bushes, hiding. When it was almost dark, I went back and got the shovel and I took her far away from the trail, really far away, like a mile or more, way down into some trees. She wasn't heavy. I dug a . . . you know. I was trying to roll her in it when I heard something and I looked up to find this . . . girl. She was staring at me, watching the whole thing. There was something wrong with her, Mags. She was crazy. She was singing to herself, in another language, like German or something, weird stuff. I don't know. But she'd seen me. There was no way to explain what she'd seen. I took the shovel and I . . . You know. It wasn't very hard. It was . . . fast. And I waited until it was light again and I put her far away, up toward the trail more.

I thought maybe . . . I don't know, that it would make it less likely they'd be found. Time was . . . it was weird, Mags. I must have been there for a whole night. It made sense at the time. I didn't mean it, Mags, it was an awful accident. If she'd just talked to me, if the other girl hadn't acted so weird."

He's finished. I need one more thing, though.

"Did the necklace and the scarf come off when you were on the ground?" I ask him.

"No. I . . . I found the scarf later. And her ID. I put it in the, the second grave. I didn't see the necklace. Later, when you told me you found it, I realized."

"She dropped them for me," I tell him. "She dropped them as a message to me."

"What . . . ?" He's done with his story. He's drained now. In just a second he'll realize what he's done. He'll get angry. Scared. I have to be ready.

"The scarf. I gave it to her. It was a message. And the ID. She was trying to tell me to pay attention. Father Anthony gave her the necklace. He knew about what happened. I think she told him the night we found her at that house. She told him. And he was willing to testify. He was willing to report it. He wrote a statement, acknowledging what happened. He gave it to her. She hid it in the box with the necklace. She was telling me to look there, but I was . . . I didn't realize. When I found the necklace. She was telling me to go look in the box. His letter told me everything. It told me about Frank."

Brian looks up. In the low light, his eyes are dark and empty.

Footsteps.

I keep eye contact with him. Very slowly, he moves his hand out from behind his leg and that's when I see it; my Glock. He's gotten it from the gun safe.

"Dad?" Lilly's standing there on the stairs in her pajamas.

"Hi, Lil," I call up, trying to keep the desperation out of my voice. "I just got home."

"Mom!" She starts to run down the stairs, but then she sees my face. "What's going on?"

"Nothing, Lil. Please go upstairs, okay? To your room. I'll be right there."

She stares at me for a minute, trying to figure it out. She knows something's wrong. "Dad? Is everyone okay? Is Uncle Danny . . . ?"

Before I can stop him, he's up the stairs. He gasps, then makes a low moaning sound. He hugs Lilly, then takes her face in his hands. He says, "Lil, I love you more than I've ever loved anyone. You're the best, best thing, Lil. The only good thing that I ever did. Never forget that." I hear the Glock clatter to the floor and then he's gone. I can hear his feet pounding on the kitchen floor.

"Call 911!" I scream at Lilly as I race after him. "Tell them I need at least two units and an ambulance."

* * *

I know where he's going.

I sprint the length of Bay Street, taking a shortcut through a backyard down toward the water. The pavilion looks sinister, looming in the tiny bit of moonlight. I sprint through, past the swing set and the lifeguard station and stand there, searching the beach in front of me, but I can't see him until I do, a bobbing head out past the floats. I kick off my shoes and wade into the water. It's still cold and I can feel numbness climb up my legs.

But I strike out, swimming straight for him, keeping an eye on the beach so I don't get too far over. I can see him ahead of me. I'm closing in.

"Brian," I call out. "Come back to the beach!" But he keeps swimming, straight out, toward Connecticut. He's a good swimmer and I can see his arms breaking the water, hear the little splashes. I'm a good swimmer, too, though, and I'm closing the distance.

And then he goes under for a minute. I don't see him at all. His head reappears, but only the top of it. We're pretty far out.

"Brian!" And then I feel him there, next to me, the weight of him.

He thought he could keep going, thought he could just slowly sink under the water. But now his survival instinct is kicking in and he's panicking as his body tires. He's grabbing for me, trying to use me as a float and I remember my lifeguard training. I've got to get him to calm down, to let me tow him back to the beach.

"Brian, let me help you," I shout at him, but he goes under again.

I dive, my hands out in front of me, feeling for him under the dark water, but he's not there.

It's only when I turn that my leg slams into something solid and I dive toward it, pushing him, pulling him up to the surface.

I get my arm around his neck and start swimming. It's slow going. He's so heavy, and though he's stopped flailing, it feels like he's working against me.

I drag him up on the sand, my back screaming at me. I'm soaked and just starting to feel the cold. But I get on top of him, pinning him down and I grab him by the ears and I hold him and even though the words mean nothing, even though I have no jurisdiction in this, I say, "Brian Giancarlo Lombardi, I place you under arrest for the murders of Erin Flaherty and Katerina Greiner. Anything you say can and will be used against you in a court of law."

But he doesn't say anything. His eyes are open. His body is limp on the sand.

Then she was quiet.

The sirens wail from up on Bay Road. I brush his hair away from his eyes and I lie down with my head on his chest to wait.

The morning he moves out, Brian and I lie on our bed one last time, staring at the picture on the bureau of Lilly as a baby. We've been talking about separating all night, yelling and accusing each other of things, fighting against it. And then I say, "I think you should move out for a bit," and he says, "Okay," and there's nothing left and we lie there, embracing because it's over.

"It was Erin," he says after a long time. "That's when it started to go wrong. It was always going to go wrong."

I don't understand what he means. I think he means it was Ireland, that it was always going to wrong once I'd been to Ireland, because of Conor, because I couldn't love Brian when I already loved Conor.

After he leaves, I get under the covers and I cry, trying not to wake up Lilly in her room next door. And the bed feels so big and empty and I think of Erin, and the way she would drape an arm over me while she slept, the smell of her, her warm hand clutching mine.

And I long for her. I cry for the end of my marriage, for the failure of it, for everything it means, but I cry, too, for Erin. And I remember what she whispered to me the night my mom died.

"She's not gone," she said. "Can't you feel her, Maggie? Can't you feel that she's here?" And I say that I can, that her love is like a cloud, always there, drifting in and out of sight.

"I used to think," she said, "that because my mom left,

it meant she didn't love me. But I think maybe her love has been here all that time, even if she couldn't be."

She smoothed my hair from my forehead and I let the tears come and she held me tight and I could hear her breathing slow and even but still she held on to me, all through that night.

50

Roly and I get the carvery lunch at the hotel in Glenmalure.

We eat well, roast beef and potatoes. A pint each since we have time to walk them off.

When we're done, we hike up into the woods and then out onto the broad boggy expanse of the Mullacor Saddle.

"Nice shoes," I tell him when we stop to look out across the mountains.

He looks down at the shiny leather hiking boots. "Thanks, D'arcy. Laura picked them up for me. You know, it's really not good for the wingtips to be immersing them in mud all the time, sure it's not."

It takes us almost an hour to reach the site where they found Erin's body. It's a half mile or so from Katerina Greiner's grave, in a little stand of trees, just as Brian described it. It's been six months now and the summer's come and gone, and you can barely see where they excavated, then filled the earth back in. Golden grass has mostly covered the site. It's late autumn and unseasonably warm, and the mountains are the way I remember them from long ago, rusty brown and purple, no small, trickling streams to be heard.

I think of her grave at St. Patrick's, the simple writing Uncle Danny chose, a small engraved flower and cross. He goes nearly every day and it's helped him, to be able to talk to her. His heart is better. He looks younger than he has in years. I thought it would kill him, finding out about Brian, but instead it's as though something's lifted.

"I didn't understand, until I read the letter from Father Anthony, why she came here," I tell him. "She'd decided to tell us what happened. She didn't care about the statute of limitations or anything. She just wanted to . . . tell the truth. And he'd told her about this place, in his letter." I can almost recite it from memory now.

Dear Erin,

You have been very, very brave and I want you to know that I am willing to testify about what I know, if you should decide that you want me to. I have struggled, as I know you have struggled, to know what to do.

Many years ago, when I was in seminary in Ireland, I went to the Wicklow Mountains with a group of other seminarians and we walked and camped in the mountains near Glendalough, a holy place where St. Kevin retreated many years ago, to be with God, and with himself. We weren't far from the Wicklow Way, when we came upon a rough stone altar in the woods. It was a mass rock, where mass would have been celebrated during the years that Catholicism was outlawed in Ireland. One of the boys who was from the area told us that *a priest had been killed there and that it was known to locals as a very holy place.*

Erin, I felt the presence of that priest, and I felt the presence of God, and I felt the presence of myself in those woods, of the very essence of myself. I have never felt so sure of my vocation, and of my humanness.

I urge you to find that place for yourself, the quiet place where you can talk to God and discover what is in your heart, what is right for you. And when you do, I am here to support you, whatever that may look like.

"She came here looking for that mass rock," I tell him. "The first time she came down, she couldn't find it, and then she just wanted to get out of Dublin, because of Brian, and she came down again, so she could look again." I pause and gaze out across the expanse of rust-colored bog. "I know they've looked and looked. I know it's unlikely. But I like to think she found it, that she experienced that peace before she died."

"And she left the necklace for you to find so you'd think of the priest."

"I think she left the scarf and the ID for me, to say, 'Maggie, pay attention. It's me.' It was the only thing she had, when she saw him. She must have known what was going to happen. And then the necklace was the message. 'Father Anthony knew. Look in the box he gave me.'"

"And you did, you found her," Roly says. "Anything going to happen to the brother and his friends?"

"I don't know." I can't talk about Frank. I haven't gotten ahold of that anger and it's always threatening to rise up and take over my body. I still have to shut it down.

"How are you, D'arcy?" Roly asks after a few minutes. "How are you holding up?"

"I'm okay now, better," I tell him. "It's been tough with Lilly. She swings back and forth between hating me and clinging to me. I'm grateful to Emer and her girlfriend for having her at their holiday house in Galway for a week. She needs a little time away from me. I saw Niamh when I was out there dropping Lilly off. She's actually doing really well."

"Grand. And how about the thing with Brenda Donaghy's family, huh?" he says. "When Griz told me they'd rung in to the tip line, I could scarcely believe it. All these years."

The call had come into the tip line in the chaotic days after they arrested Cathal Deasey. Ann Forde, seventy-two, of Limerick, had seen the call for any information about a Brenda Donaghy Flaherty who had left Ireland in the late '60s or early '70s. It had taken her a few weeks to remember that her sister Brigid had loved the name Brenda, had seen it on a television program once and had thought it was beautiful and dramatic.

She told me that Brigid had gone to New York in 1968. She had stayed in touch for a few months and then she hadn't. They weren't a close family and she assumed that Brigid had just wanted to start over.

In 1983 Ann had moved back to Ireland from London, and into her mother's flat in Balbriggan. One day a package came from the States, from a man in Texas who said he'd been Brigid's landlord. She had passed away, from heart failure, he said the doctors told him, and here was her driver's license and did Ann want her things? The license said Brigid Forde, which had been her actual name. Donaghy was her mother's maiden name and she liked to use it. Brenda Donaghy had been an invention, a wish. I met Ann at the Skerries South beach right after Lilly and I arrived and I showed her a picture of Erin and told her what had happened.

I turn to look at Roly. He's squinting into the sun, looking out across the golden brown bog.

"How about you?" I ask him. "You're kind of the big man these days, huh? You got Cathal Deasey, you'll get the conviction on Teresa and June, on Niamh."

"Couldn't have done it without you, D'arcy. You're a bit of a celebrity, too, you know."

"Ah, you would have gotten him. You had the thing on the truck and you would have figured out about Croydon. Or Griz would have." I smile at him.

"I don't know. We were so fixed on Niall Deasey, we didn't think about the fact that Cathal Deasey had the same roots over here. That he knew the area, too. That the mountains meant something to him. That he would have come over to visit for Petey Deasey's eightieth birthday party. We're checking other murders in the UK now. During the years that he and Niall were running the garage over there, he got around a lot. We've got some psych stuff, too. Apparently he had kind of a love/hate thing with his father. He worshipped him and he resented him, for making him English rather than Irish, for abandoning him."

"How did Niall Deasey take it?"

"He was shocked, so he was," Roly says. "I really think he didn't know his brother was a psychopath."

"What about John White?" I ask him. "You decided what you're going to do about him?"

"I'm going to let that sit for right now, thank you very much," Roly says. "That's the last fucking thing I need." He glares at me a little.

"No judgment here," I say. "We do what we have to do."

"Anyway, thanks, D'arcy. For all you did."

He smiles and puts an arm around me and we stay there for a long time, feeling the last of the day on our backs, looking out across the hills and valleys. He's warm and solid. We don't turn around and head back until we've soaked up every last bit of the dying sun.

* * *

A few days later, I'm walking down Grafton Street.

Grafton Street in November.

It's full of tourists and I dodge them, heading down to the bottom. Someone's playing a Lady Gaga song on a saw. Someone else is playing the fiddle badly, trying for "Danny Boy."

The air smells of peat smoke and apples. There's not a rain cloud in sight.

I cross Nassau Street with a thick clot of students, the girls young and bright and laughing, teetering in high-heeled boots. The city feels familiar to me now, the dark faces of buildings, the distant mountains, the way the clouds run across the sky. Something leaps within me when I see the gray archway and I duck under it, standing there for a moment in the frigid shade. The table offering student tours looks exactly the same. The group of girls are still ahead of me, shouting and joking.

On the other side of the arch, in the courtyard, the sun is shining, Even Lecky looks happy today.

I have that feeling of coming down off a mountain and into a valley, a warm, homecoming sort of feeling. *Ireland.*

I sit down on the cement wall by the library, where the sun can reach my face for as long as it lasts. I have an *Irish Times* and a coffee and nowhere to be.

It's two hours before I look up and I see him coming out of the main doors and down the steps.

He's looking down, his hair flopping over his forehead, his shoulders bent, his frame thinner in profile. It feels like I'm getting a glimpse into time, the way it will line his face and gray his hair, the way his shoulders will carry years.

He looks up.

Conor.

Finally, Conor.

Erin is leaving for Dublin on a bitter Saturday morning early in January, a new beginning, a fresh start for a new year.

I wake up early and do seven miles on the roads that wind down toward the water. I finish up on the beach, my sneakers turning up the wet gray sand and pebbles along the shore. Long Island Sound is dark and rough, the wind whipping up little meringues of whitecaps here and there. The air is thick with salt water; I can't tell if it's raining or if the wind is lifting it up from the Sound, but I can feel my soaked ponytail slapping against the collar of my running jacket.

I see her once I'm past the big houses west of the Tide Club. She's wearing one of Uncle Danny's old yellow raincoats and standing on the beach, smoking and looking out across the water. I slow my pace and jog up to her, letting her hear me. She drops the cigarette on the beach, grinds it into the sand with her heel. When she turns her face toward me, her cheeks are pink, her mouth grim. We're still careful around each other, her hurt feelings a haze around her body. I've only seen her once since Christmas Day, and that was at the bar, where we could pretend nothing had happened, that nothing had changed.

"You all packed?" I ask her, huffing the cold air. I run my hands over my face, wiping off the salty rain. It is rain, I realize, coming faster now. Out in the bay, a Boston Whaler chugs slowly through the water.

"Yeah. My dad's loading my stuff into the car. I wanted

to say goodbye to the beach, you know?" When she turns to look at me, the hood falls back and her hair, curly in the wet air, springs out around her face. She has on her leather jacket under the raincoat, the scarf I gave her for Christmas, her claddagh necklace, the amethyst heart held by the little silver hands, glistening with a tiny drop of rain.

She looks down the beach toward Jessica's house and something crosses her face, a little spasm of sorrow tugging her mouth down. She and Jessica are going to miss each other.

"You can look at it from over there," I tell her, pointing vaguely to the mouth of the Sound, to the ocean, to Ireland.

"What? Oh. . . ." She smiles. "Yeah."

"How's Danny?" I bend over, pulling up on my toes. I don't want my Achilles seizing up again.

"Trying to pretend he doesn't care but I think he's kind of a mess. He said California was one thing. Or Florida. But Ireland feels really far away. You'll check on him, won't you? You and your dad?"

"Of course. I'll be at the bar."

She looks up, a flash of concern crossing her face. "I know. He appreciates it. He feels like, really guilty you didn't go back to finish school out there."

"So not his fault." I bend again to stretch my right hamstring. I can still smell cigarette smoke, mixing with her perfume, Anaïs Anaïs, and I have a sudden flashback to the pile of magazine samples she used to keep on her dresser, before she saved up enough money working at the bar to buy a whole bottle.

I take a deep breath, start, stop, start again. "Are you sure about this?"

She looks back at the water one more time and then turns around.

"Bye, Mags," she says. She doesn't move to hug me. She starts walking.

"Good luck."

She turns around. Her eyes are bright against the gray sky, the exact blue of my eyes, of my mother's eyes, of our grandmother's and countless unknown ancestors who crossed that ocean behind me. "It's going to be okay, Mags," she says. "It's really going to be okay. I just need . . . it's going to be okay."

The wind picks up. A gull wheels overhead and drops a clamshell on the rocks. And then she smiles, a huge, glorious smile that crinkles her eyes and lifts her whole face toward the thin light. She's so beautiful I can't help but smile back.

"Love ya, Mags," she says.

"I'm sorry," I whisper, but I don't know if she hears me.

I watch her as she walks up toward the house, a bright, shining yellow form glowing through the gray. I wait until I can't see her anymore.

Acknowledgments

....

The seeds of this story were planted many years ago, when I was living in Dublin, Ireland, in the mid-nineties. Though it departs immediately from the details of the cases that inspired it, I am ever mindful of the loss and grief that is always with the families and friends of the women still missing in Ireland, and of the tireless work of the men and women who worked those cases. I hope they will one day have answers to their questions.

Dubliners know that there is no pub called the Raven in Temple Bar and no pub called O'Brien's on Pearse Street. I've replaced actual places with these invented ones to give myself a bit of license, but all of the other pubs in this book are indeed ones you'd pass while crossing Dublin. Drumkee and Ballyclash are likewise invented townlands in the midst of actual places.

Dubliners will also know that the Serious Crime Review squad does not work out of the Pearse Street Garda Station. I have built them an extension for their offices there for sentimental reasons of my own. I am forever indebted to members of the Garda Síochána for being willing to share their expertise and experiences. Any stretchings of truth or departures from protocol or regulations for the purposes of the story are mine and mine alone.

Acknowledgments

Thank you to Gillian Fallon for her keen eye and deft pen. They both made this book so much better.

So much gratitude goes out to Esmond Harmsworth at Aevitas Creative Management, for his support and expertise over many years, and to Kelley Ragland, for putting me back in the game and helping me to make this the book I wanted it to be. I'm so incredibly delighted to have come full circle with you. Thank you to Madeline Houpt for all of her help, to Ivy McFadden for so many heroic saves and rescues in the course of copyediting, and to everyone at Minotaur Books for their work on behalf of Maggie and her book.

To Sarah Piel and Lisa Christie, thank you for reading multiple, raggedy early versions. You are true friends (and true friends to books and authors).

To Paula McLoughlin, thank you for the bed in Dublin and the chats and the mass rock inspiration and the friendship!

In a way, this book is a love letter to Dublin and Ireland, though it's the twisted kind, where you make terrible things happen in a beloved place. I'm grateful to the city, and to the "families" I was lucky enough to be a part of there. Thank you to the Morehampton House crew and my amazing Rosary Terrace women (those who lived there and those who were just passing through), and my Trinity M.Phil classmates and professors, in particular Thomas Kilroy, who gave me a bit of encouragement at a crucial moment. Thanks also to the Dublin Writer's Workshop, circa 1994, and to everyone who listened to me read my tentative words in the Hairy Lemon and told me to keep going.

Thanks to the Upper Valley Gaeilgeoiri and most especially Maura Naughton. Irish lessons are one of my favorite parts of my week and I am so grateful to you for your friendship, cups of tea, and for sharing a beautiful language with me. *Go raibh míle maith agat, a Mhaura!*

My parents, David and Susan Taylor, gave me the gift of unconditional love and support . . . and lots and lots of books. Thank you, Mom and Dad.

Matt Dunne, thank you for your belief in me, your endless love and support and patience, and for keeping life really interesting.

To Judson, Abe, and Cora: When you were little, you made it hard to write! But having you, raising you, and loving you has opened the lid of a box filled with all of the most beautiful, magical, terrible, weird, and wonderful things in the world. You have given me the gift of making me want desperately to write about it all—and making it possible for me to do it now. Thank you.